WELCOME TO
PASSPORT TO READING
A beginning reader's ticket to a brand-new world!

Every book in this program is designed to build read-along and read-alone skills, level by level, through engaging and enriching stories. As the reader turns each page, he or she will become more confident with new vocabulary, sight words, and comprehension.

These PASSPORT TO READING levels will help you choose the perfect book for every reader.

READING TOGETHER
Read short words in simple sentence structures together to begin a reader's journey.

READING OUT LOUD
Encourage developing readers to sound out words in more complex stories with simple vocabulary.

READING INDEPENDENTLY
Newly independent readers gain confidence reading more complex sentences with higher word counts.

READY TO READ MORE
Readers prepare for chapter books with fewer illustrations and longer paragraphs.

This book features sight words from the educator-supported Dolch Sight Words List. This encourages the reader to recognize commonly used vocabulary words, increasing reading speed and fluency.

For more information, please visit passporttoreadingbooks.com.

Enjoy the journey!

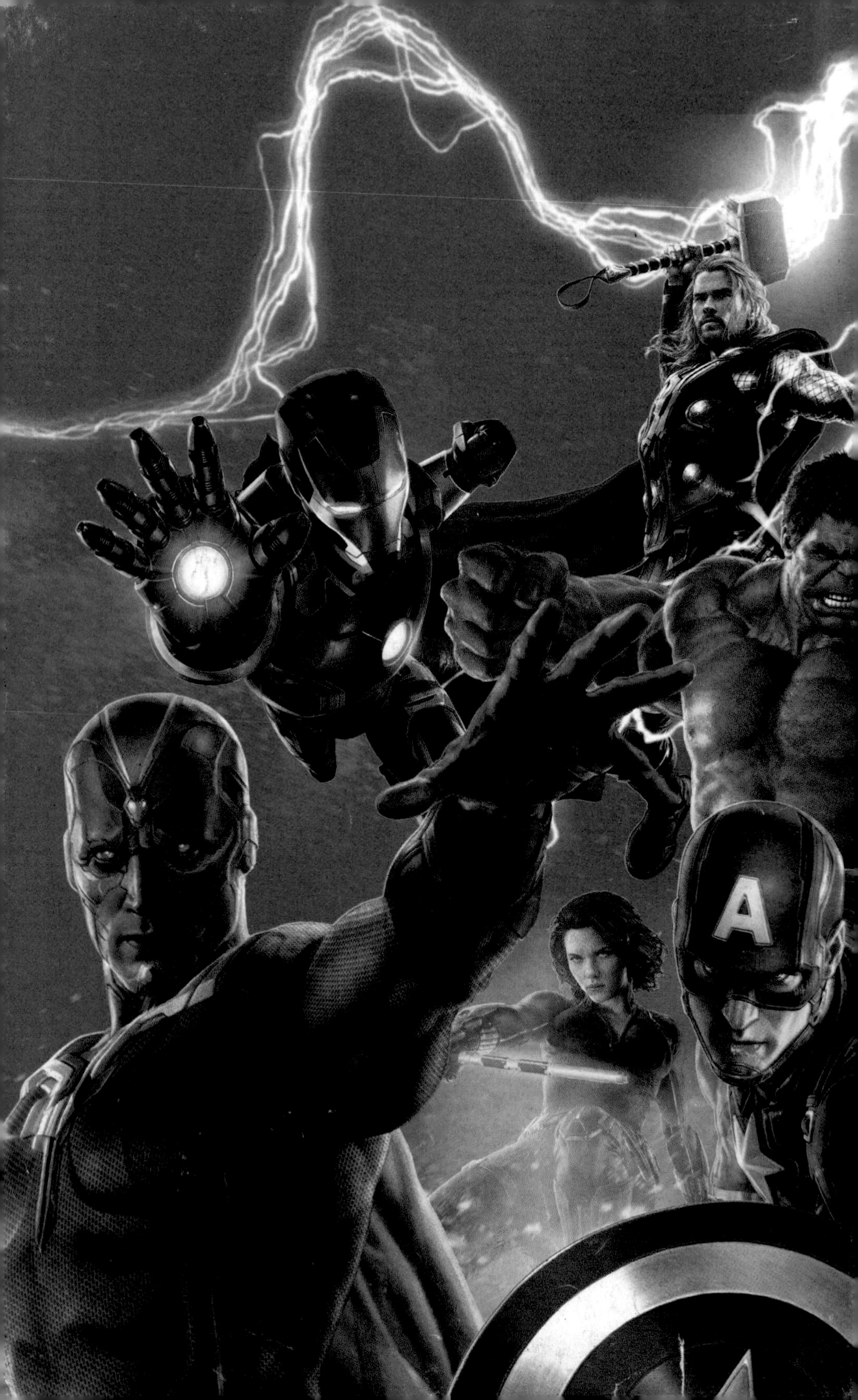

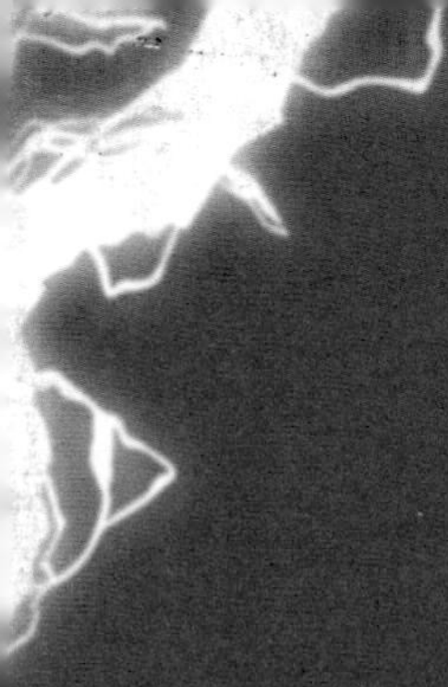

MARVEL

MARVEL CINEMATIC UNIVERSE

READING RUMBLE

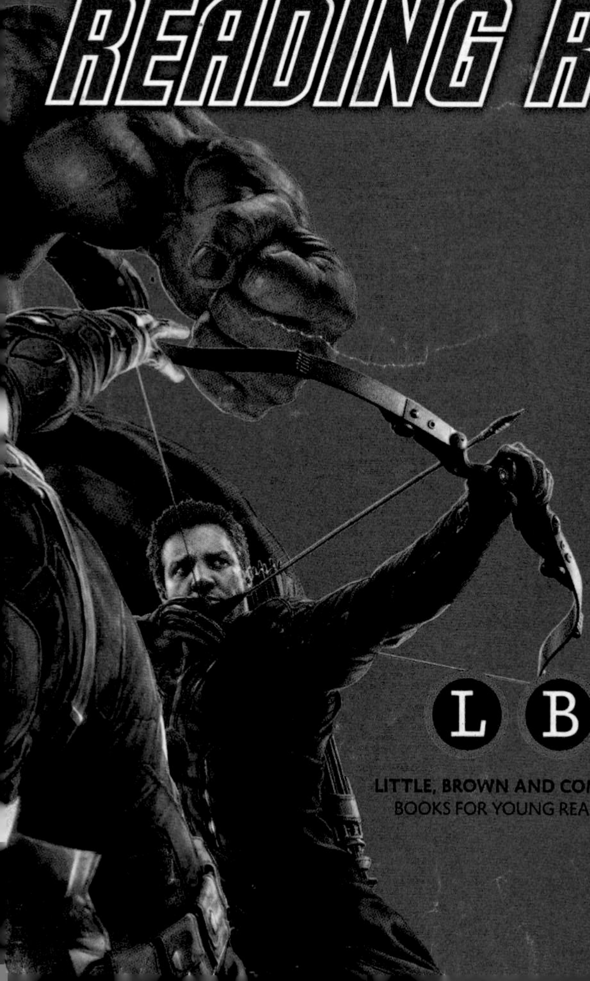

LB

LITTLE, BROWN AND COMPANY
BOOKS FOR YOUNG READERS

Little, Brown and Company

Hachette Book Group
1290 Avenue of the Americas, New York, NY 10104
Visit us at lb-kids.com

Little, Brown and Company is a division of Hachette Book Group, Inc.
The Little, Brown name and logo are trademarks of Hachette Book Group, Inc.

The publisher is not responsible for websites (or their content) that are not owned by the publisher.

First Edition: April 2016
Captain America: The Winter Soldier: Falcon Takes Flight originally published in March 2014 by Disney Publishing Worldwide
Avengers: Assemble! Originally published in April 2012 by Disney Publishing Worldwide
Avengers: Age of Ultron: Friends and Foes originally published in April 2015 by Little, Brown and Company
Avengers: Age of Ultron: Hulk to the Rescue originally published in April 2015 by Little, Brown and Company
Ant-Man: I Am Ant-Man originally published in June 2015 by Little, Brown and Company
Guardians of the Galaxy: Friends and Foes originally published in July 2014 by Little, Brown and Company

LCCN 2015960172

ISBN 978-0-316-27147-9 (pb)

ISBN 978-0-316-27171-4 (paper over board)

10 9 8 7 6 5 4 3 2 1

CW

Printed in the United States of America

Passport to Reading titles are leveled by independet reviewers applying the standards developed by Irene Fountas and Gay Su Pinnell in *Matching Books to Readers: Using Leveled Books in Guided Reading*, Heinemann, 1999.

TABLE OF CONTENTS

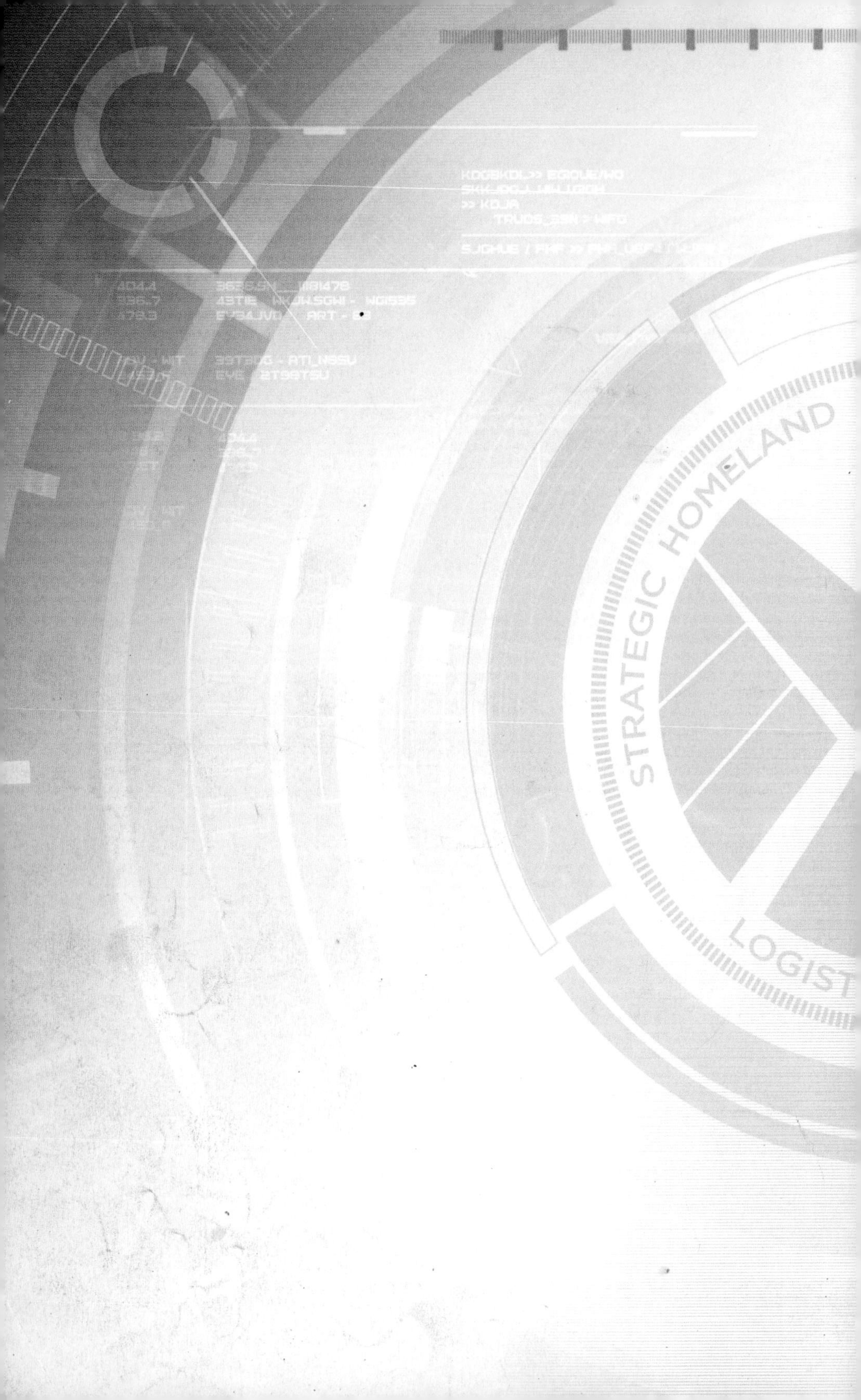
STRATEGIC HOMELAND
LOGIST

MARVEL
CAPTAIN AMERICA
THE WINTER SOLDIER
FALCON TAKES FLIGHT

BY
Adam Davis

BASED ON THE SCREENPLAY BY
Christopher Markus & Stephen McFeely

PRODUCED BY
Kevin Feige, p.g.a.

DIRECTED BY
Anthony and Joe Russo

ILLUSTRATED BY
Ron Lim, Cam Smith, and Lee Duhig

STRATEGIC HOMELAND I

LOGISTI

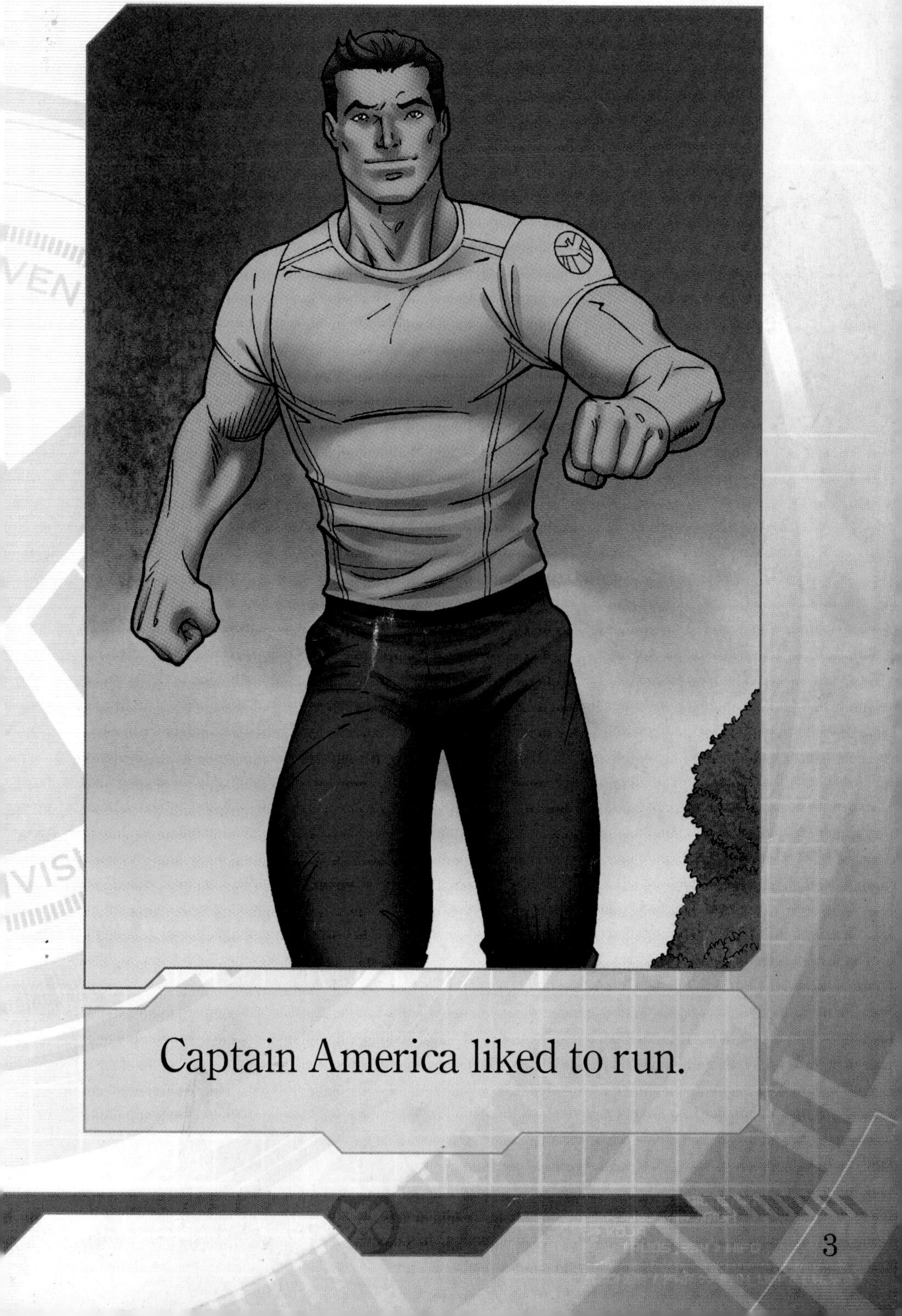

Captain America liked to run.

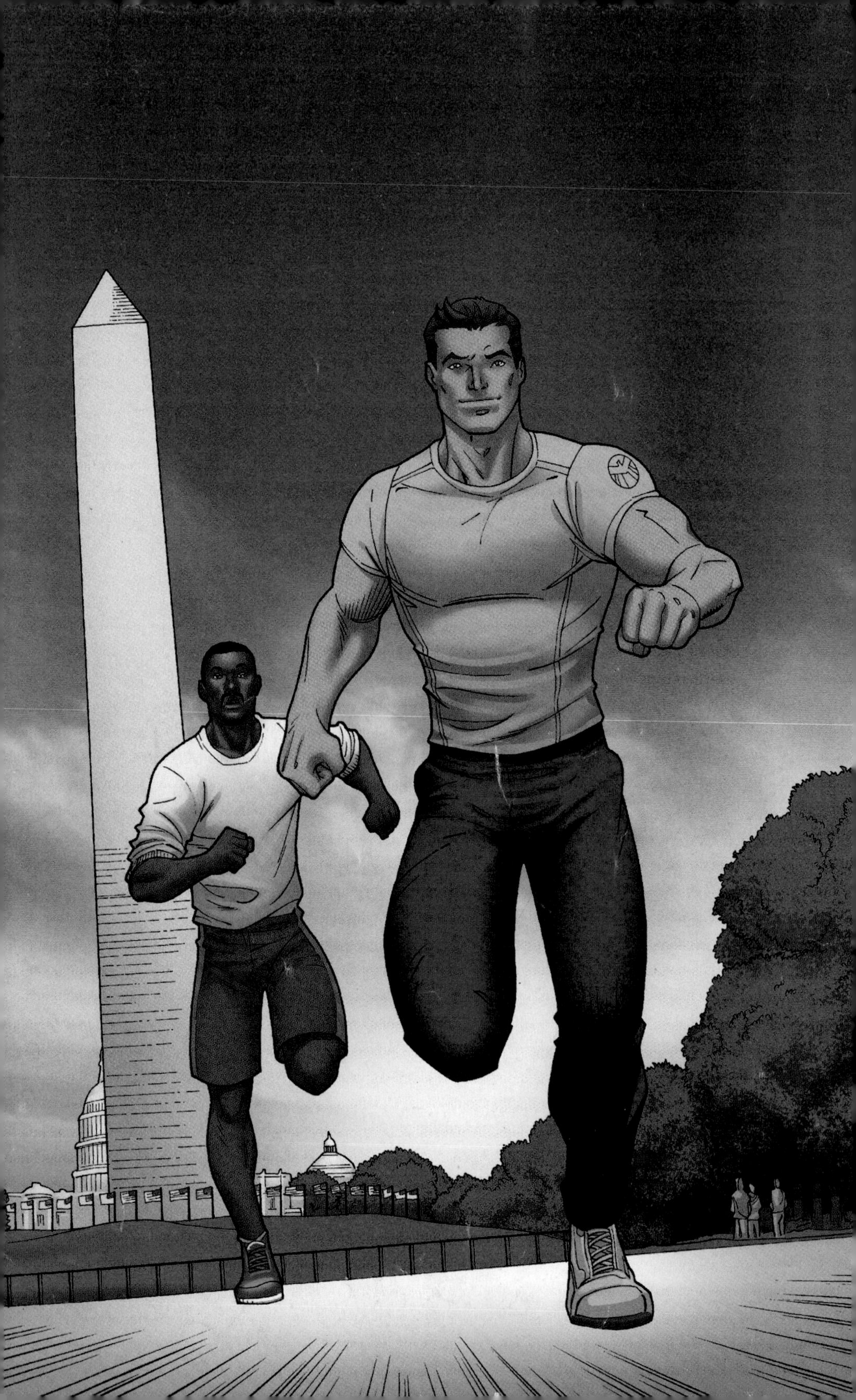

He ran every morning.

One morning, he met another
person who also liked to run.
His name was Sam Wilson.

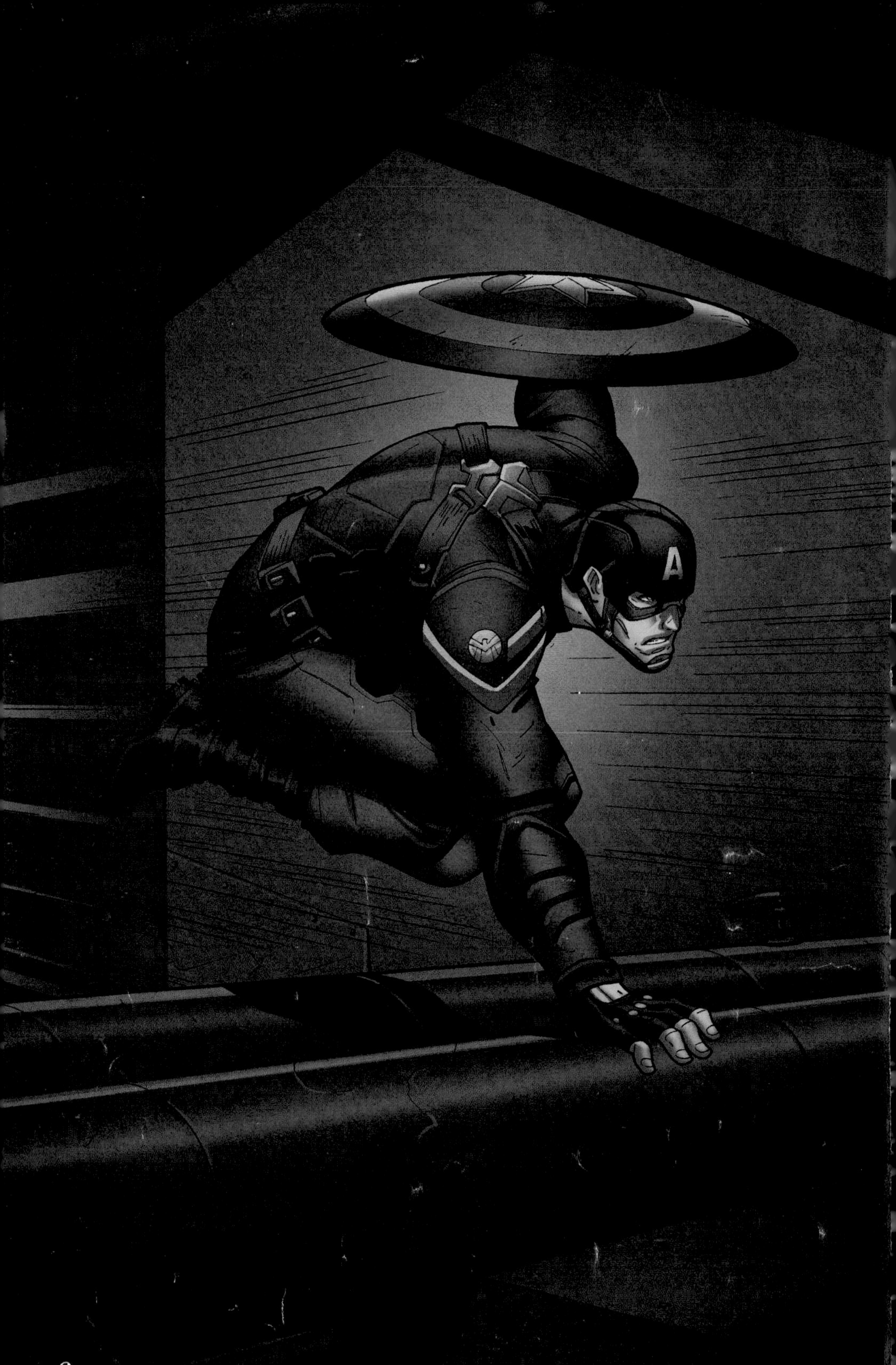

Sam and Captain America

had something in common.

Both were soldiers in the military.

Sam was now retired.

But Captain America

still had top secret missions.

Captain America worked to
fight bad guys and rescue hostages.
Sam worked to help other
veterans like himself.
They both had different jobs.
Yet both were important.

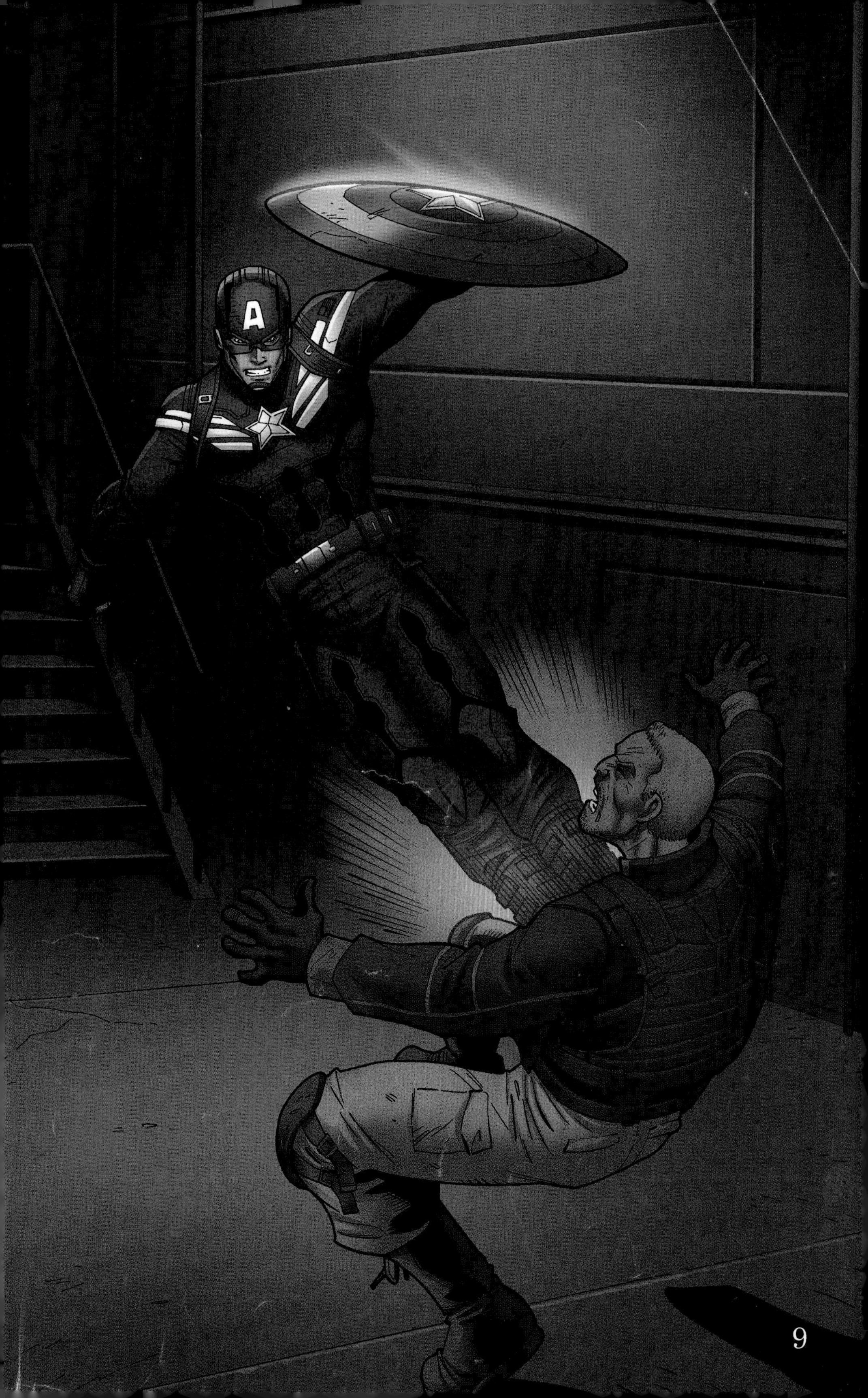

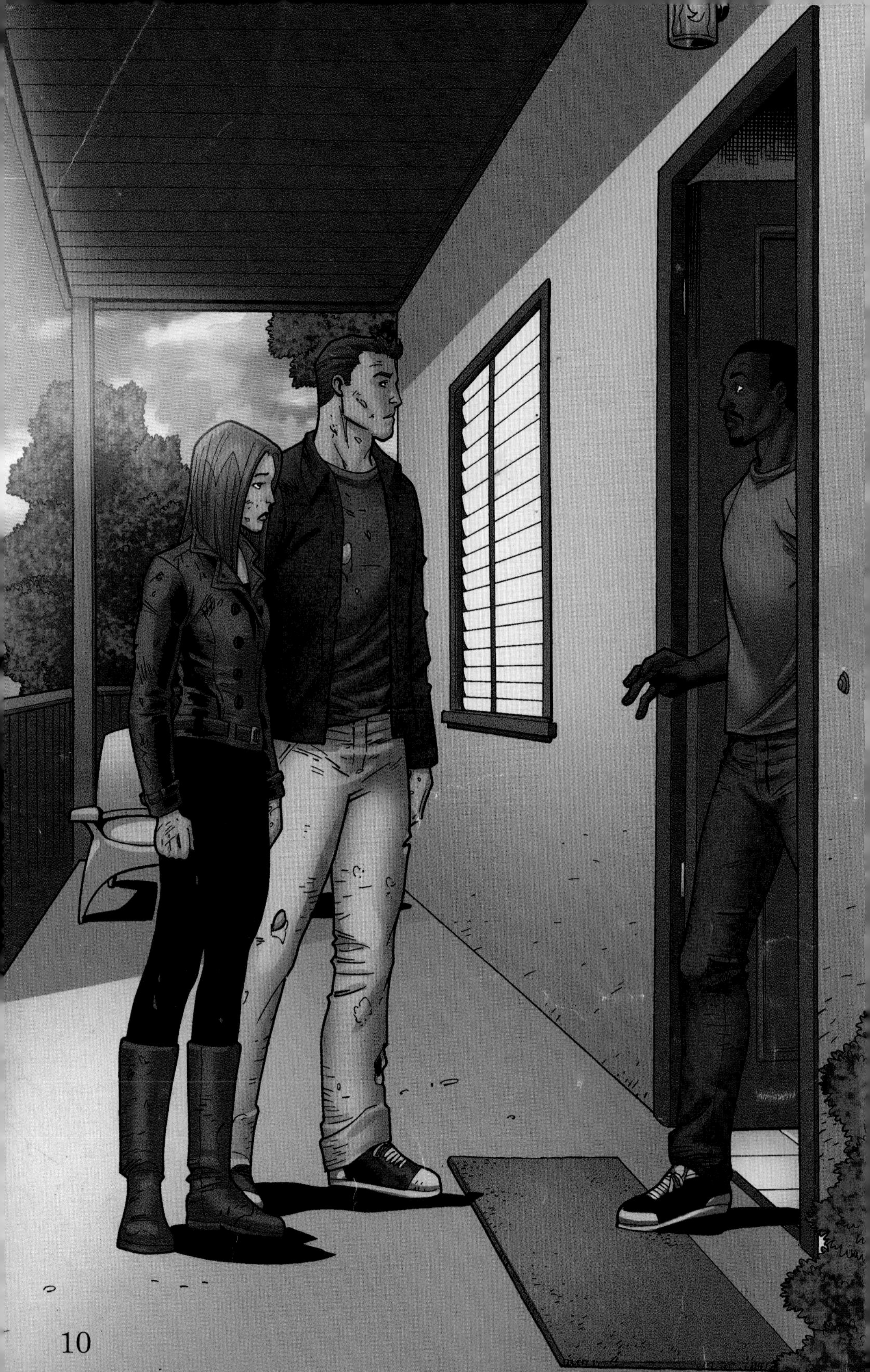

Captain America and Black
Widow went to Sam one day.

They had a problem.

They needed help.

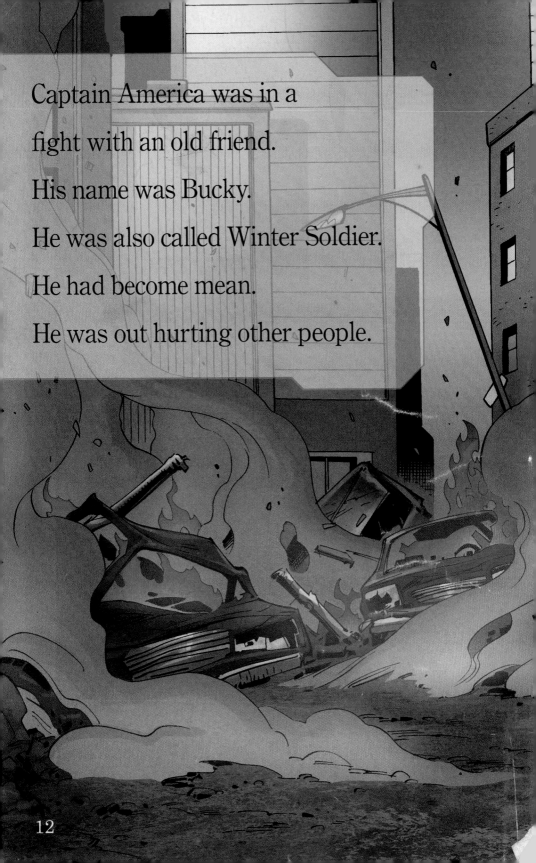

Captain America was in a
fight with an old friend.

His name was Bucky.

He was also called Winter Soldier.

He had become mean.

He was out hurting other people.

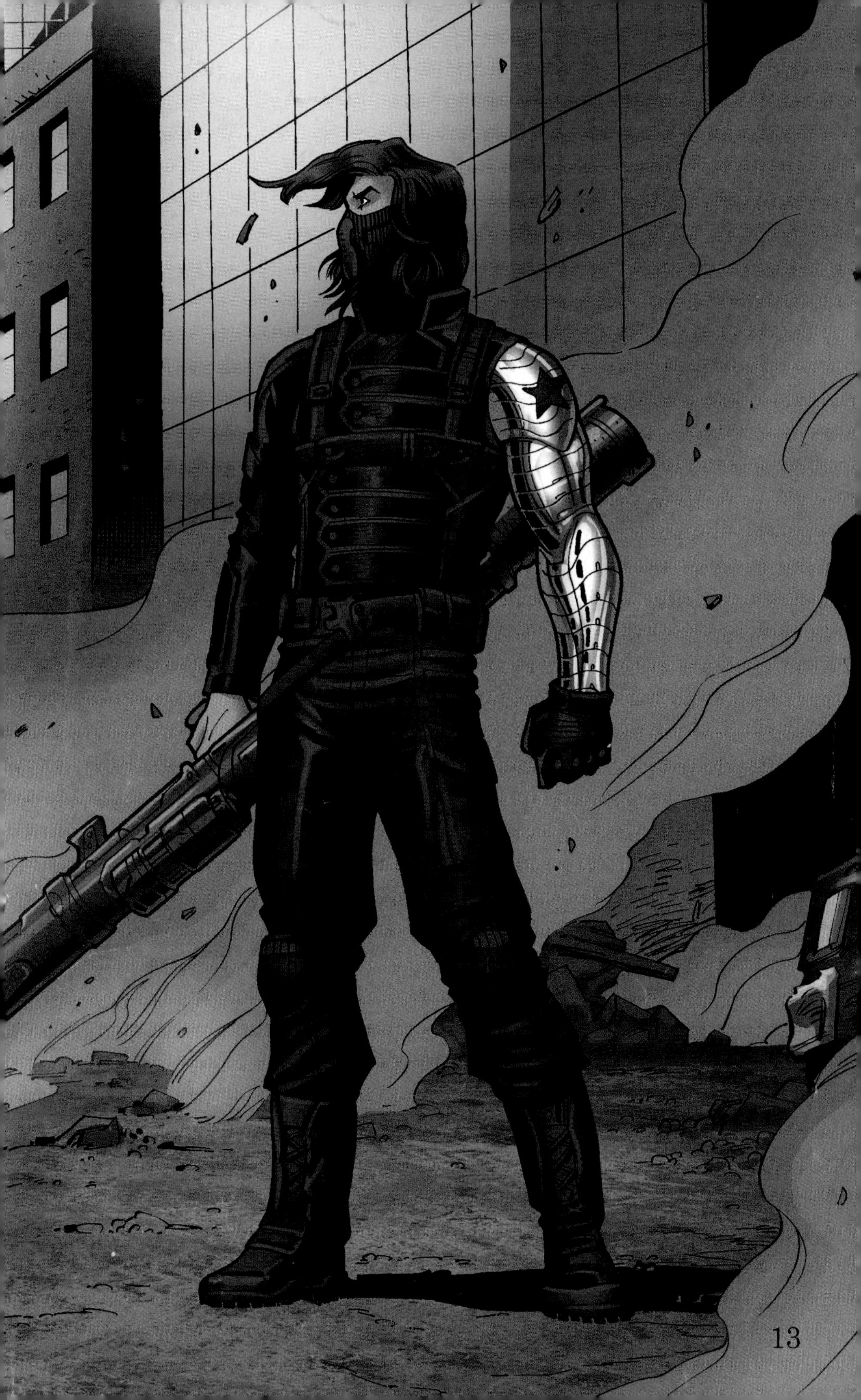

Sam didn't have
to think about it.
Of course he would help!
Captain America was a fellow
soldier in need. Sam Wilson
would answer the call!

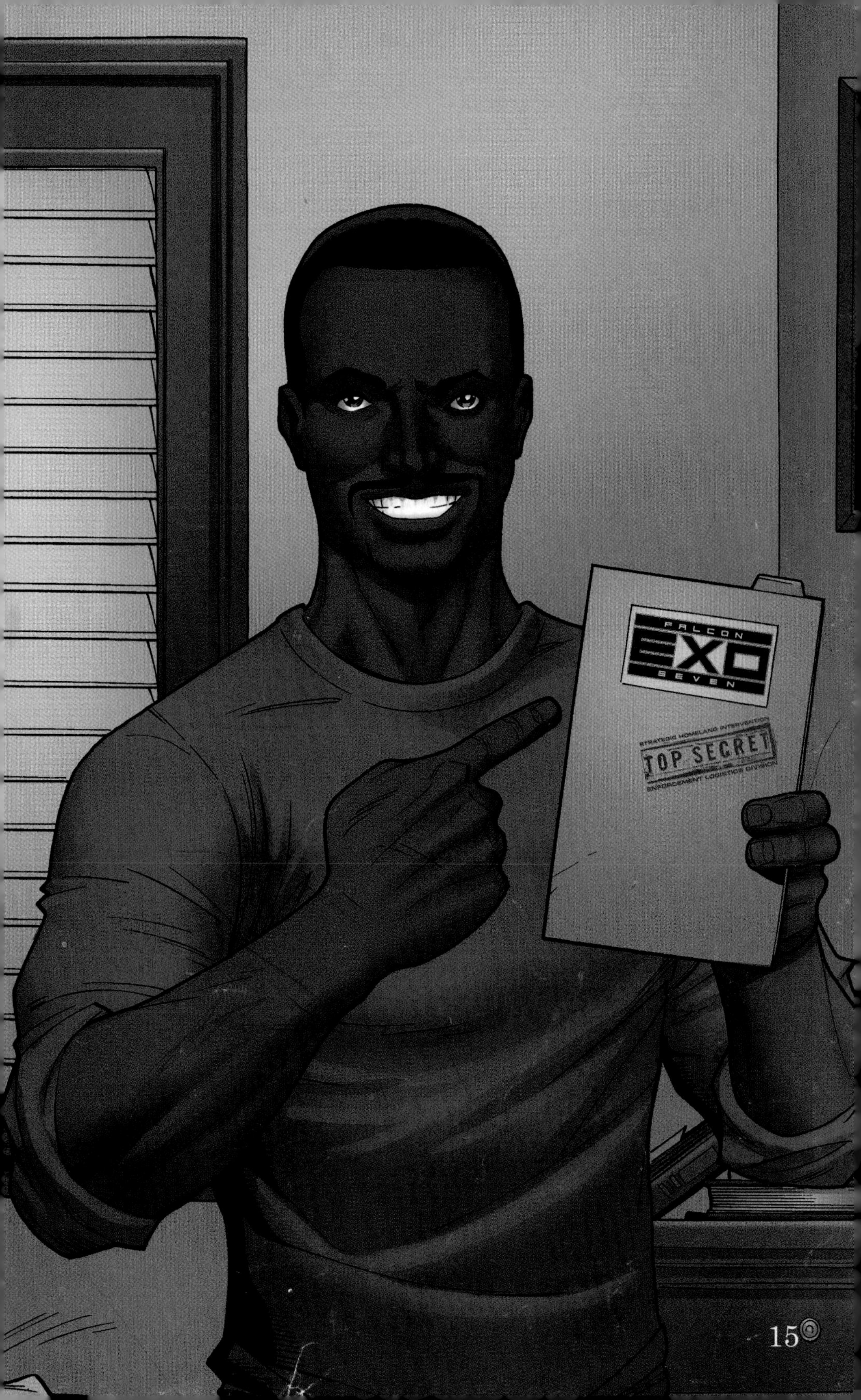
FALCON
EXO
SEVEN
STRATEGIC HOMELAND INTERVENTION
TOP SECRET
ENFORCEMENT LOGISTICS DIVISION

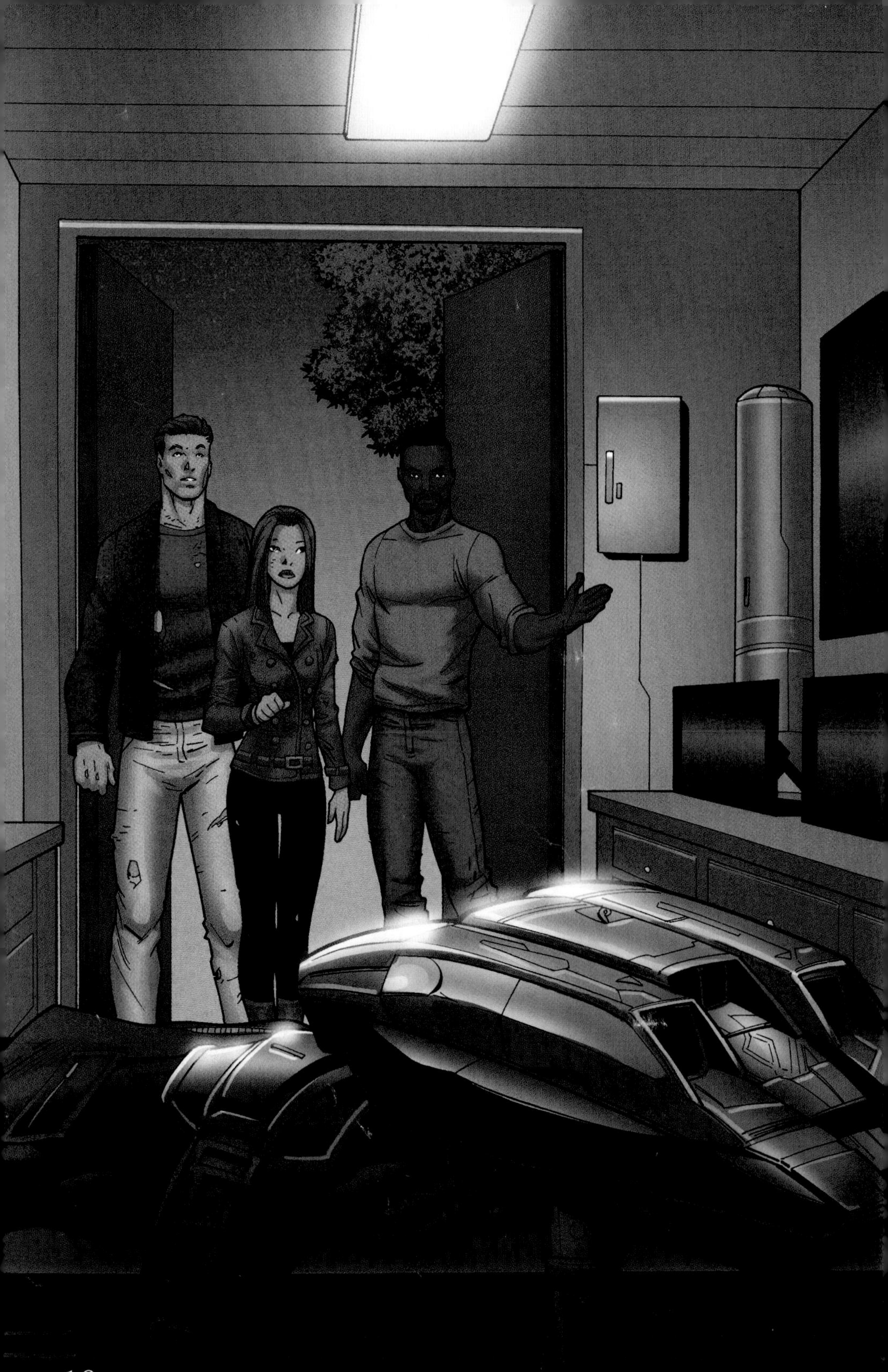

Captain America wore a heroic suit.

So Sam decided to wear one, too!

It was called the EXO-7 FALCON

wing suit. Sam used to wear one

when he was a soldier.

It was time to wear it again!

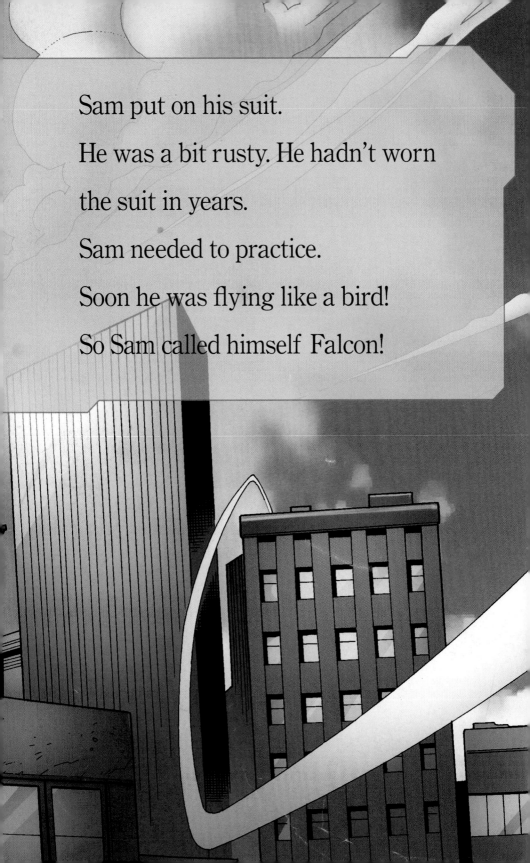

Sam put on his suit.

He was a bit rusty. He hadn't worn

the suit in years.

Sam needed to practice.

Soon he was flying like a bird!

So Sam called himself Falcon!

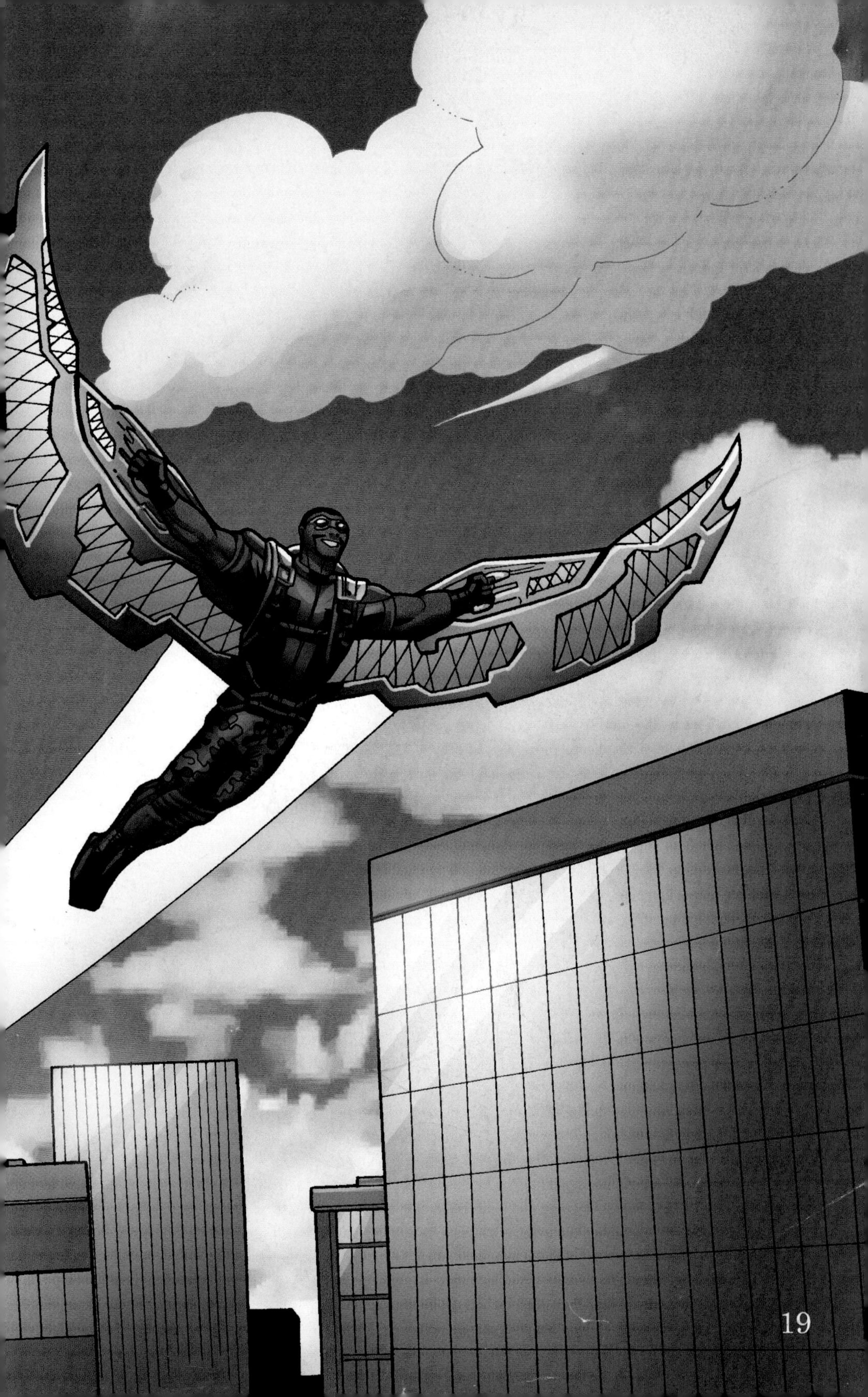

The Heroes searched for Bucky.

They didn't have to search for long!

Bucky was in a helicopter!

He went after the Super Heroes.

Falcon picked up Captain America
and they attacked the helicopter!

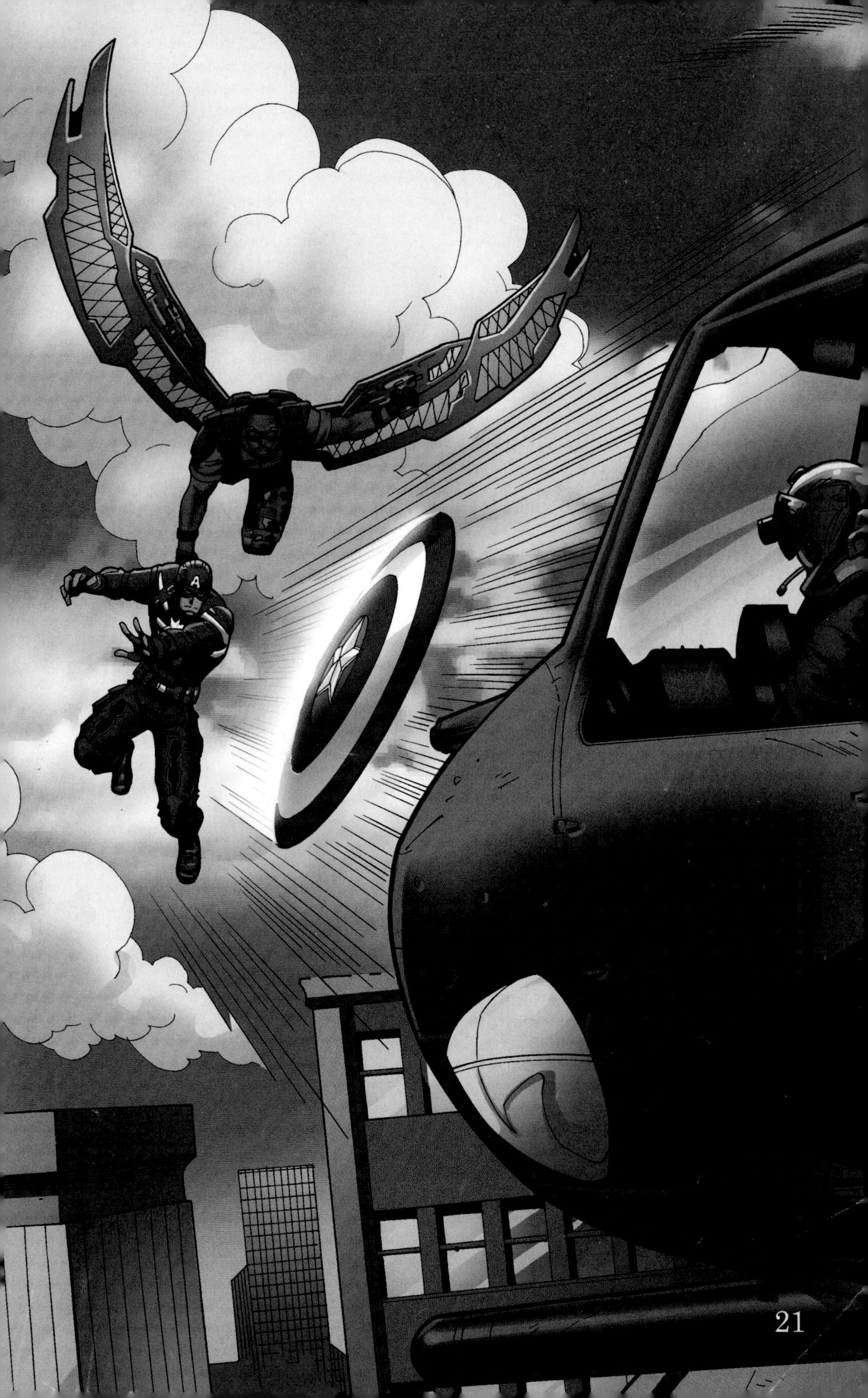

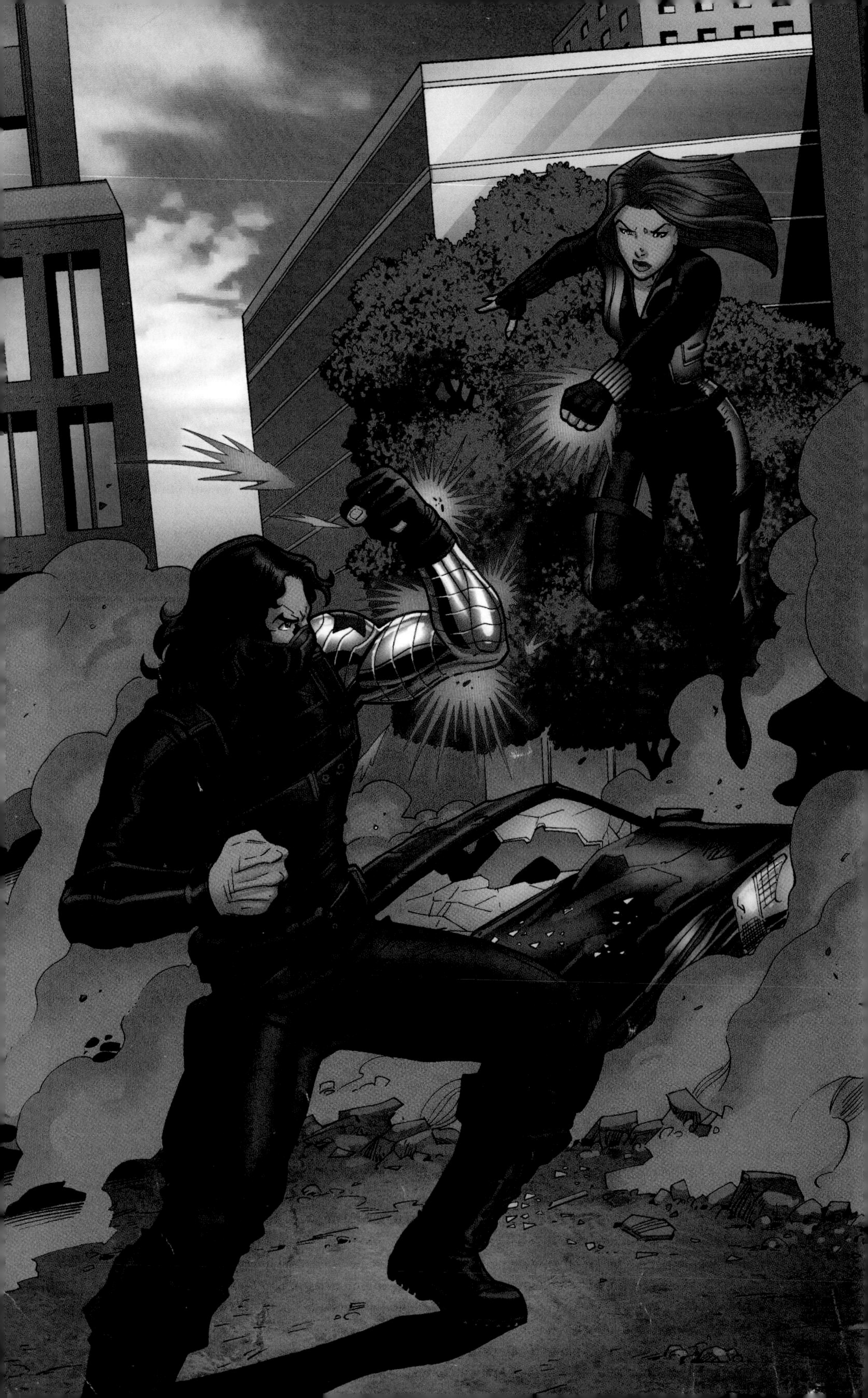

Bucky leaped from the helicopter.

He landed on the street below.

Black Widow attacked Bucky.

She fired her Widow's Bites.

He blocked them with his metal arm.

Bucky was strong!

Falcon was also in a fight.

He found some goons on a rooftop.

Falcon swooped in and attacked.

He kicked them to the ground.

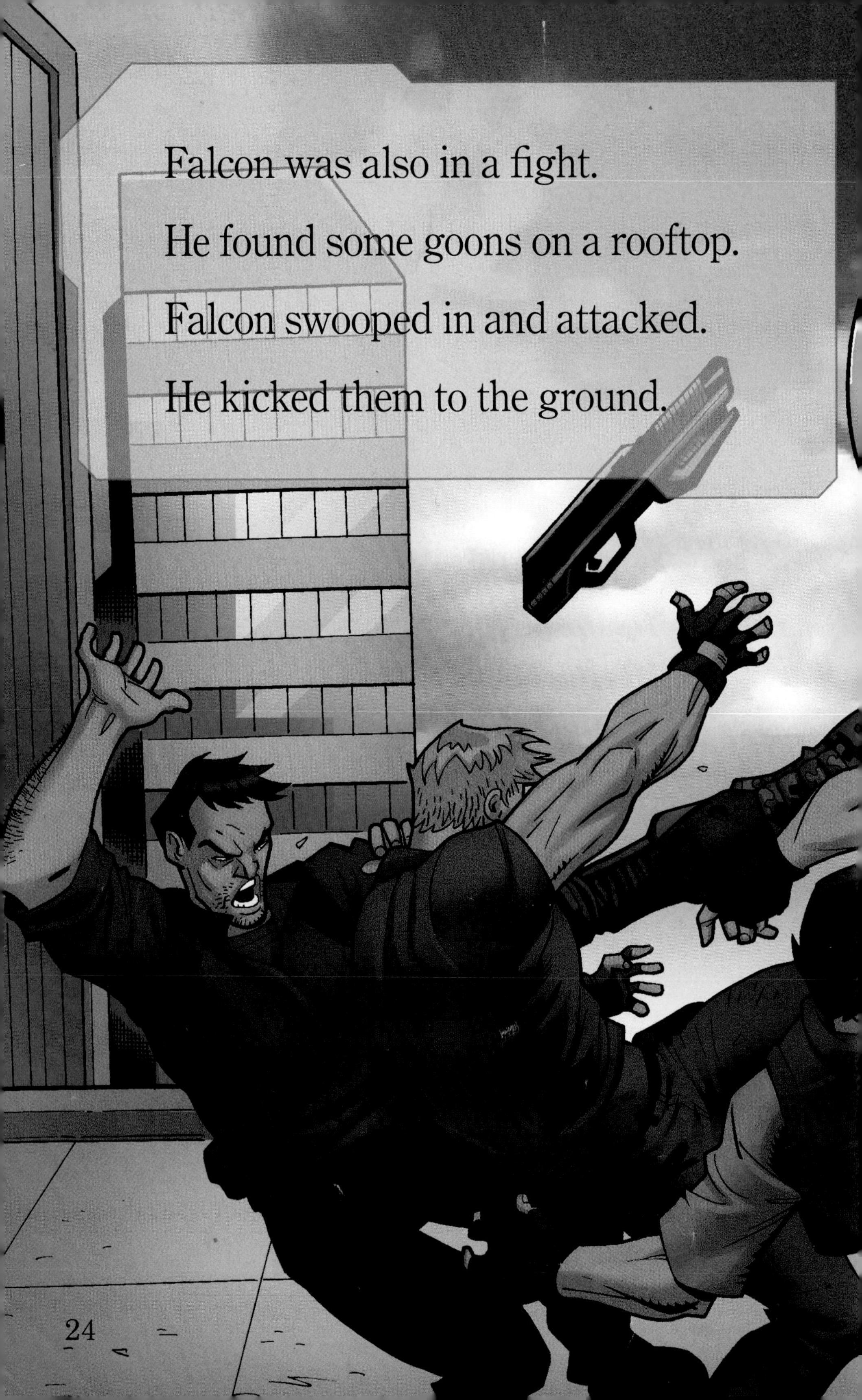

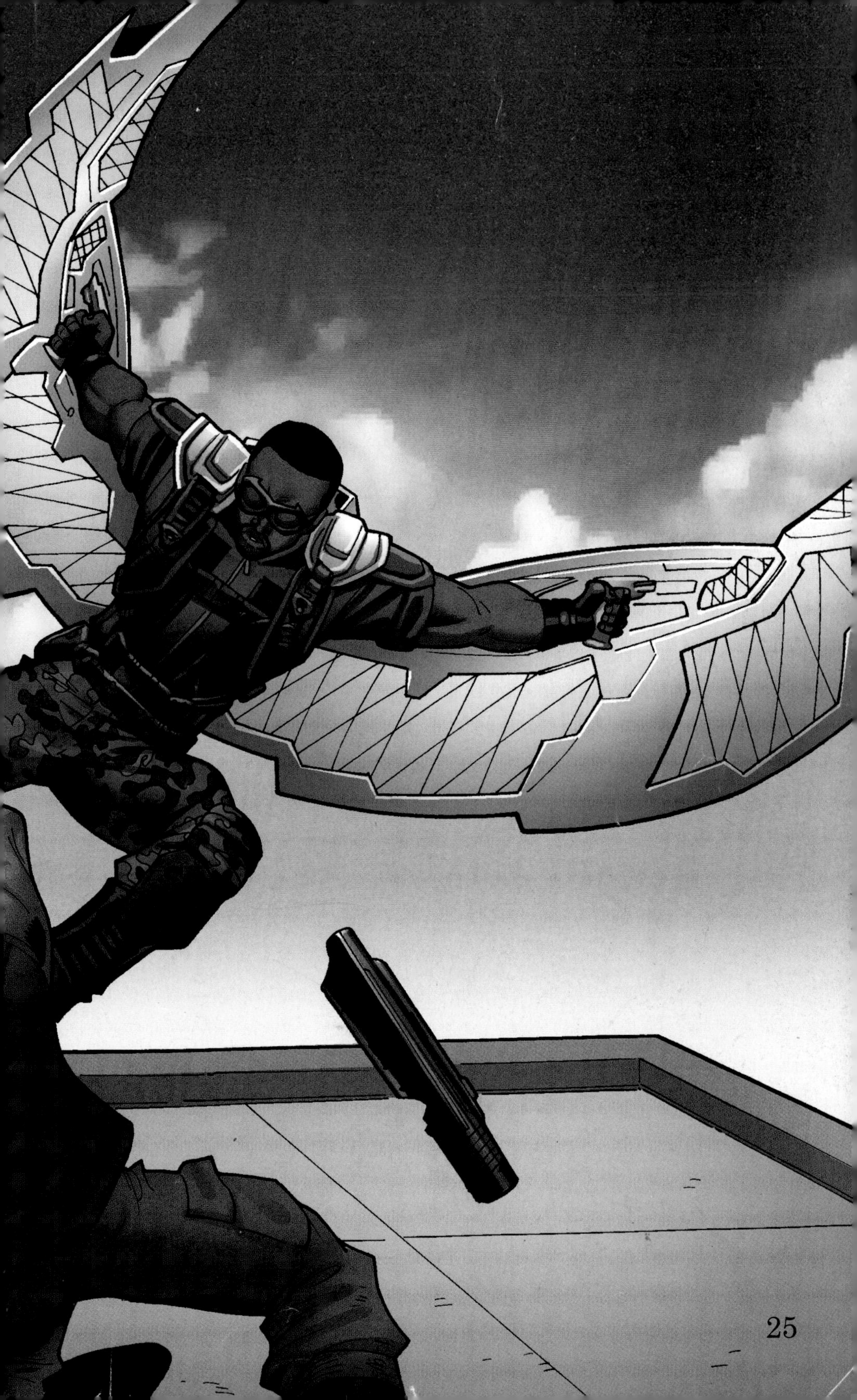

It was now Falcon's turn

to fight Bucky.

Falcon dove down from the sky.

He smashed into Bucky!

Bucky hit Falcon with his metal arm.

It was a great fight!

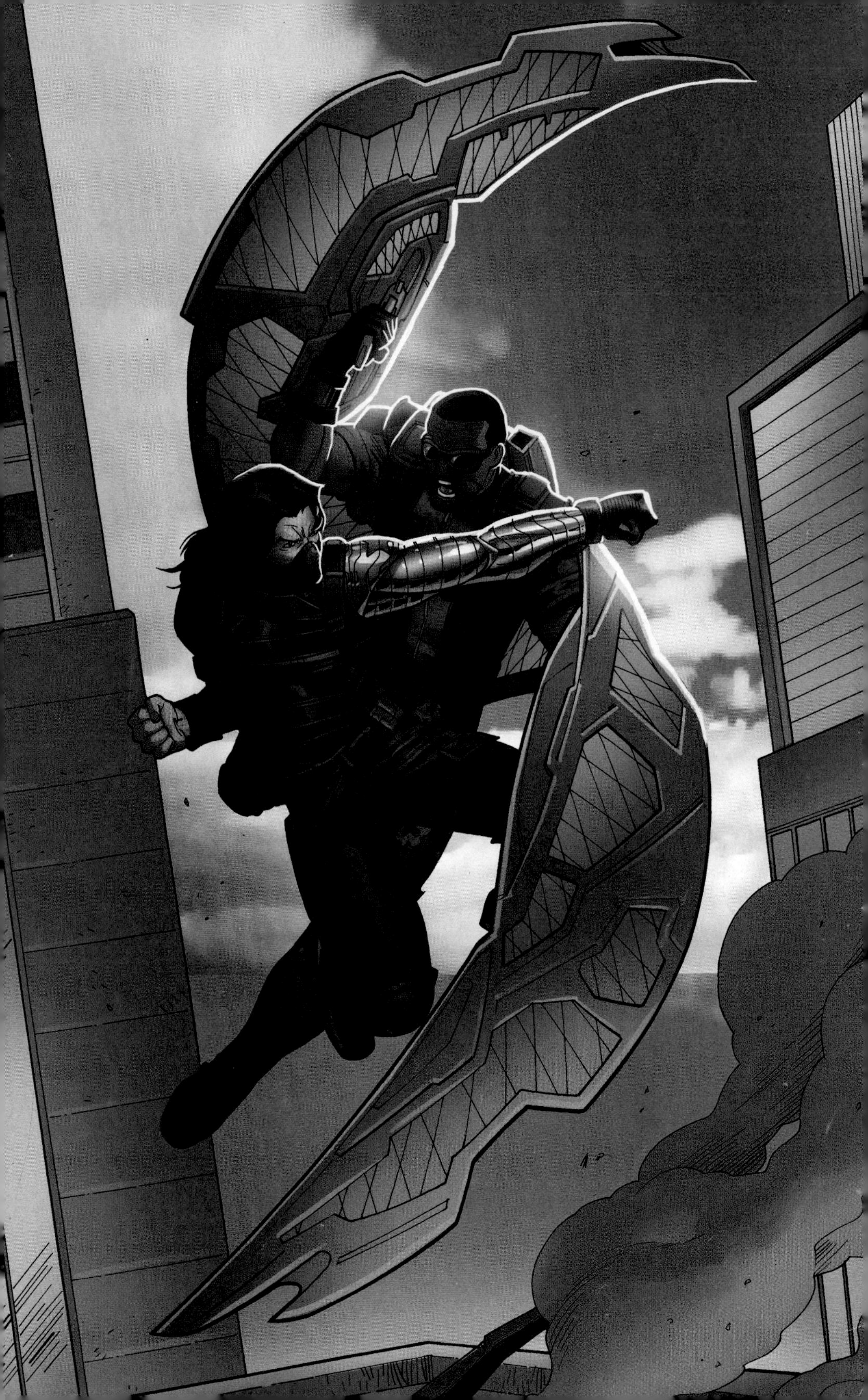

Next up was Captain America.
Cap attacked Bucky with his shield.

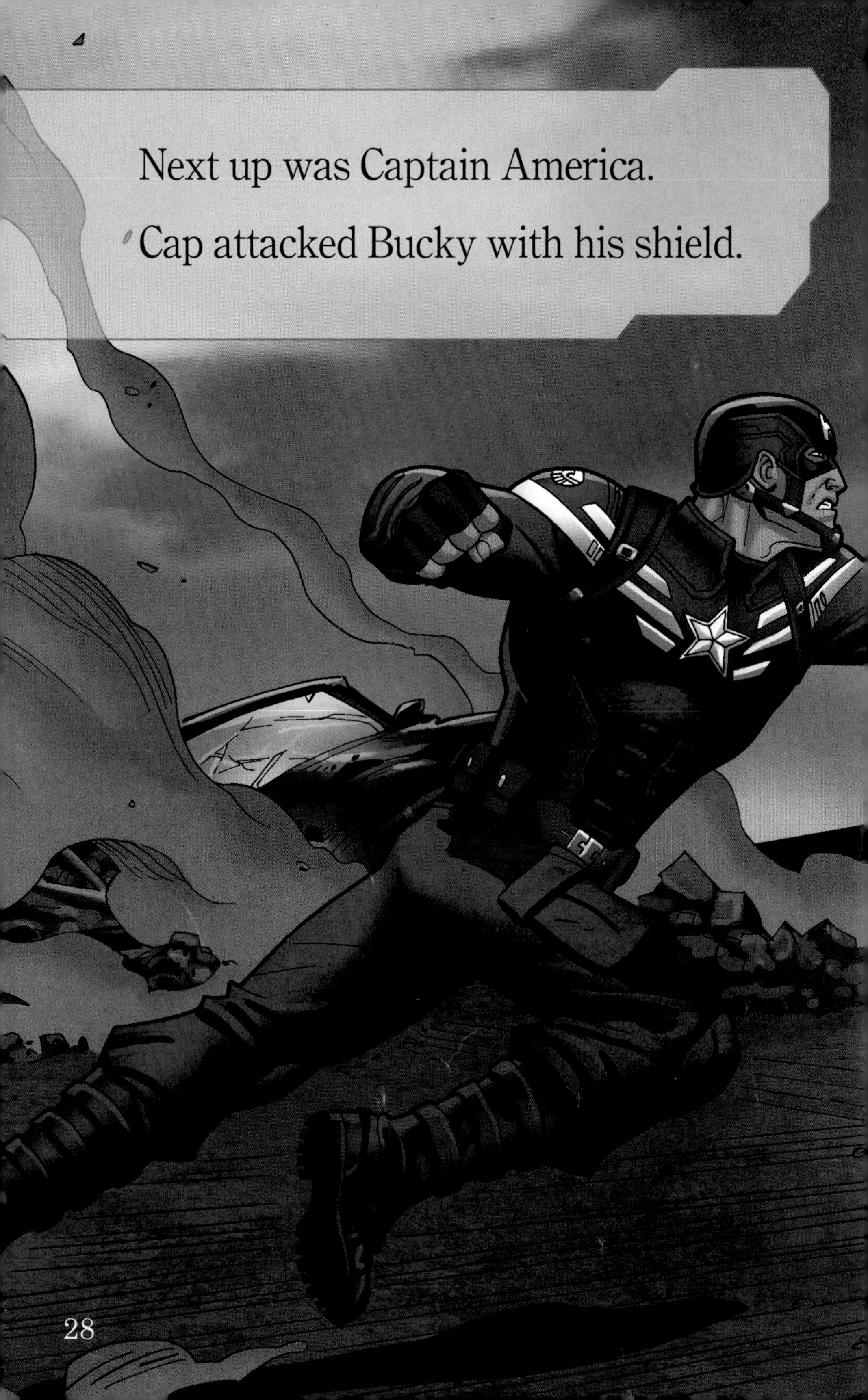

His metal fist punched the metal shield.

CRACK!

This was going to be a tough fight!

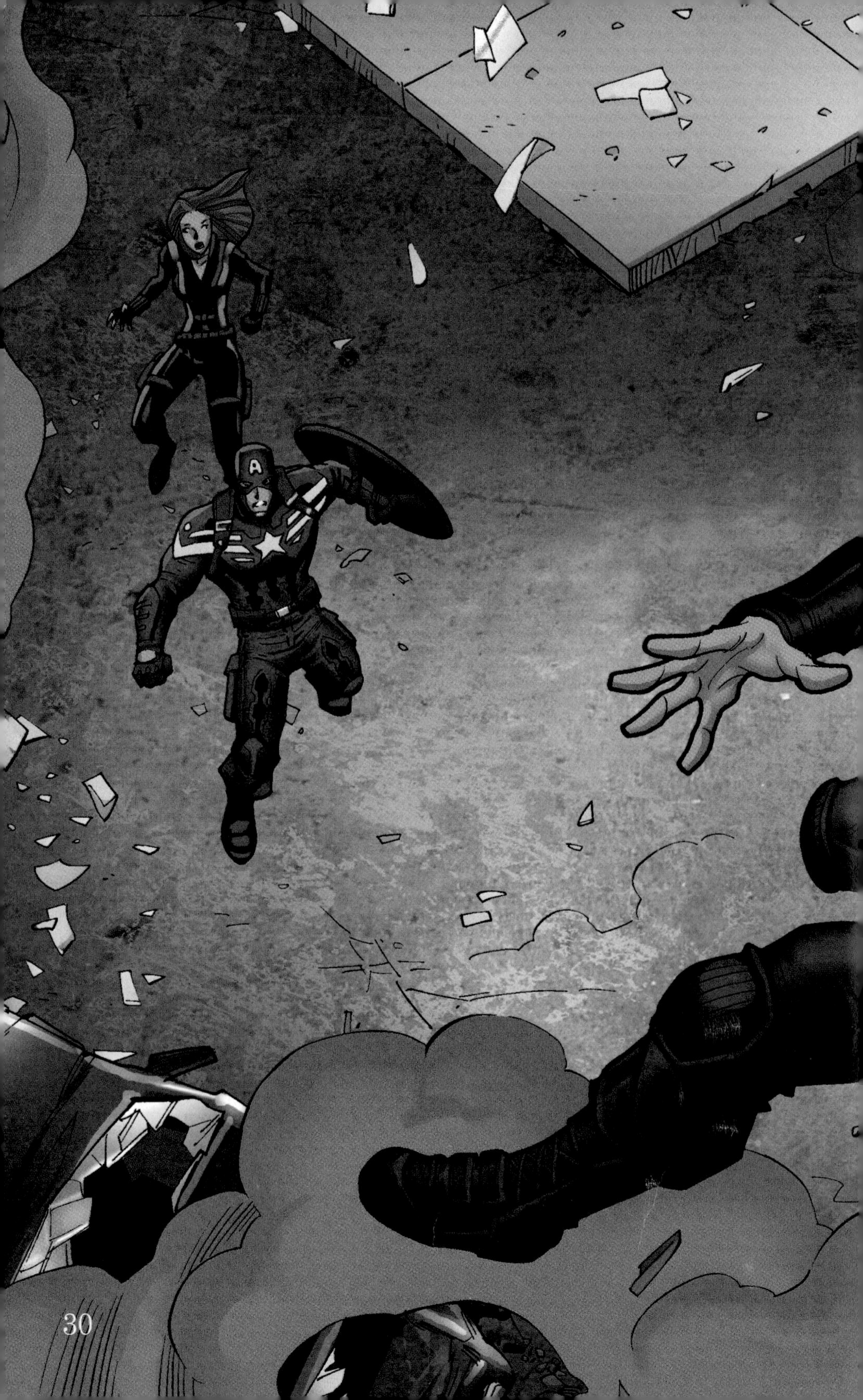

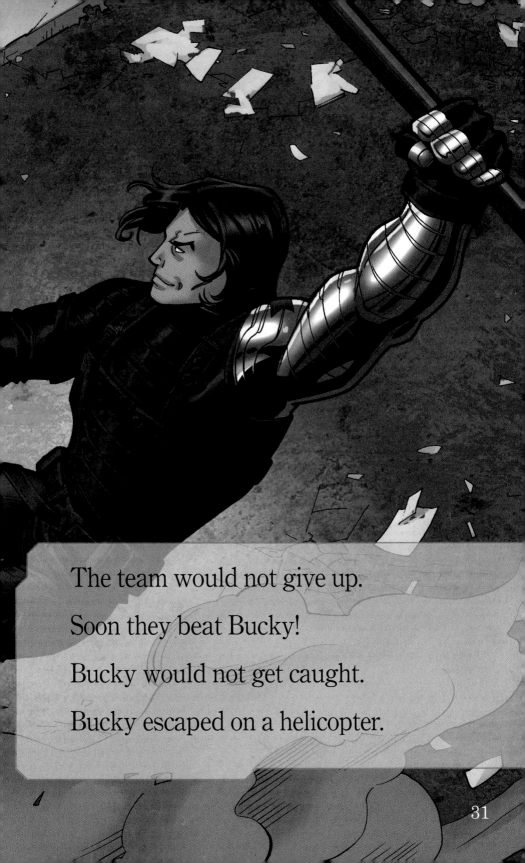

The team would not give up.

Soon they beat Bucky!

Bucky would not get caught.

Bucky escaped on a helicopter.

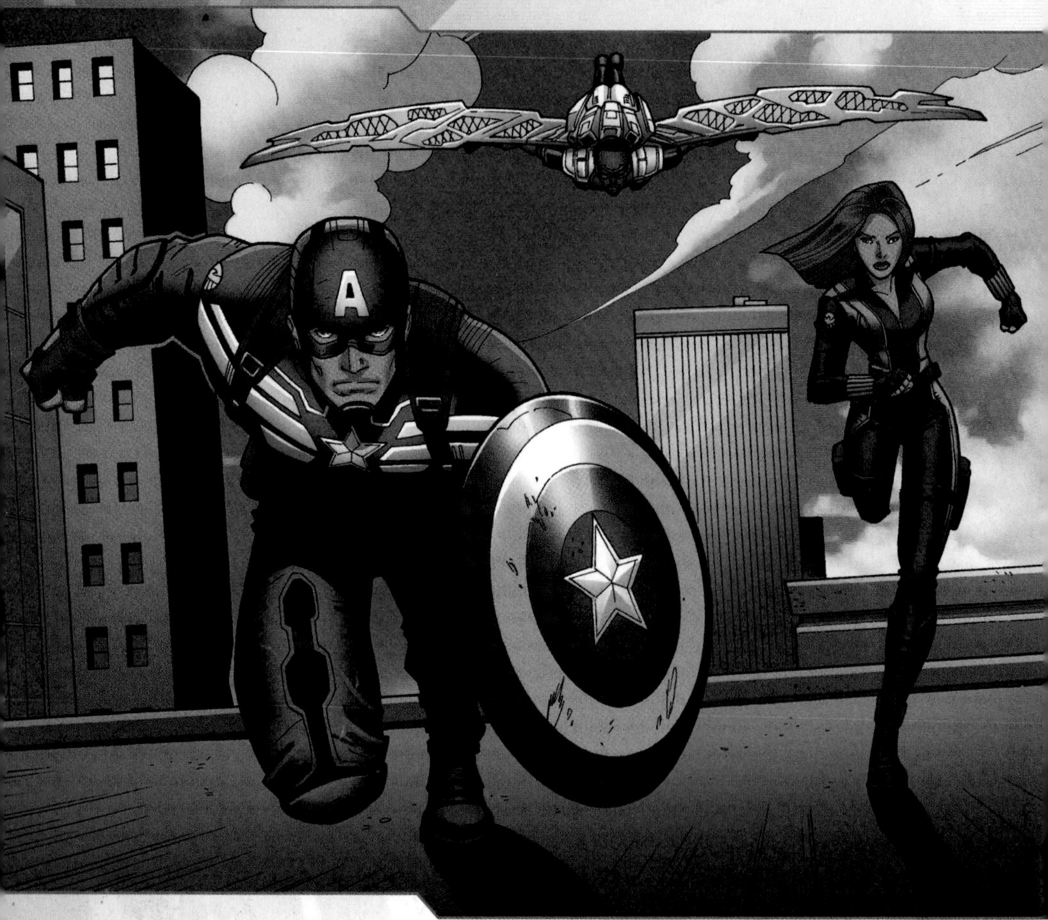

Captain America had lost a friend.

He also made a new friend.

His name was Falcon!

MARVEL

THE AVENGERS

» AVENGERS: ASSEMBLE!

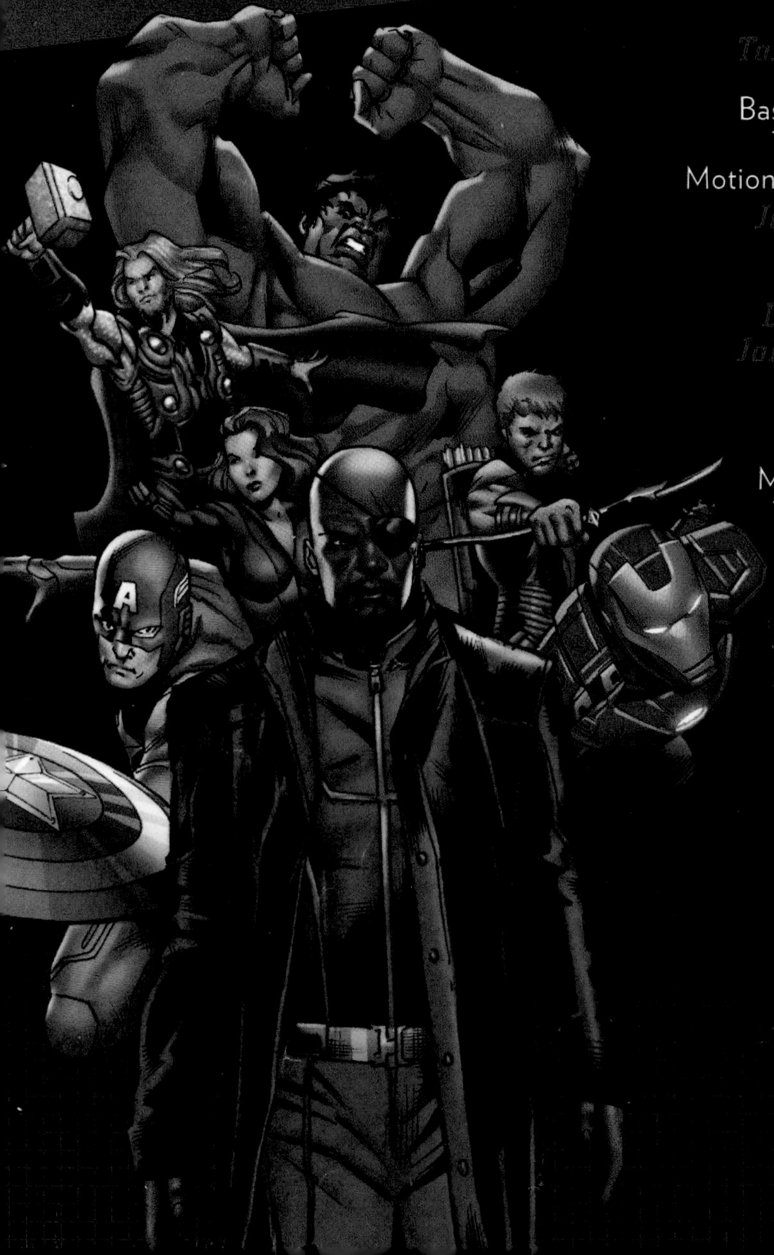

Written by
Tomas Palacios

Based on Marvel's
The Avengers
Motion Picture Written by
Joss Whedon

Illustrated by
Lee Garbett,
John Lucas, and
Lee Duhig

Based on
Marvel Comics'
The Avengers

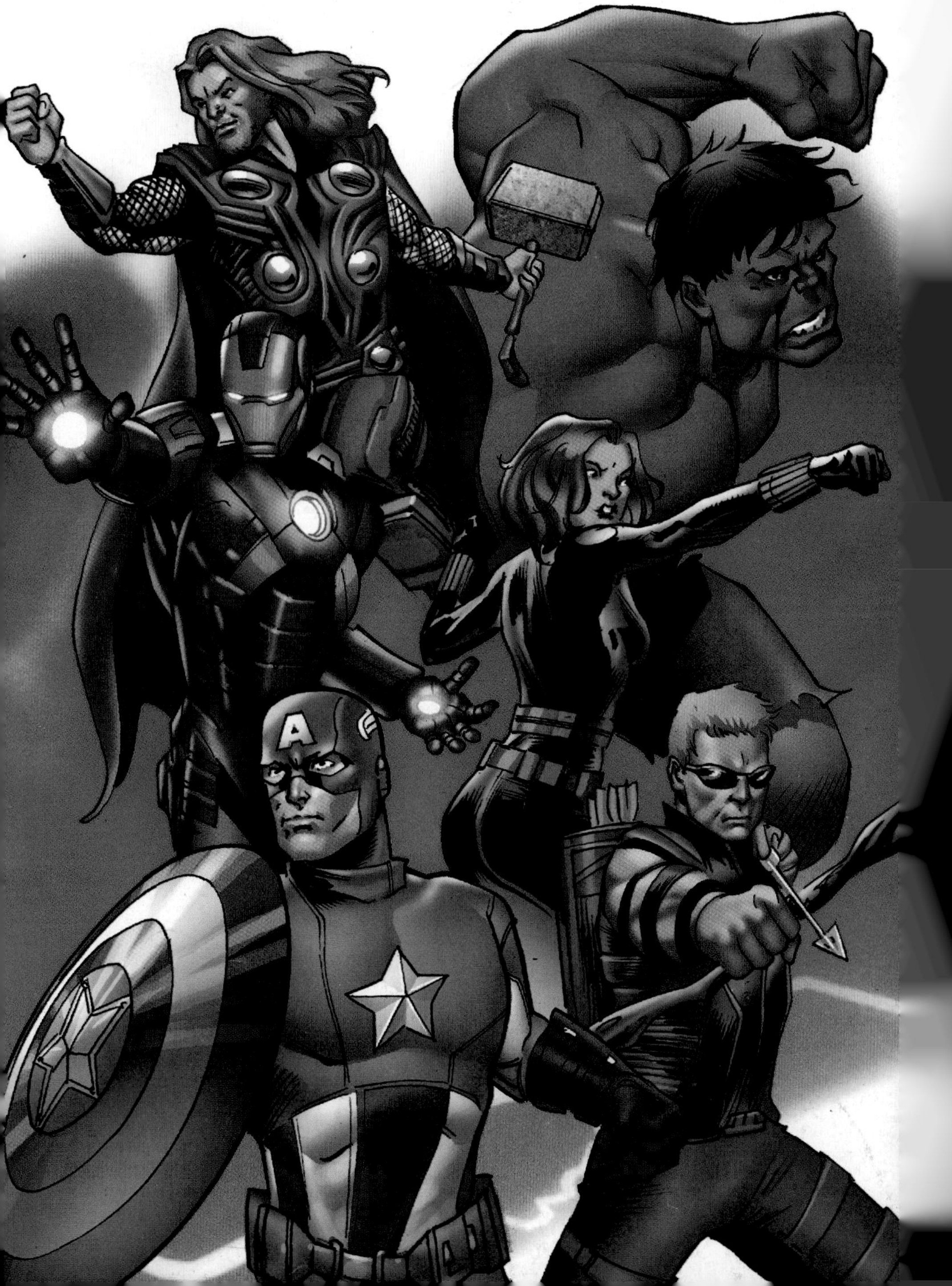

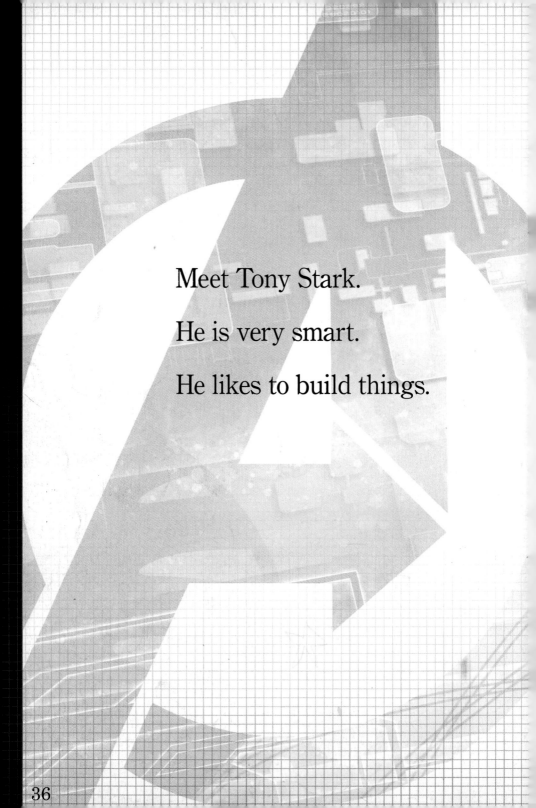

Meet Tony Stark.

He is very smart.

He likes to build things.

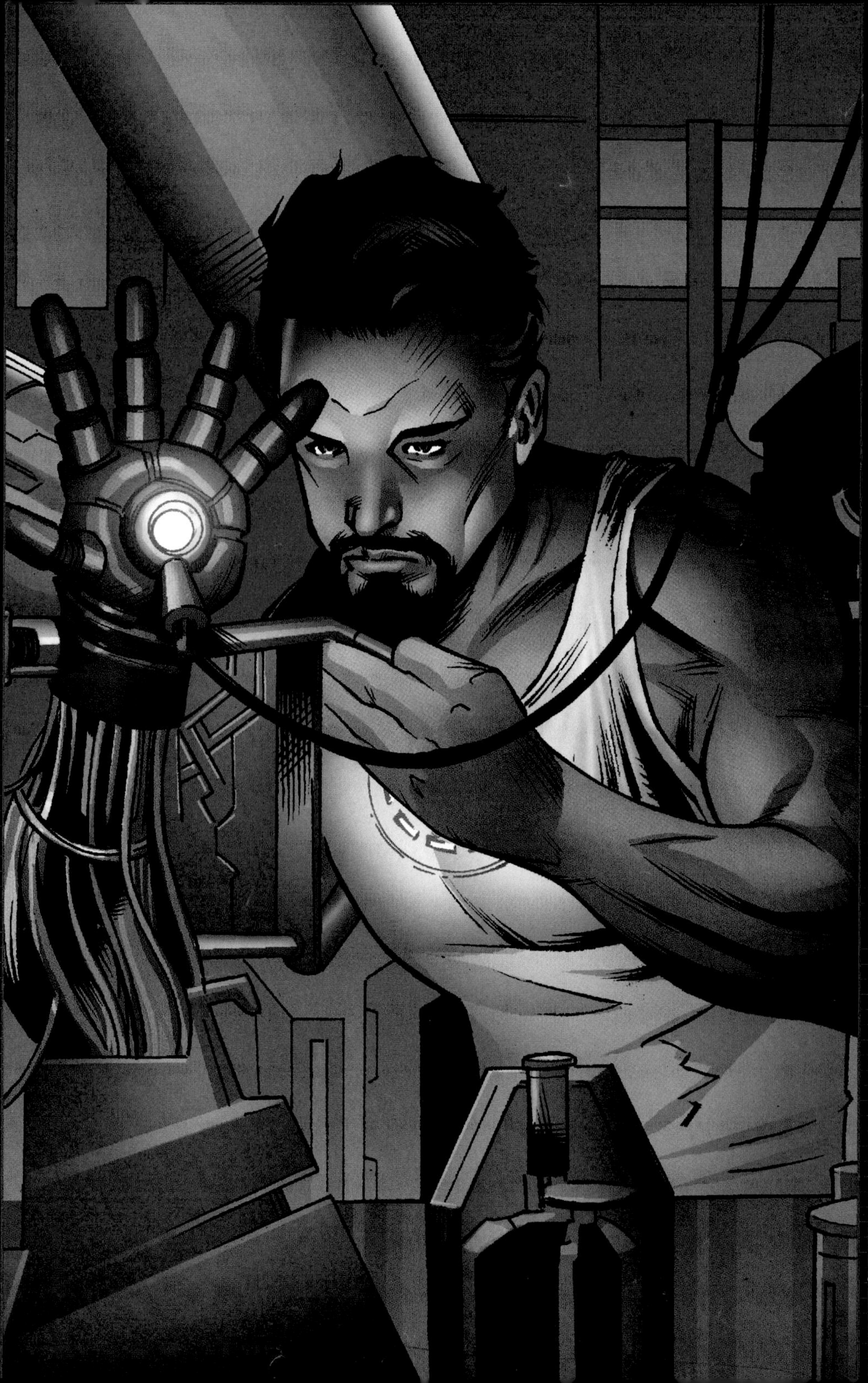

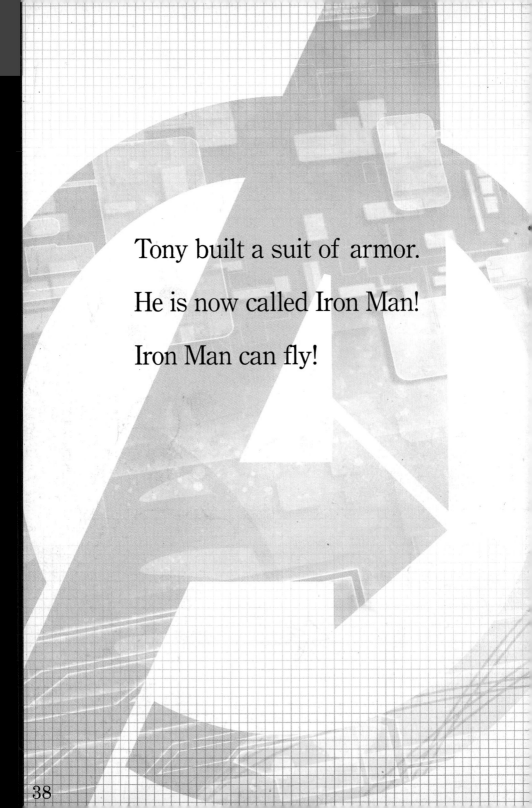

Tony built a suit of armor.

He is now called Iron Man!

Iron Man can fly!

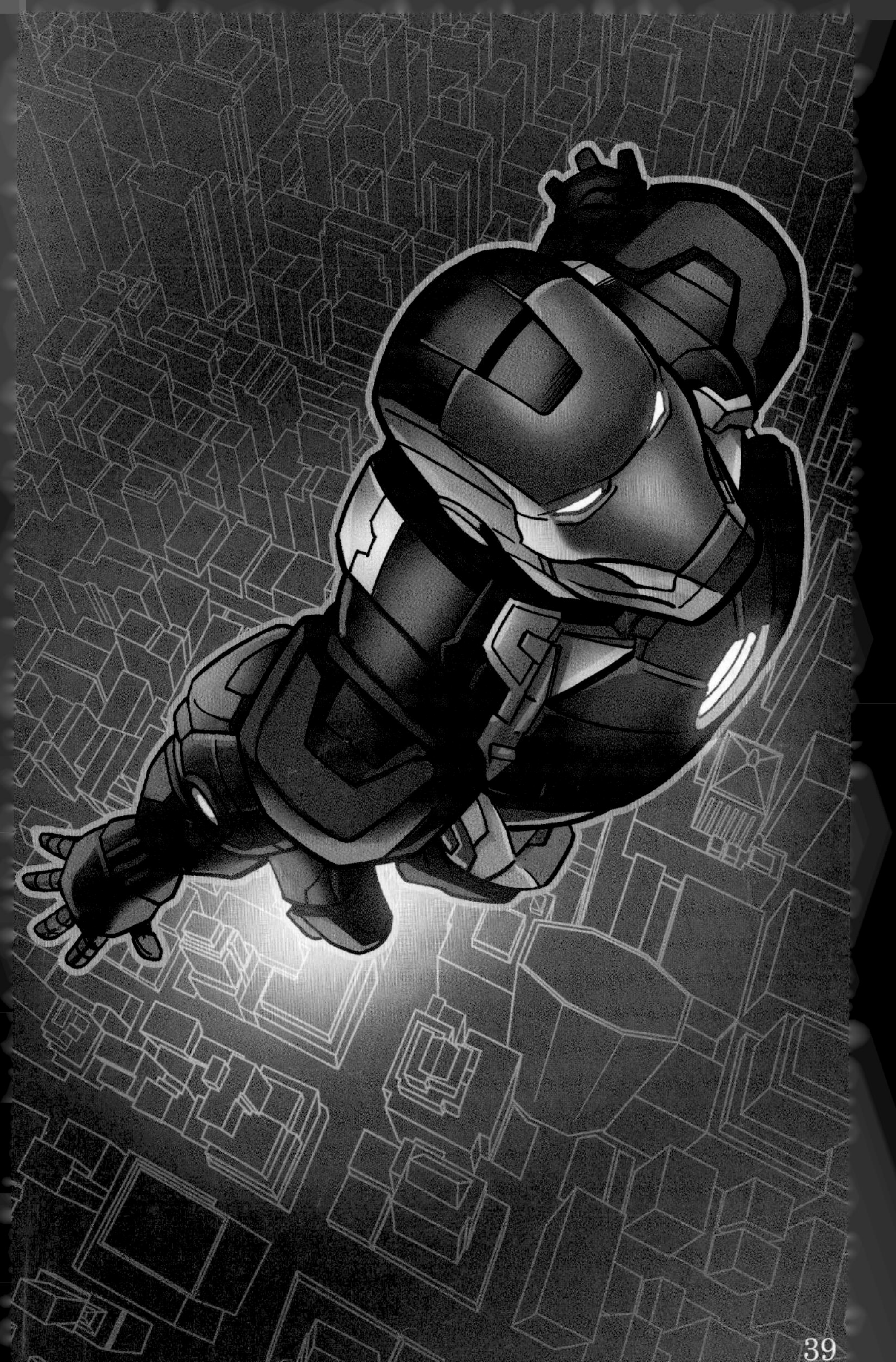

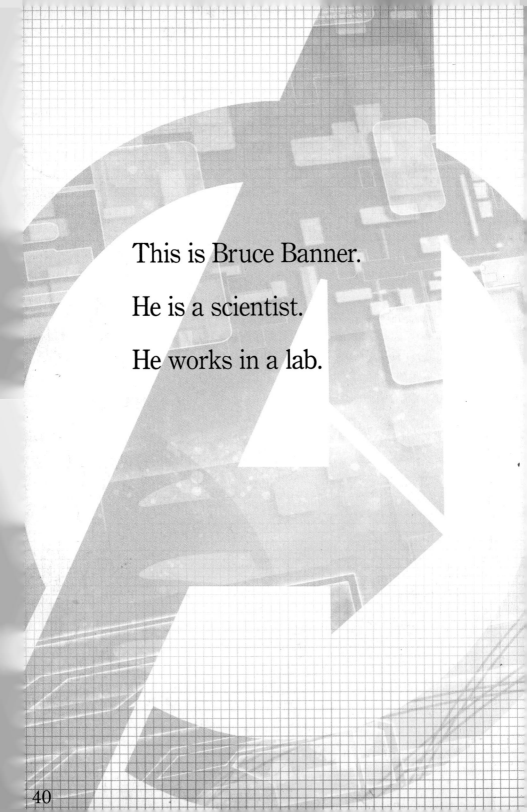

This is Bruce Banner.

He is a scientist.

He works in a lab.

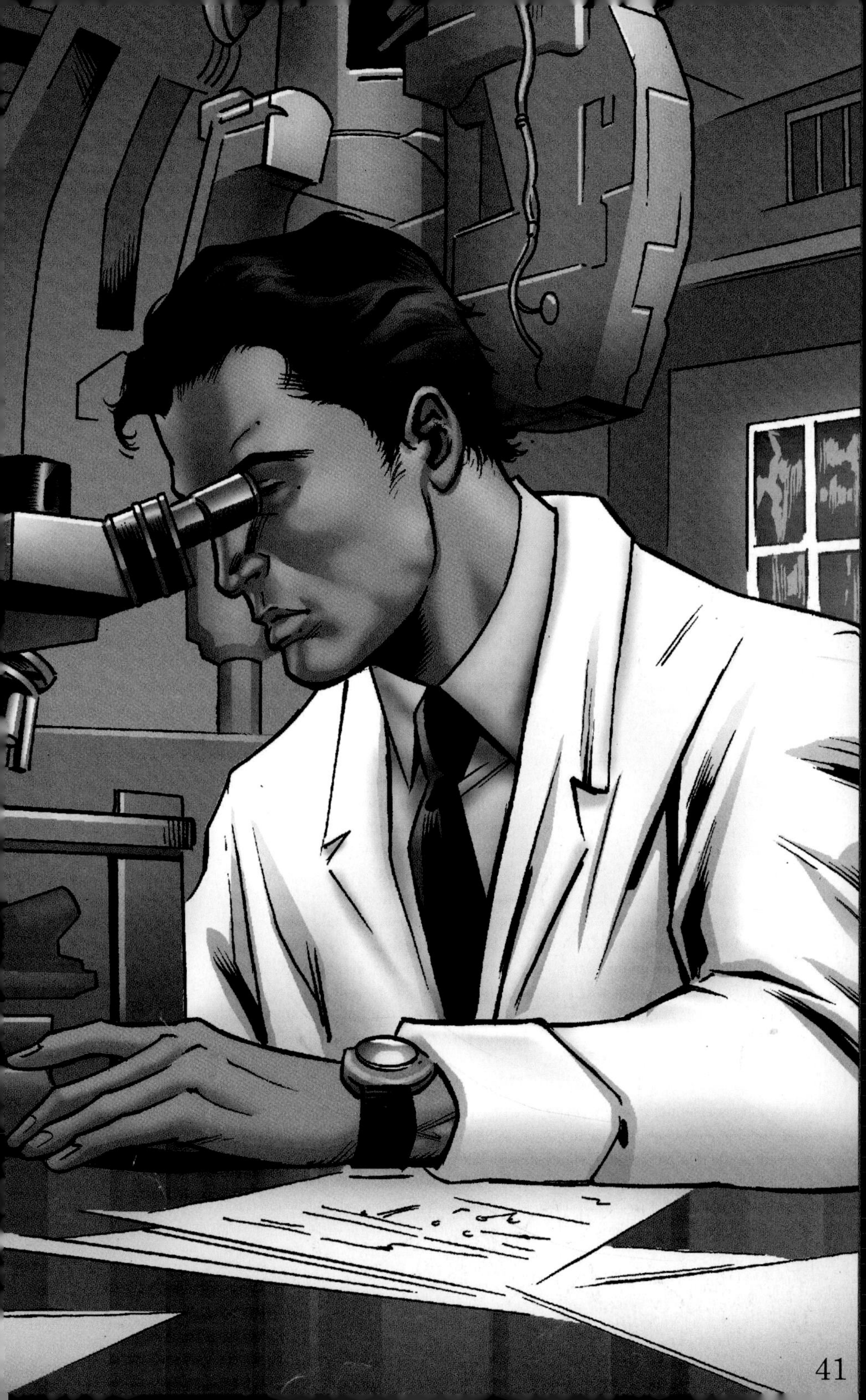

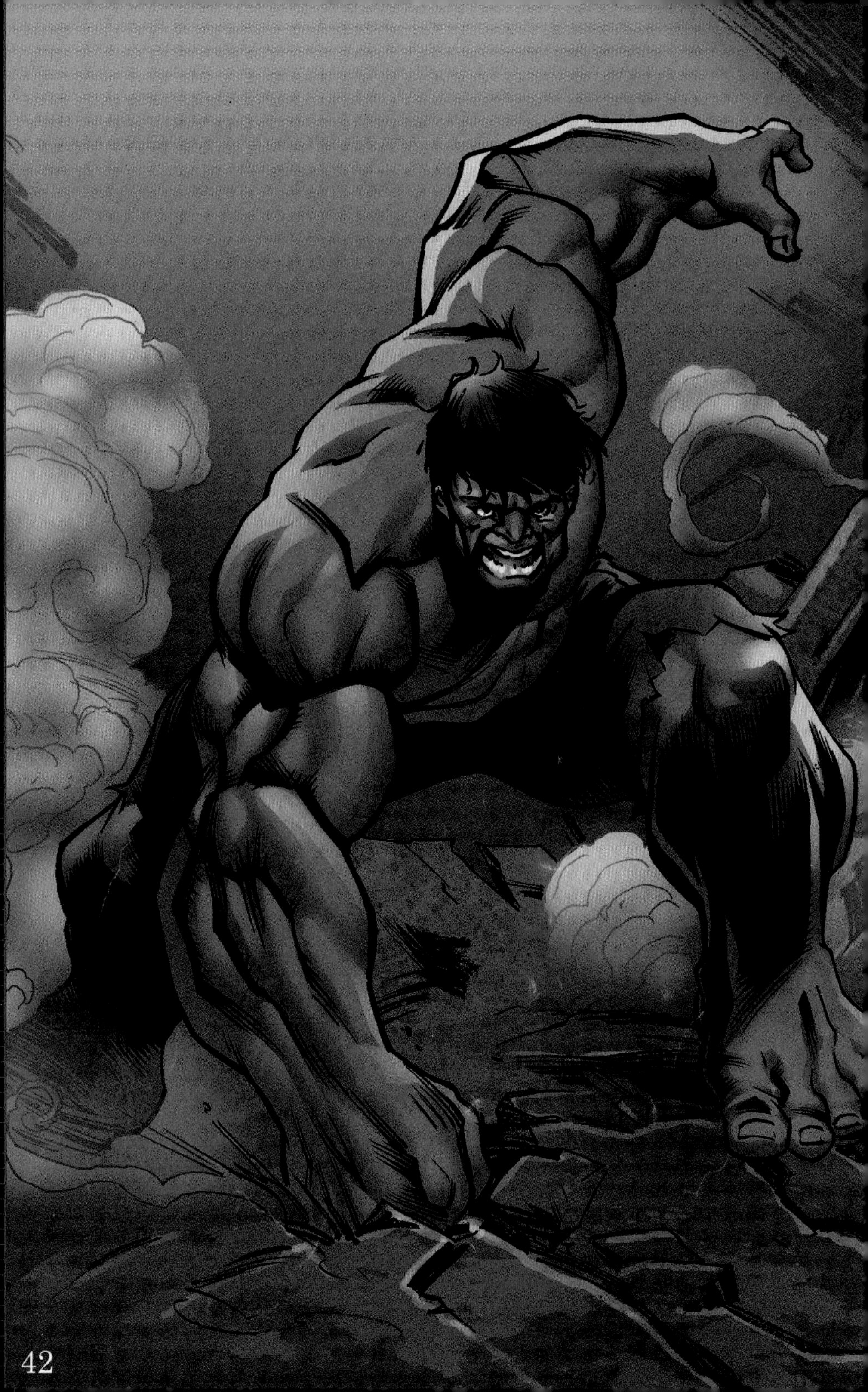

When Bruce gets angry,

he turns into the Hulk!

The Hulk is very big

and green!

Next is Thor.

He is from another world.

Thor has a magical hammer.

He can control lightning!

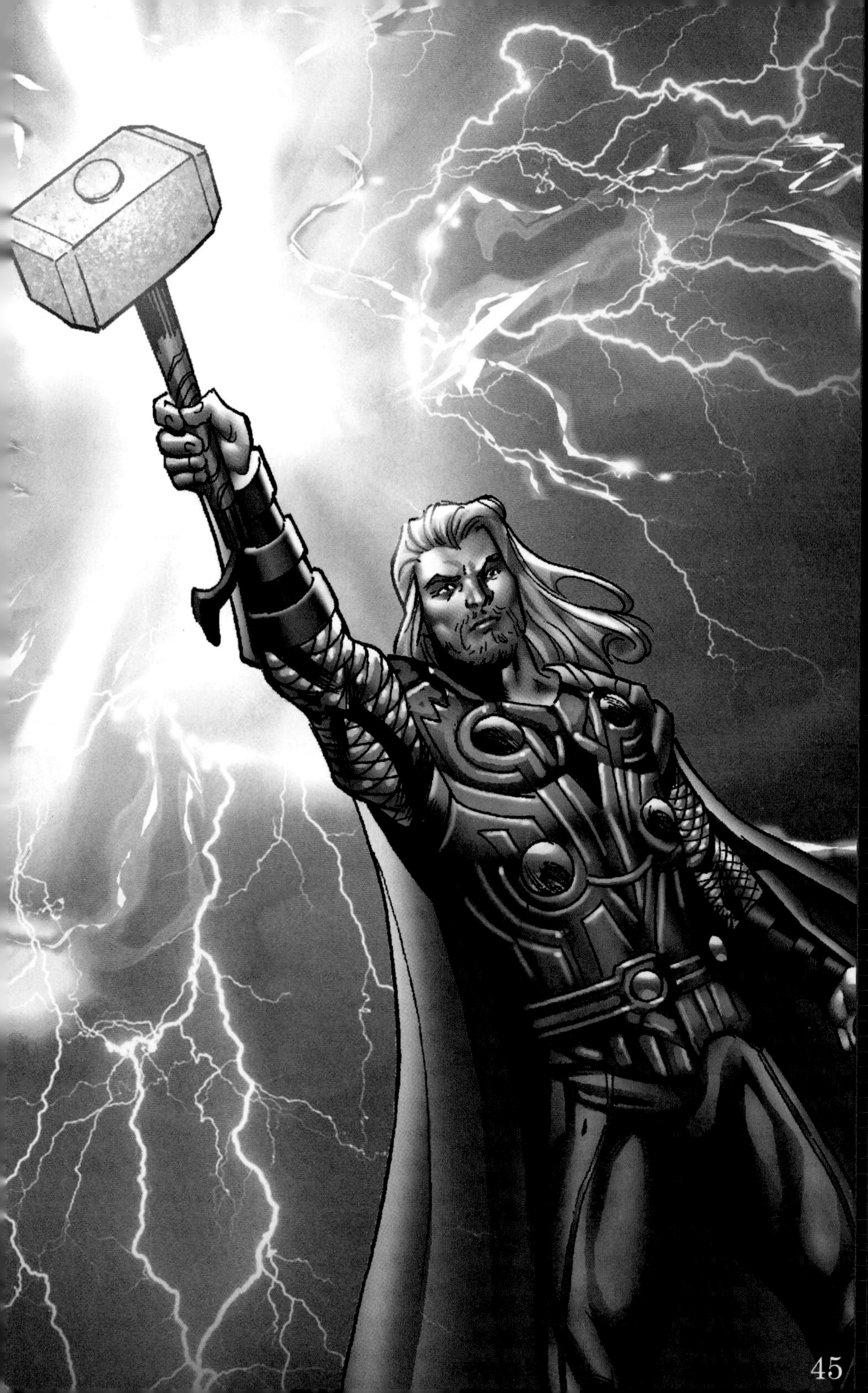

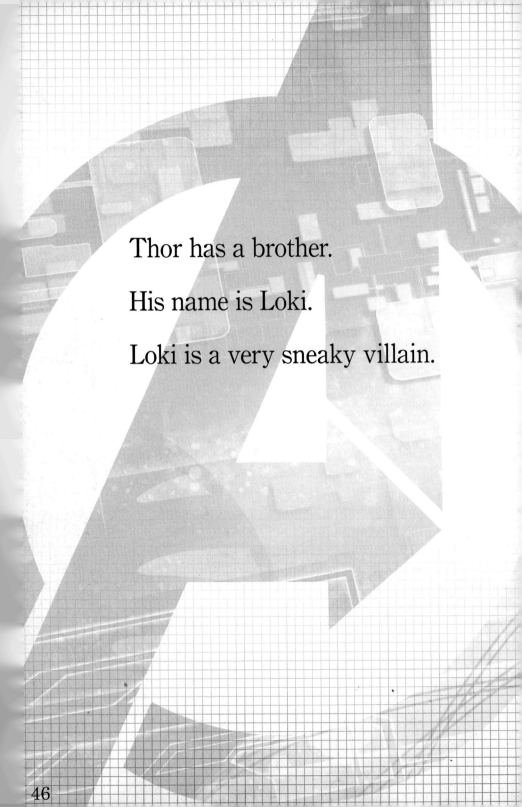

Thor has a brother.

His name is Loki.

Loki is a very sneaky villain.

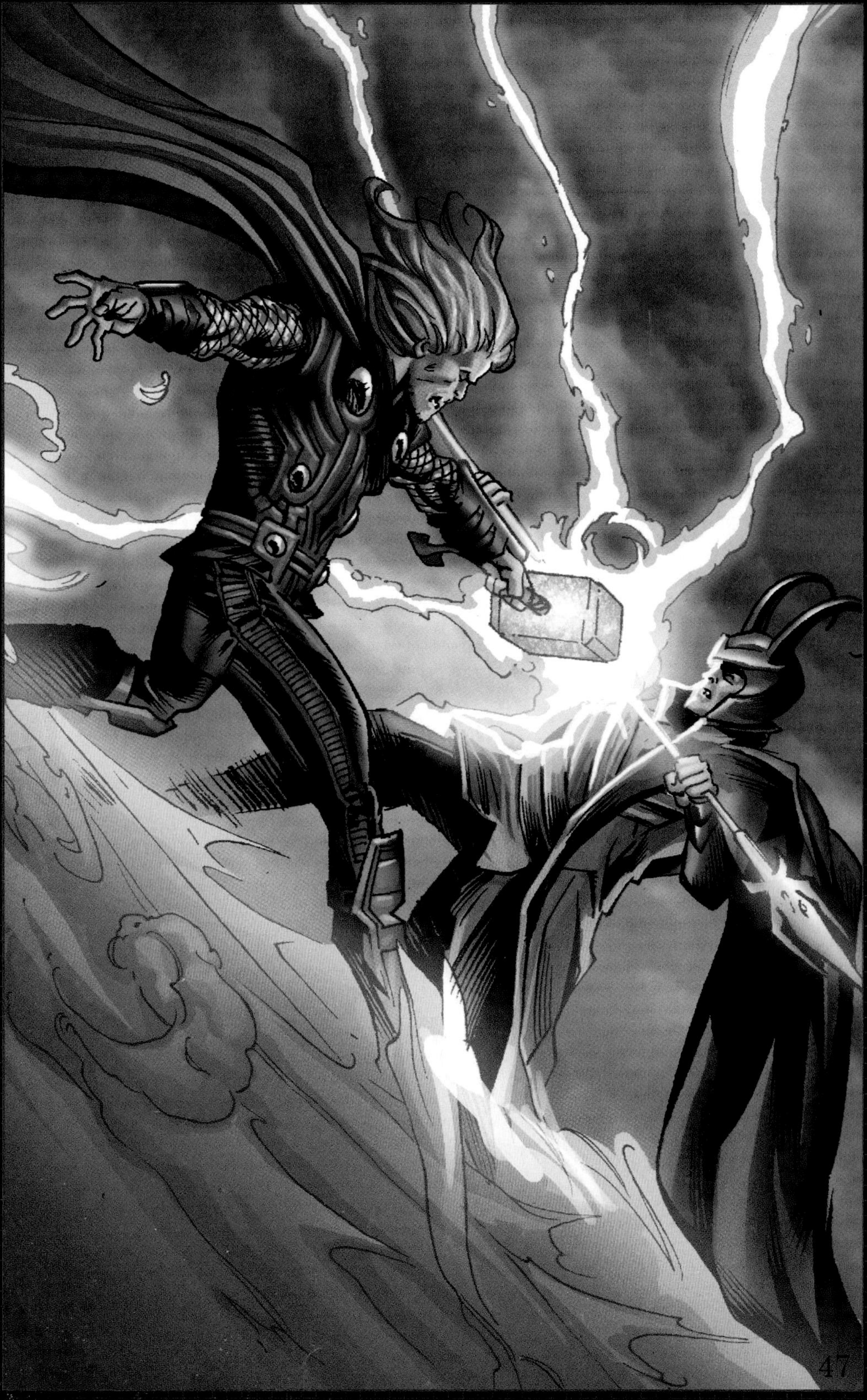

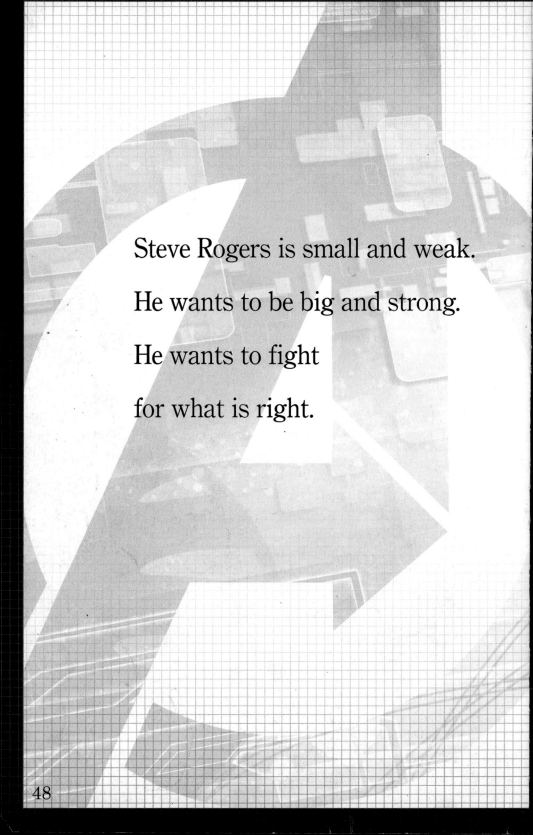

Steve Rogers is small and weak.

He wants to be big and strong.

He wants to fight

for what is right.

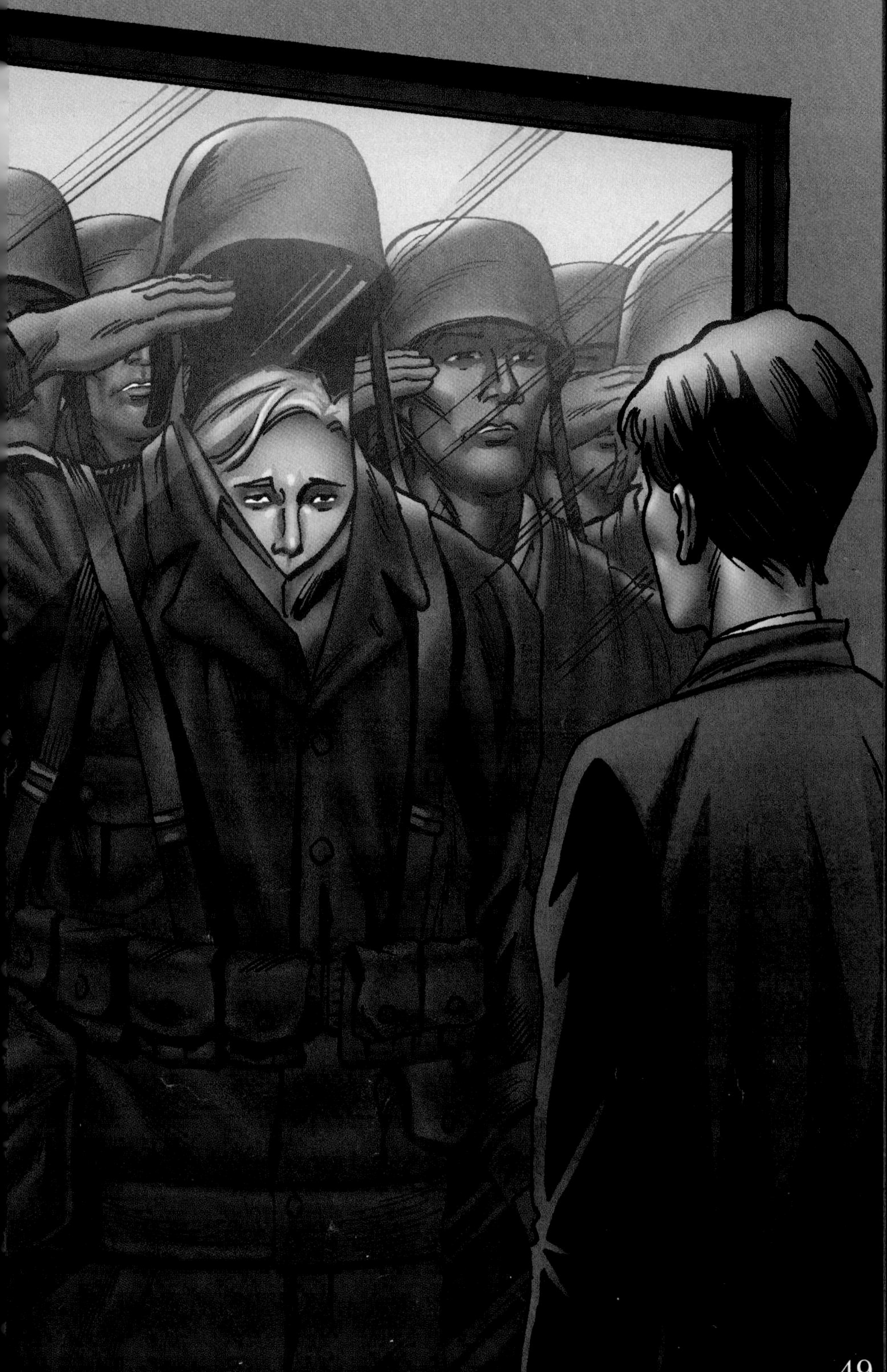

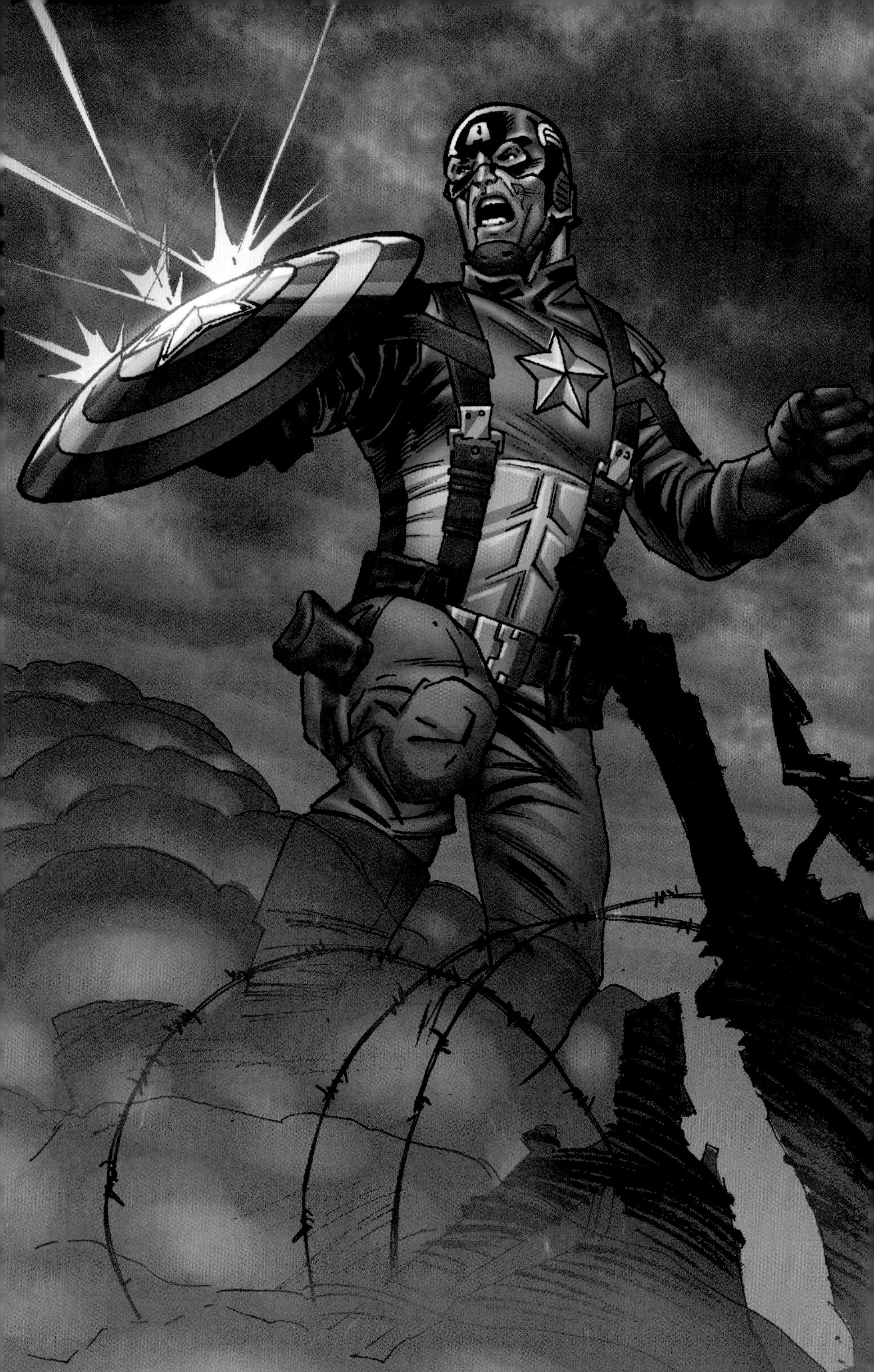

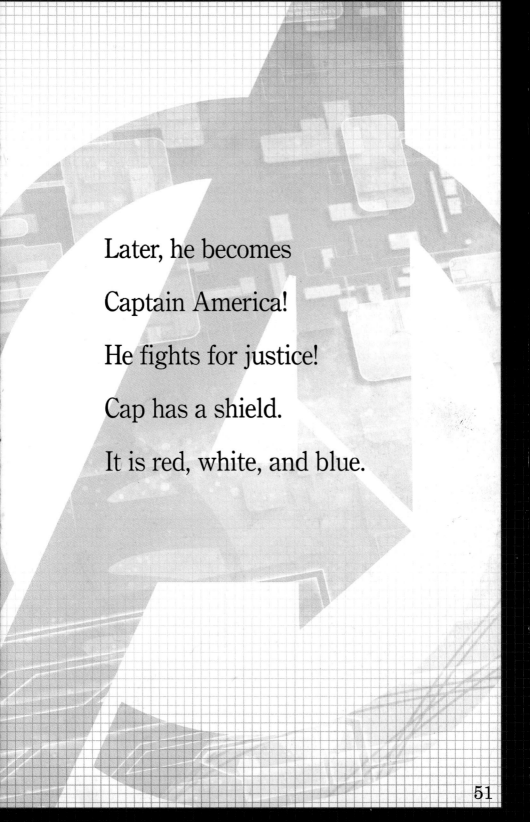

Later, he becomes

Captain America!

He fights for justice!

Cap has a shield.

It is red, white, and blue.

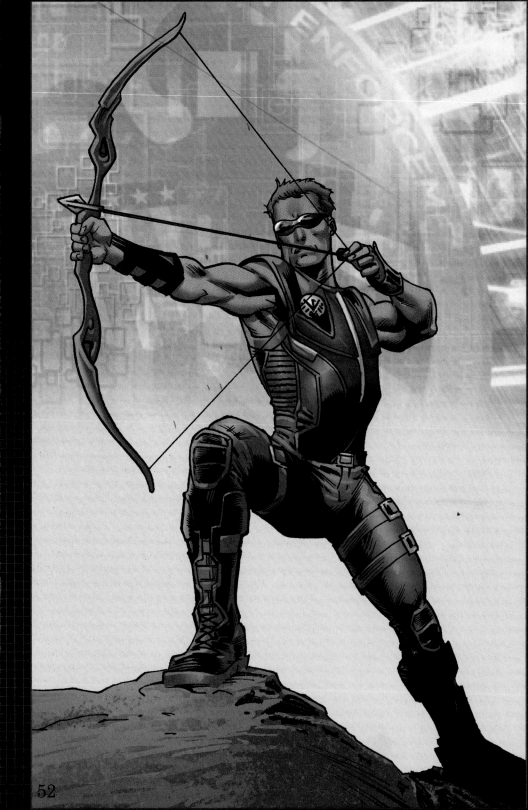

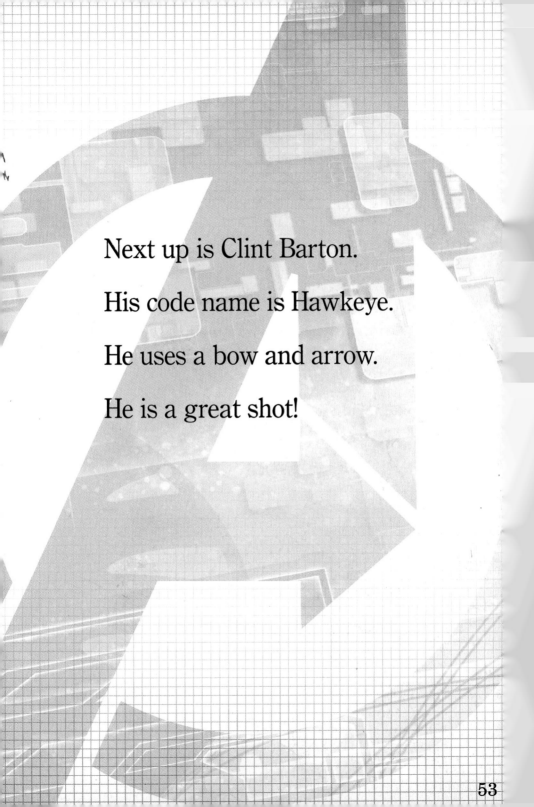

Next up is Clint Barton.

His code name is Hawkeye.

He uses a bow and arrow.

He is a great shot!

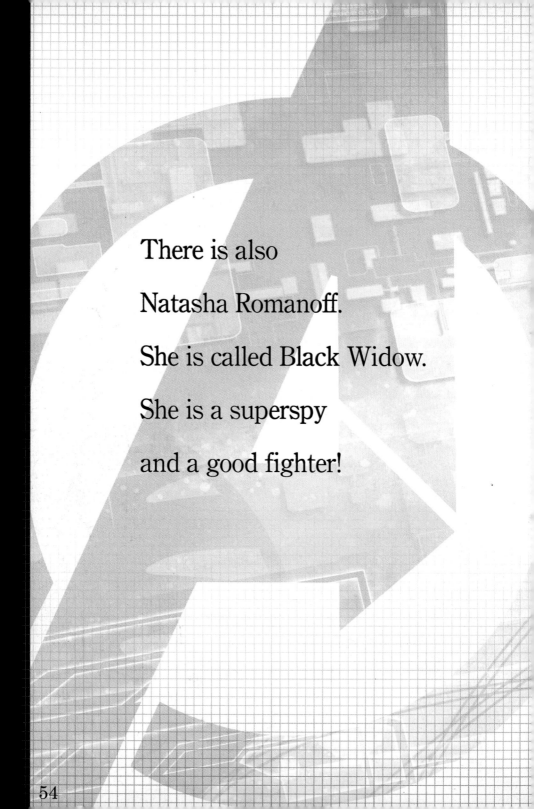

There is also

Natasha Romanoff.

She is called Black Widow.

She is a superspy

and a good fighter!

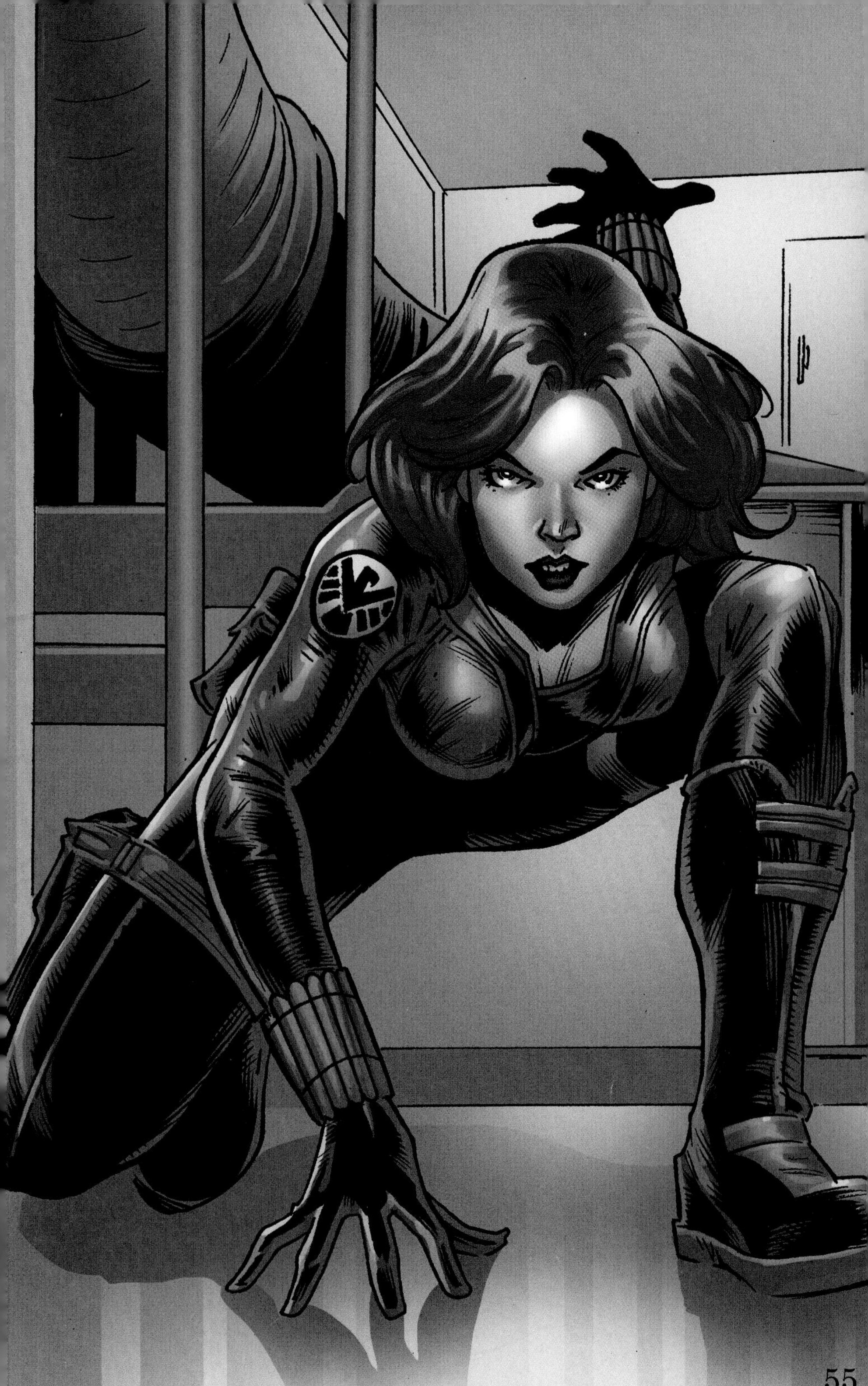

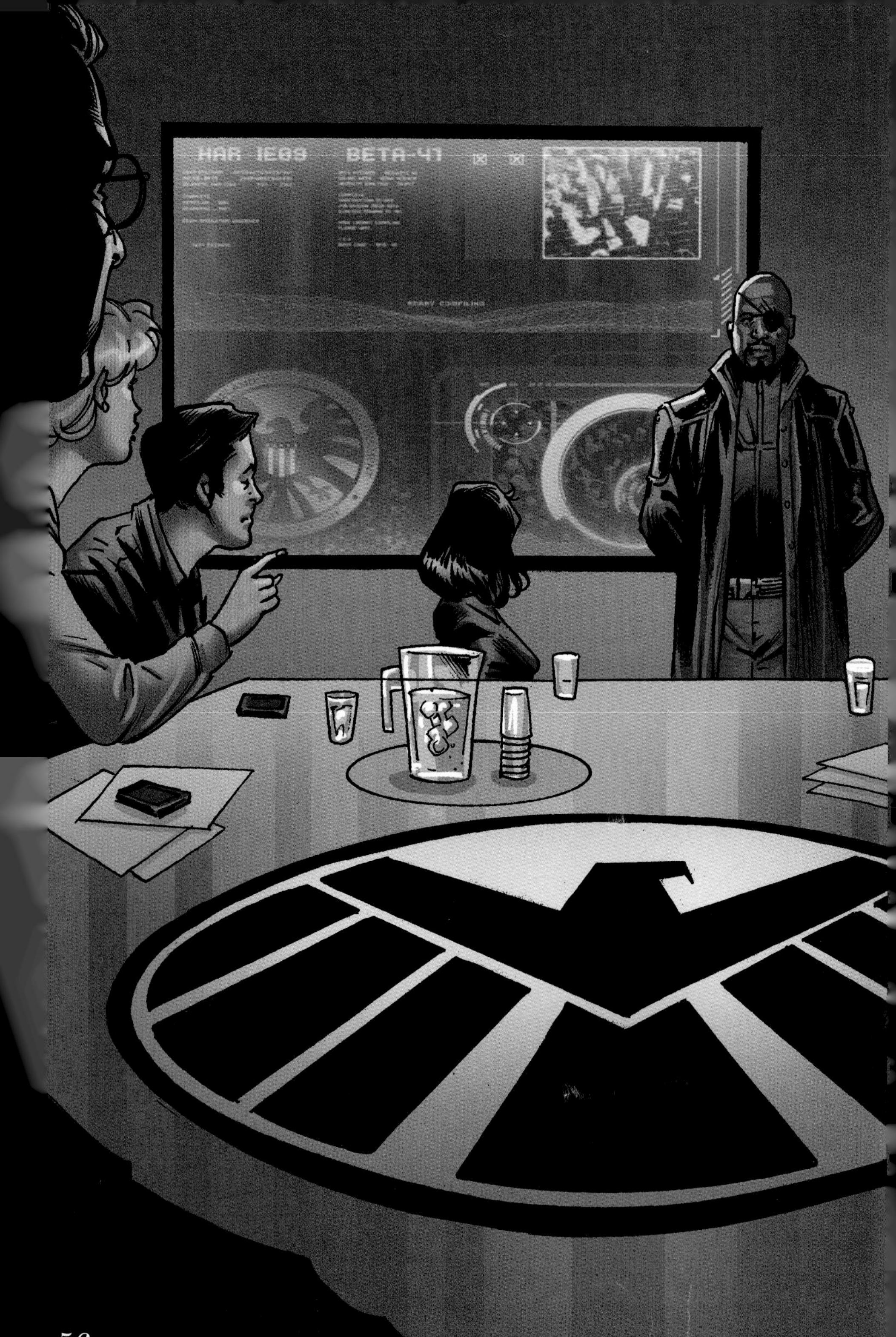
BETA-41
ARRAY COMPILING

Finally, there is Nick Fury.

He is the leader of S.H.I.E.L.D.

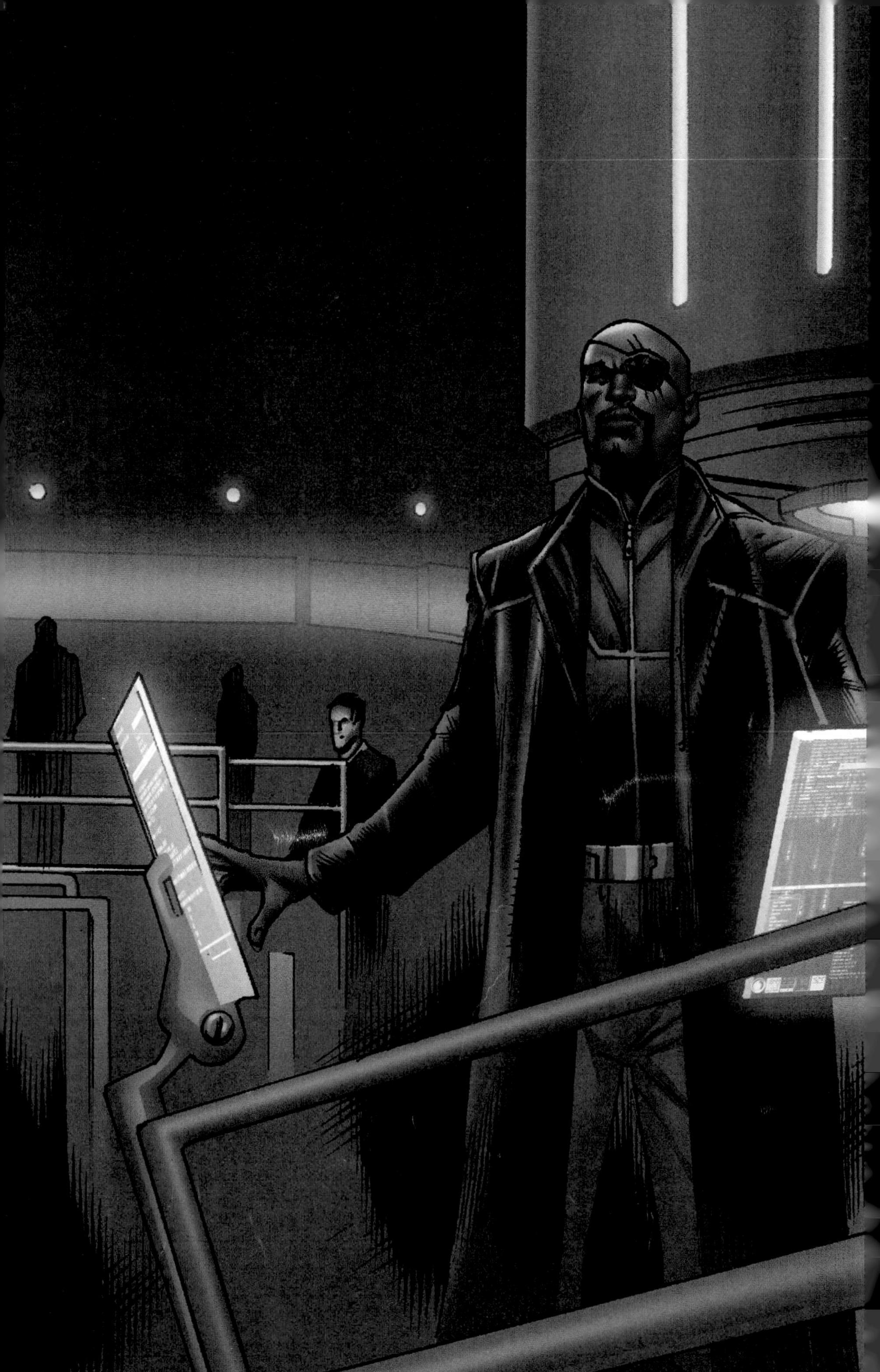

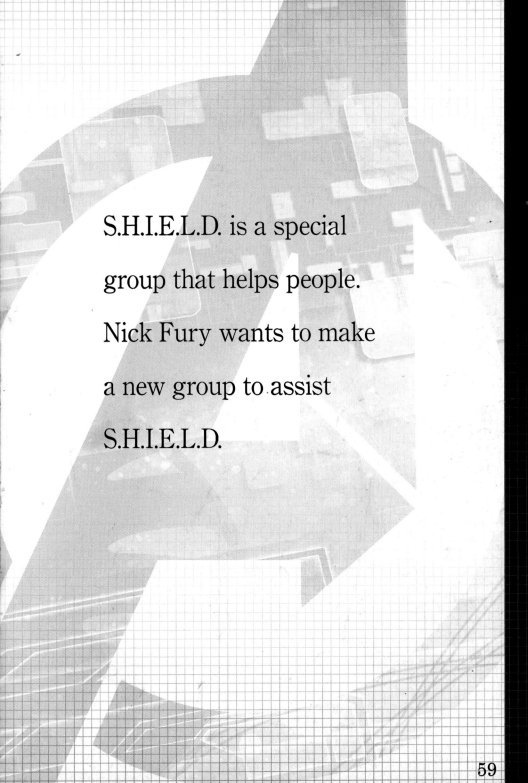

S.H.I.E.L.D. is a special

group that helps people.

Nick Fury wants to make

a new group to assist

S.H.I.E.L.D.

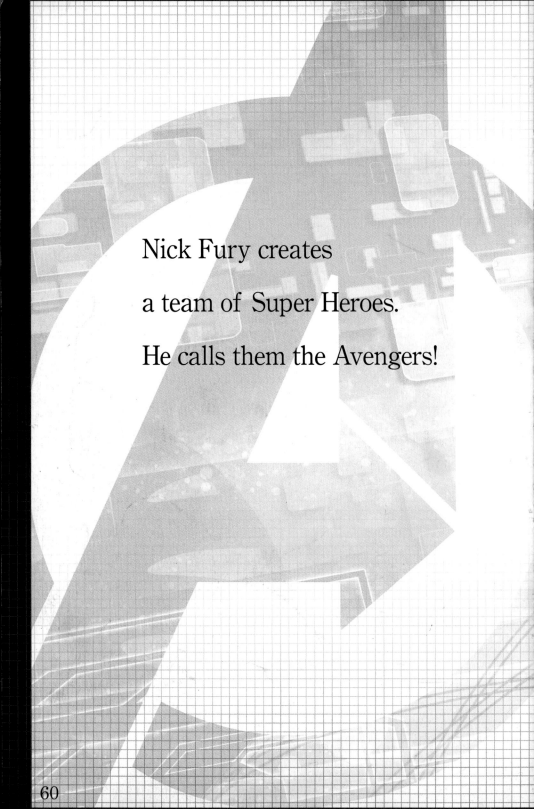

Nick Fury creates

a team of Super Heroes.

He calls them the Avengers!

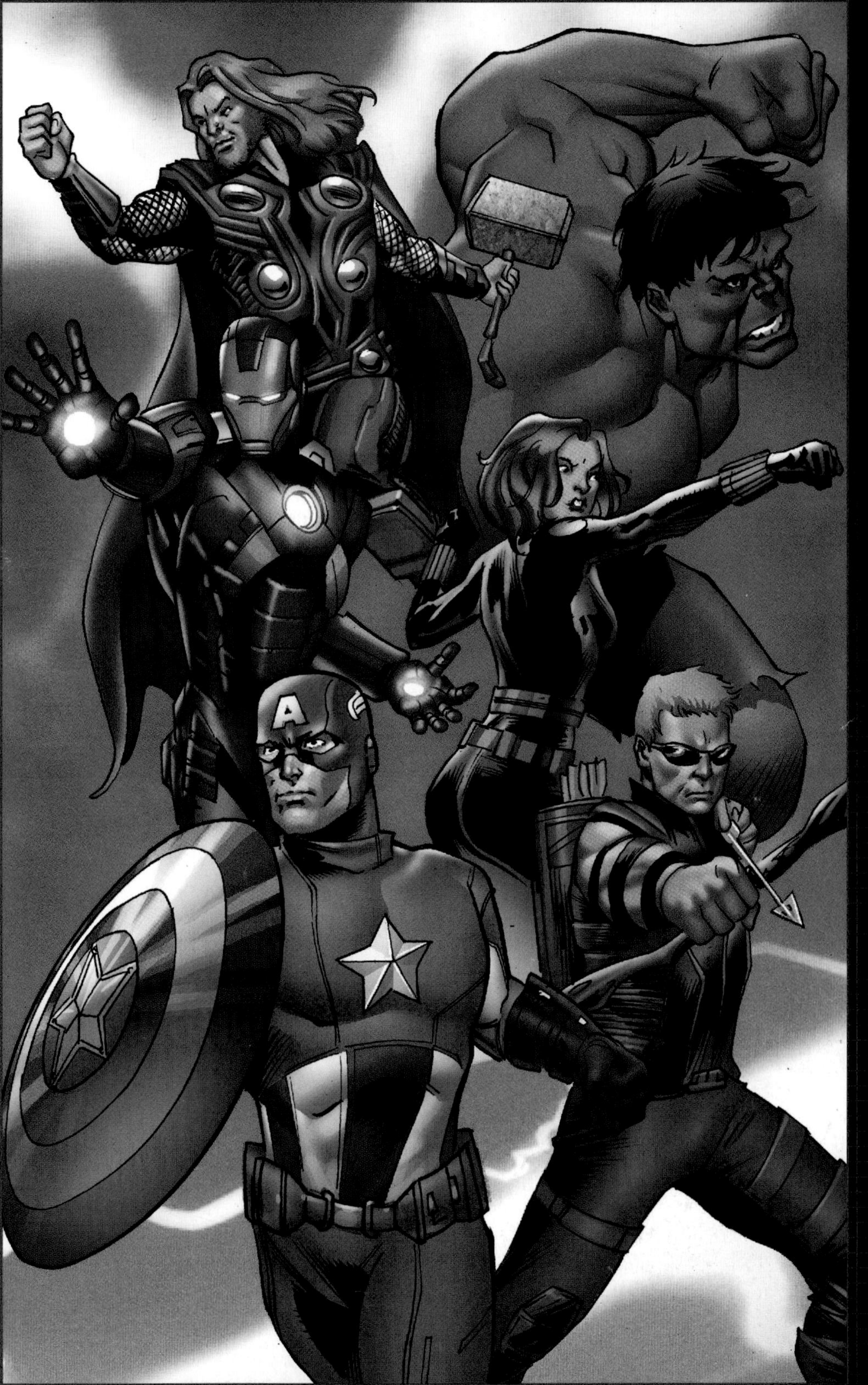

The Avengers fight for good.

They use their powers

to stop bad guys.

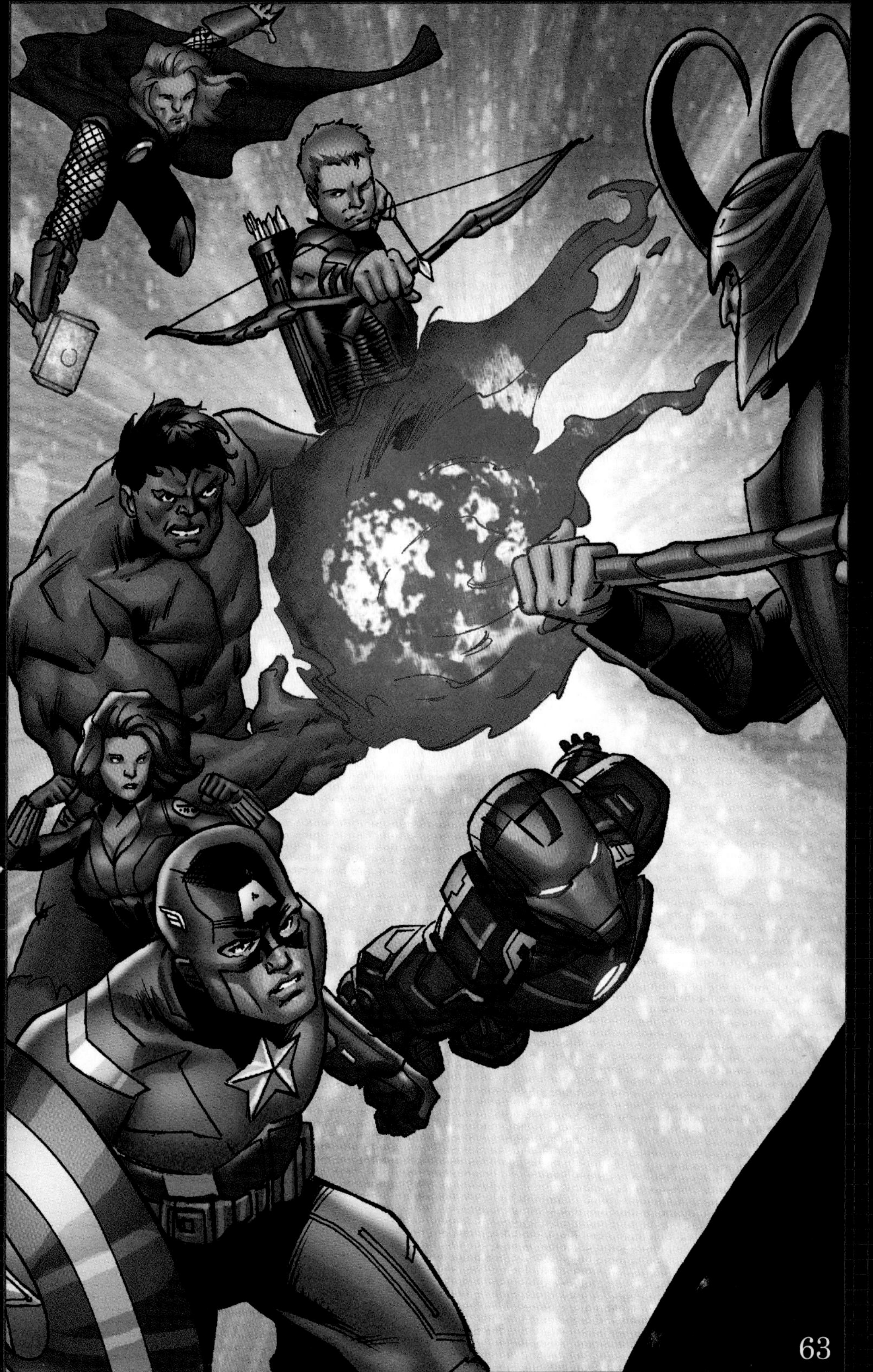

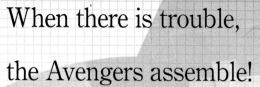

When there is trouble,

the Avengers assemble!

AGE OF ULTRON

Friends and Foes

By **Tomas Palacios**
Illustrated by **Ron Lim, Andy Smith, and Andy Troy**
Based on the Screenplay by **Joss Whedon**
Produced by **Kevin Feige, p.g.a.**
Directed by **Joss Whedon**

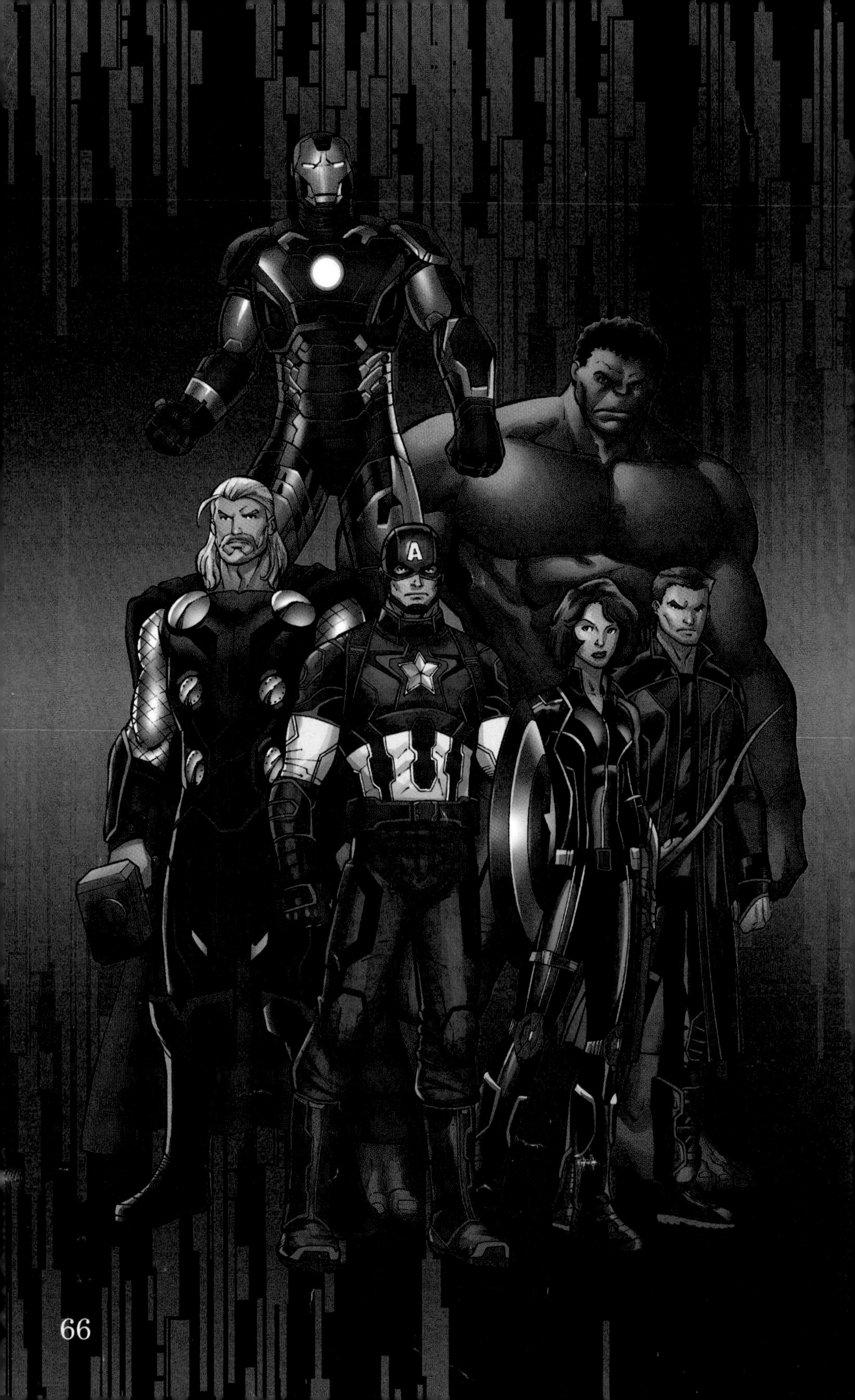

Attention, AVENGERS fans!
Look for these words
when you read this book.
Can you spot them all?

scepter

robot

shield

arrow

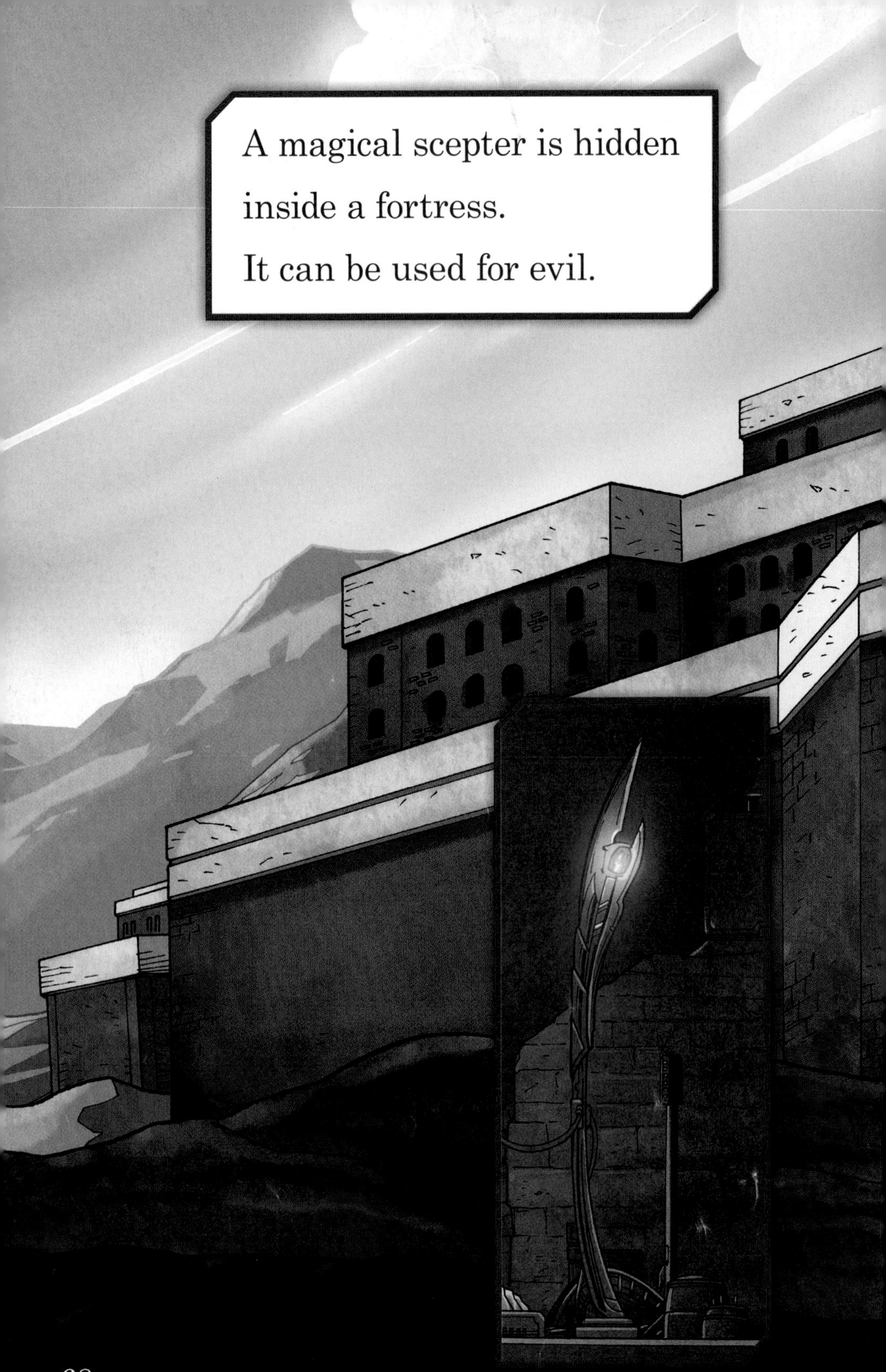
A magical scepter is hidden inside a fortress.
It can be used for evil.

The Avengers must get the scepter.
They do not want it to fall into
the wrong hands.
They want to protect it from villains.

Tony Stark is Iron Man.
Iron Man's suit is very strong.
He can fly and fire missiles.

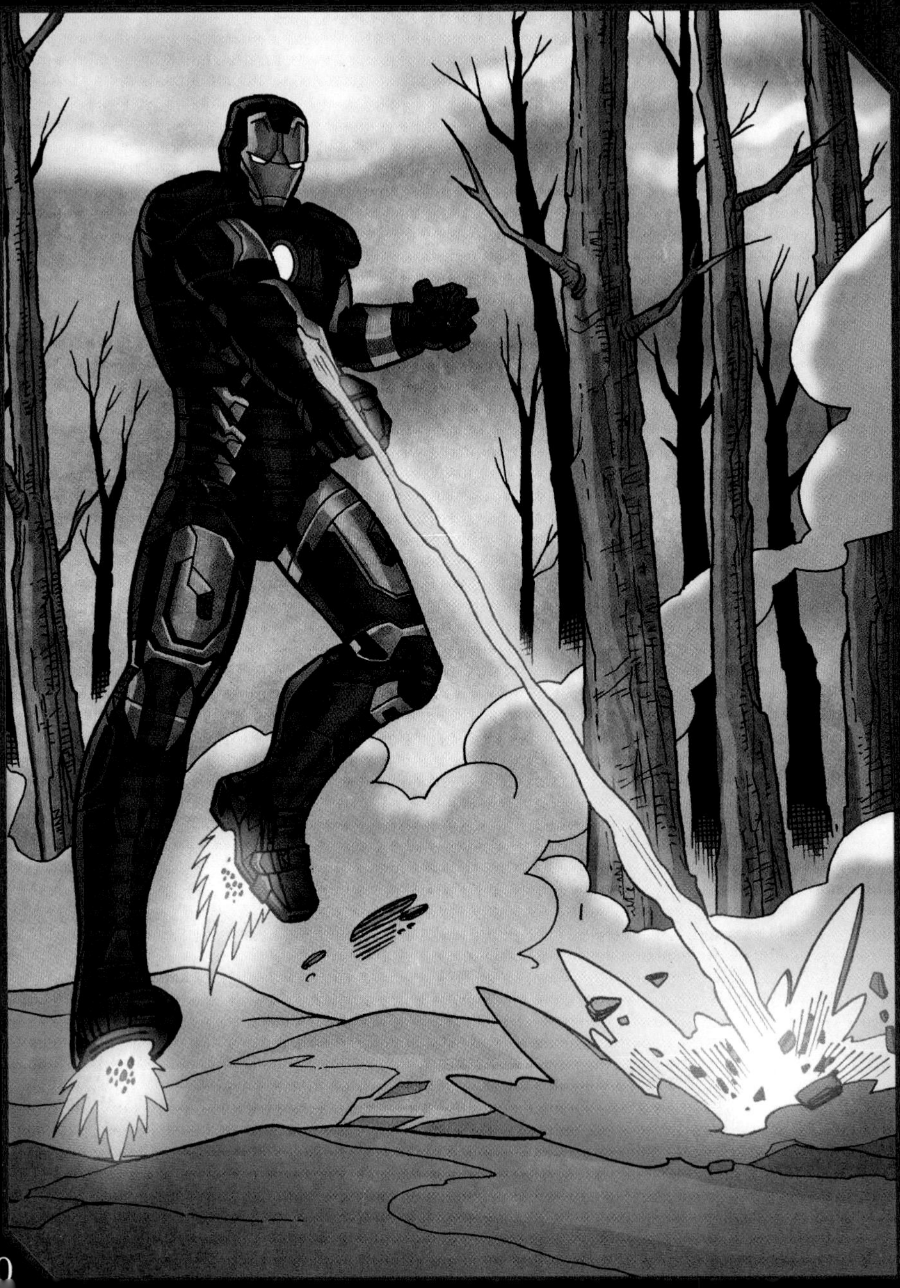

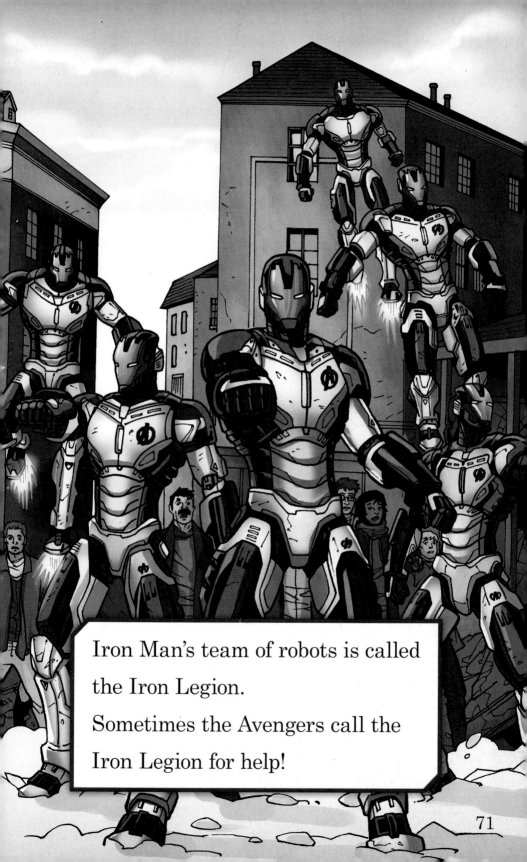

Iron Man's team of robots is called the Iron Legion.
Sometimes the Avengers call the Iron Legion for help!

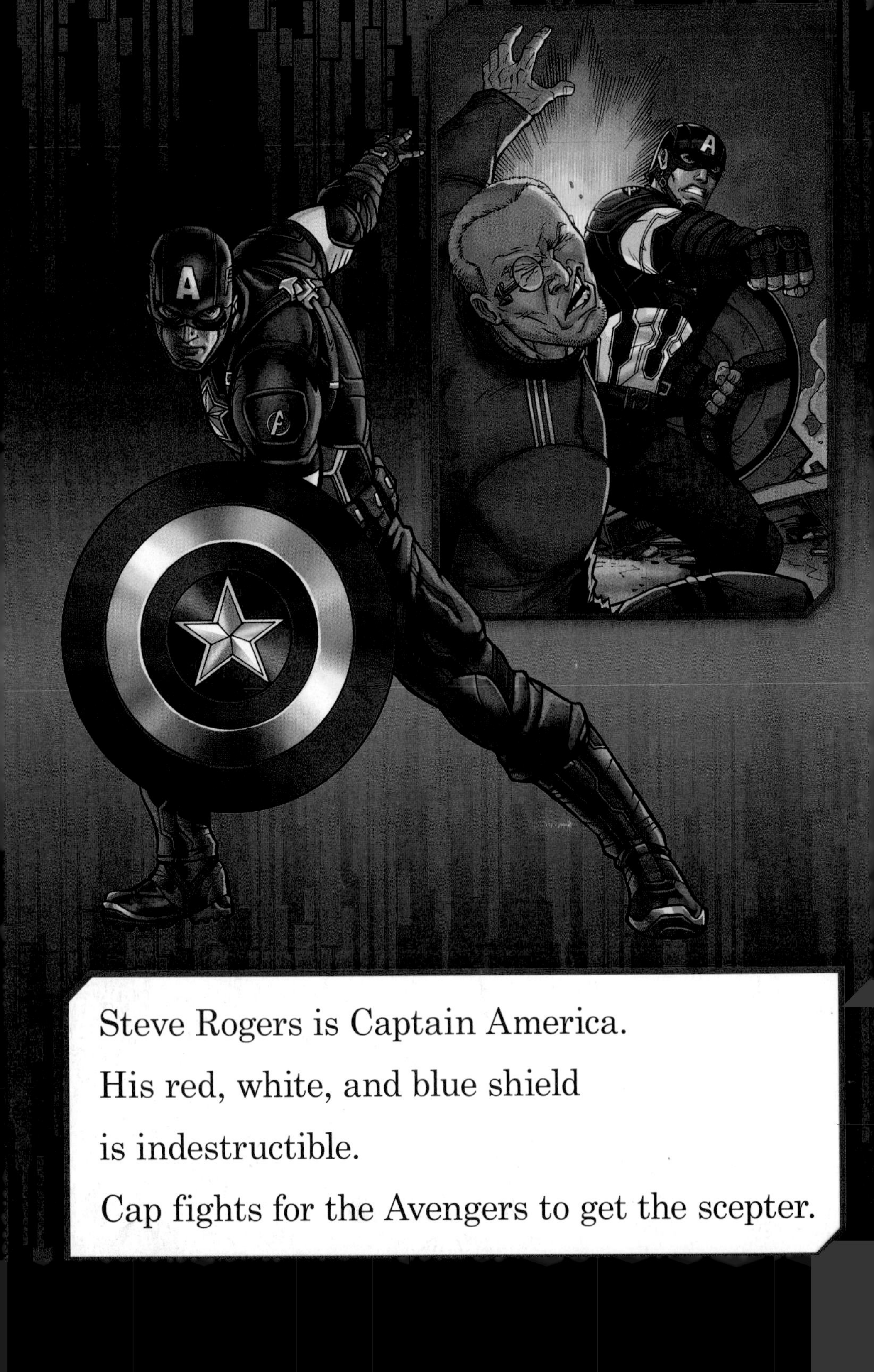

Steve Rogers is Captain America.
His red, white, and blue shield
is indestructible.
Cap fights for the Avengers to get the scepter.

The Incredible Hulk is the
strongest Avenger.
He is not always big and green.
When he is calm,
he is scientist Bruce Banner.

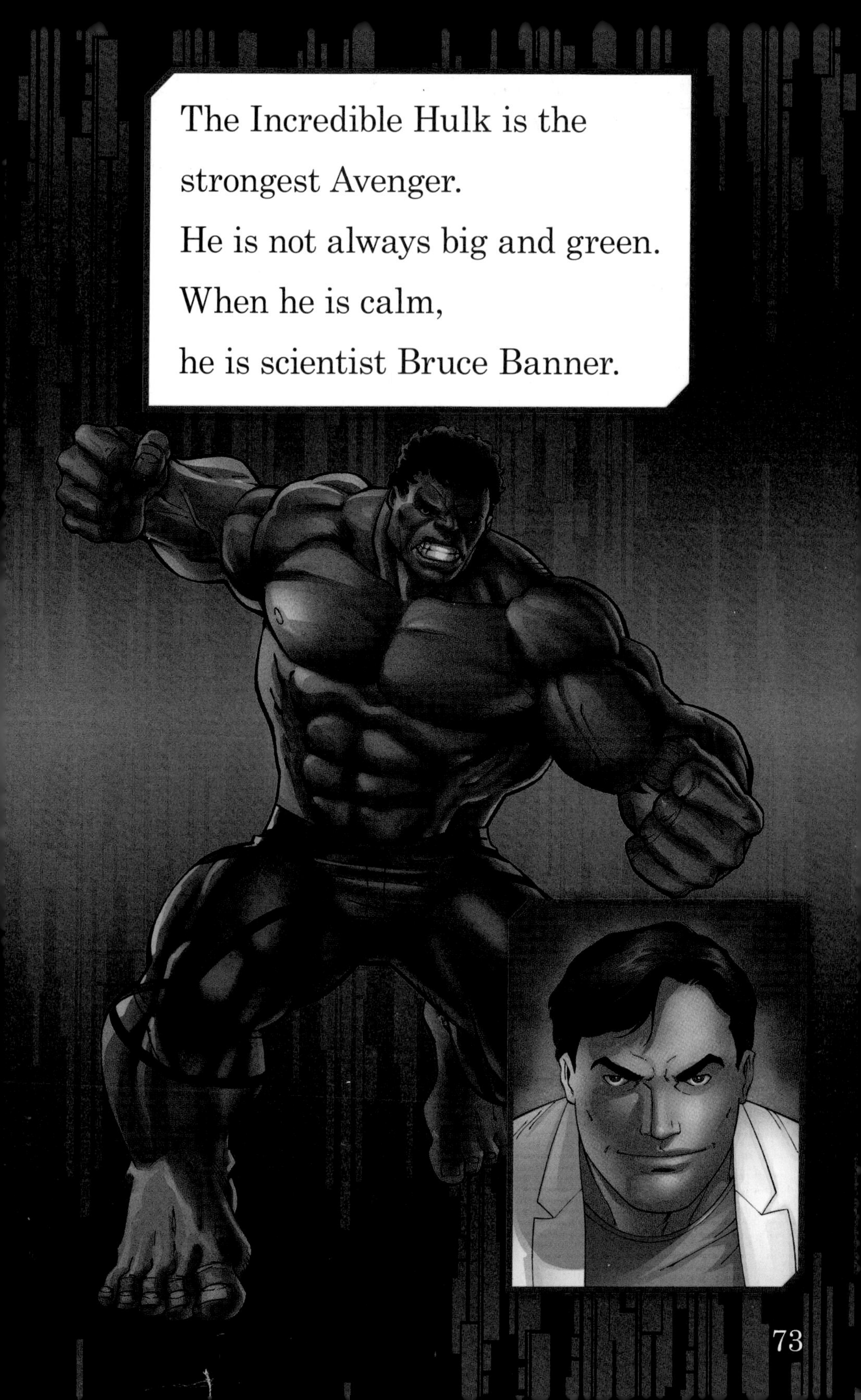

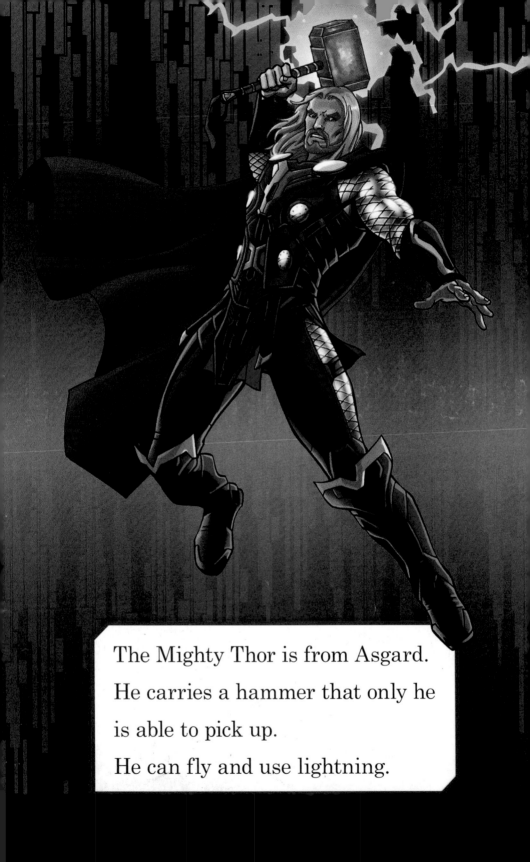

The Mighty Thor is from Asgard.
He carries a hammer that only he
is able to pick up.
He can fly and use lightning.

Hawkeye never misses a shot.
He uses his bow and special arrows
to stop enemies.

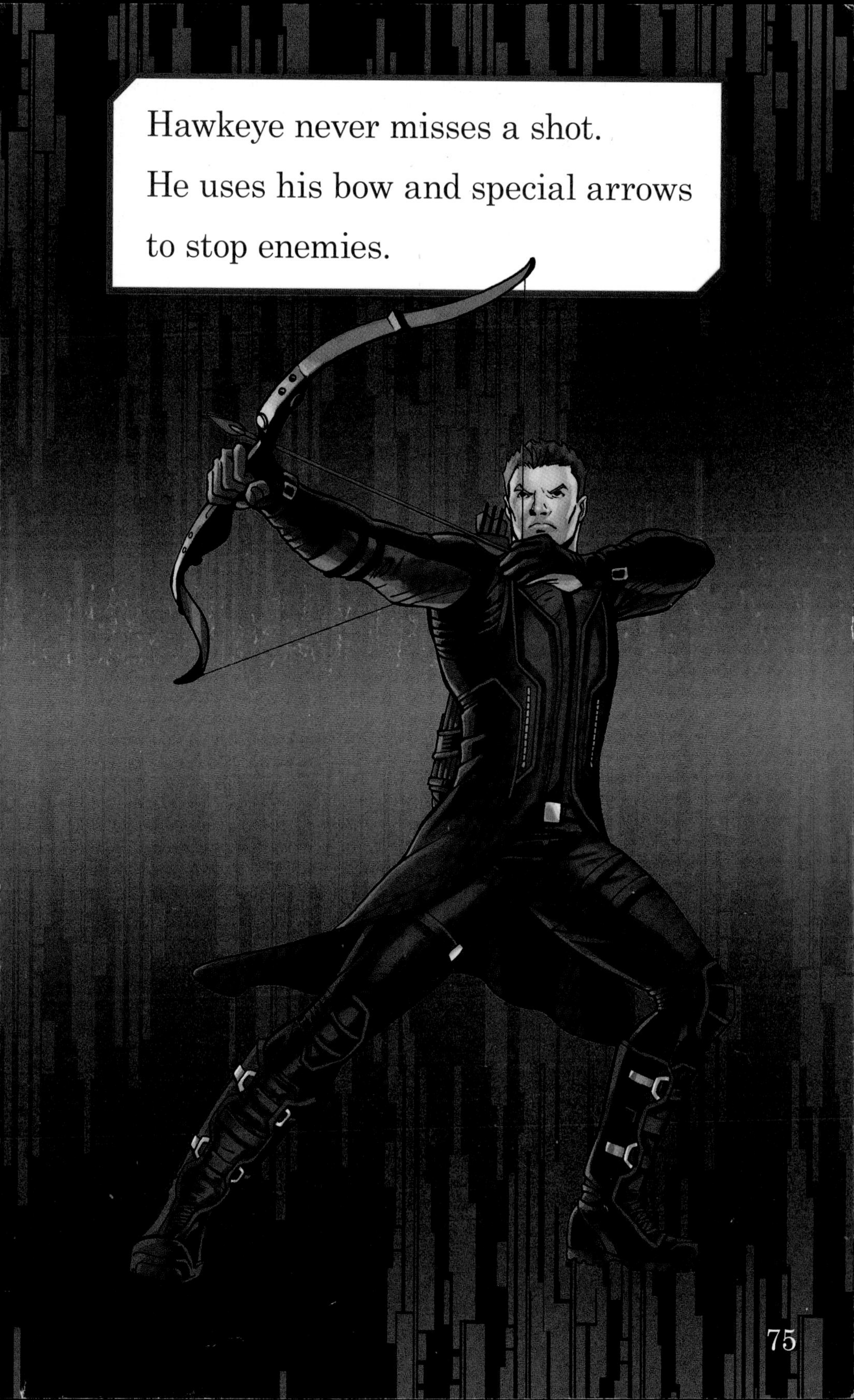

Black Widow is a super-spy who fights hard.
She has weapons on her wrist
called Widow's Bites.
They zap enemies.

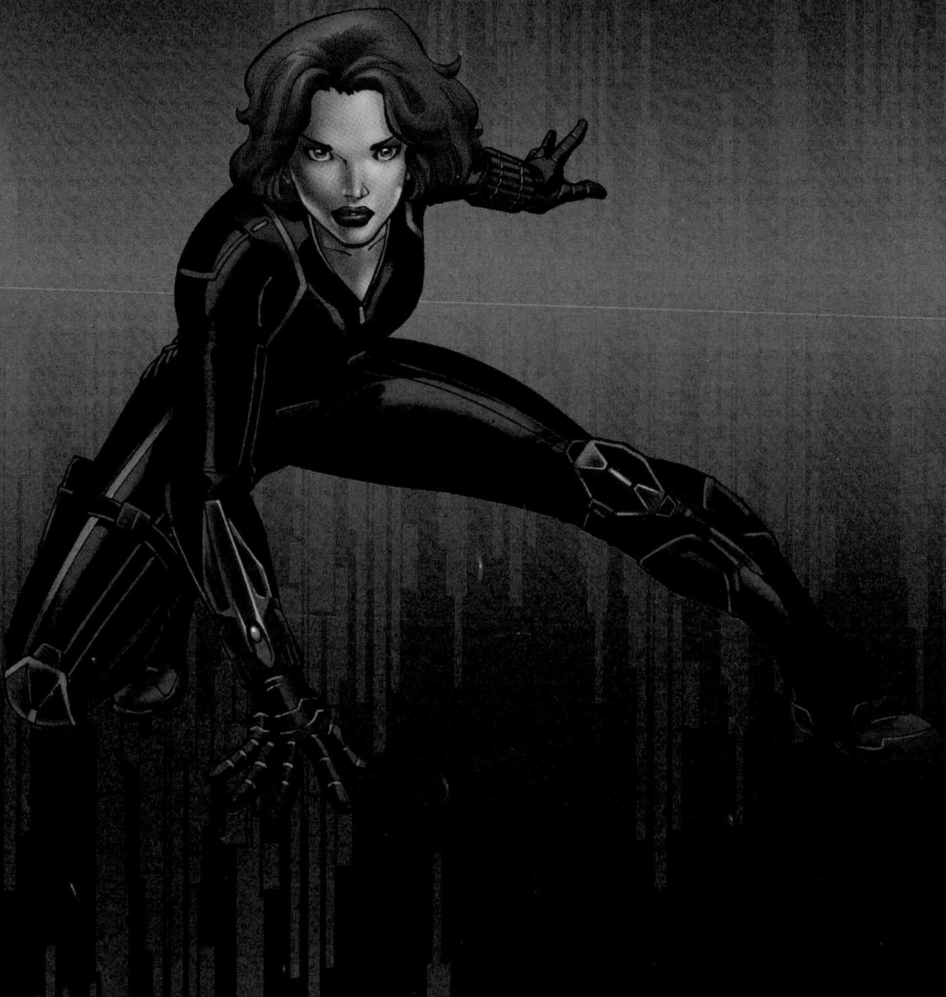

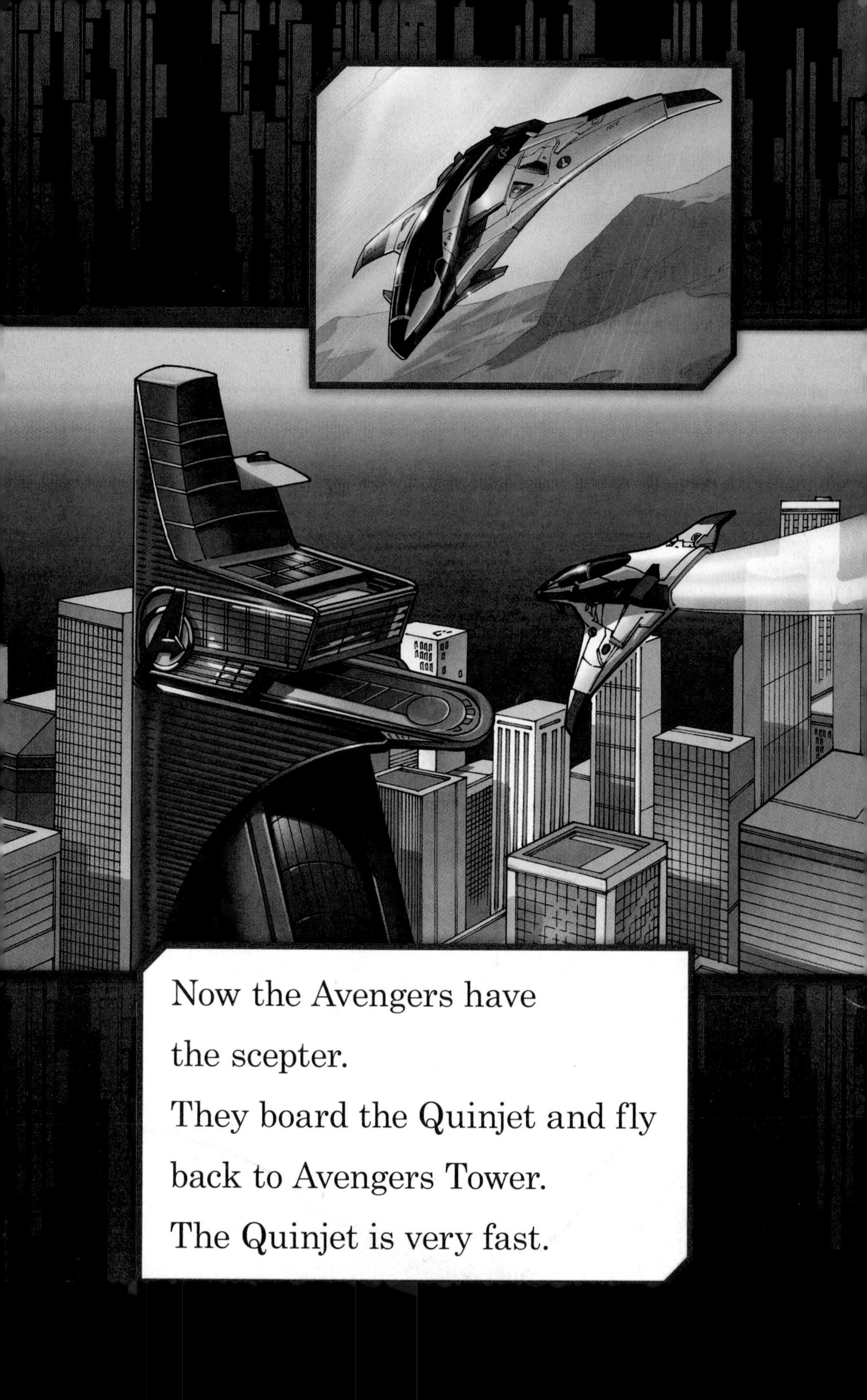

Now the Avengers have
the scepter.
They board the Quinjet and fly
back to Avengers Tower.
The Quinjet is very fast.

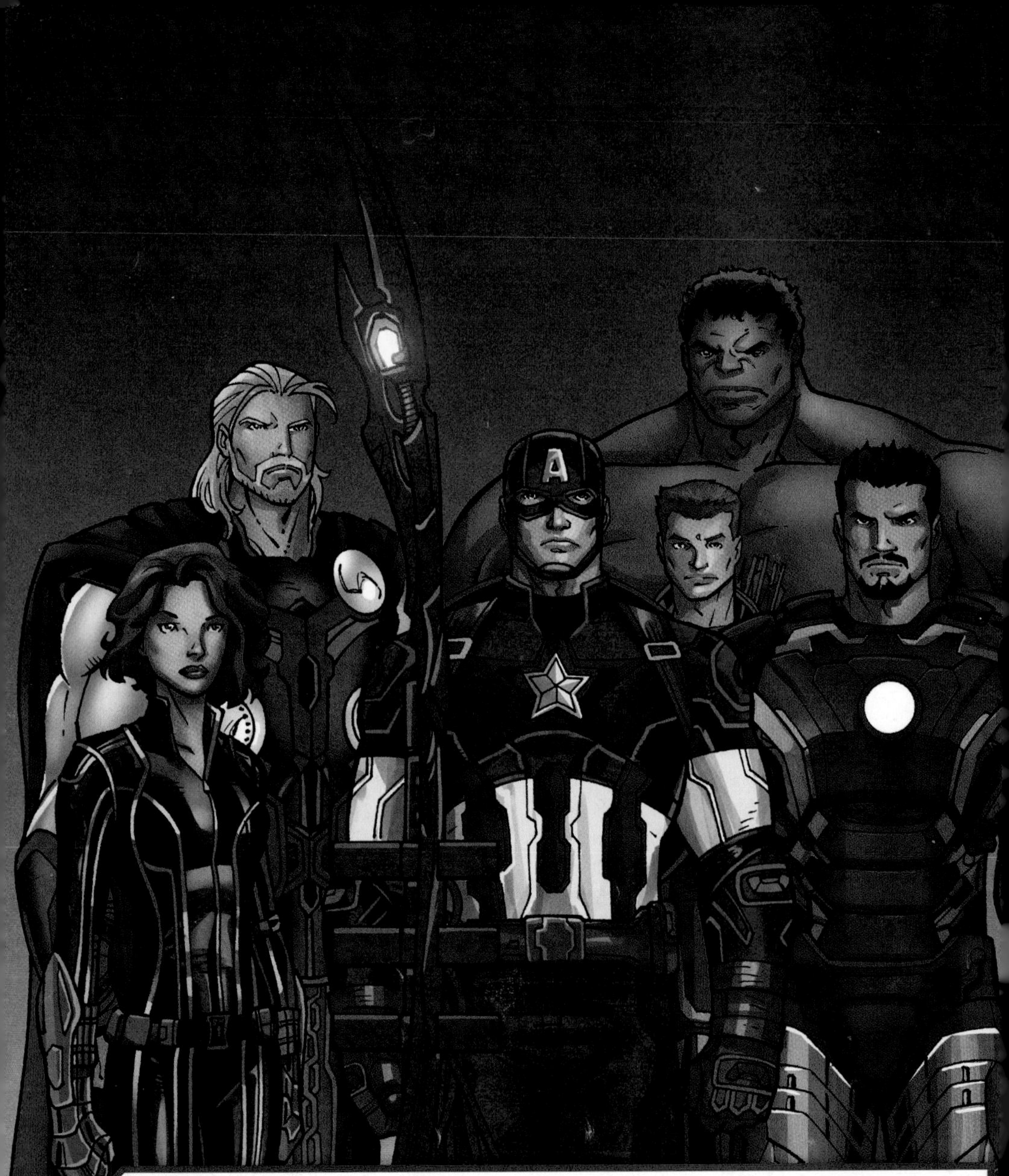

The Avengers study the scepter.
They learn how much power it possesses
and what it is capable of doing.
The Avengers must protect it from all threats.

One threat is Ultron.
He wants the scepter from the Avengers.
He wants to take over the world.

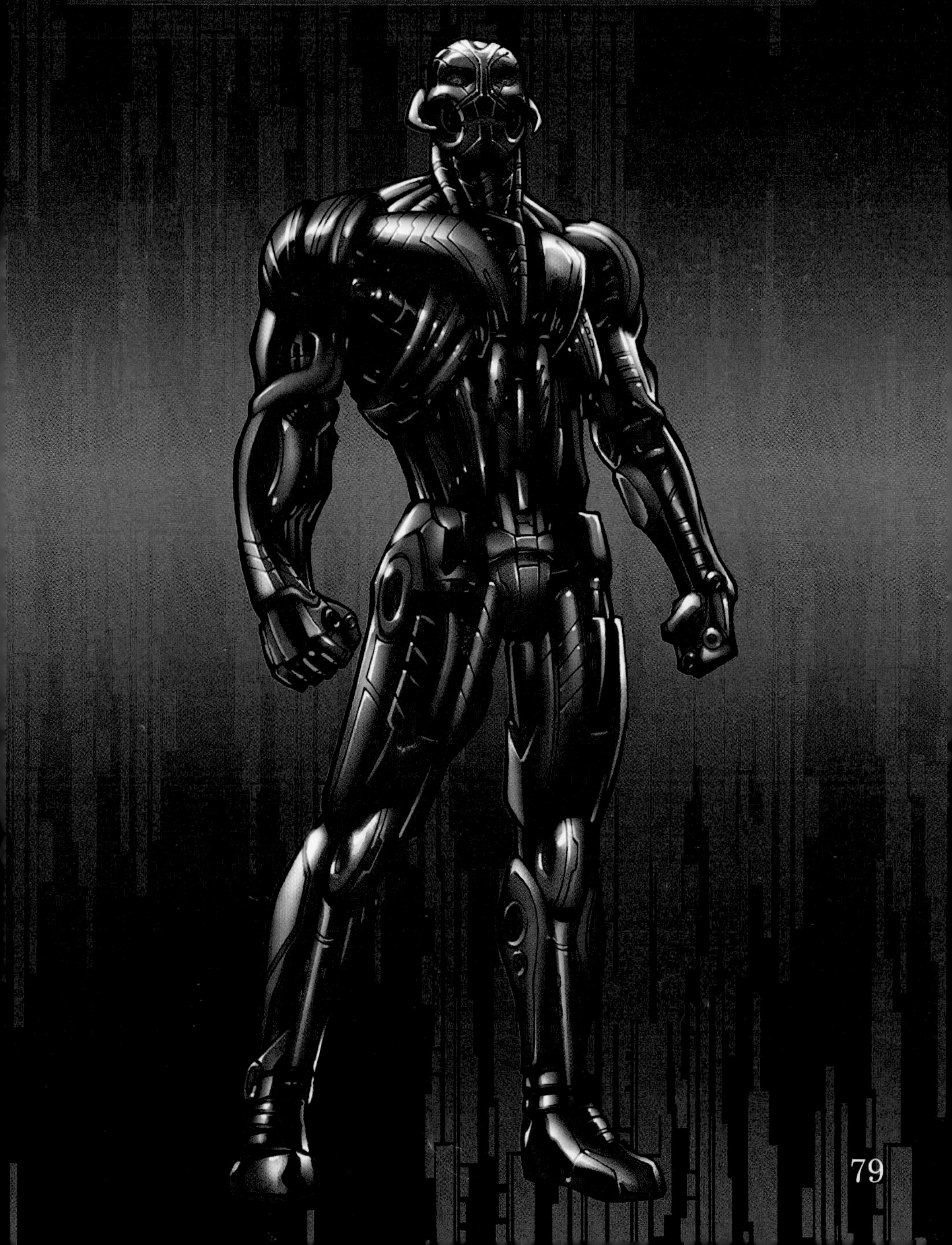

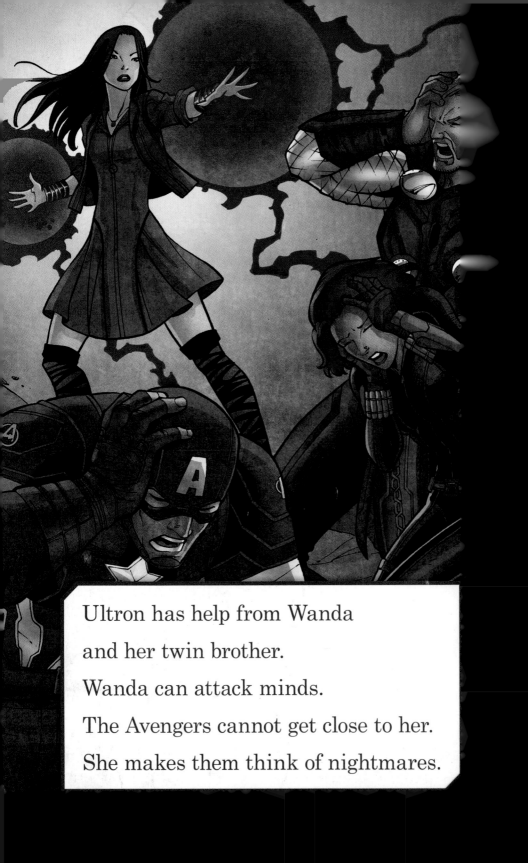

Ultron has help from Wanda
and her twin brother.
Wanda can attack minds.
The Avengers cannot get close to her.
She makes them think of nightmares.

Pietro is Wanda's brother.

He is so fast that no Avengers
can catch him.

Together the twins try to help Ultron
get the scepter from the Avengers.

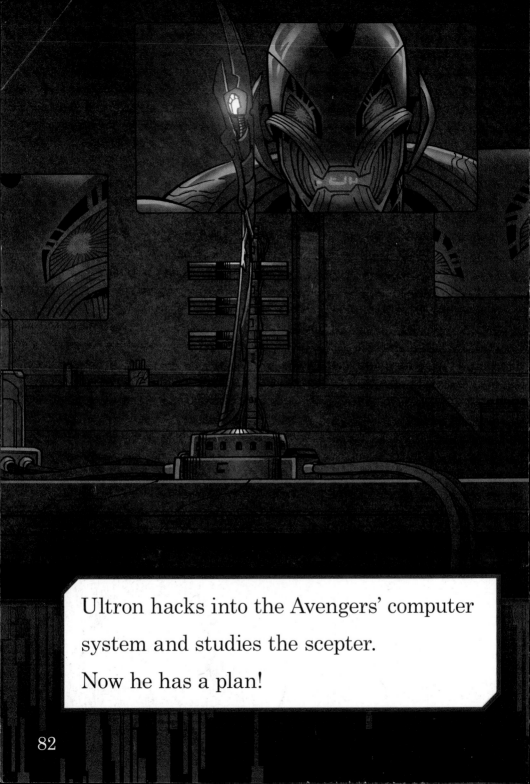

Ultron hacks into the Avengers' computer system and studies the scepter.

Now he has a plan!

Ultron takes over the Iron Legion.
They must now obey Ultron.
The robots burst through the window
and attack the Avengers!

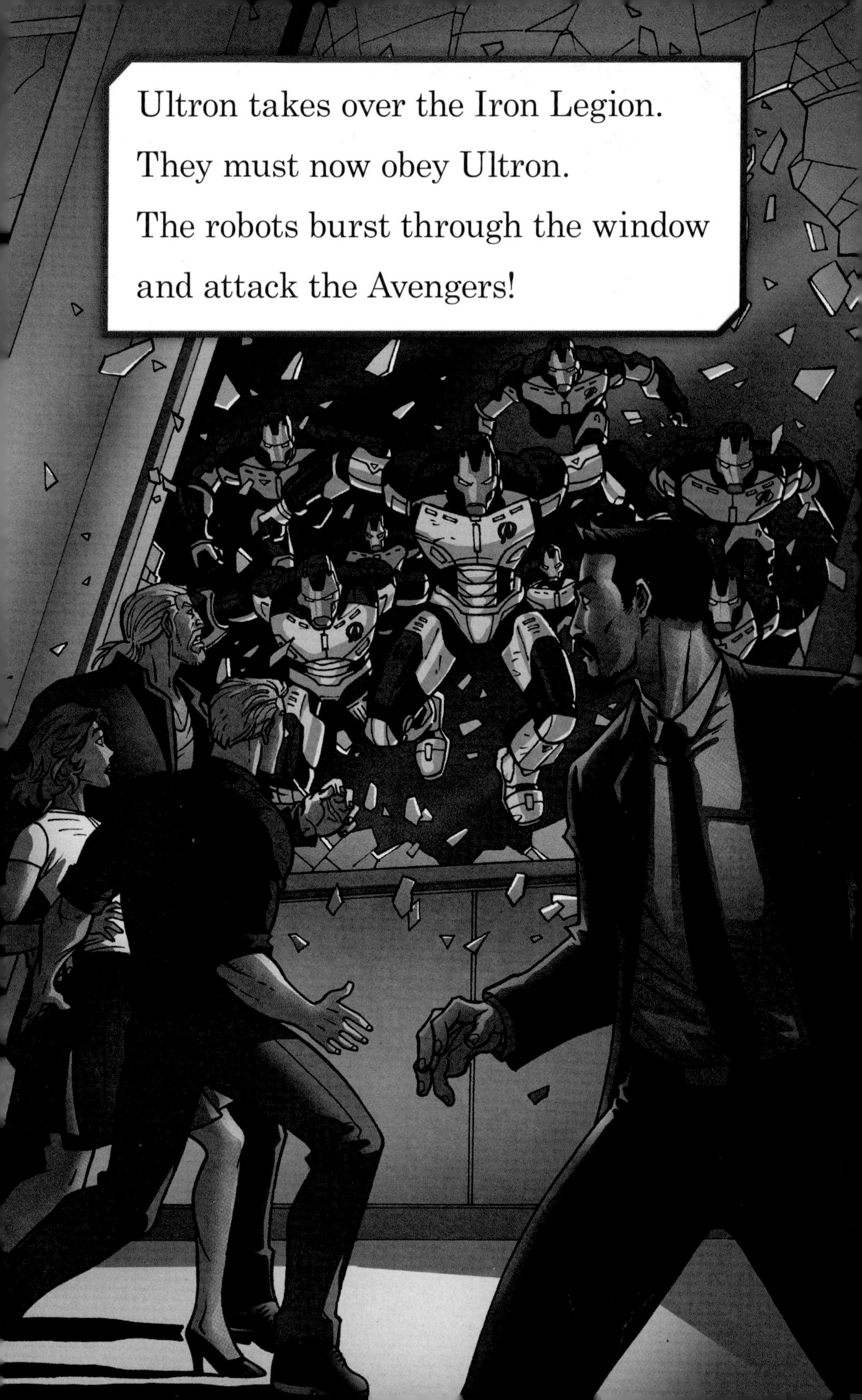

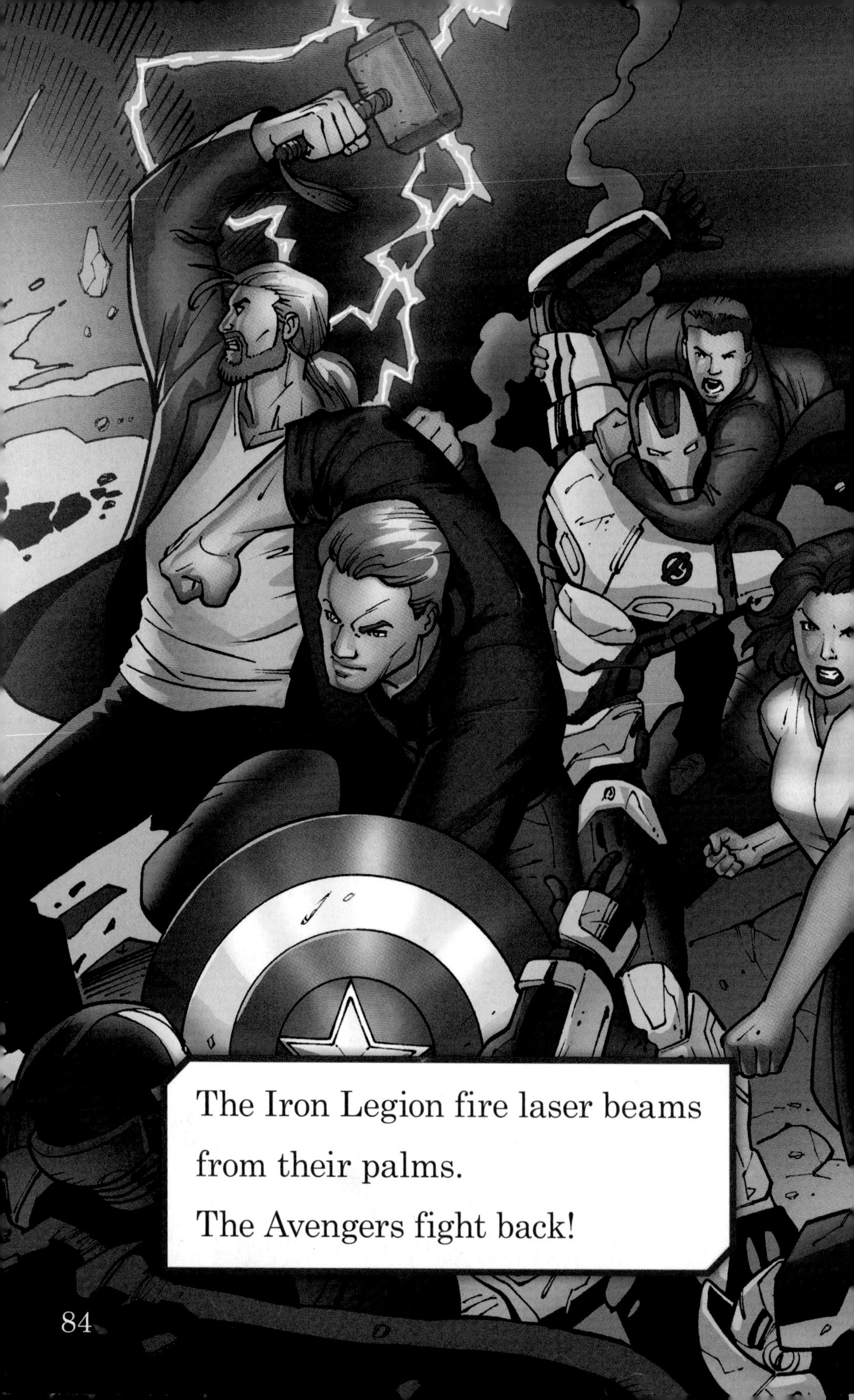

The Iron Legion fire laser beams from their palms.
The Avengers fight back!

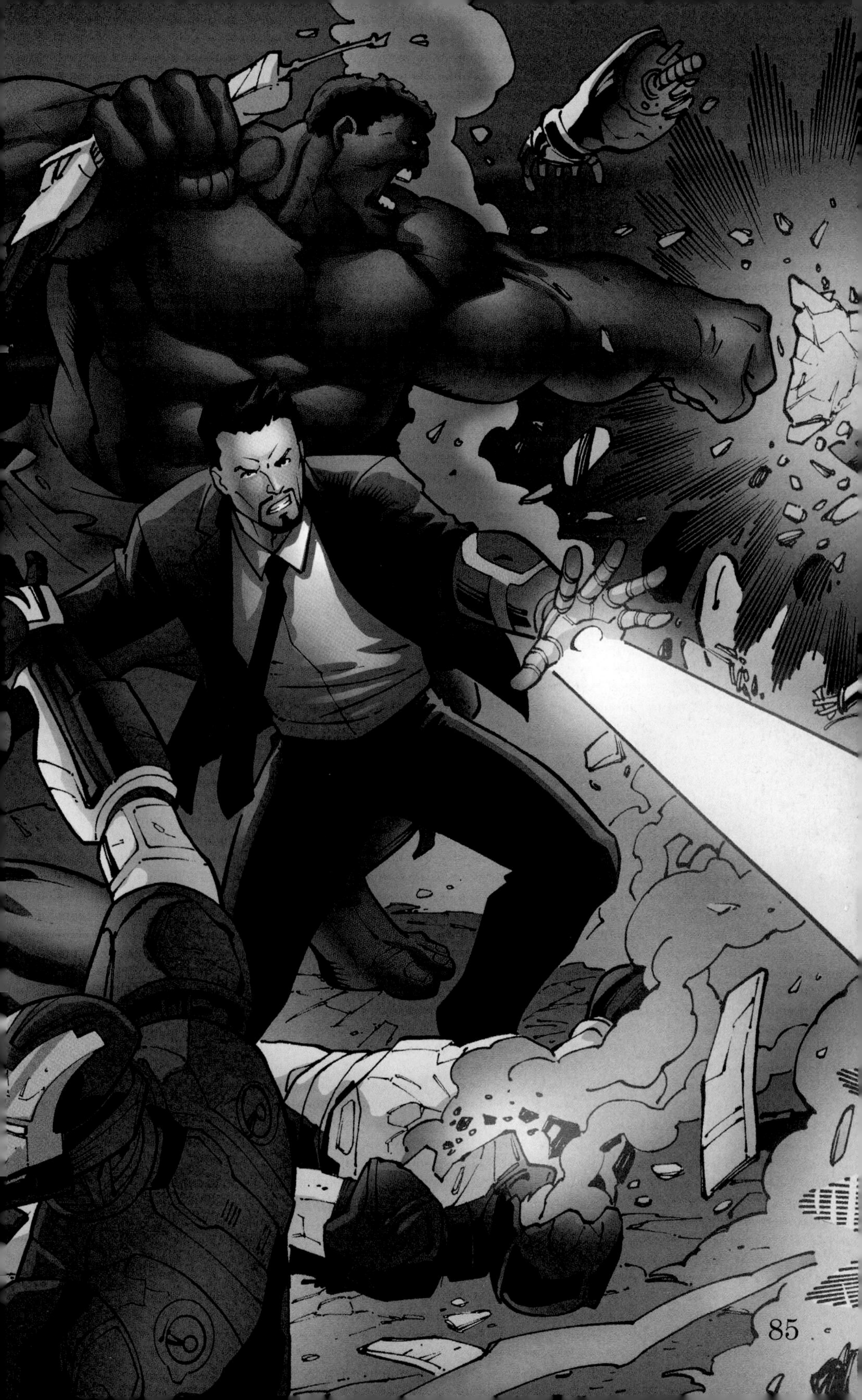

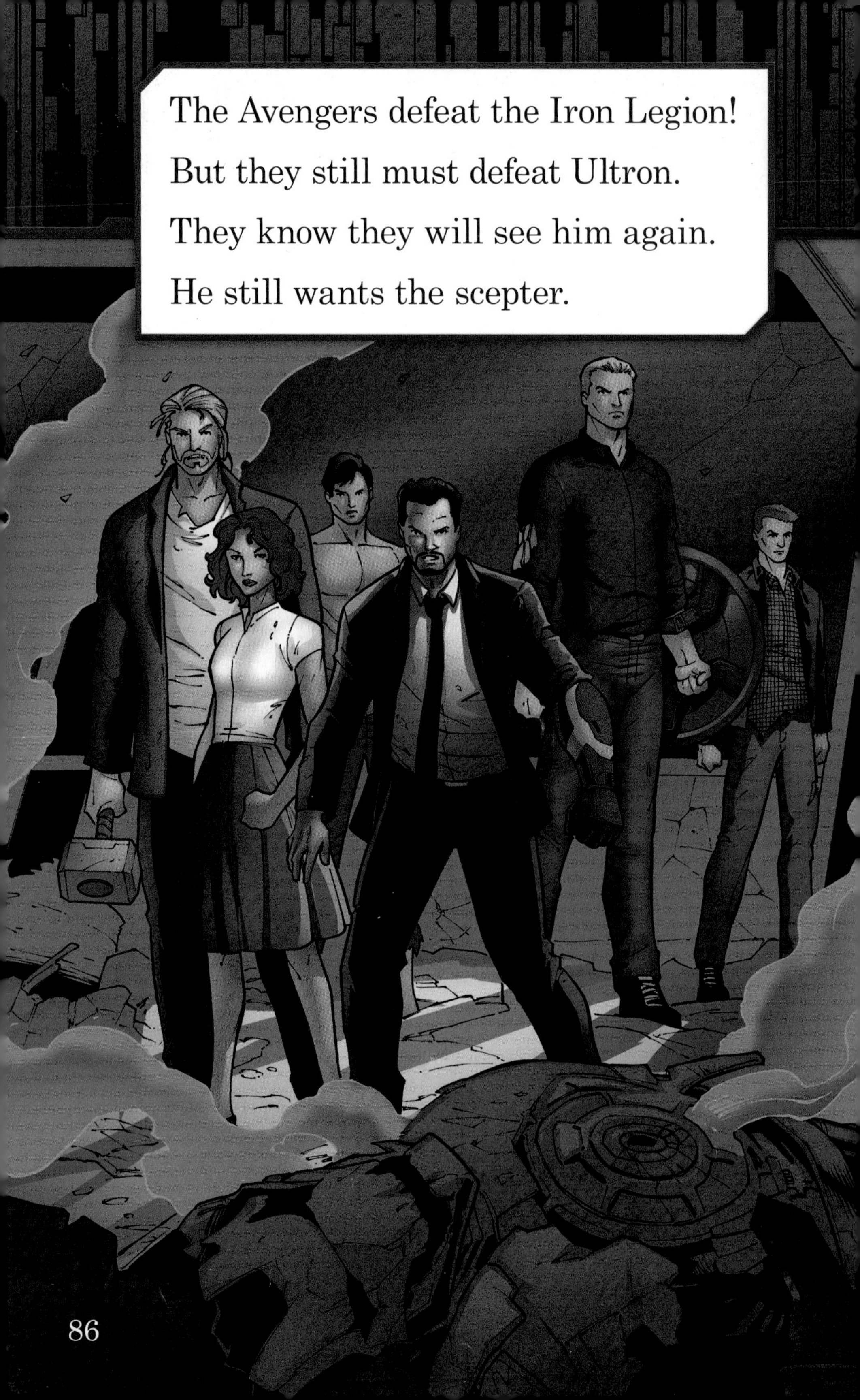
The Avengers defeat the Iron Legion!
But they still must defeat Ultron.
They know they will see him again.
He still wants the scepter.

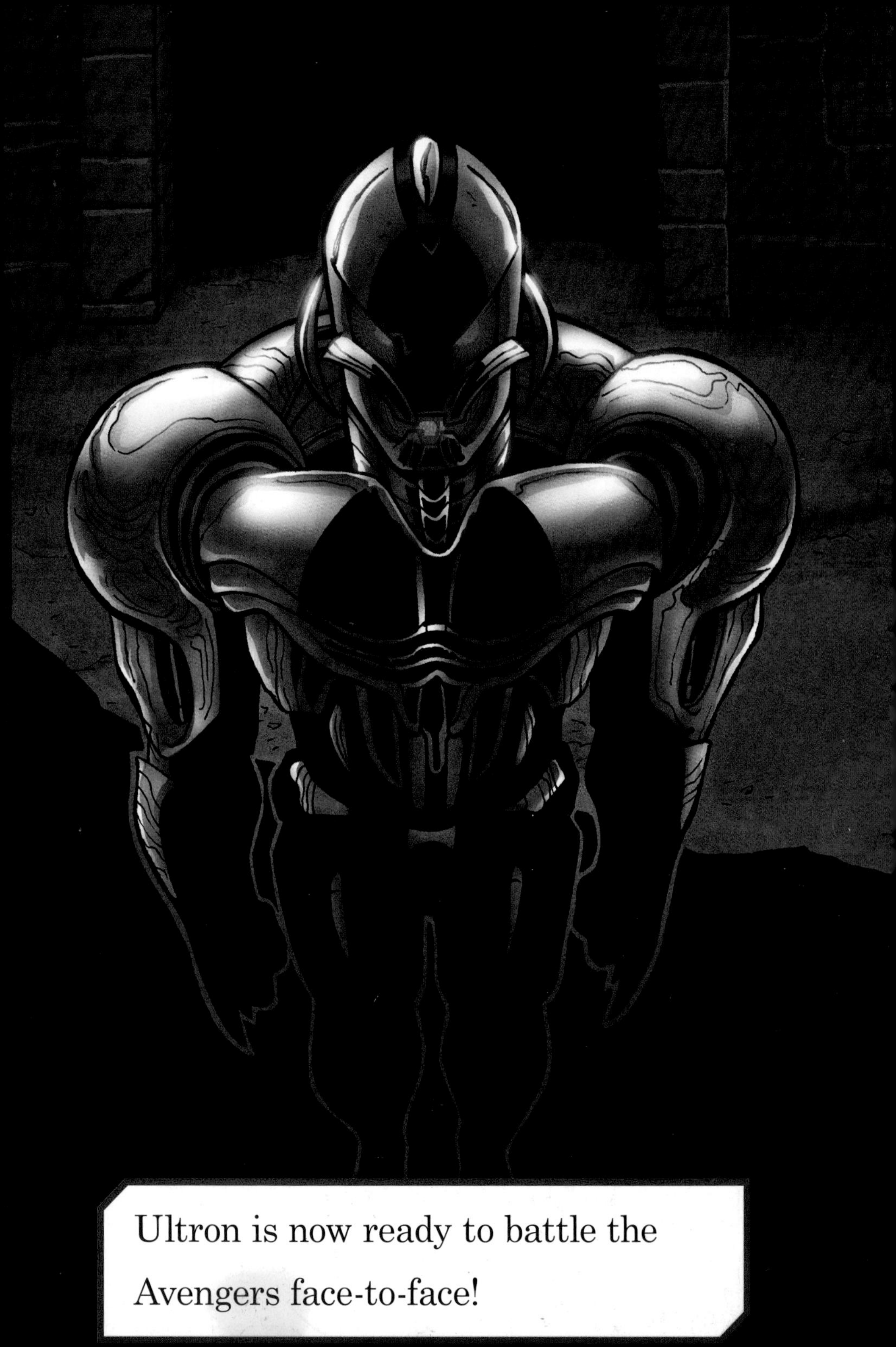
Ultron is now ready to battle the Avengers face-to-face!

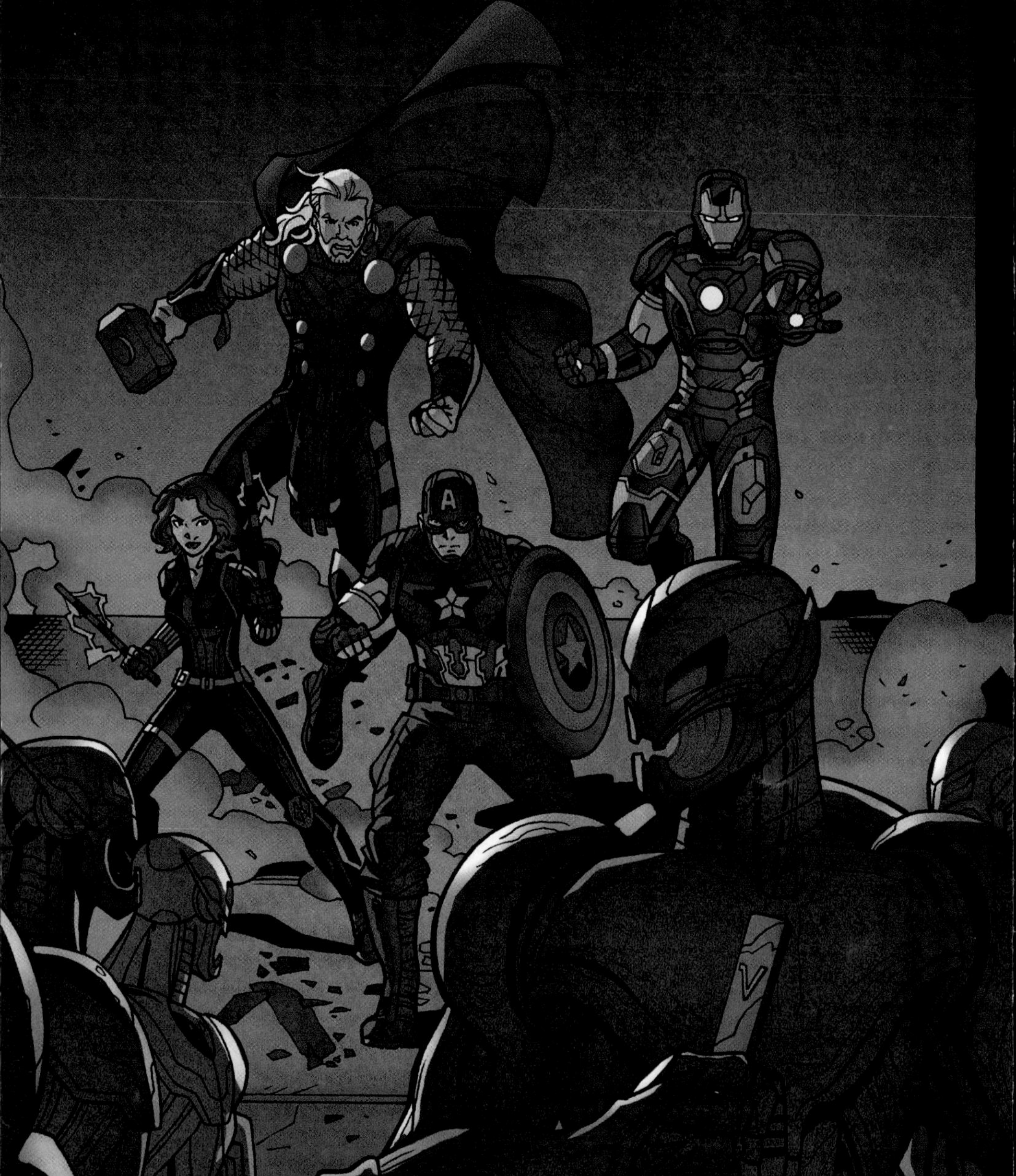

The Avengers find Ultron in South Africa.
He is with an army of Sentries.

The Avengers jump into battle!

But there are too many Sentries!

The Avengers cannot keep up.

The Hulk roars!

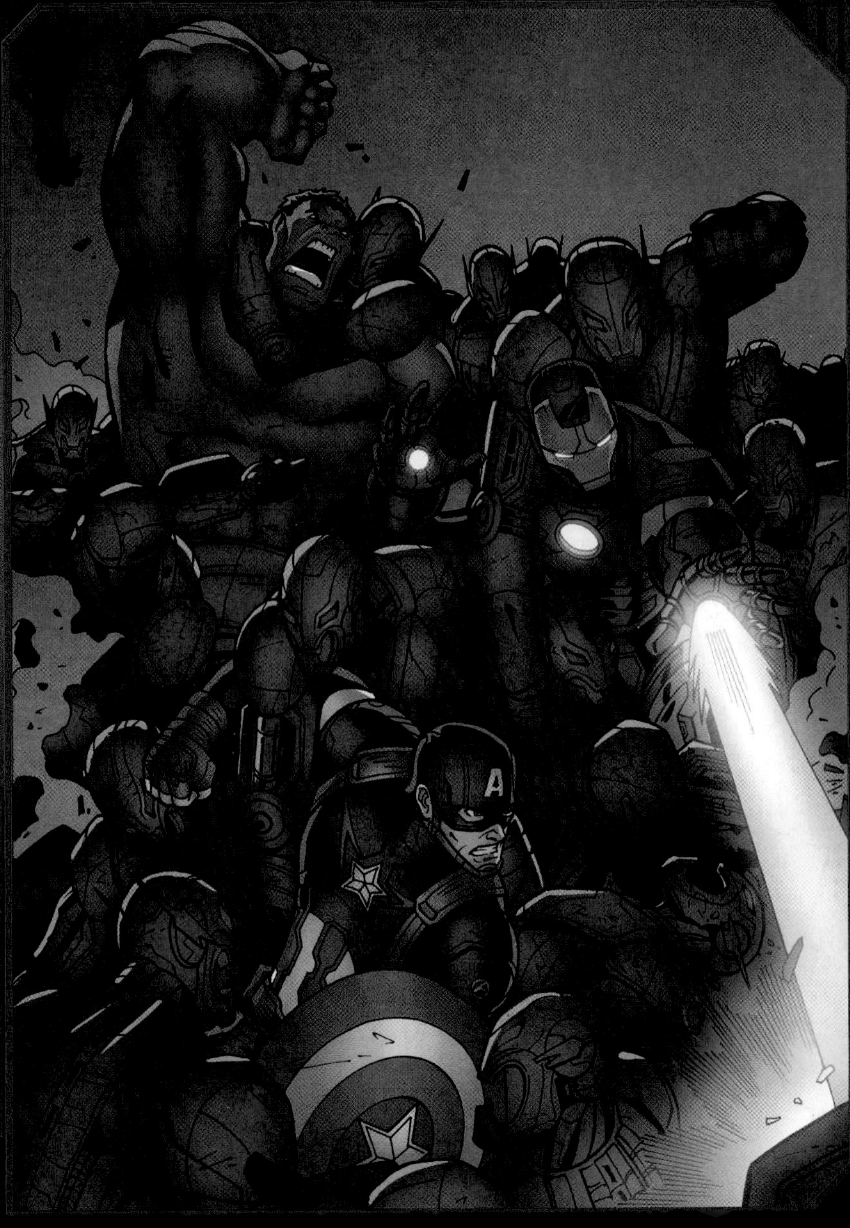

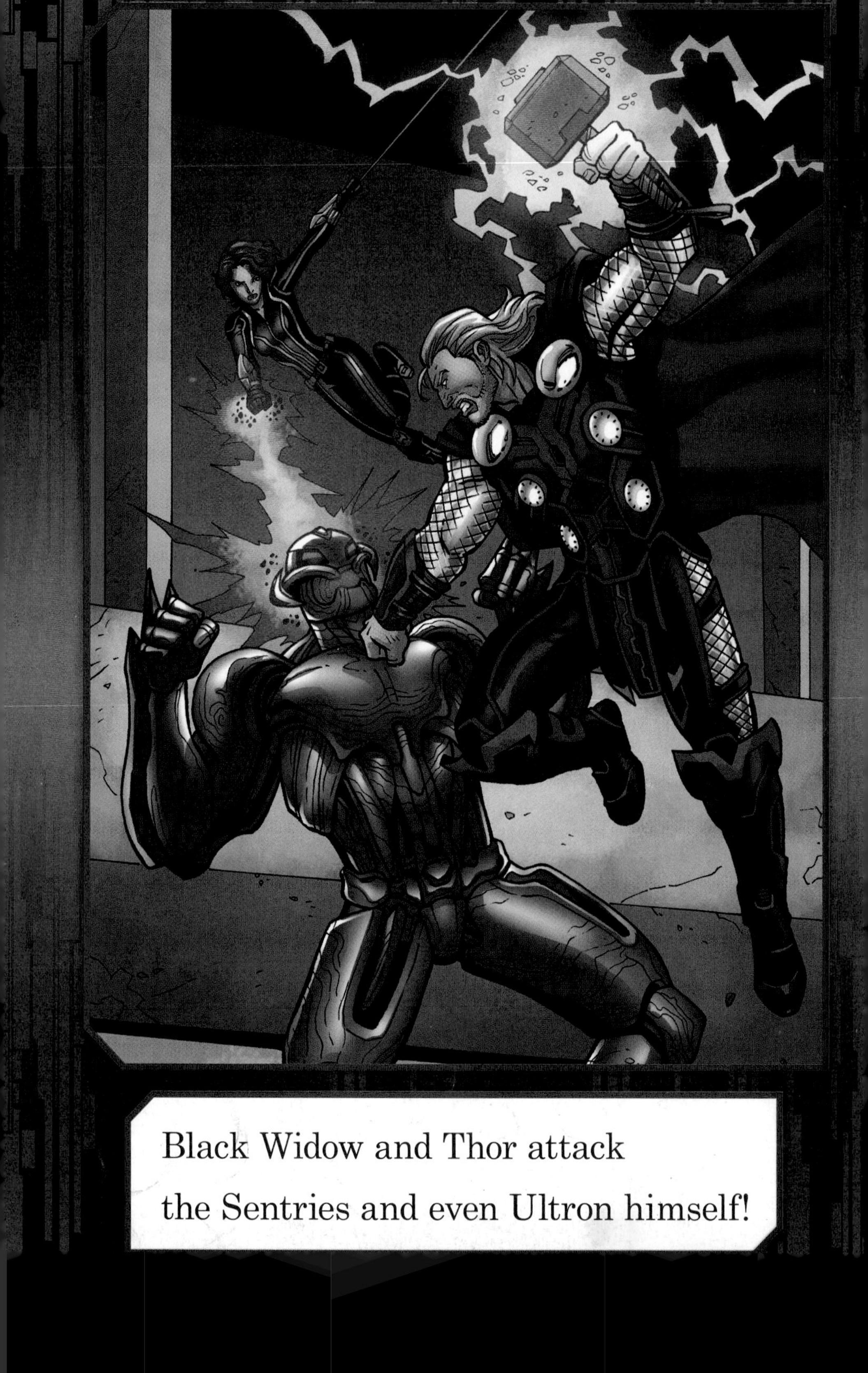

Black Widow and Thor attack
the Sentries and even Ultron himself!

Iron Man lands a blow against Ultron!
It seems to be working!
The Sentries are getting weak!
Time for the team to come together
and finish them off!

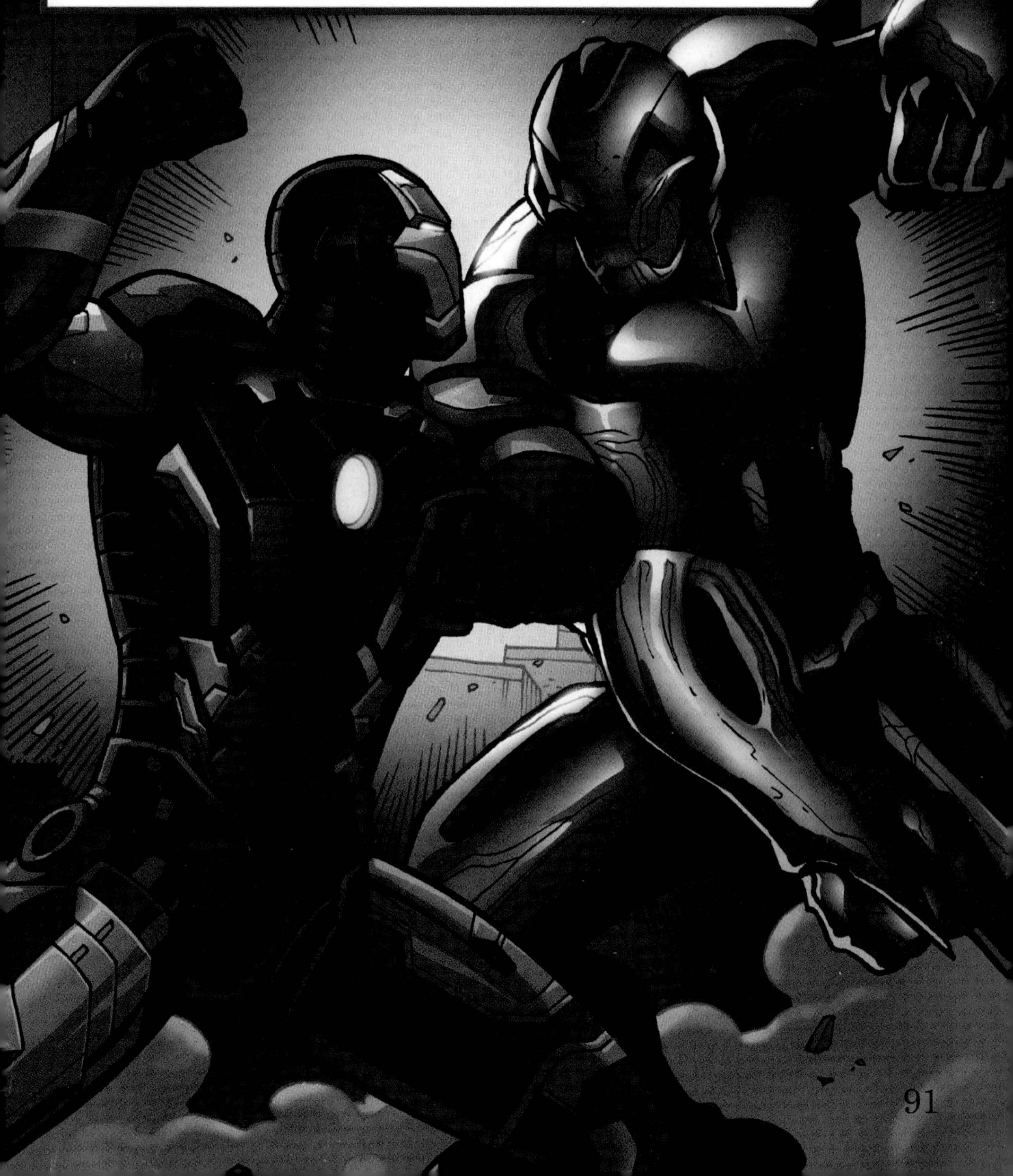

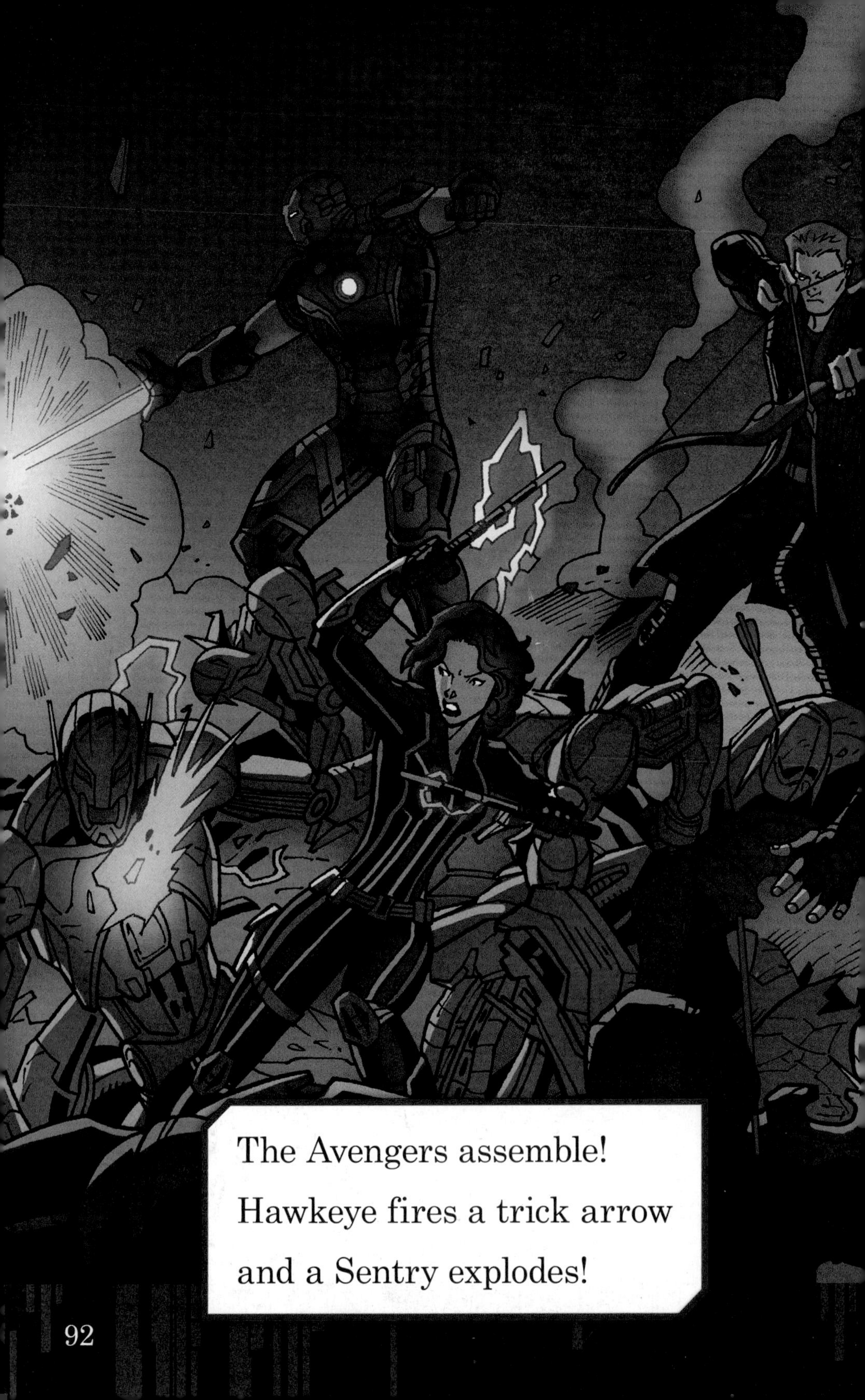

The Avengers assemble!
Hawkeye fires a trick arrow
and a Sentry explodes!

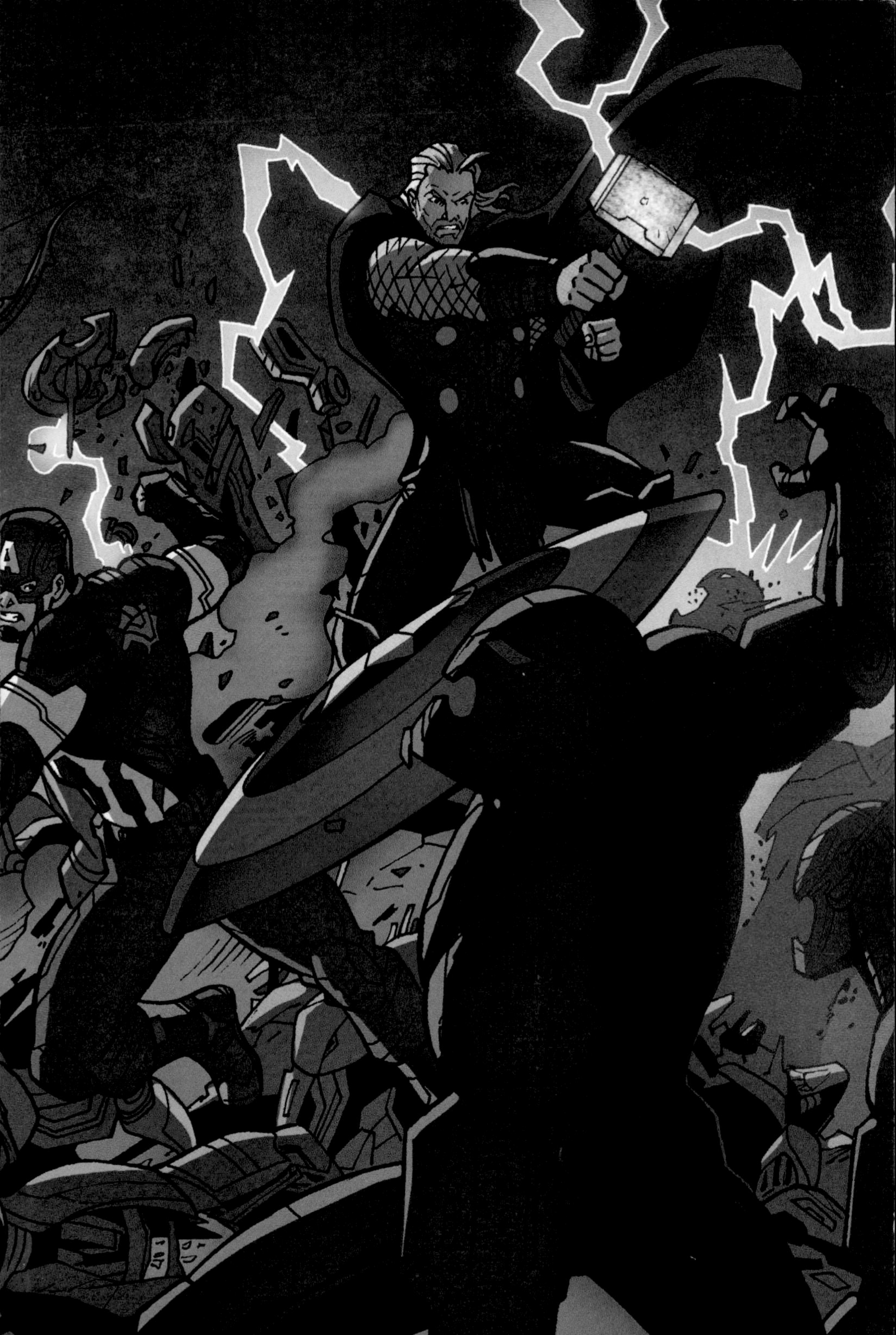

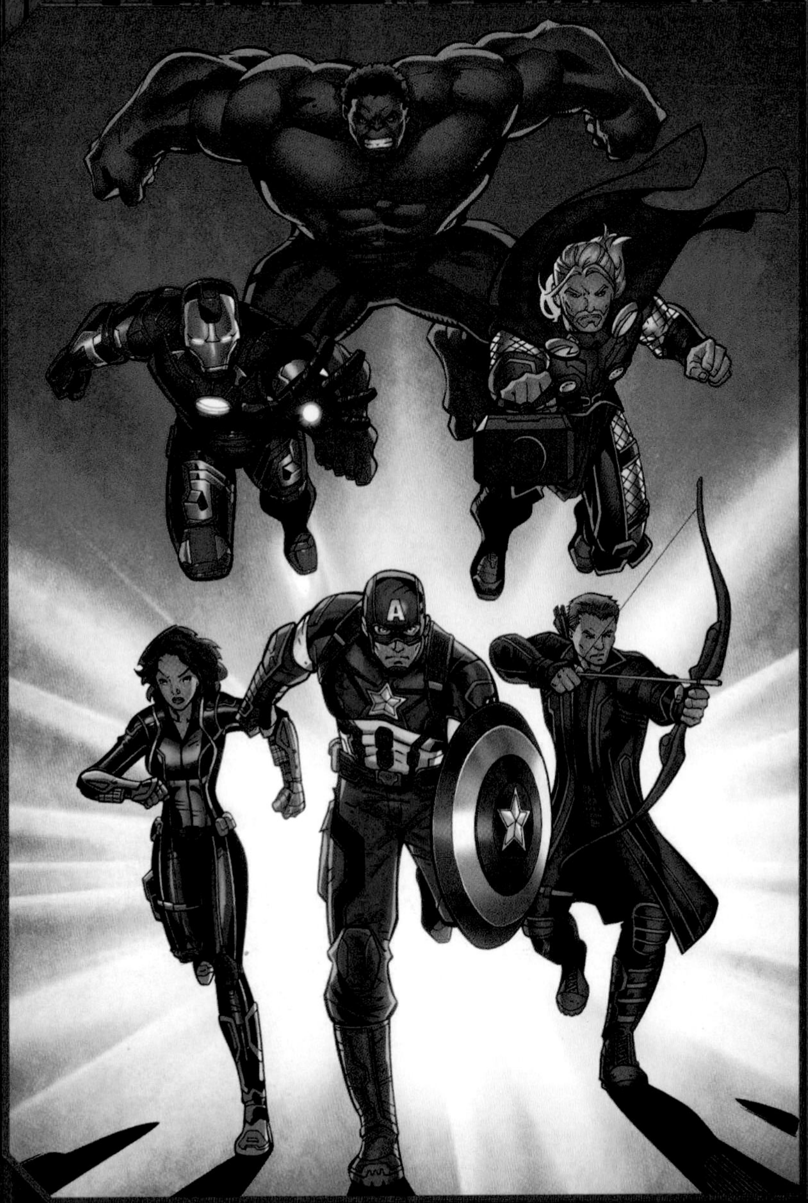

The Avengers stopped Ultron,
but the evil robot will return.
The Avengers will assemble
and save the day once again!

MARVEL
AVENGERS
AGE OF ULTRON

Hulk to the Rescue

By Adam Davis
Illustrated by Ron Lim, Andy Smith, and Andy Troy
Based on the Screenplay by Joss Whedon
Produced by Kevin Feige, p.g.a.
Directed by Joss Whedon

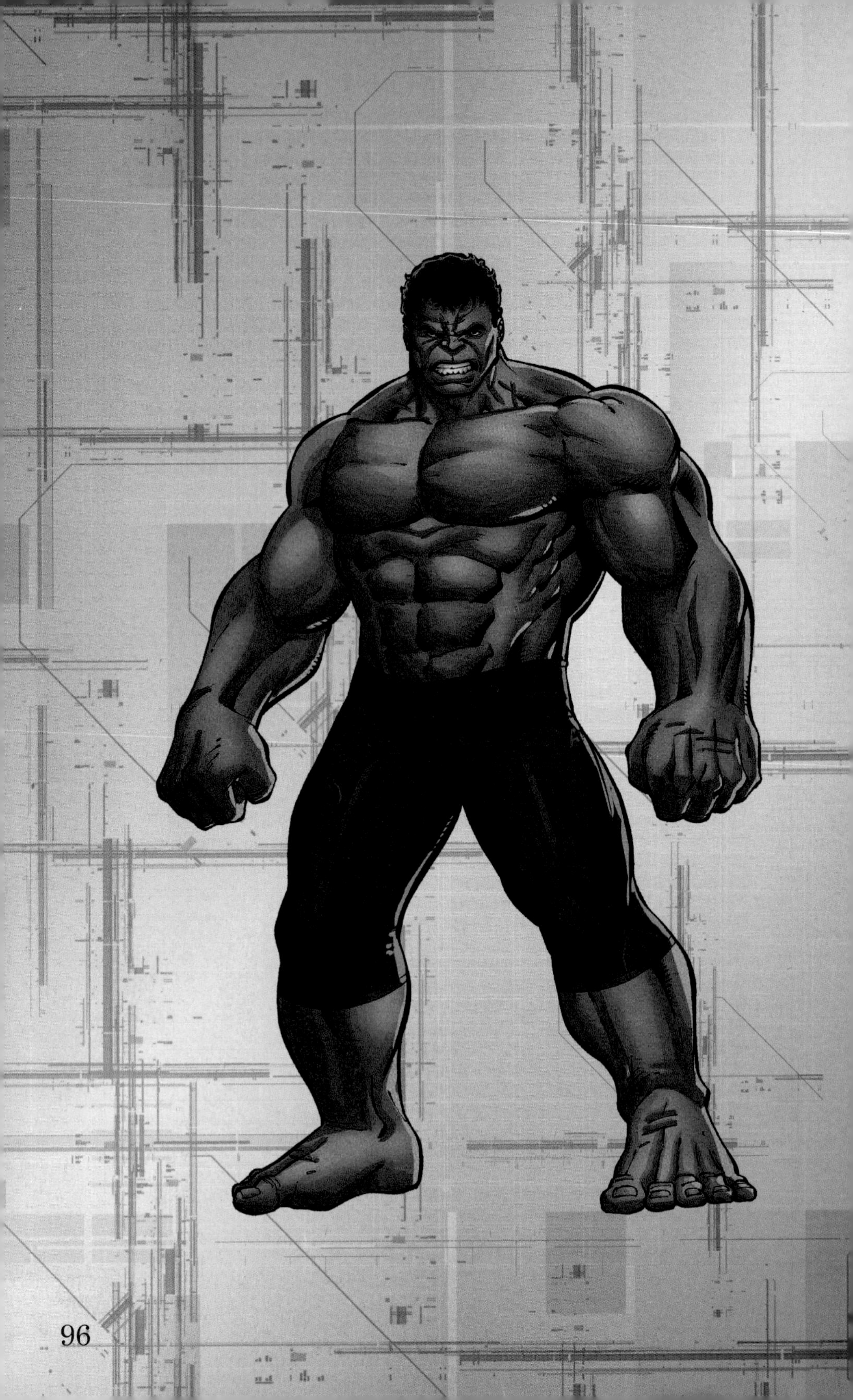

Attention, AVENGERS fans!
Look for these words
when you read this book.
Can you spot them all?

robot

metal

army

hammer

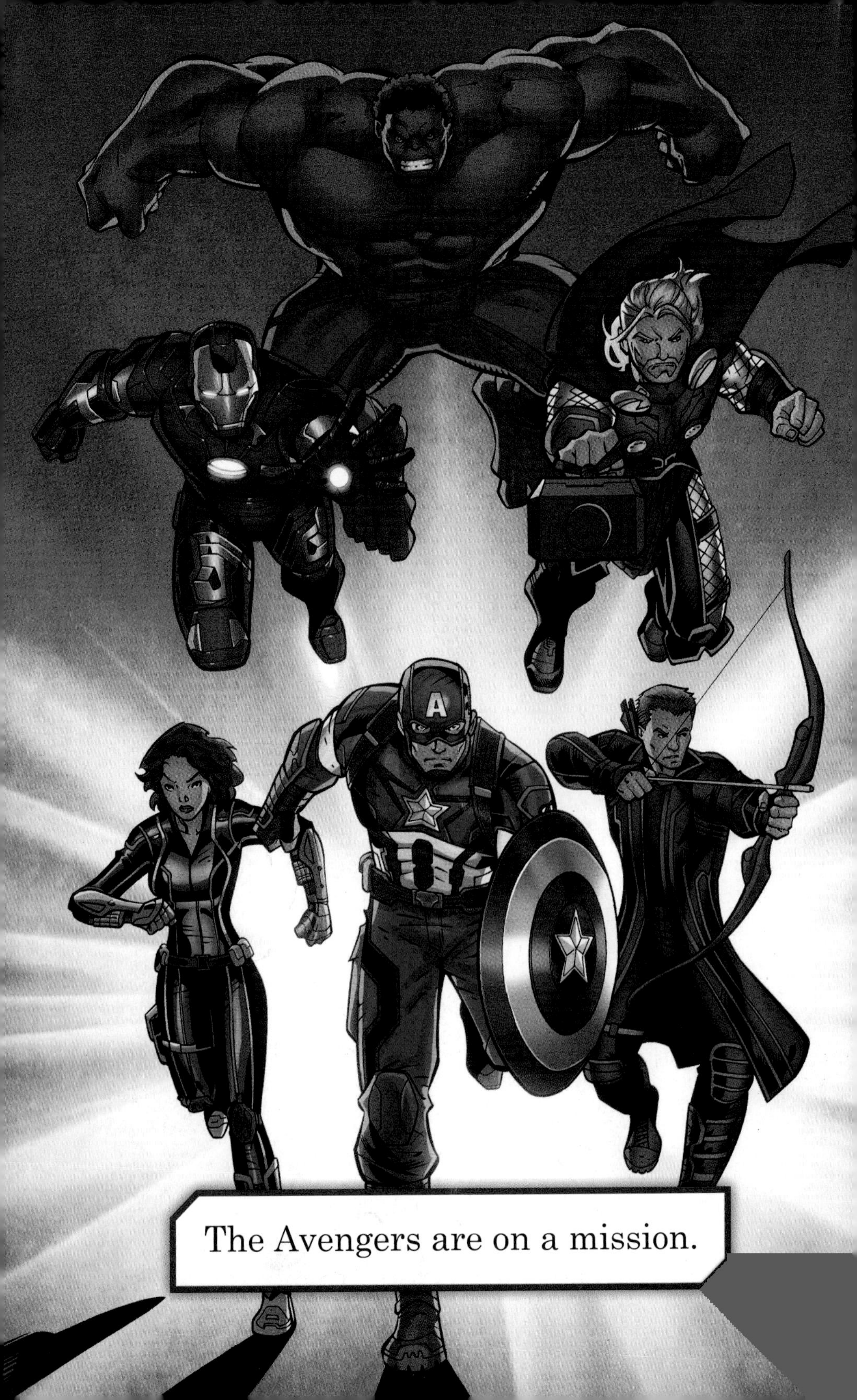
The Avengers are on a mission.

They must defeat an evil robot named Ultron.

He wants to take over the world.

Ultron wants a special metal.
It will make him so strong that
the Avengers cannot stop him!

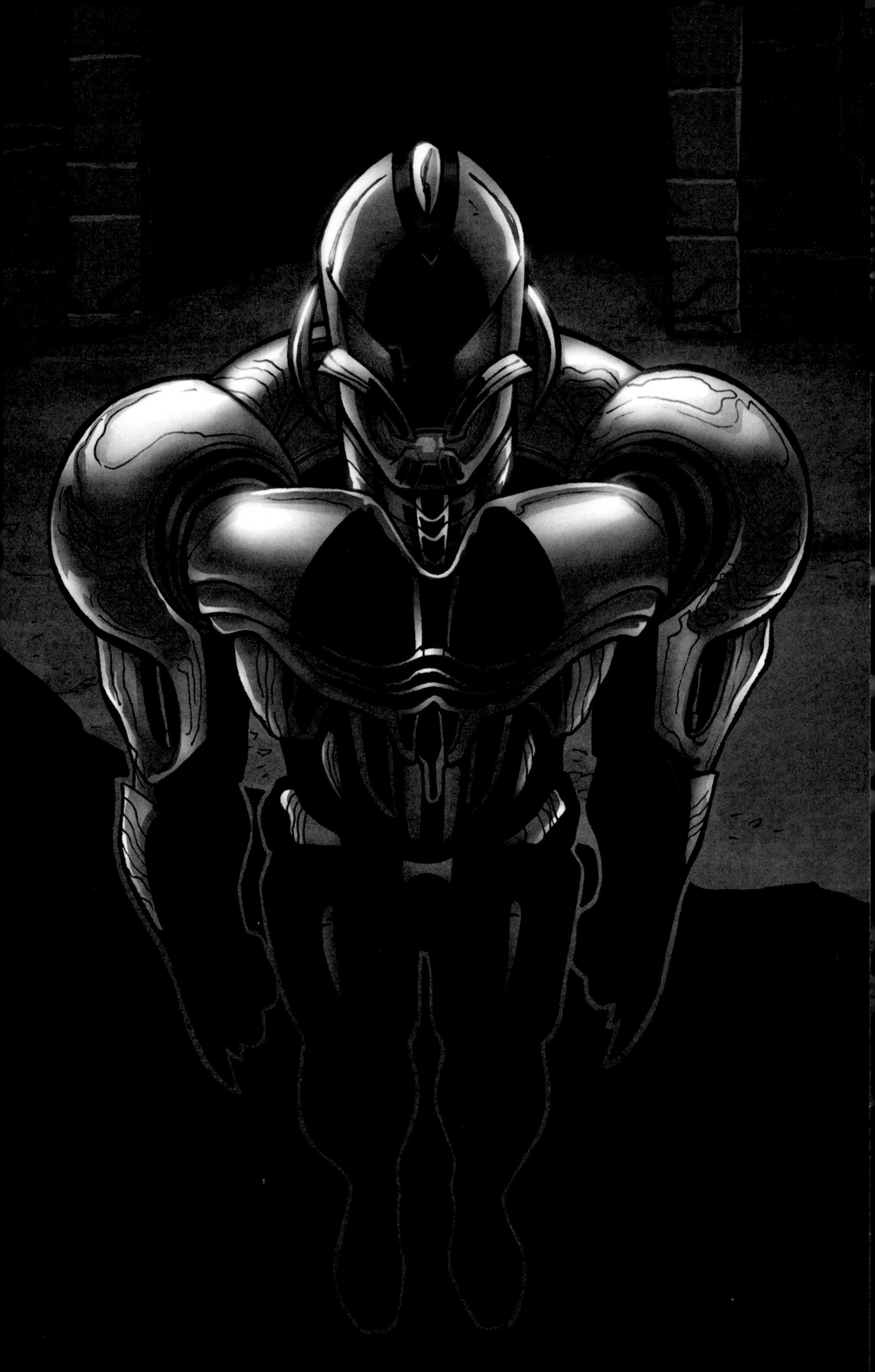

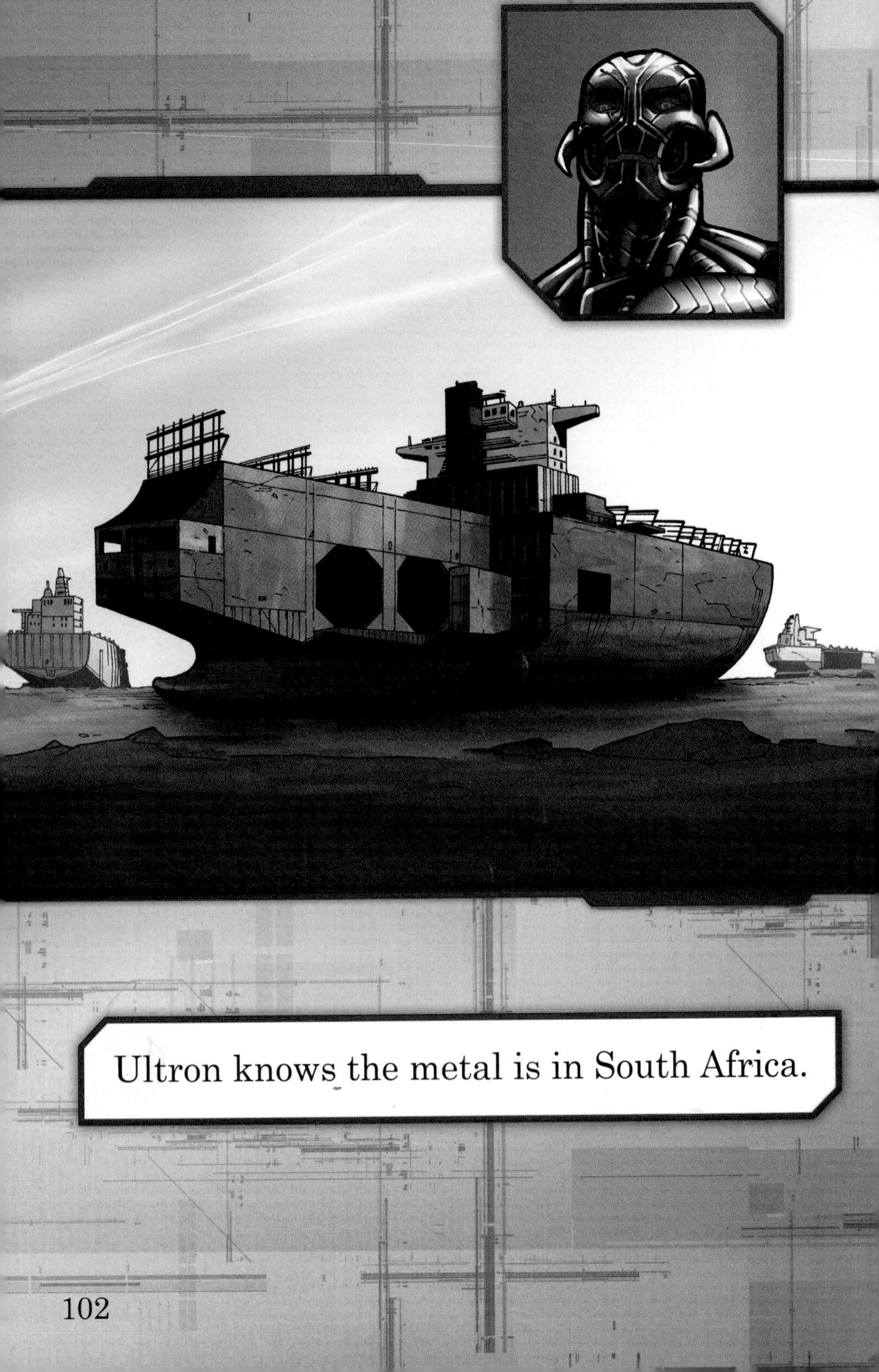

Ultron knows the metal is in South Africa.

He can get it from a man named Klaue.
Klaue sells bad things to bad people.

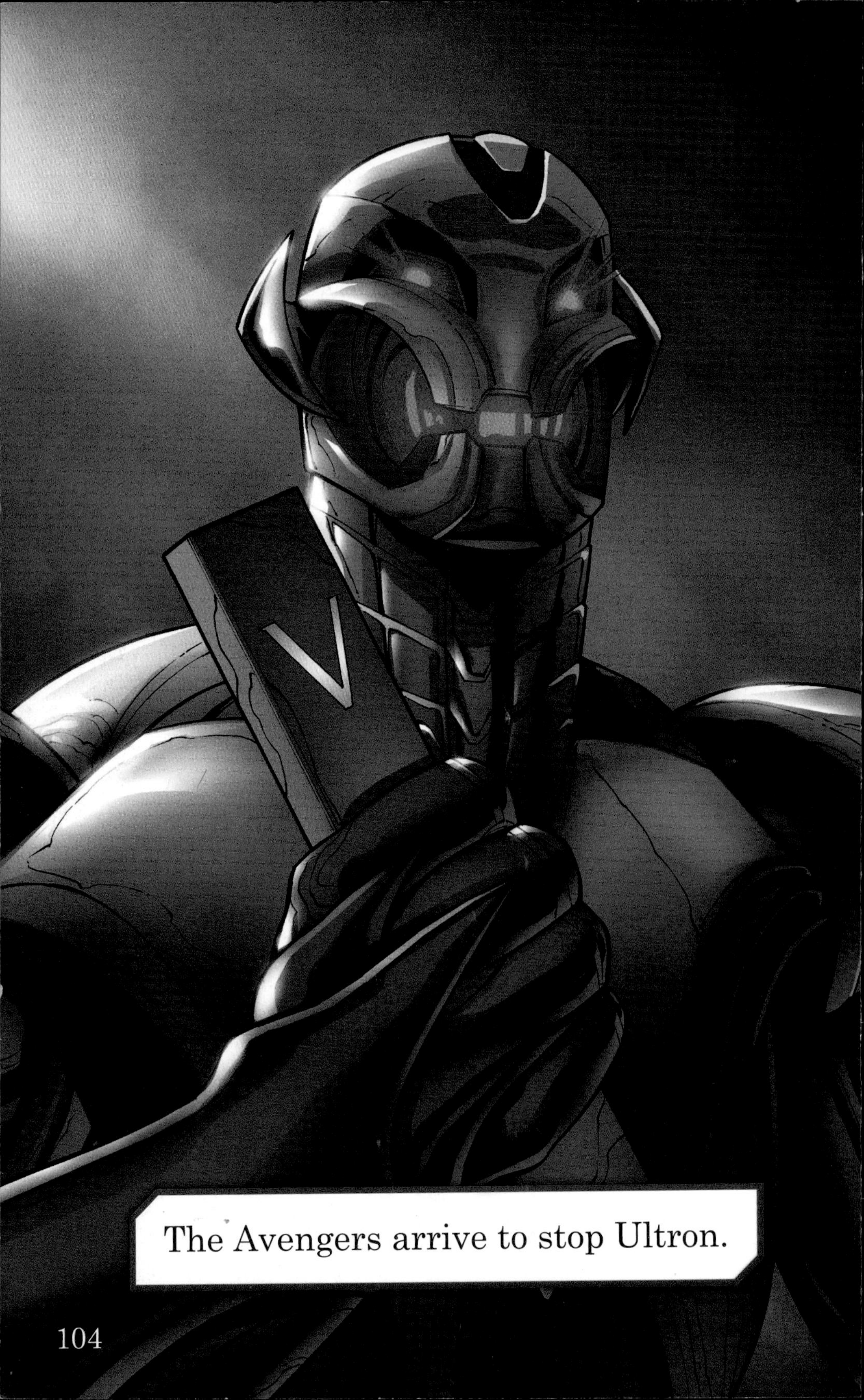
The Avengers arrive to stop Ultron.

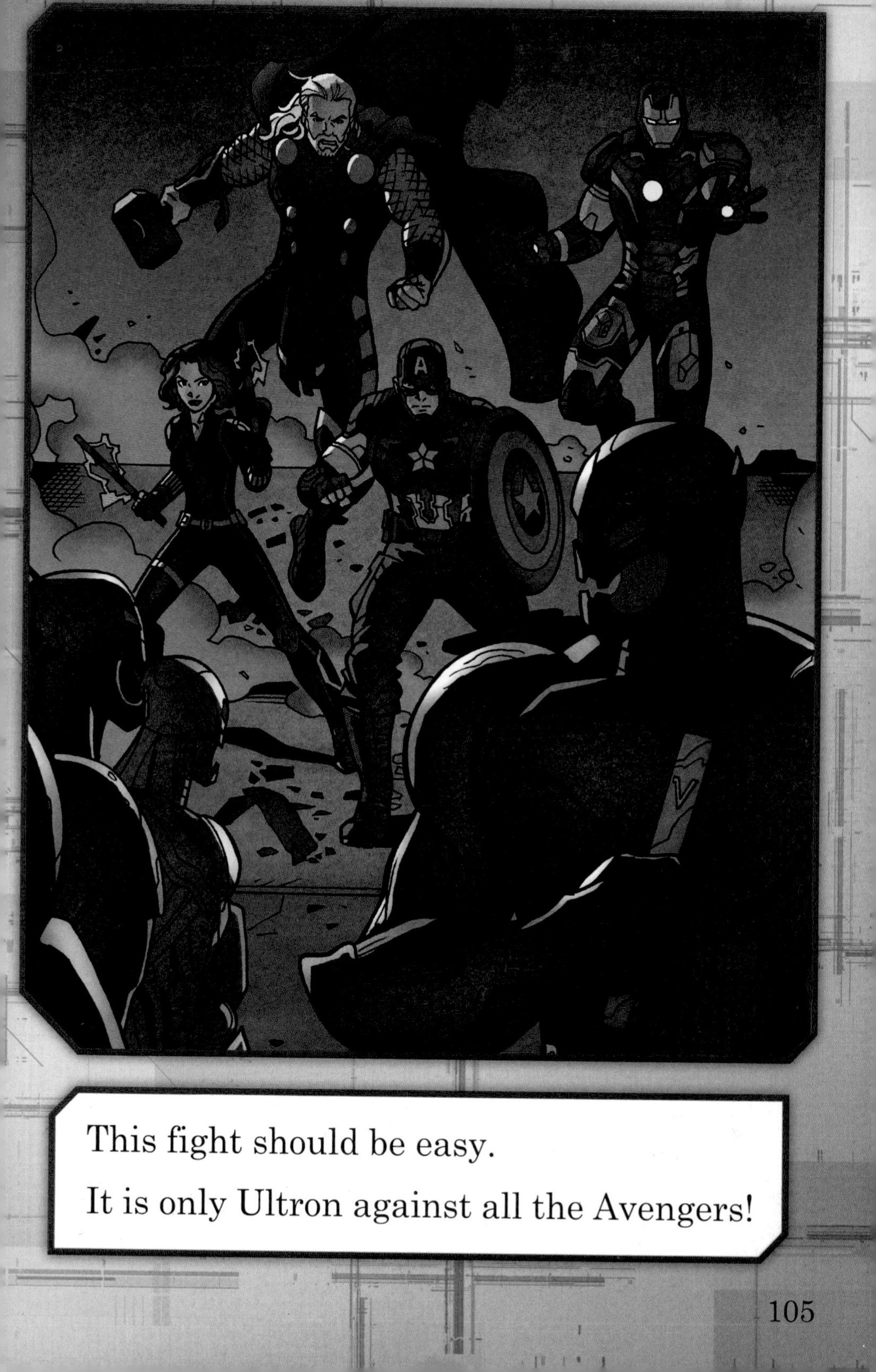

This fight should be easy.
It is only Ultron against all the Avengers!

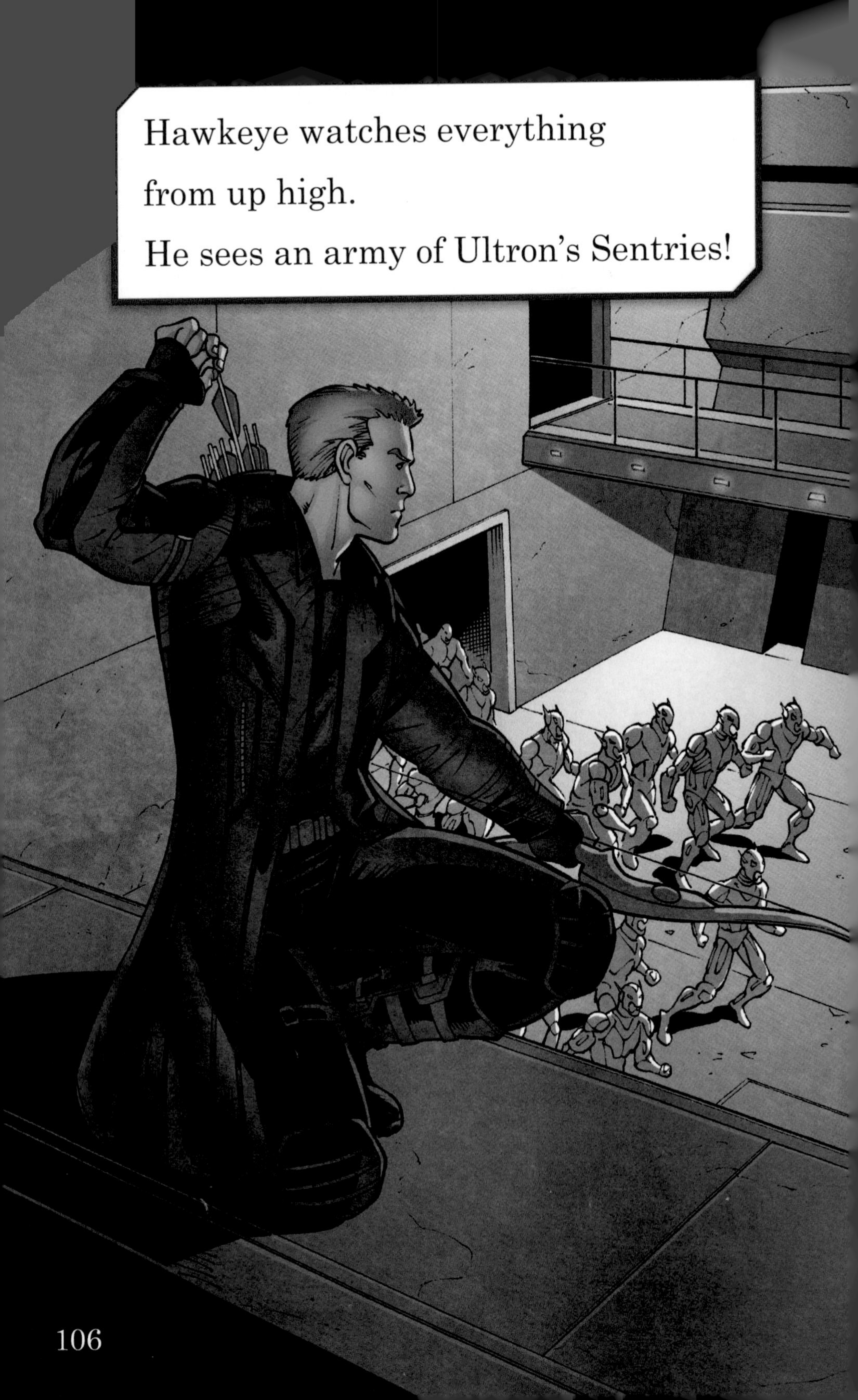
Hawkeye watches everything from up high.
He sees an army of Ultron's Sentries!

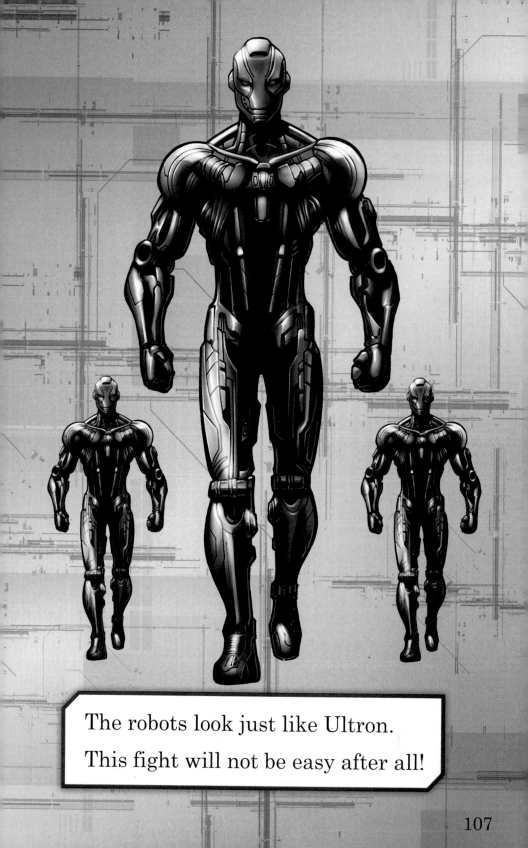

The robots look just like Ultron.
This fight will not be easy after all!

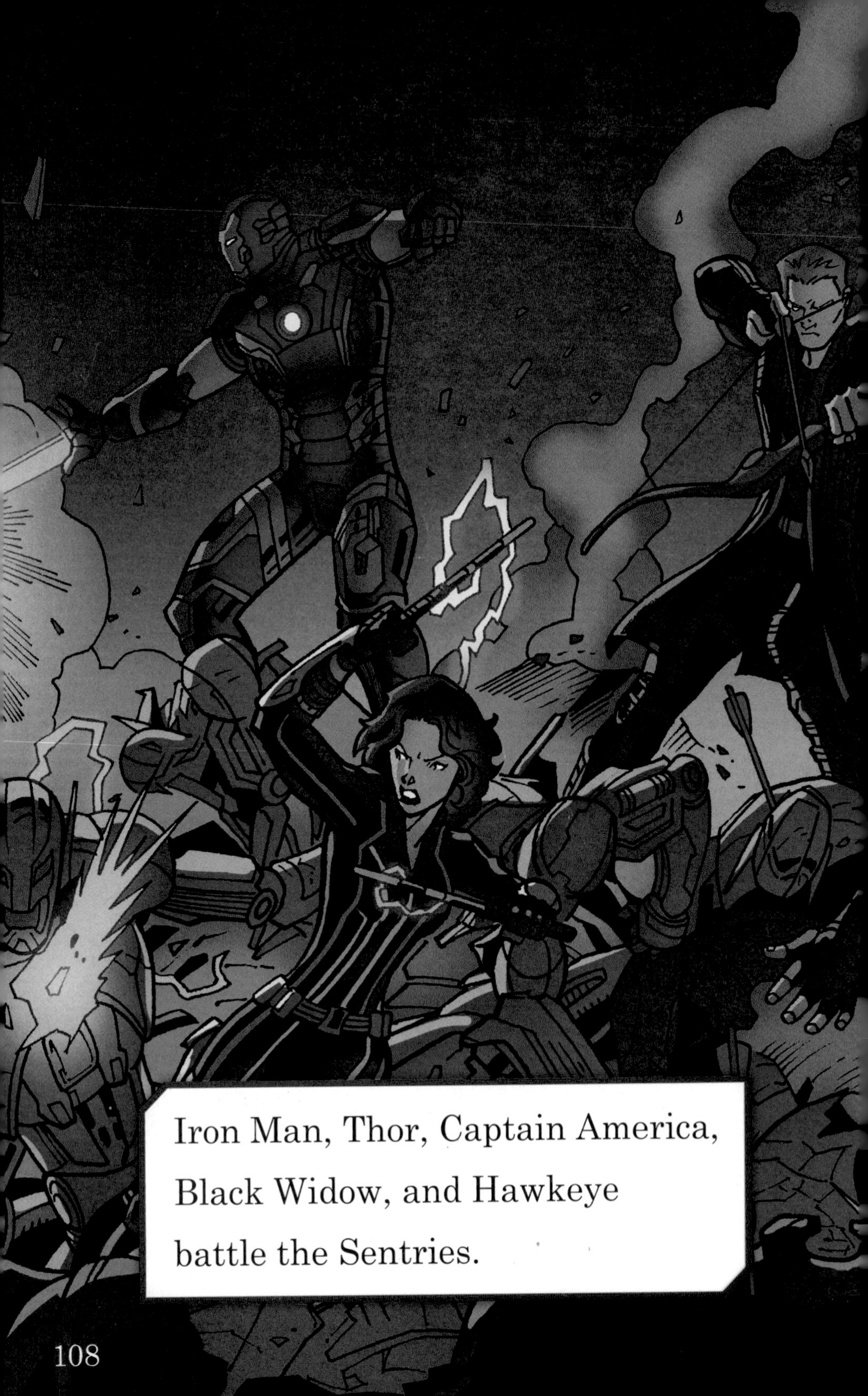
Iron Man, Thor, Captain America, Black Widow, and Hawkeye battle the Sentries.

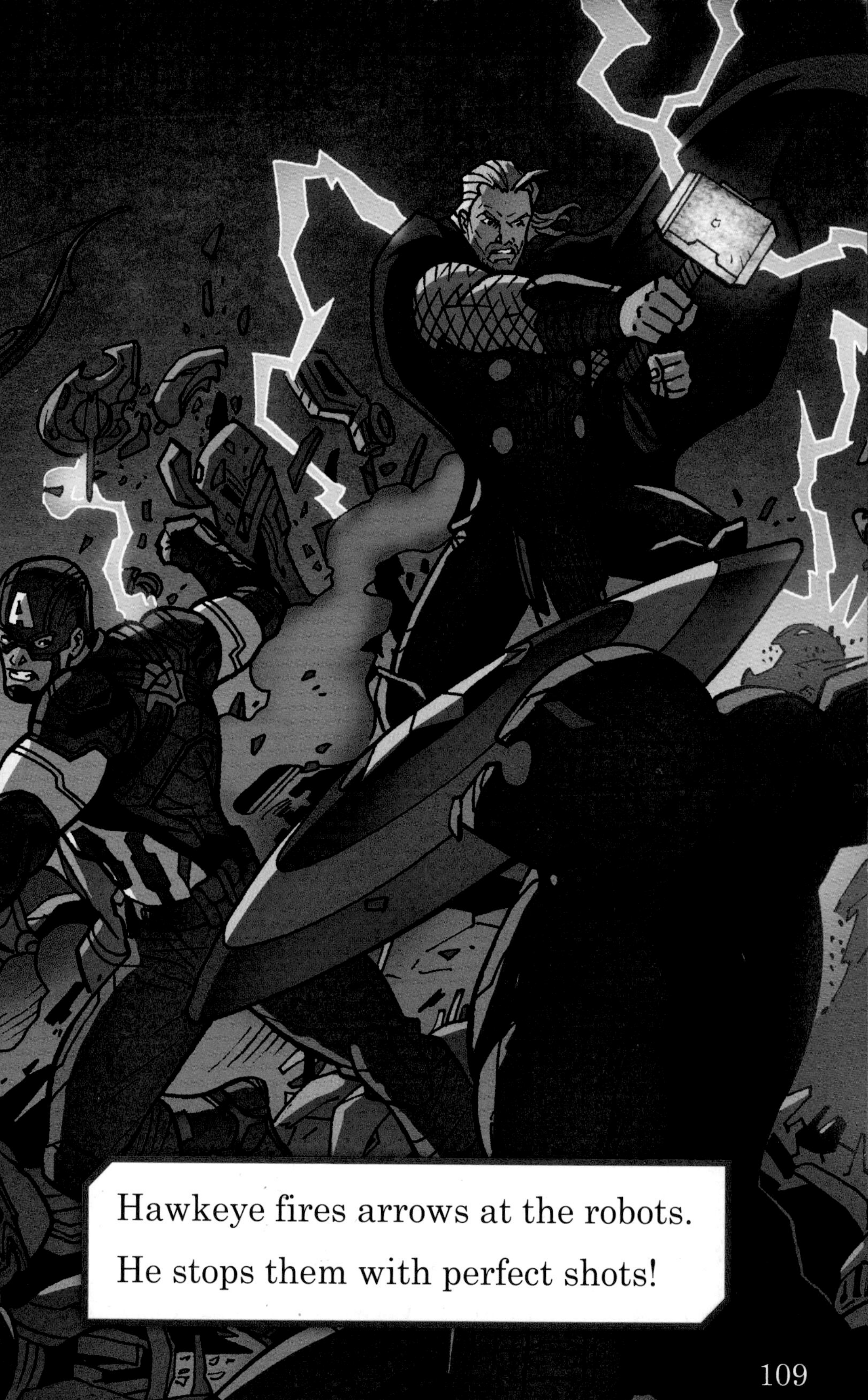

Hawkeye fires arrows at the robots.
He stops them with perfect shots!

Black Widow and Thor fight Ultron.

Widow uses her Widow's Bites.

Thor uses his mighty fists and hammer.

Ultron is tough.

The blows do not damage his metal body!

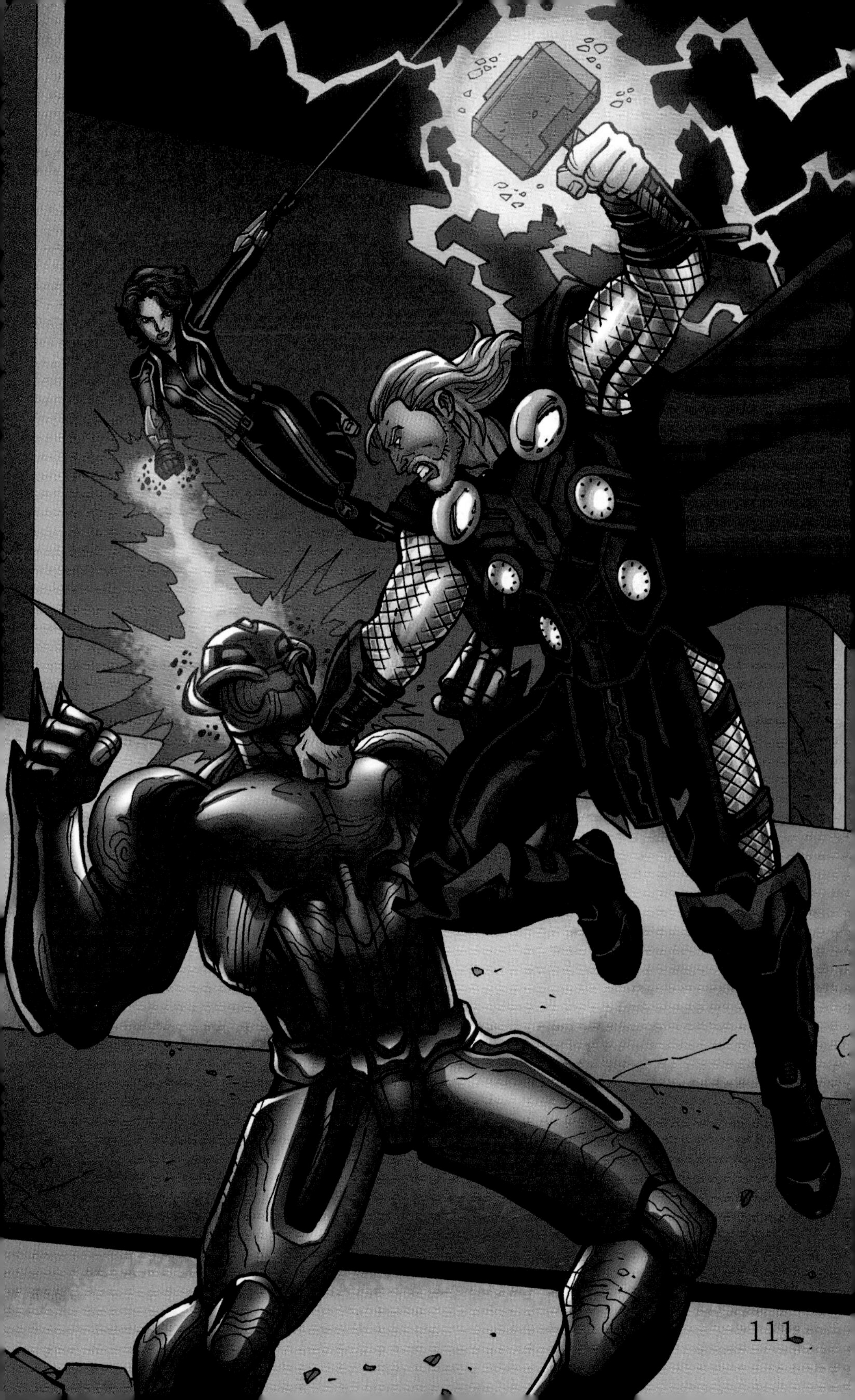

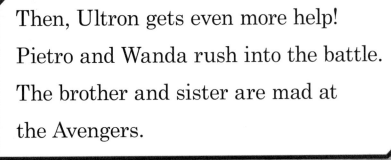

Then, Ultron gets even more help! Pietro and Wanda rush into the battle. The brother and sister are mad at the Avengers.

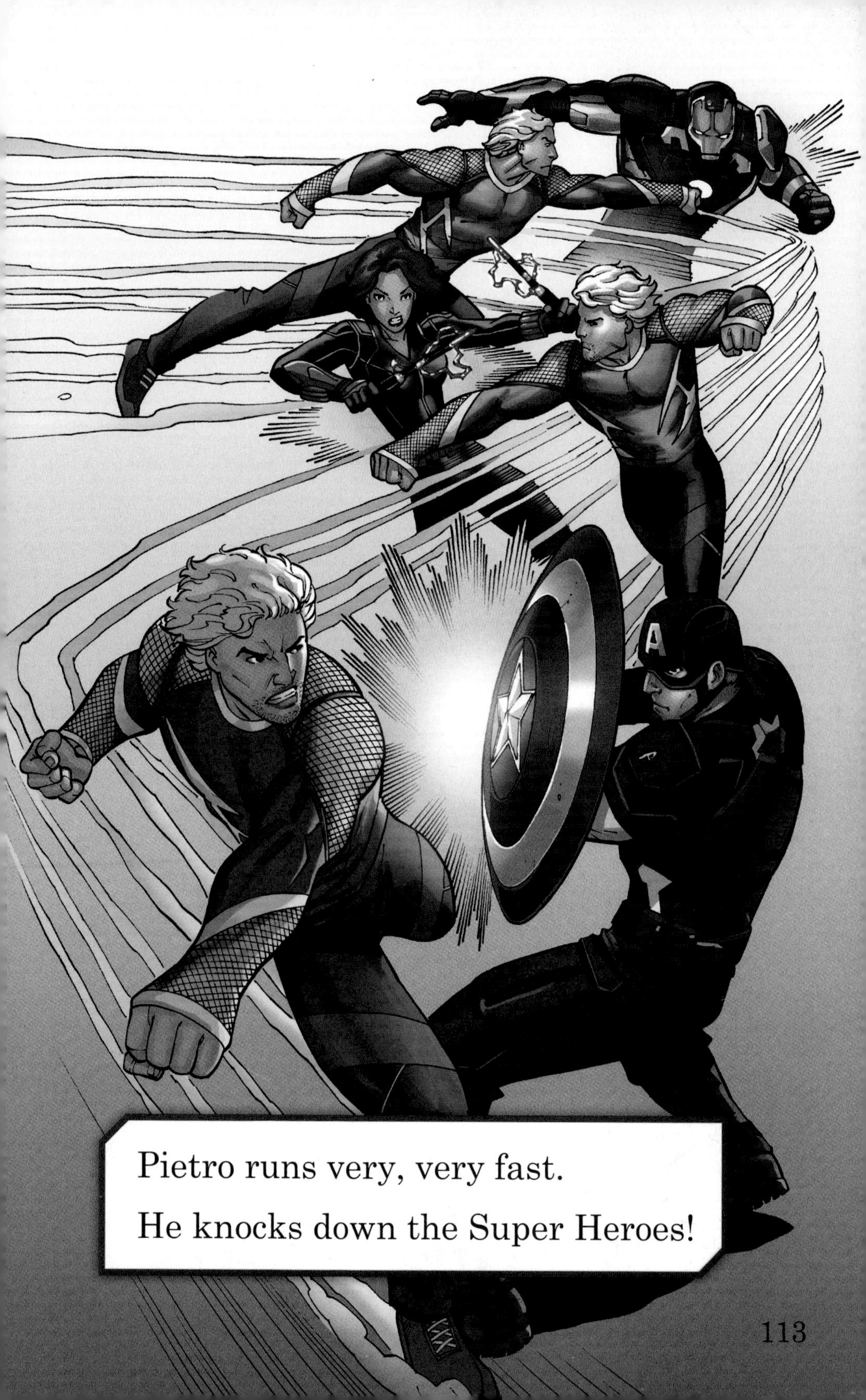
Pietro runs very, very fast.
He knocks down the Super Heroes!

Wanda has powers, too.

She uses strange energy to hurt

the Avengers' minds.

Thor, Black Widow, and

Captain America cannot stop her.

She is too strong.

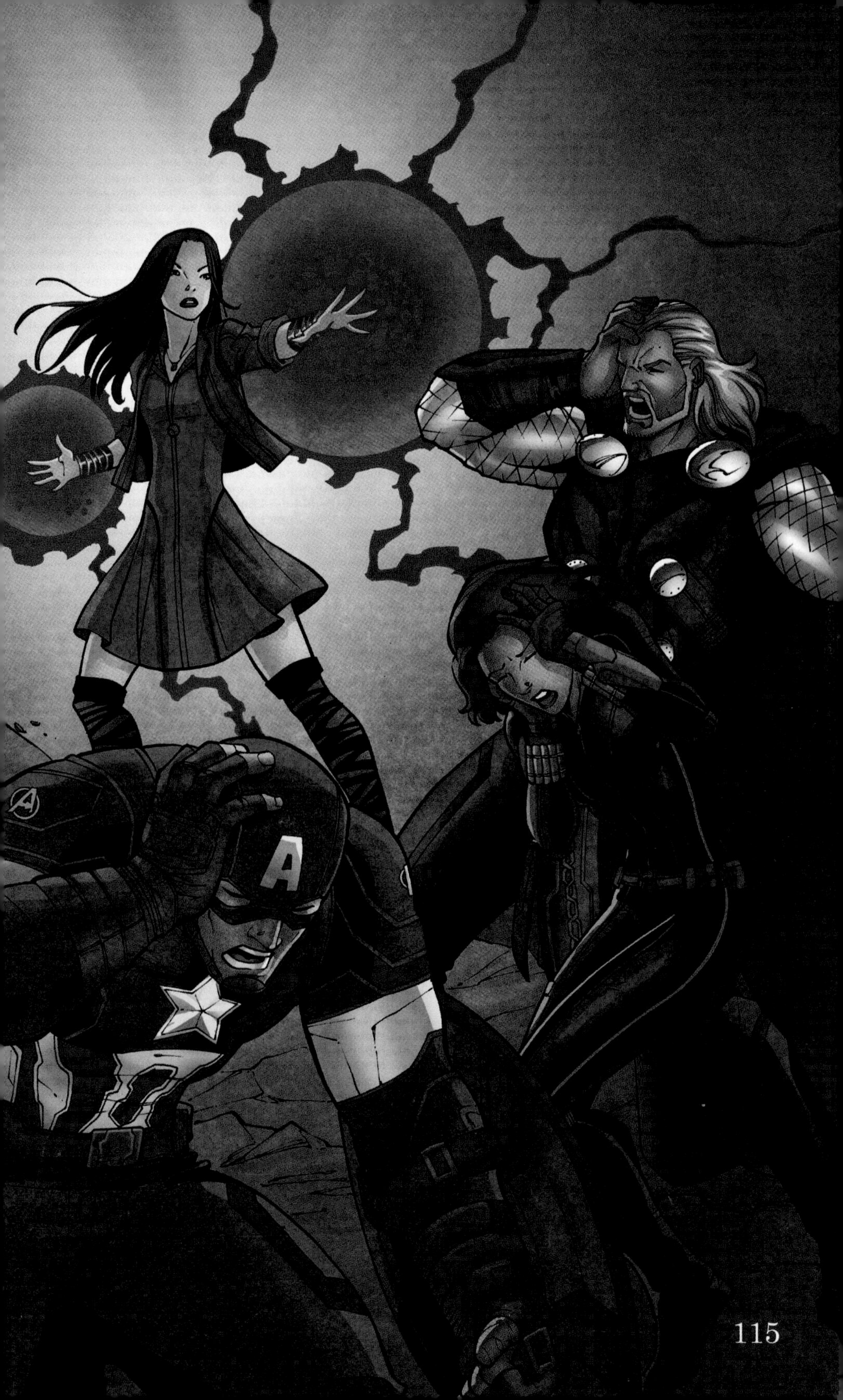

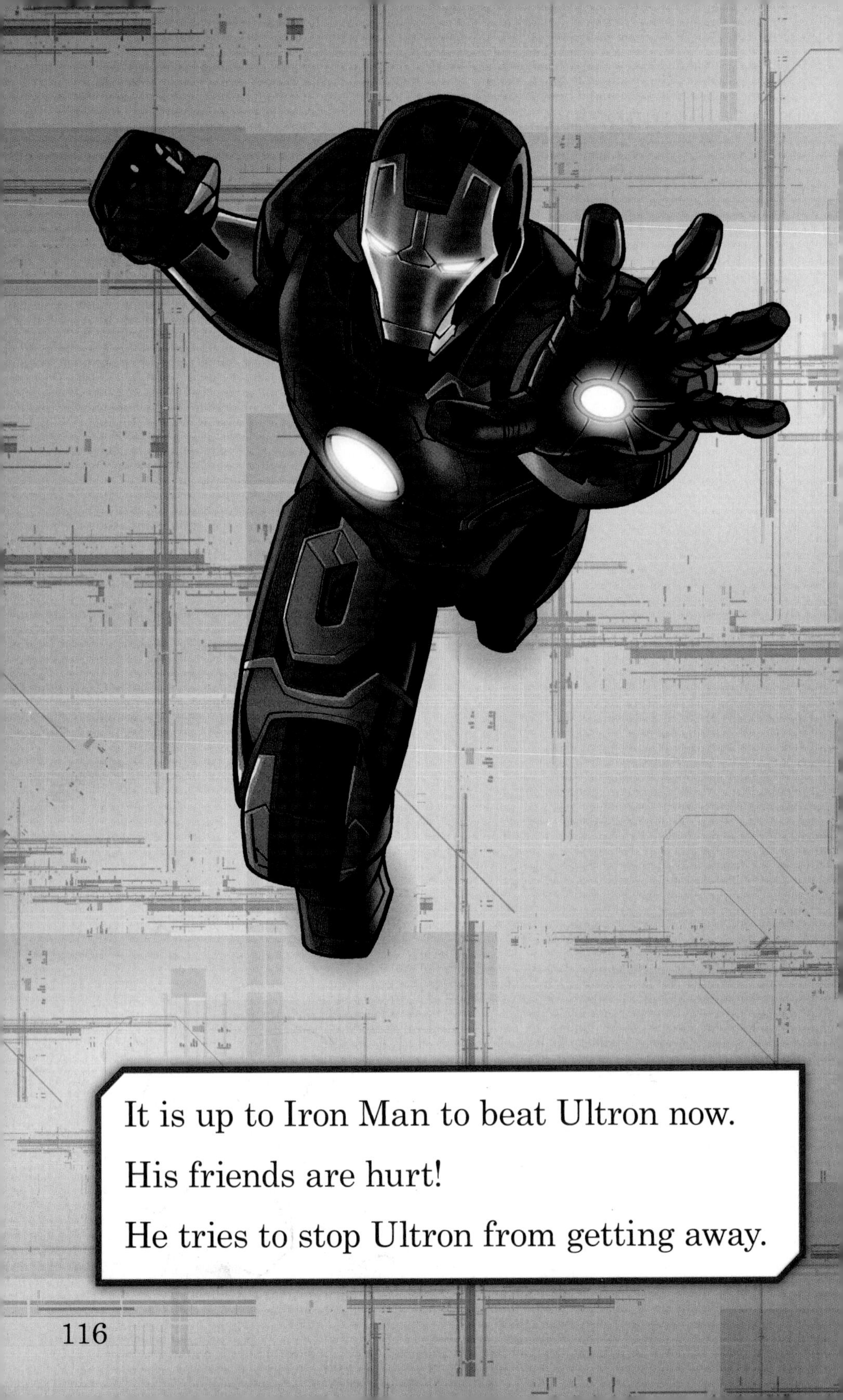

It is up to Iron Man to beat Ultron now.
His friends are hurt!
He tries to stop Ultron from getting away.

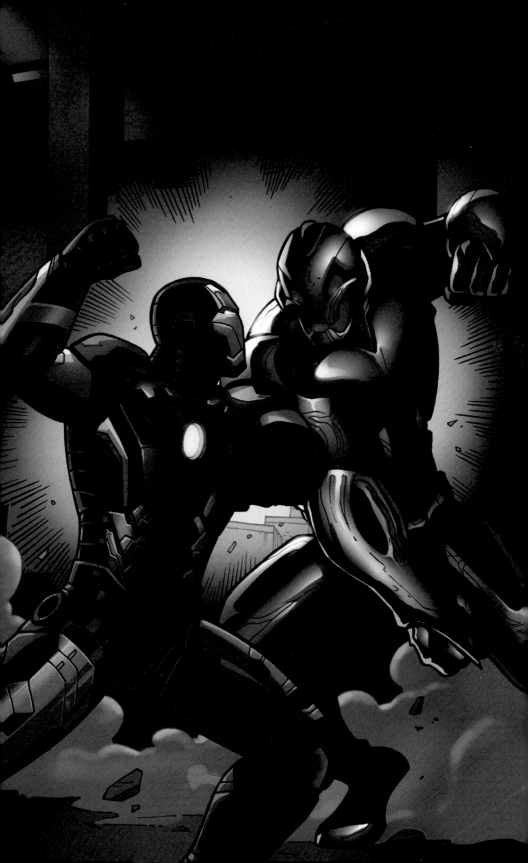

Ultron is too powerful.

Even Iron Man's armor cannot hurt his metal body.

It looks like the Avengers are losing!

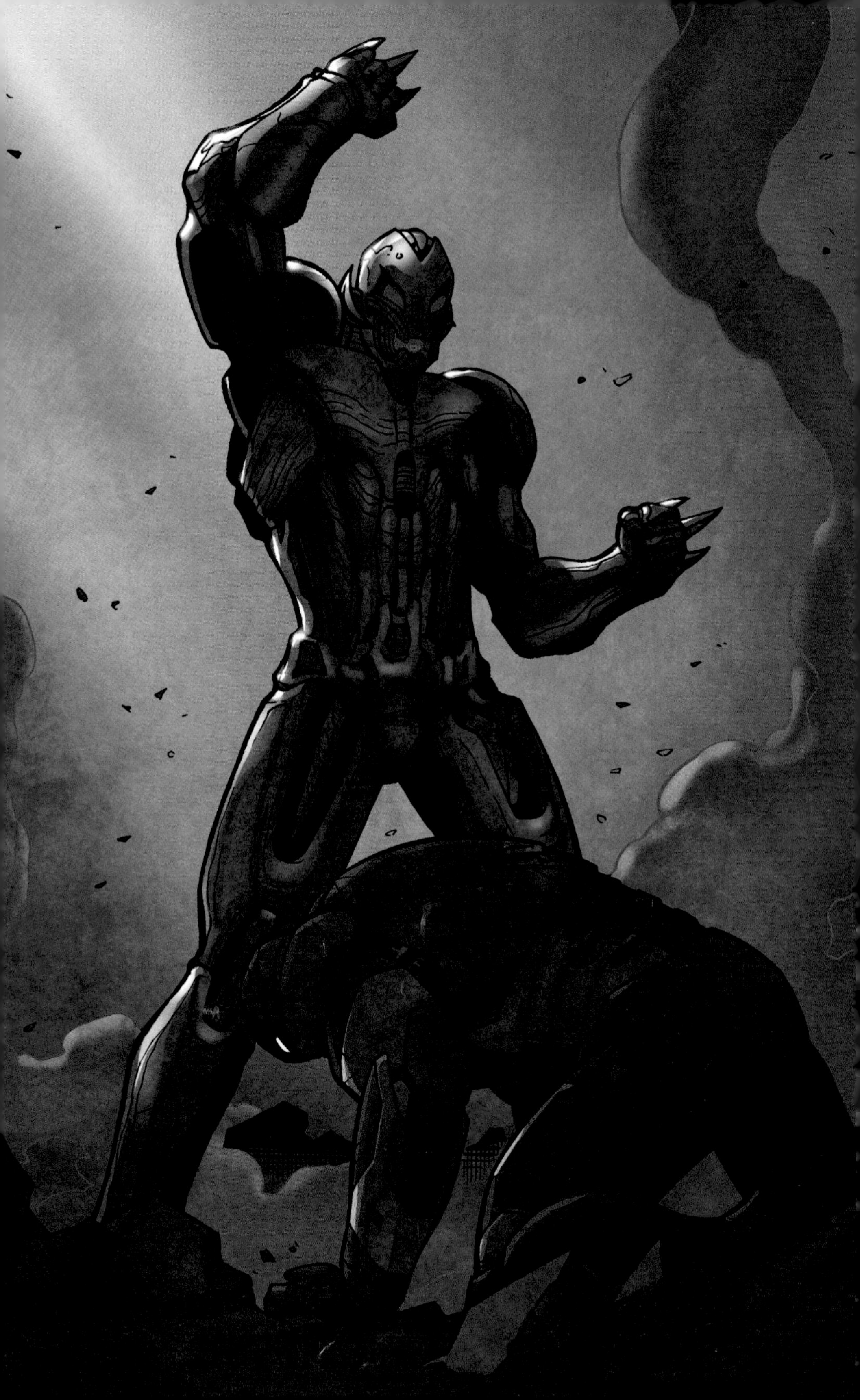

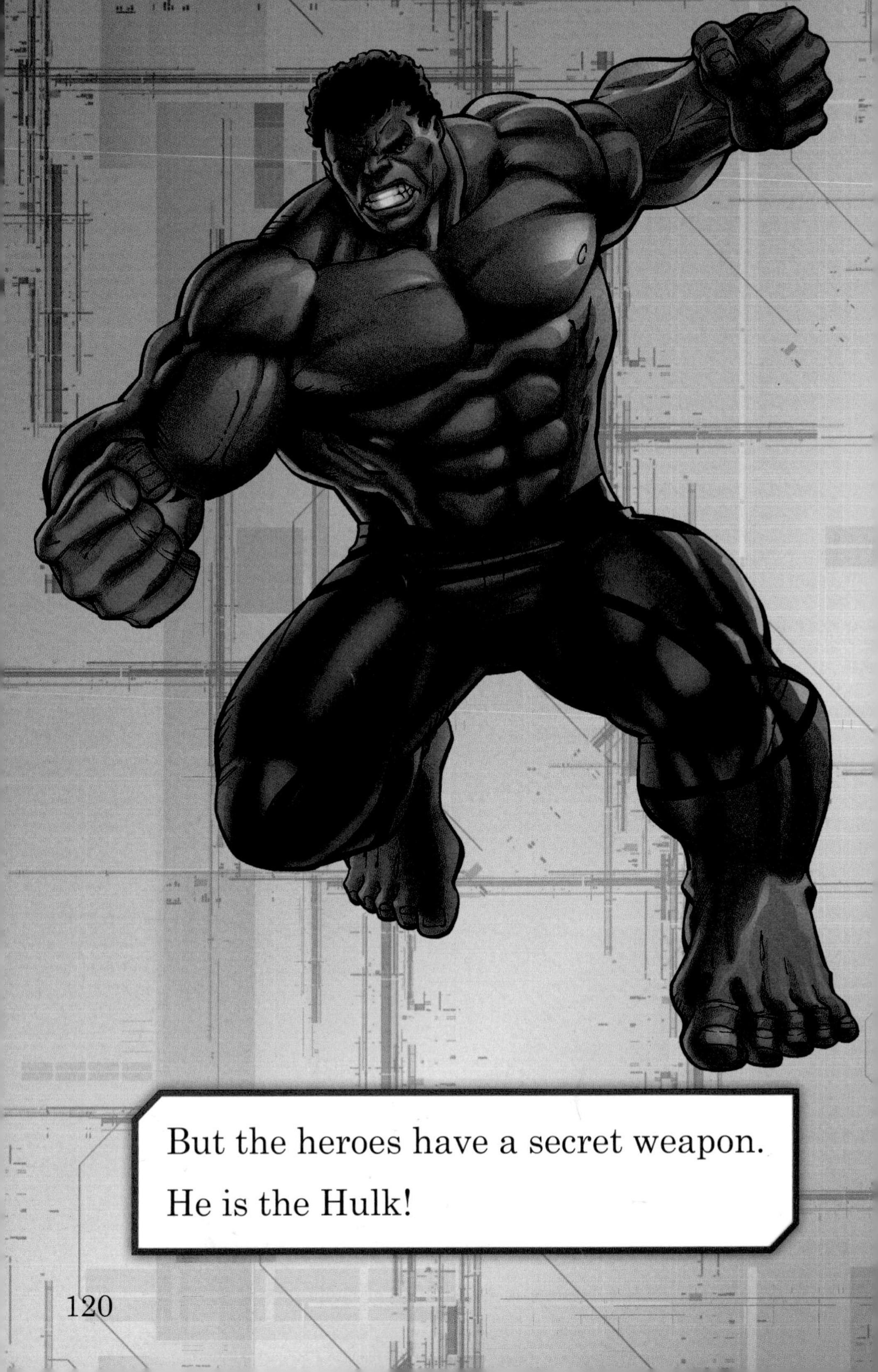

But the heroes have a secret weapon.
He is the Hulk!

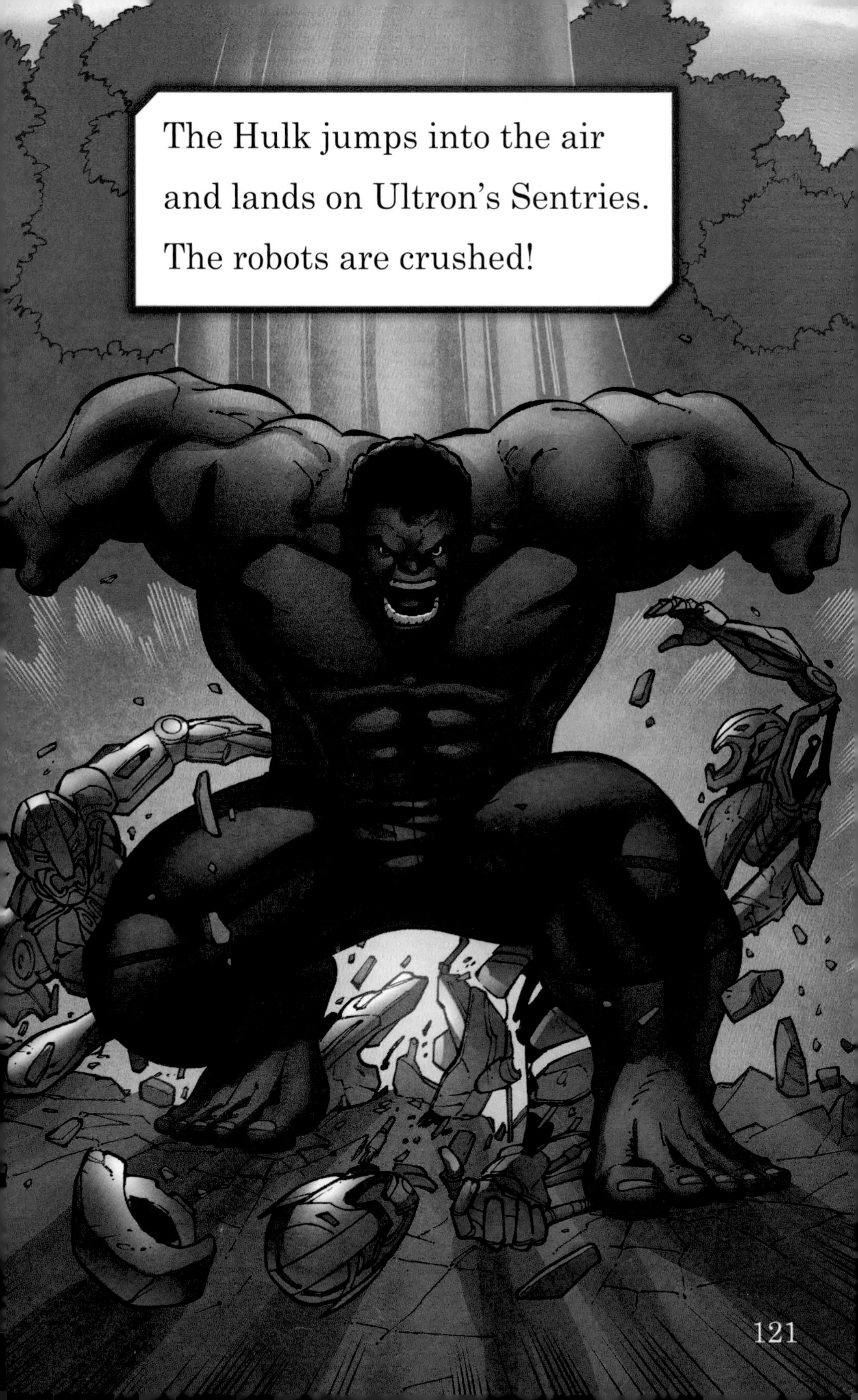
The Hulk jumps into the air and lands on Ultron's Sentries. The robots are crushed!

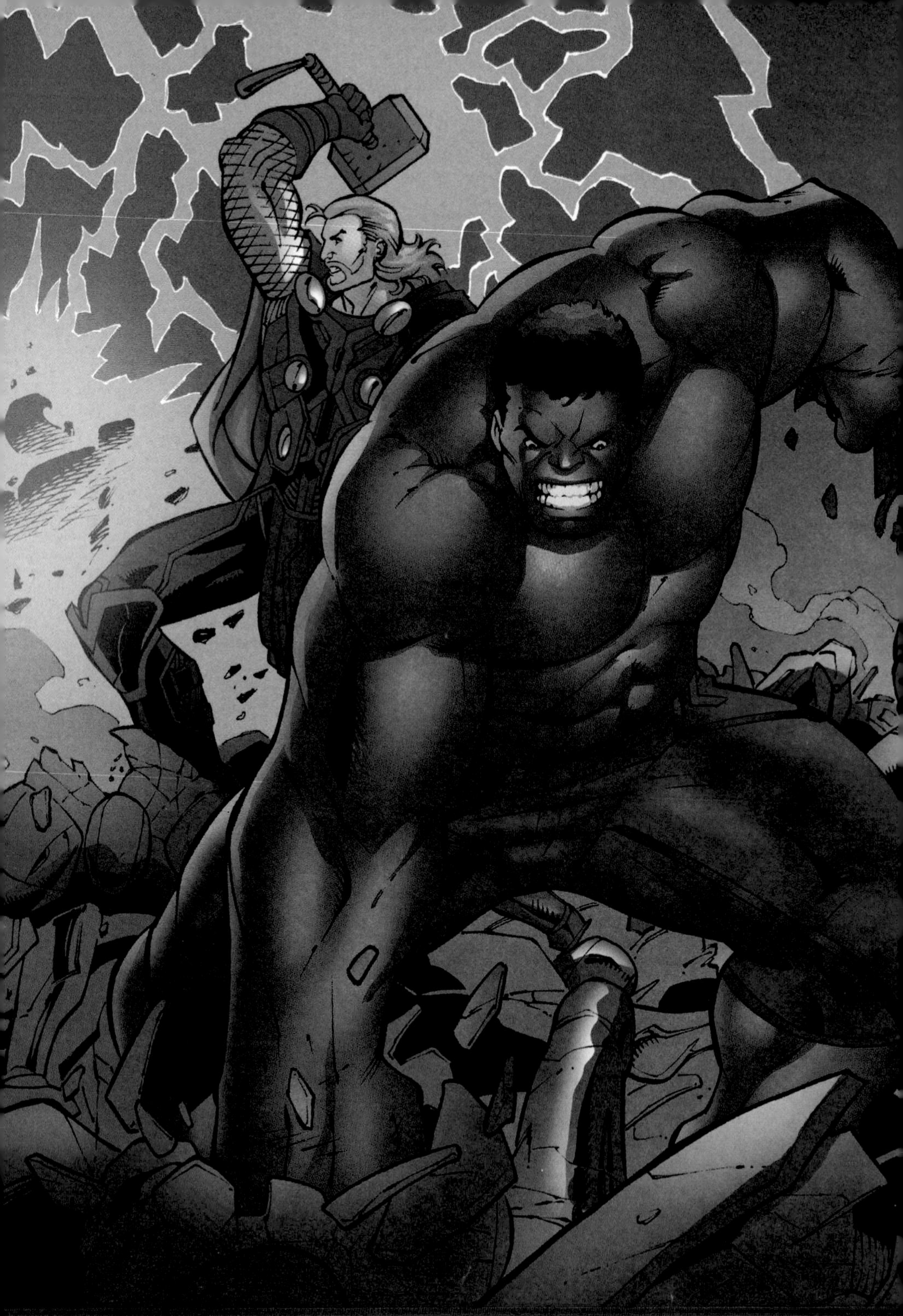

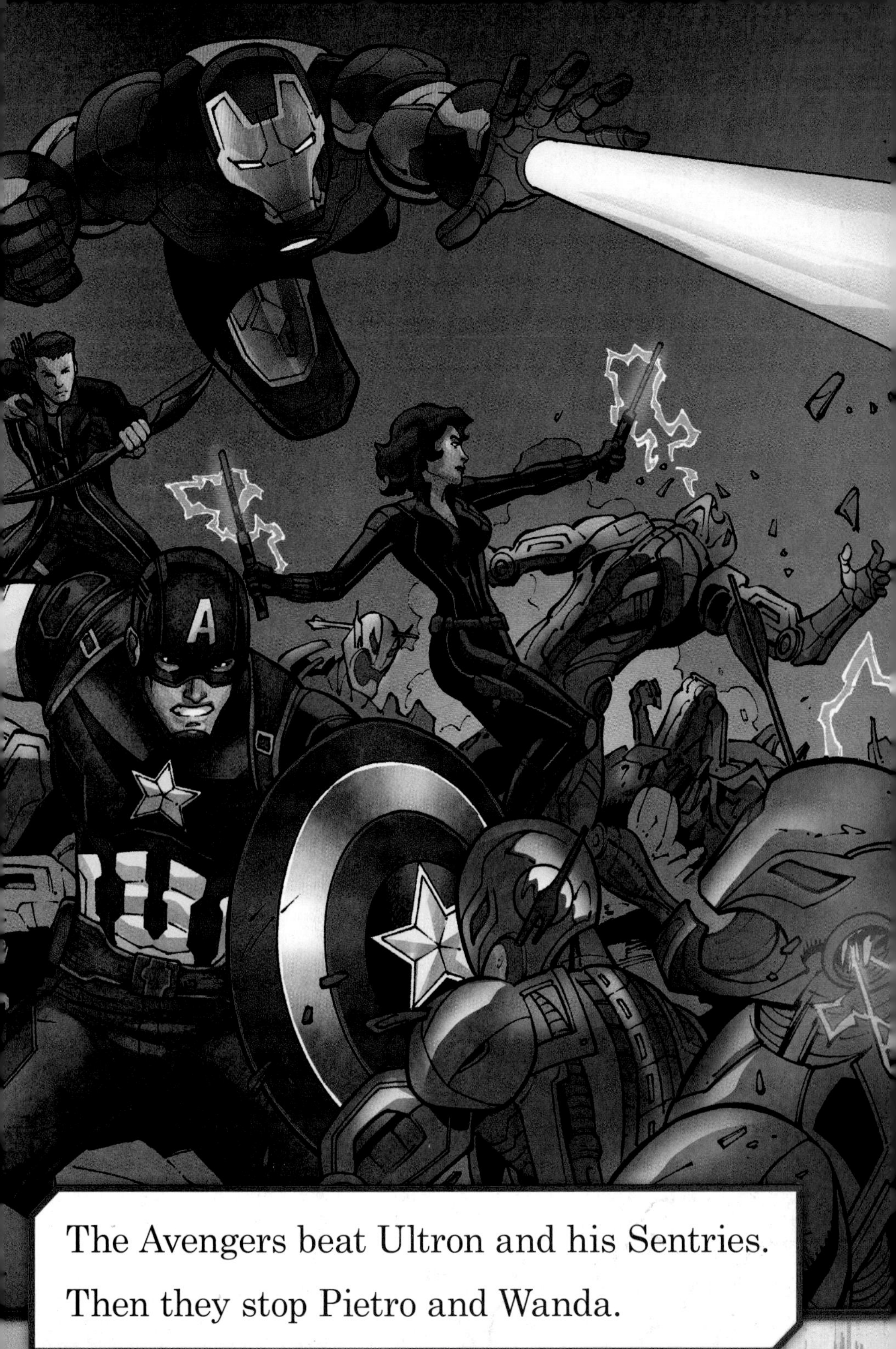

The Avengers beat Ultron and his Sentries.
Then they stop Pietro and Wanda.

The heroes are a team, but the Hulk is the one who saves the day!

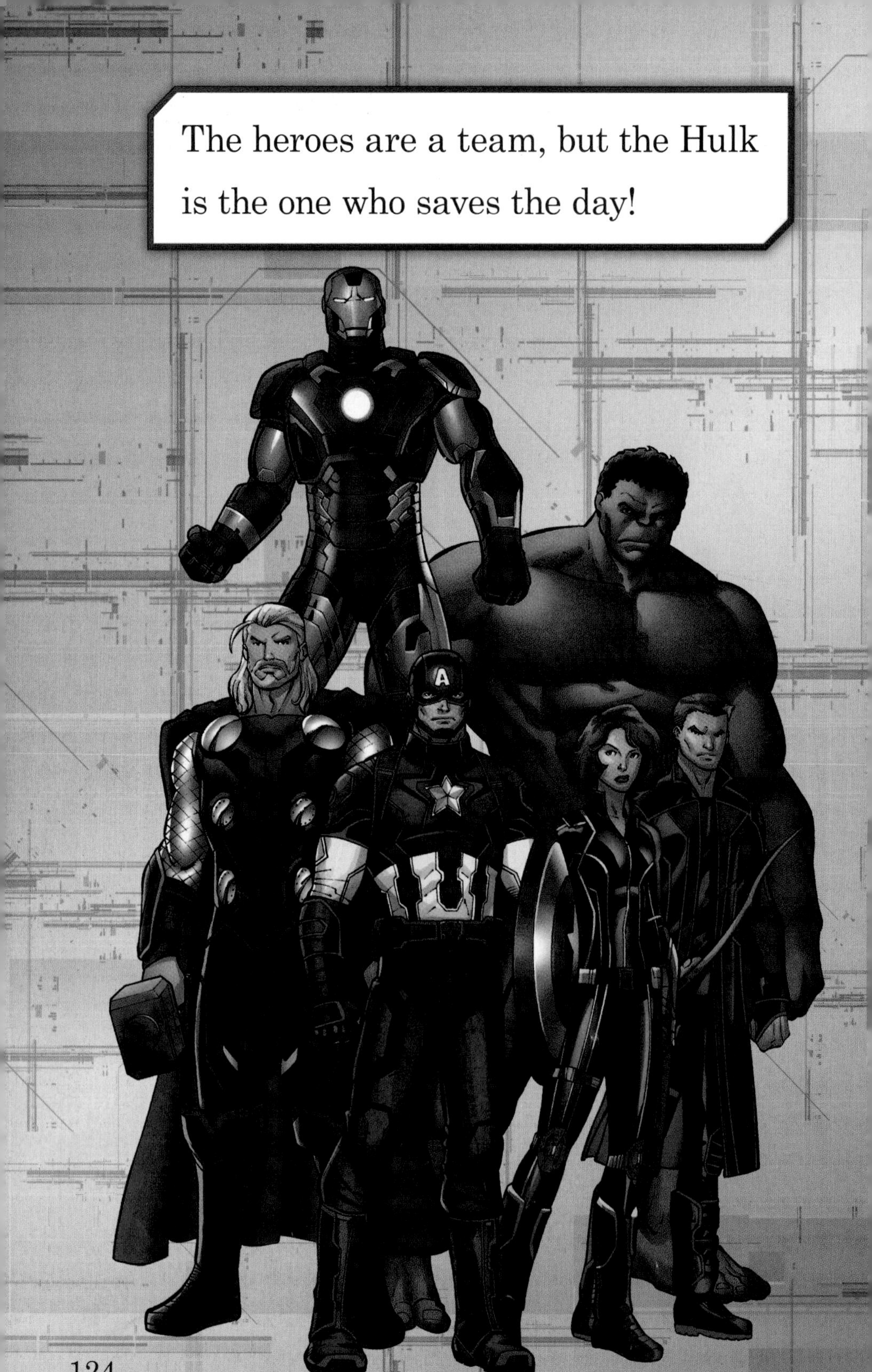

MARVEL
ANT-MAN

I AM ANT-MAN

By Tomas Palacios
Illustrated by Ron Lim, Andy Smith, and Andy Troy
Inspired by Marvel's Ant-Man
Based on the Screenplay by Adam McKay & Paul Rudd
Story by Edgar Wright & Joe Cornish
Produced by Kevin Feige, p.g.a.
Directed by Peyton Reed

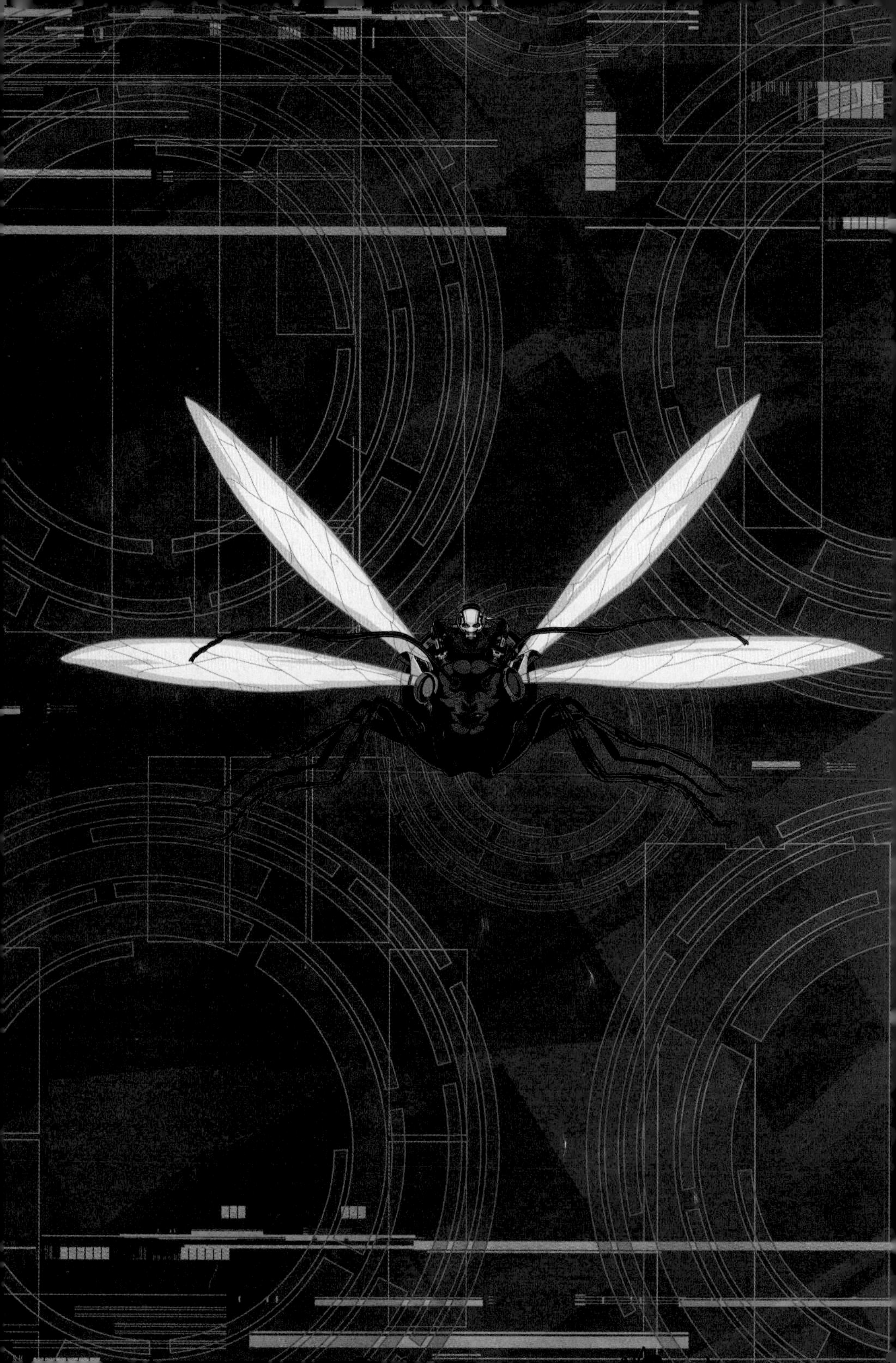

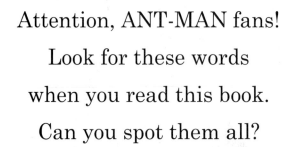

Attention, ANT-MAN fans!
Look for these words
when you read this book.
Can you spot them all?

suit

helmet

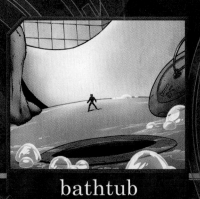

bathtub

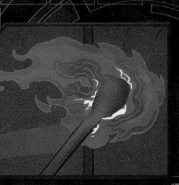

match

Scott Lang did a bad thing.

He stole a lot of money.

Scott went away for a few years,

and now he wants to be good.

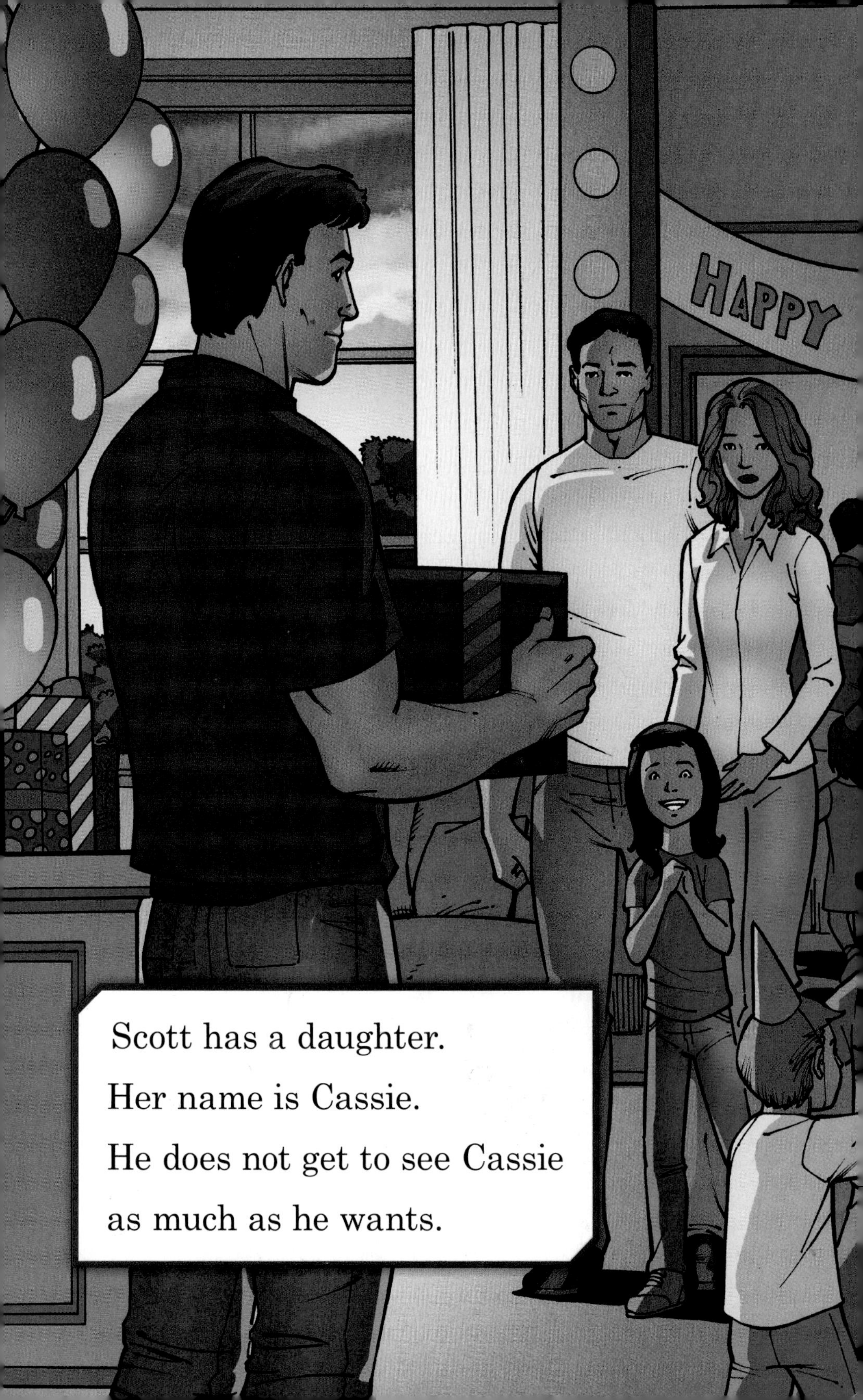
HAPPY
Scott has a daughter.
Her name is Cassie.
He does not get to see Cassie
as much as he wants.

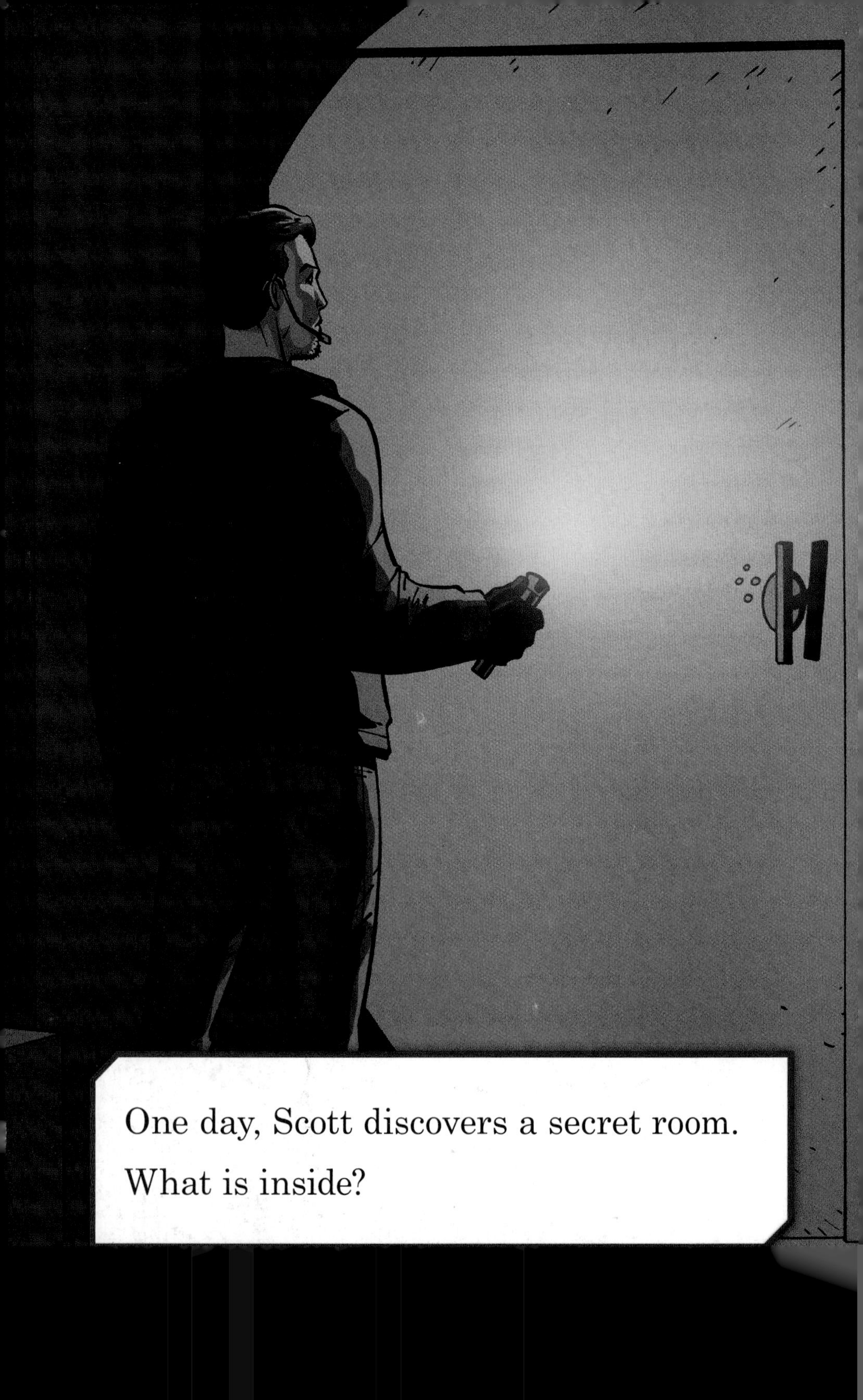
One day, Scott discovers a secret room. What is inside?

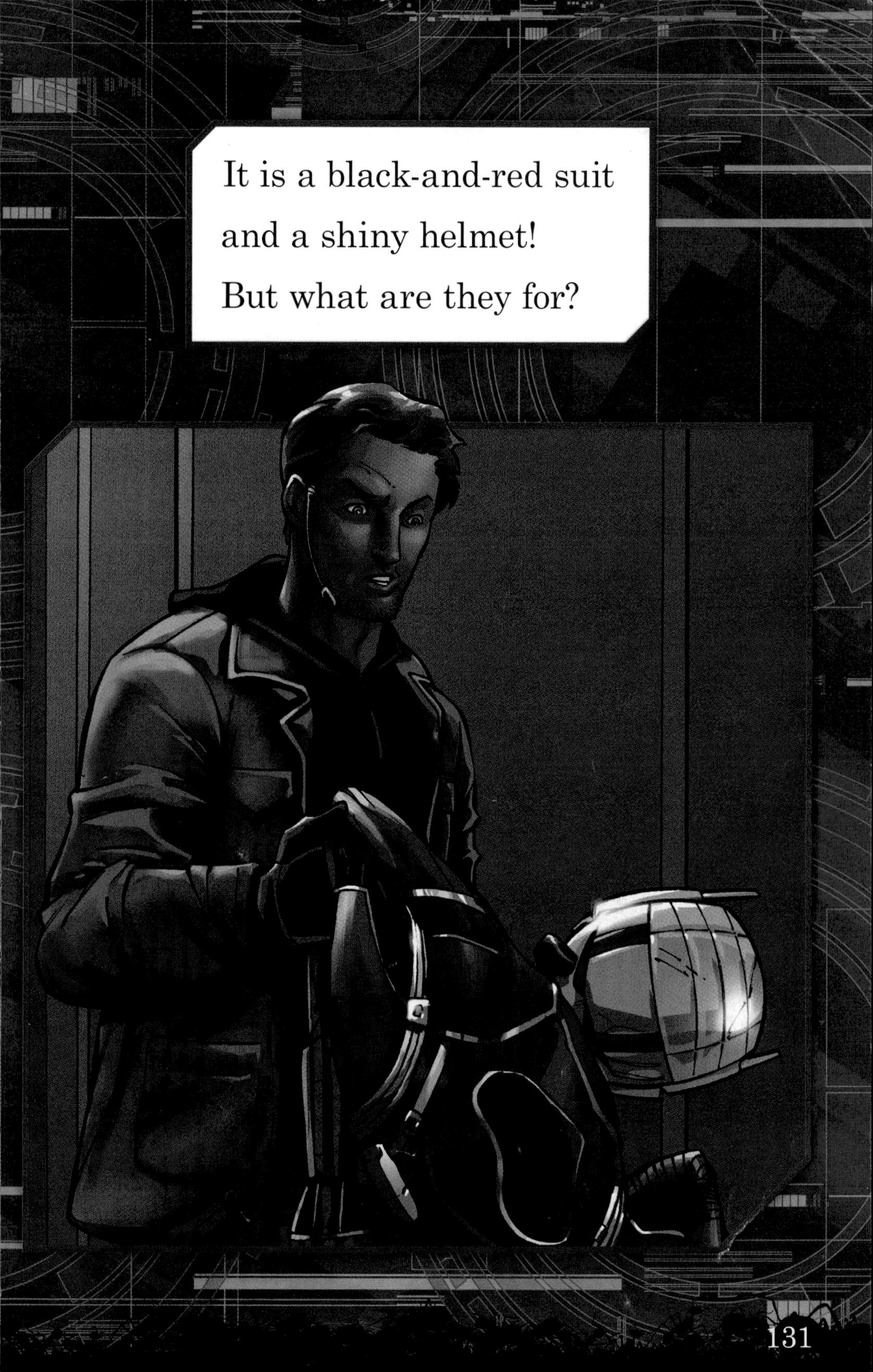
It is a black-and-red suit
and a shiny helmet!
But what are they for?

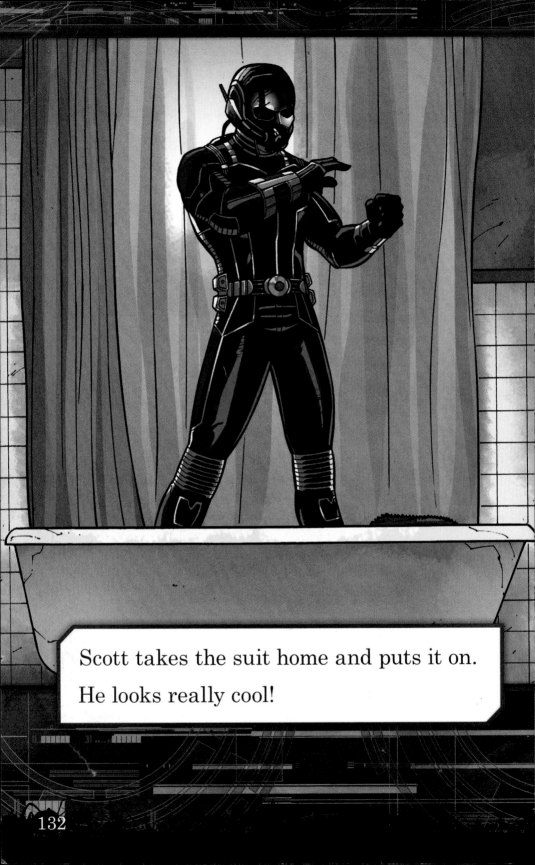

Scott takes the suit home and puts it on.

He looks really cool!

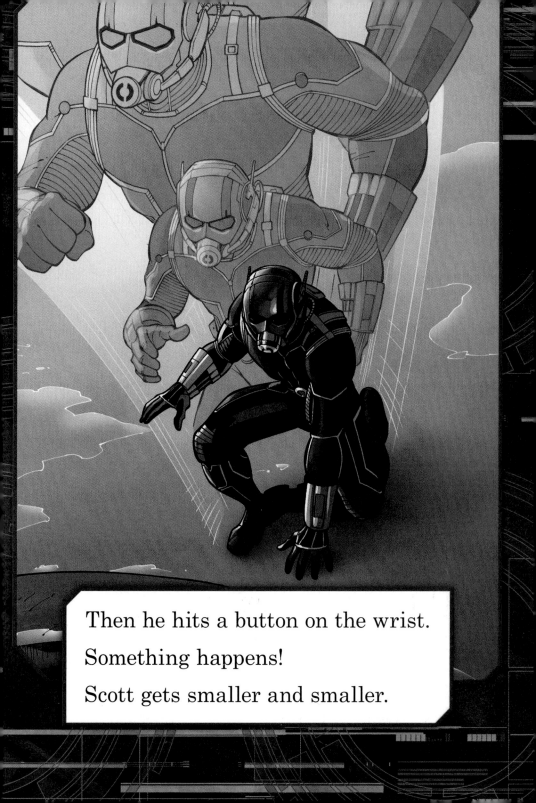

Then he hits a button on the wrist.

Something happens!

Scott gets smaller and smaller.

Scott is the size of an ant and is inside the bathtub! He sees a new world, and everything around him is bigger than before.

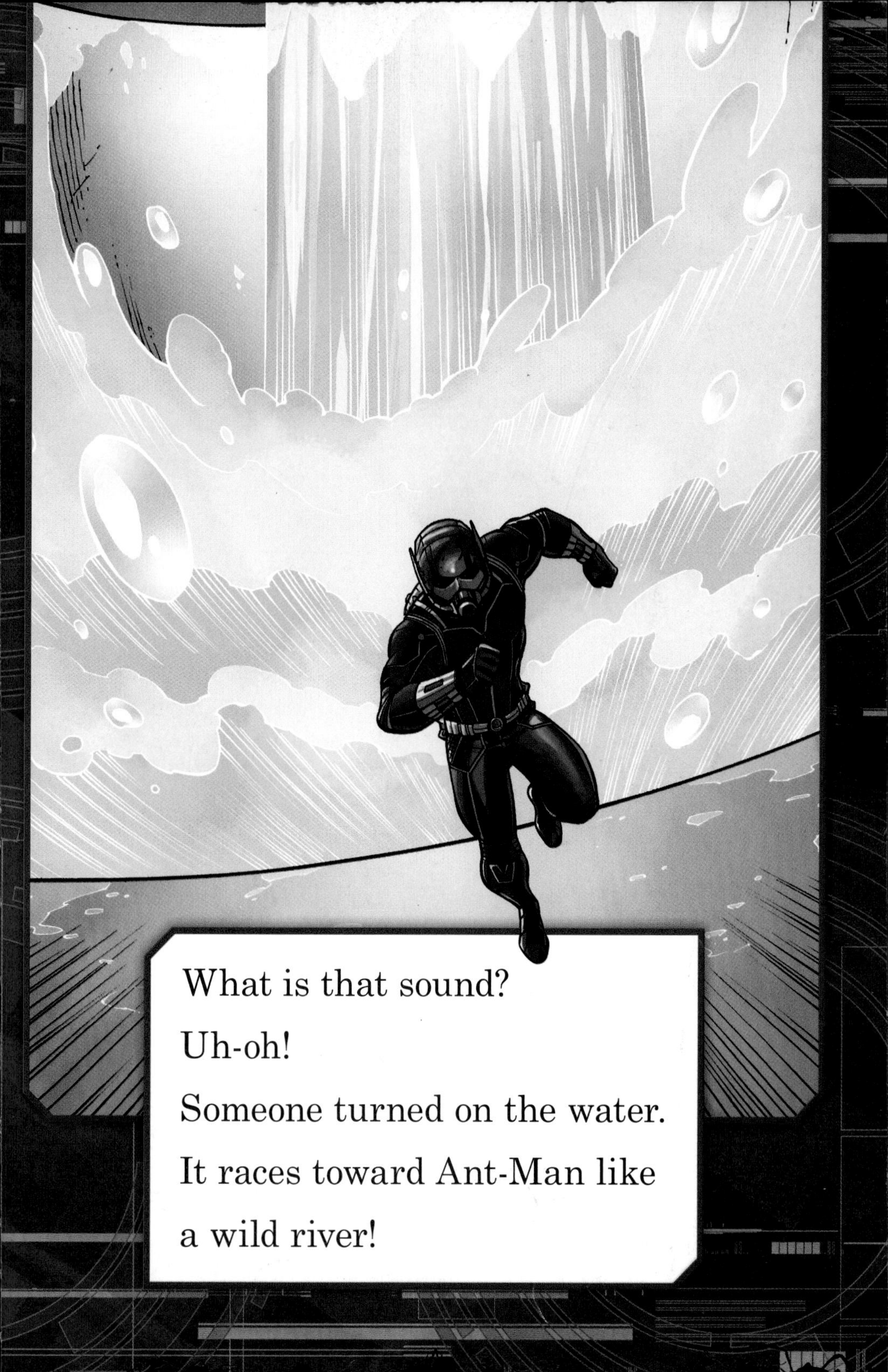

What is that sound?
Uh-oh!
Someone turned on the water.
It races toward Ant-Man like
a wild river!

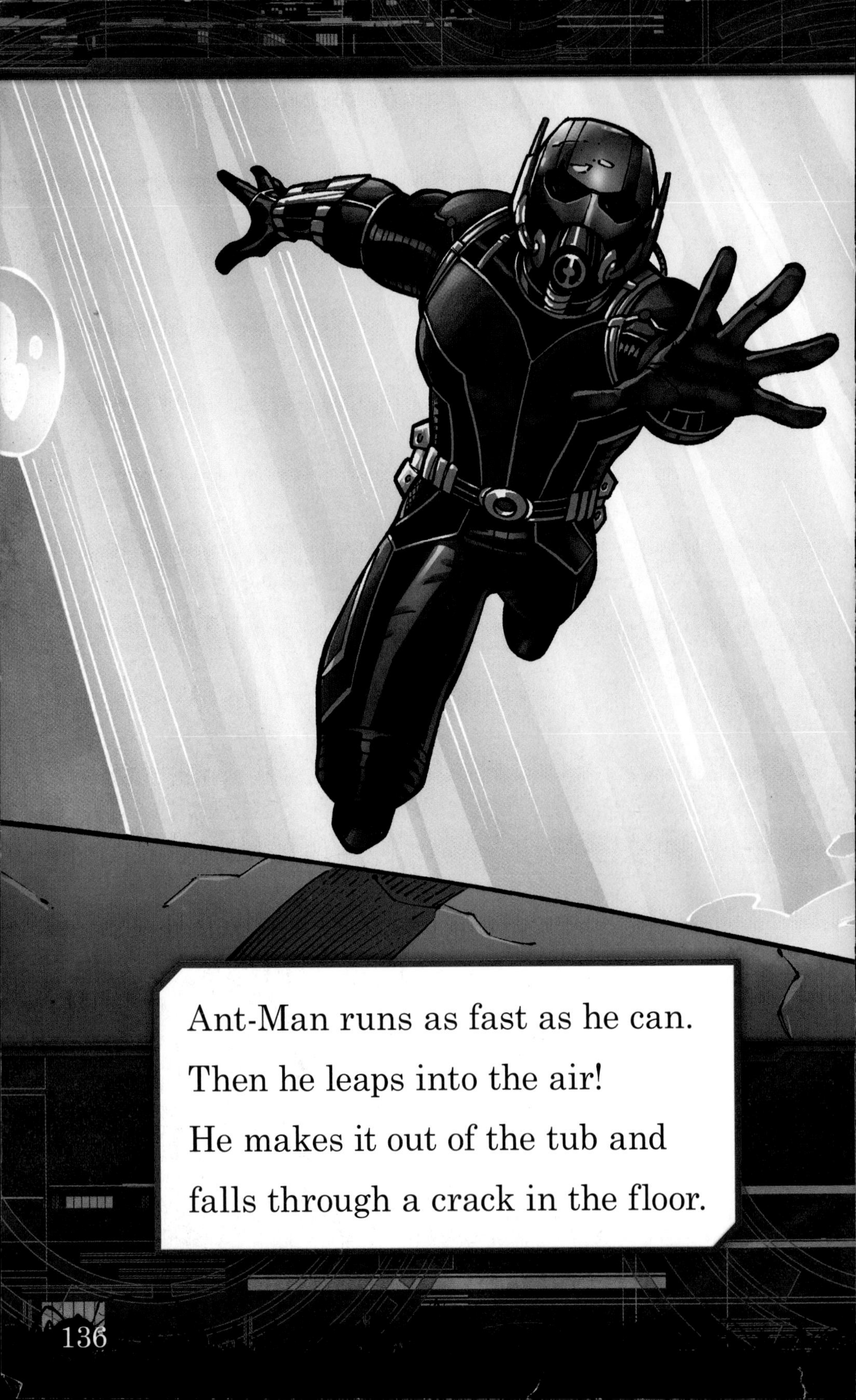

Ant-Man runs as fast as he can.
Then he leaps into the air!
He makes it out of the tub and
falls through a crack in the floor.

Ant-Man lands in the apartment below.
He tries to be very quiet
so he does not bother the puppy.
But the puppy hears Ant-Man.
He gets up to chase him!

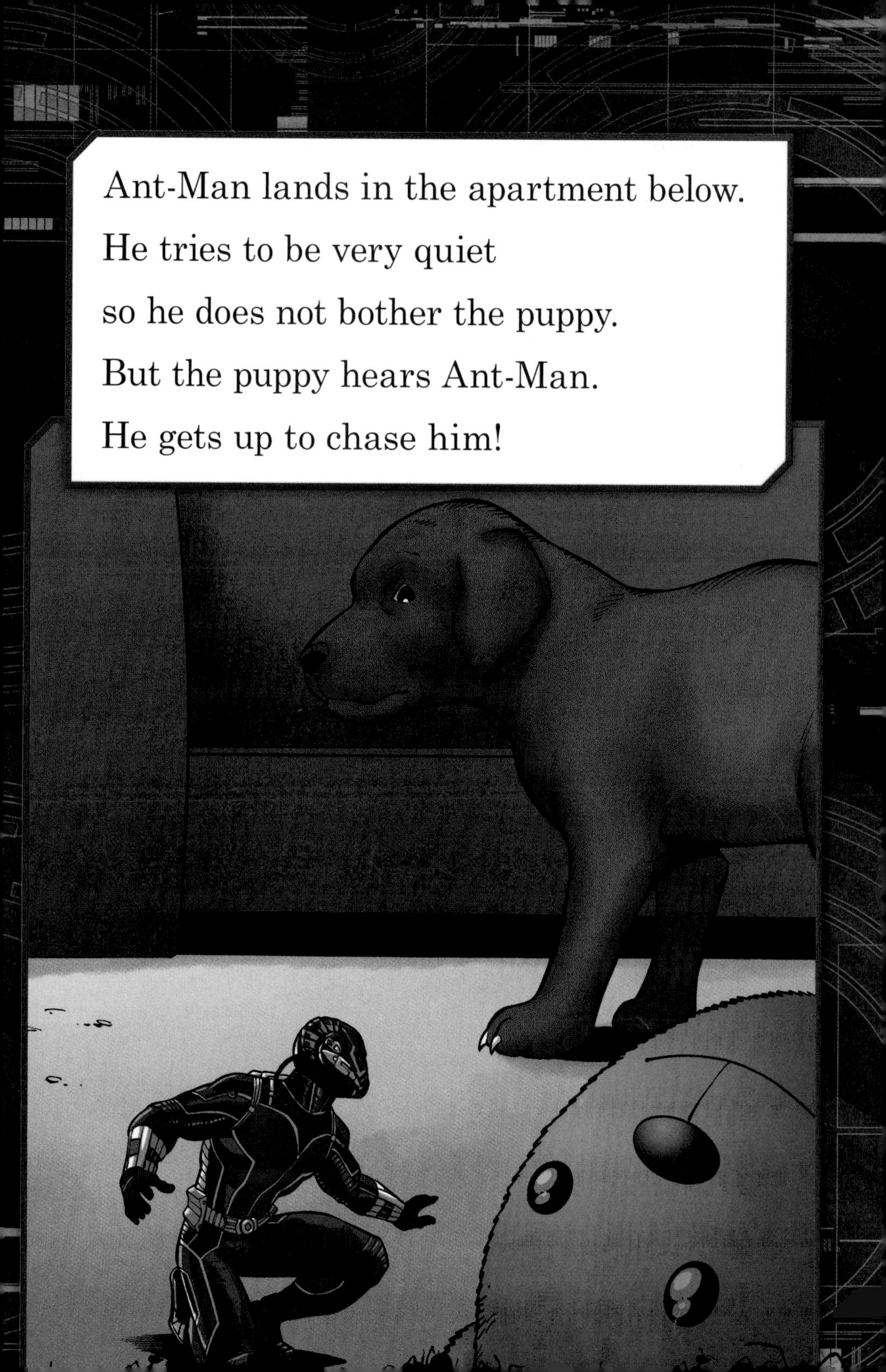

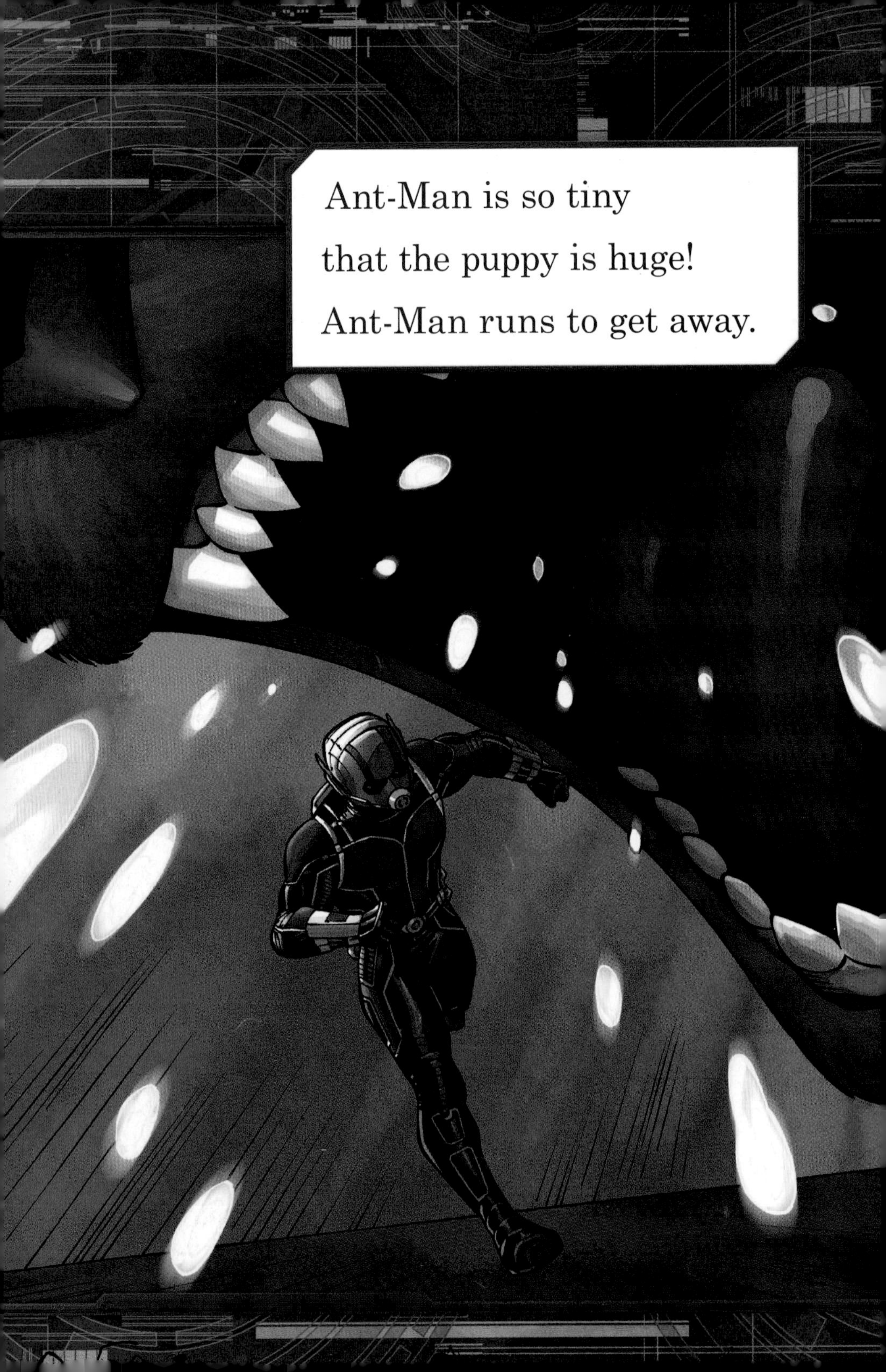
Ant-Man is so tiny
that the puppy is huge!
Ant-Man runs to get away.

Ant-Man learns he is faster when he is small.
He escapes the puppy and lands on something that spins and spins and spins! What is it?

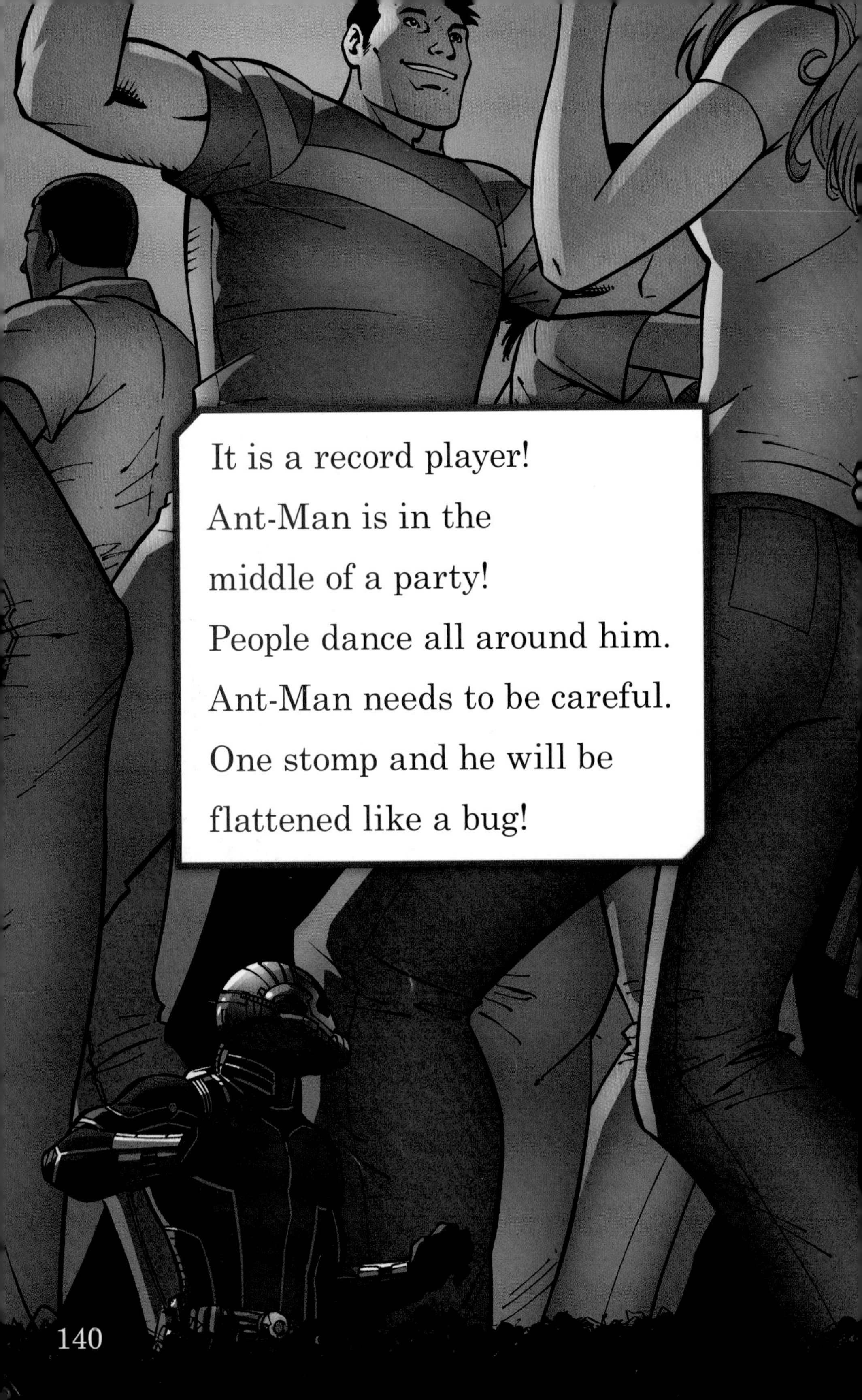

It is a record player!
Ant-Man is in the
middle of a party!
People dance all around him.
Ant-Man needs to be careful.
One stomp and he will be
flattened like a bug!

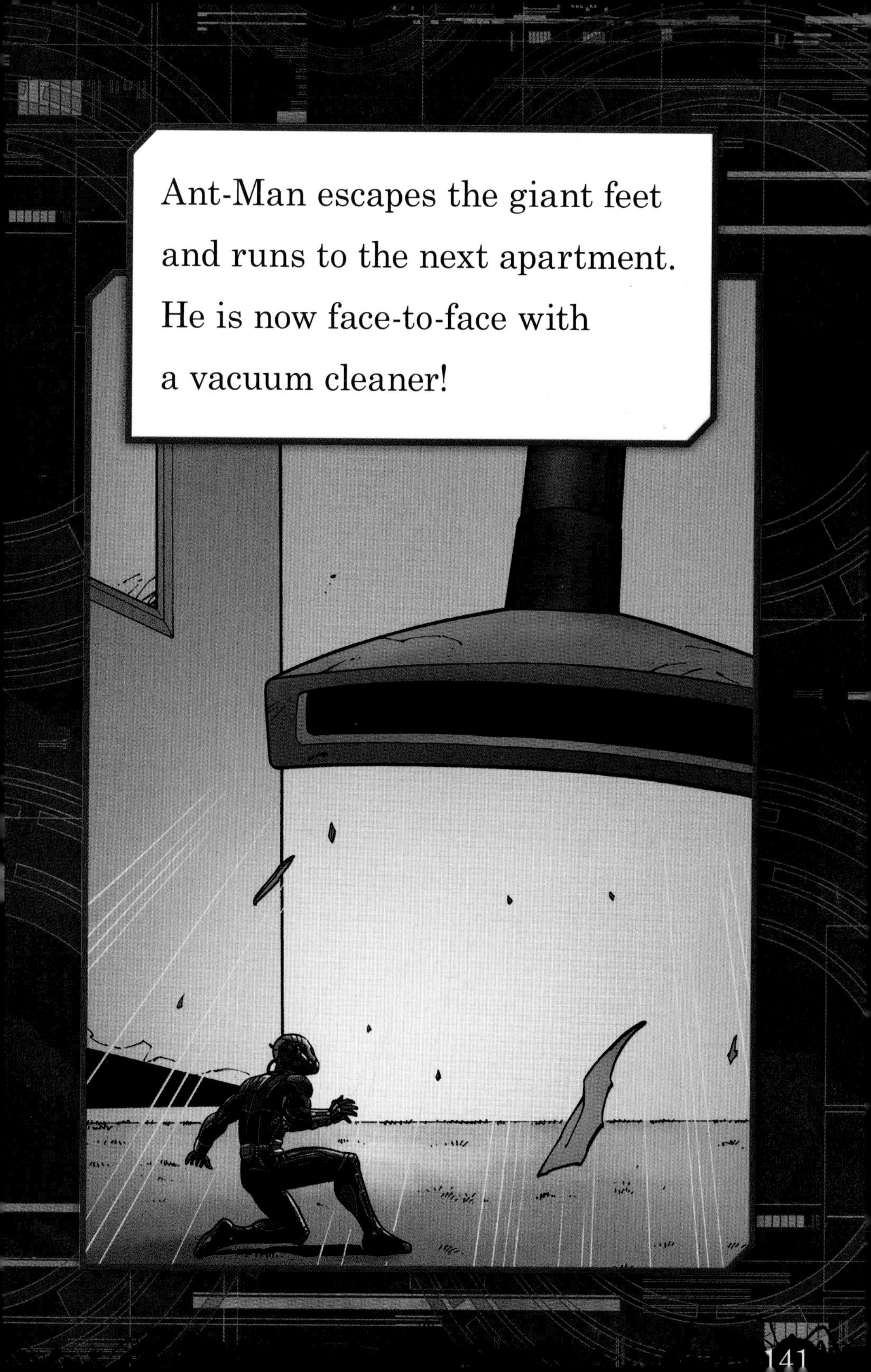
Ant-Man escapes the giant feet and runs to the next apartment. He is now face-to-face with a vacuum cleaner!

Ant-Man gets sucked into the machine!
He spins and twists and ends up
in the dust bag.
It is full of crumbs and dirt the size
of gigantic rocks!
How will he get out?

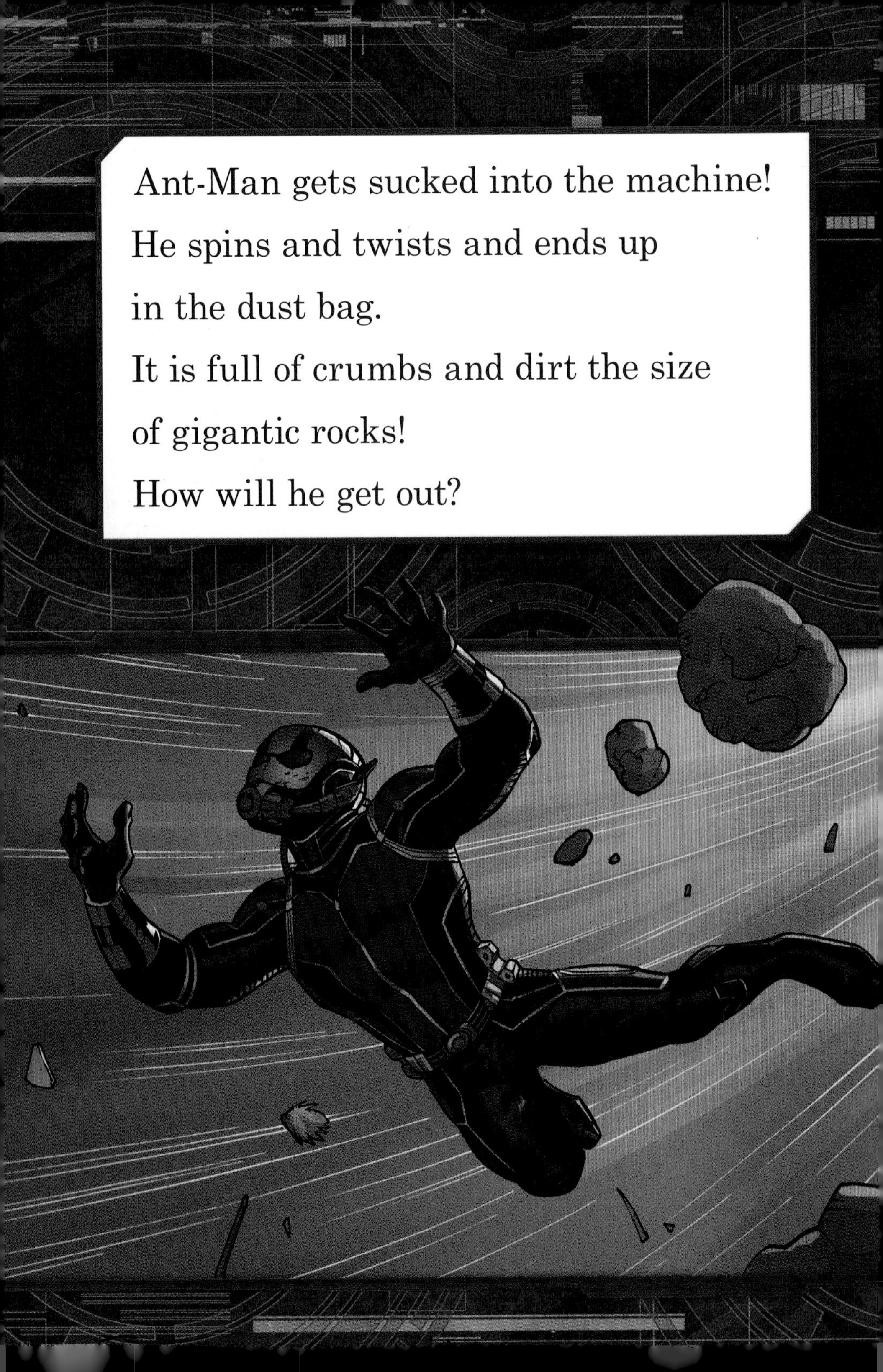

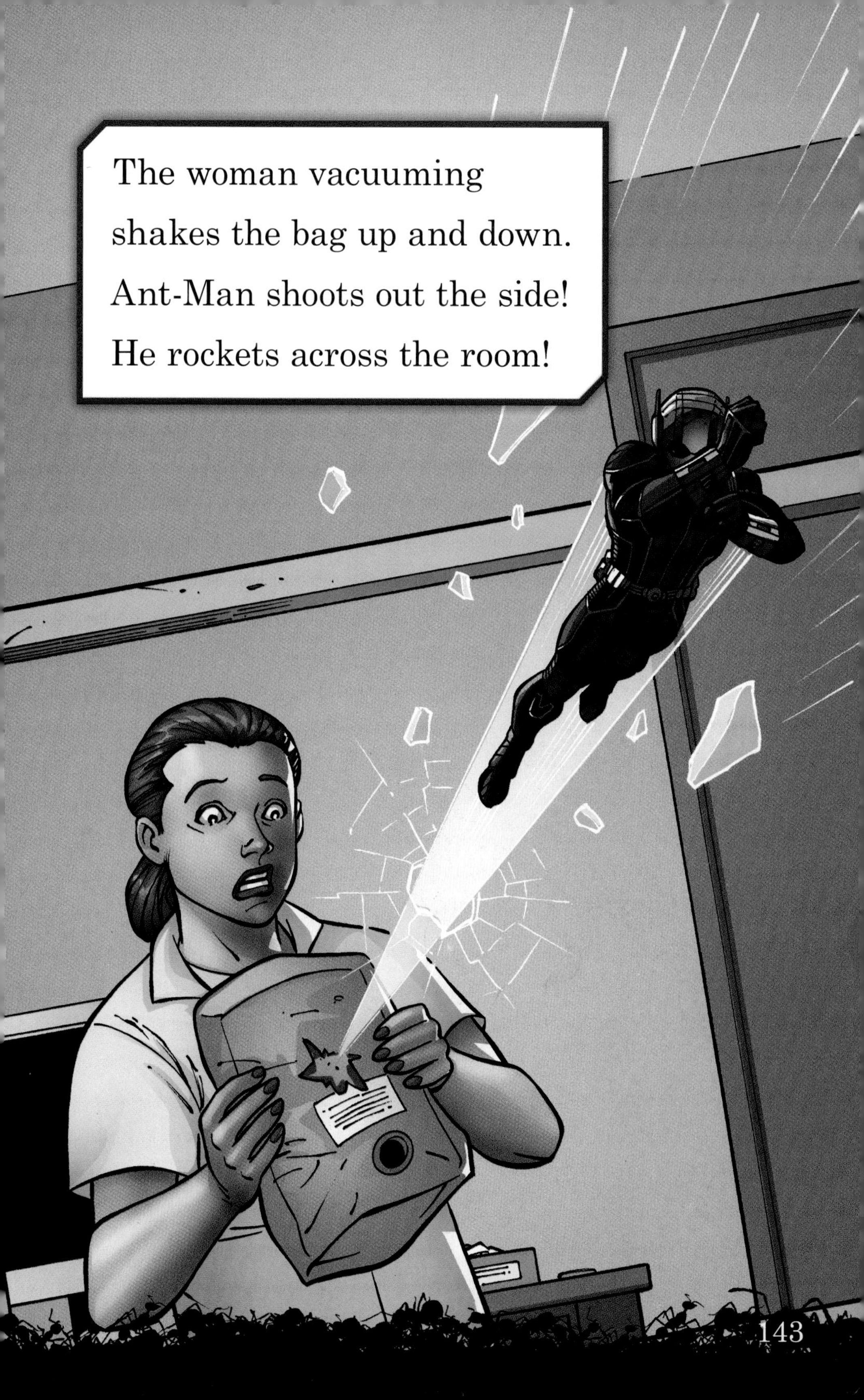
The woman vacuuming shakes the bag up and down. Ant-Man shoots out the side! He rockets across the room!

Ant-Man lands on a car with a hard thump! He dents the roof! Ant-Man learns he is tougher when he is small!

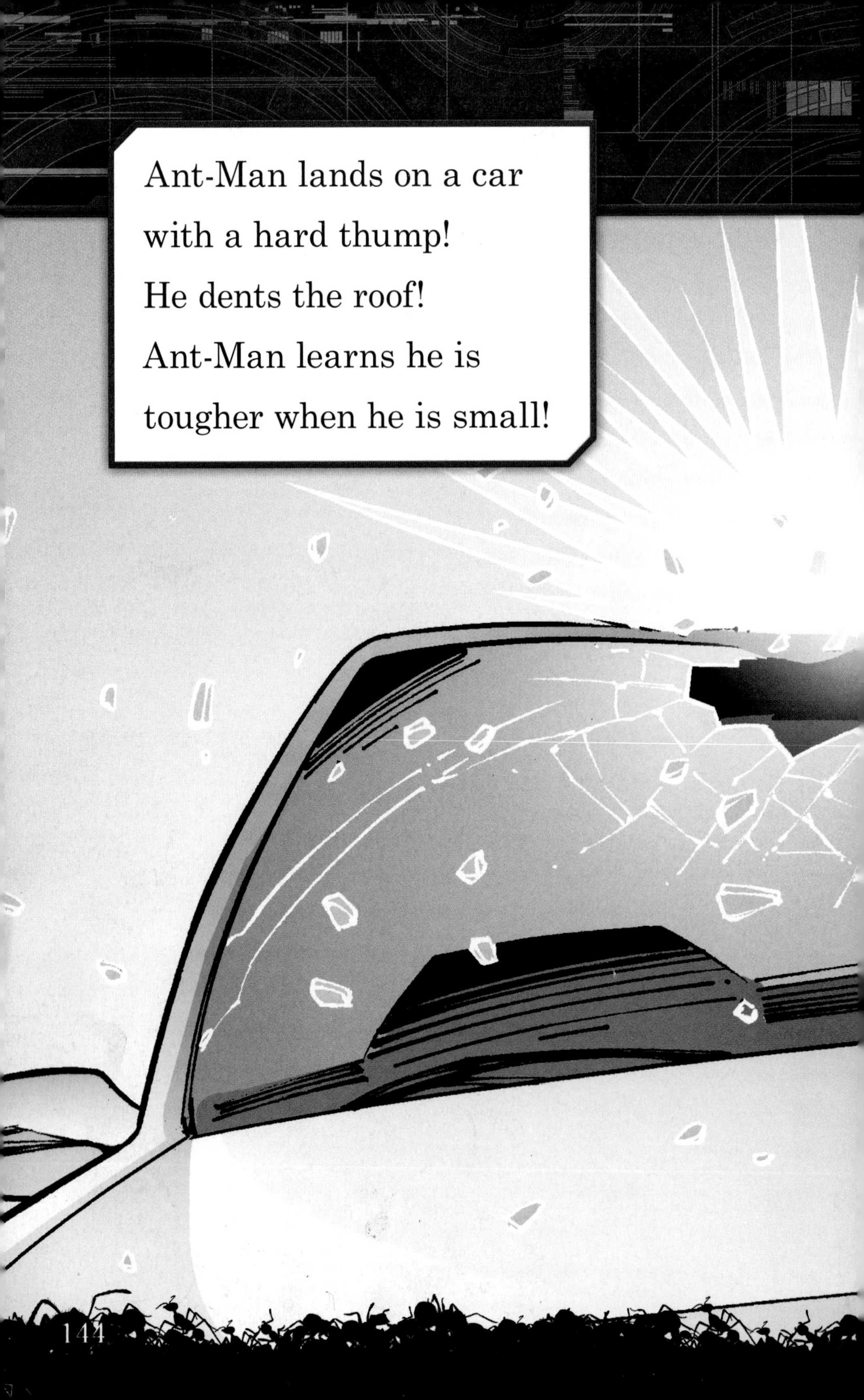

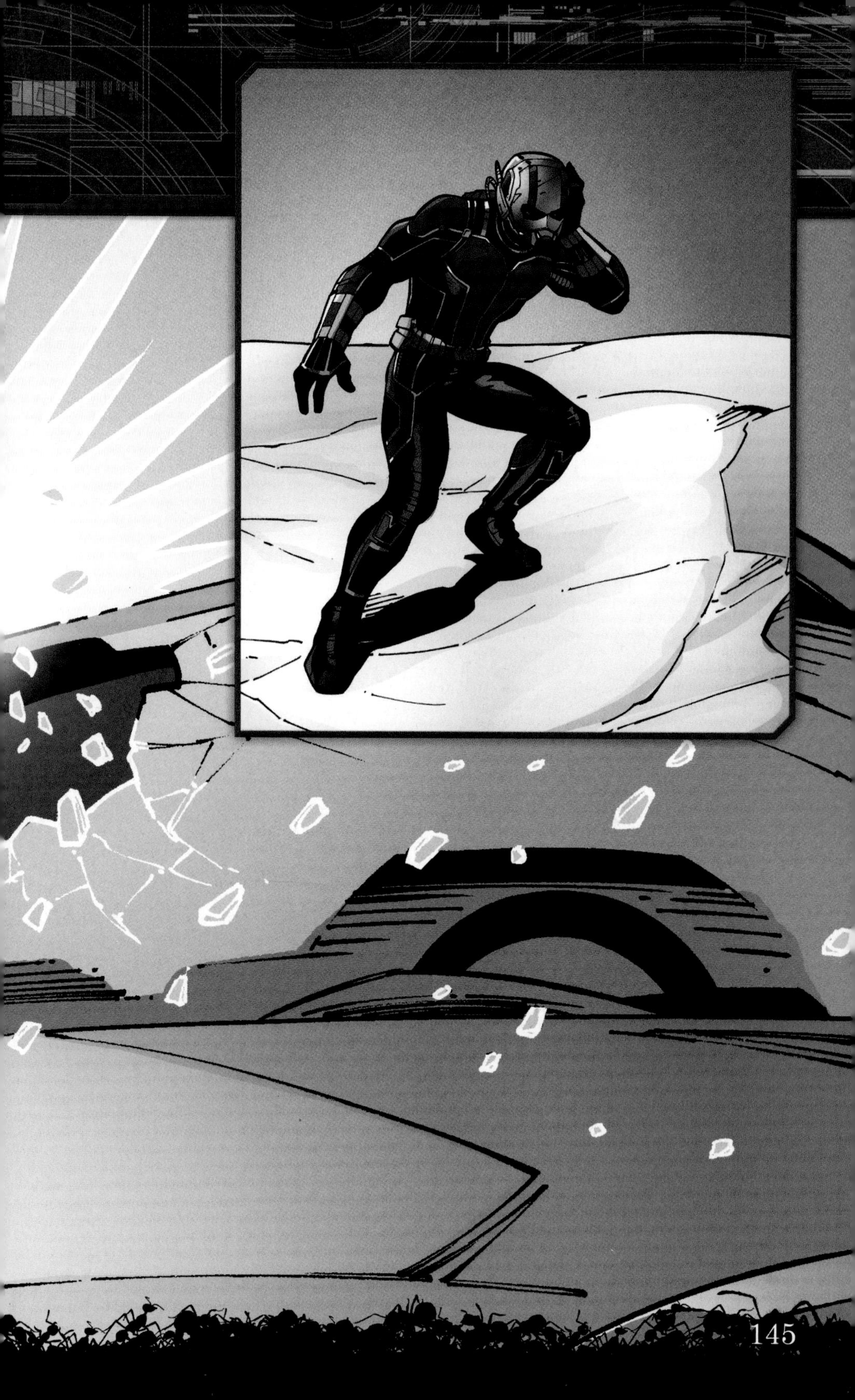

Ant-Man soon sees
a group of ants.
They circle around him.

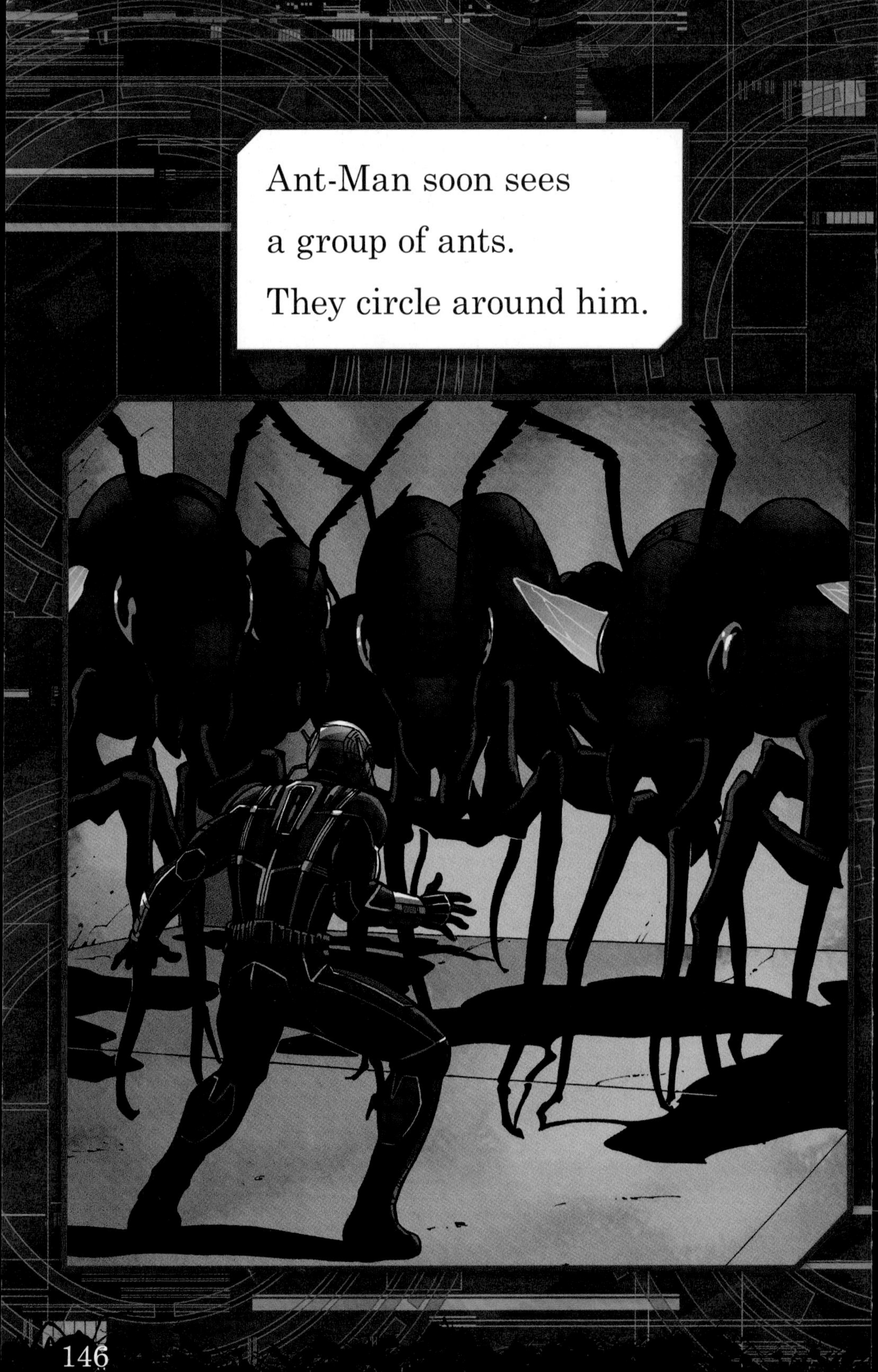

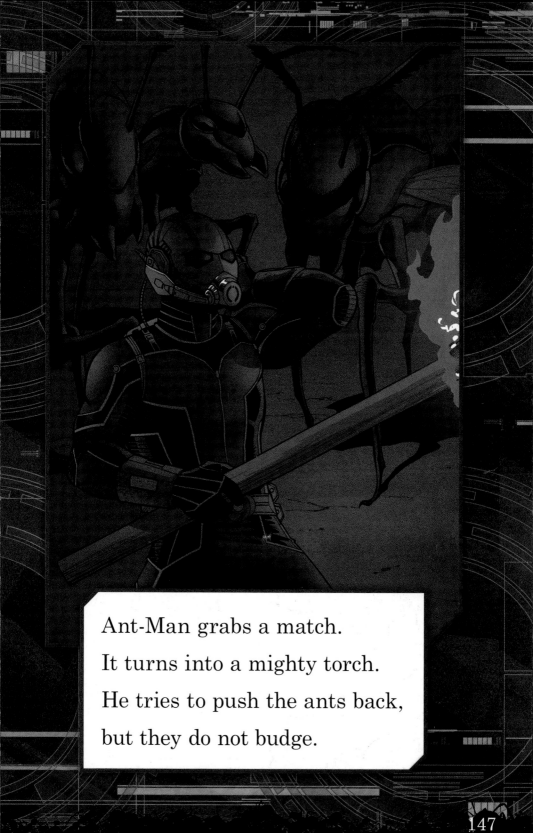

Ant-Man grabs a match.
It turns into a mighty torch.
He tries to push the ants back,
but they do not budge.

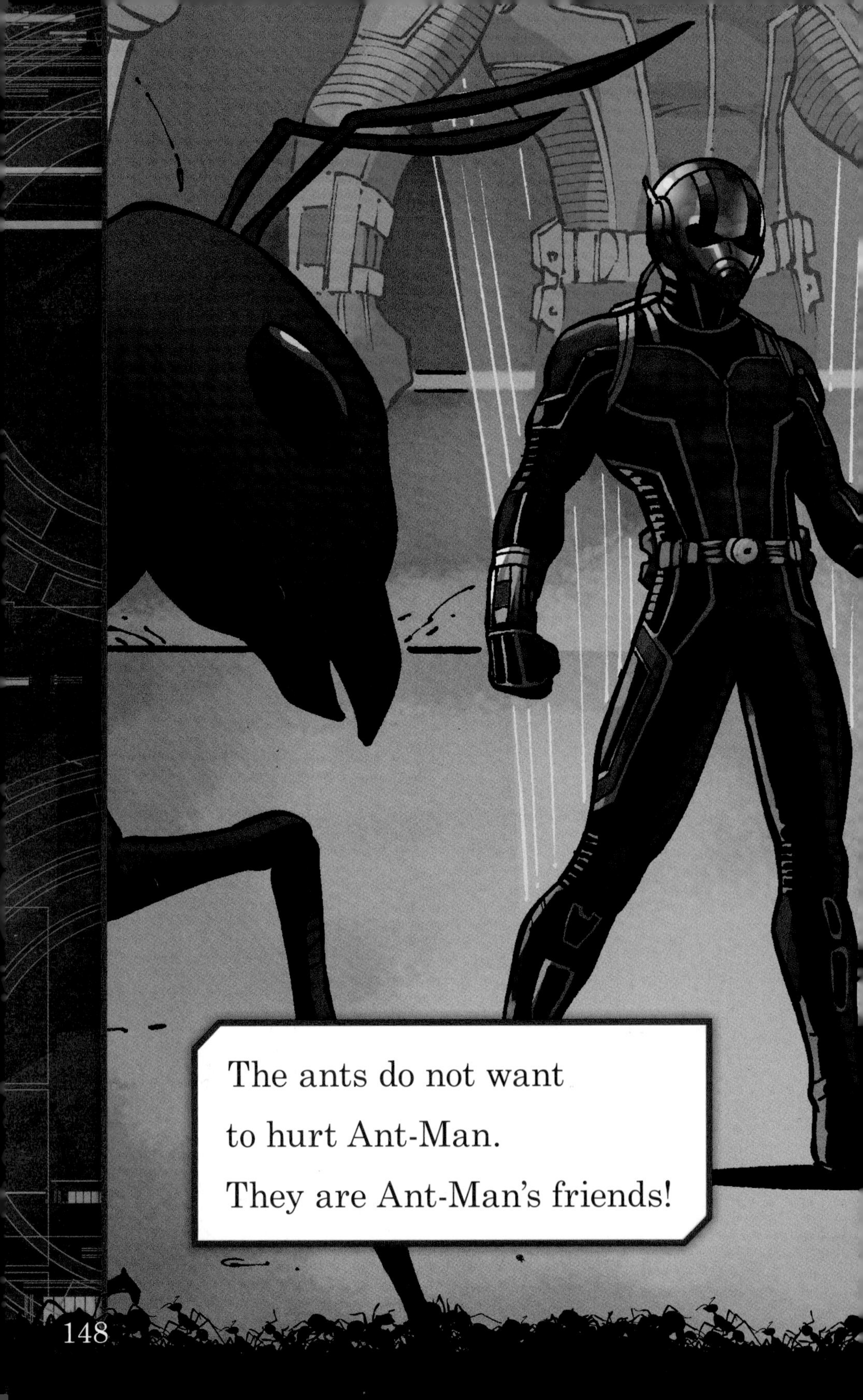

The ants do not want
to hurt Ant-Man.
They are Ant-Man's friends!

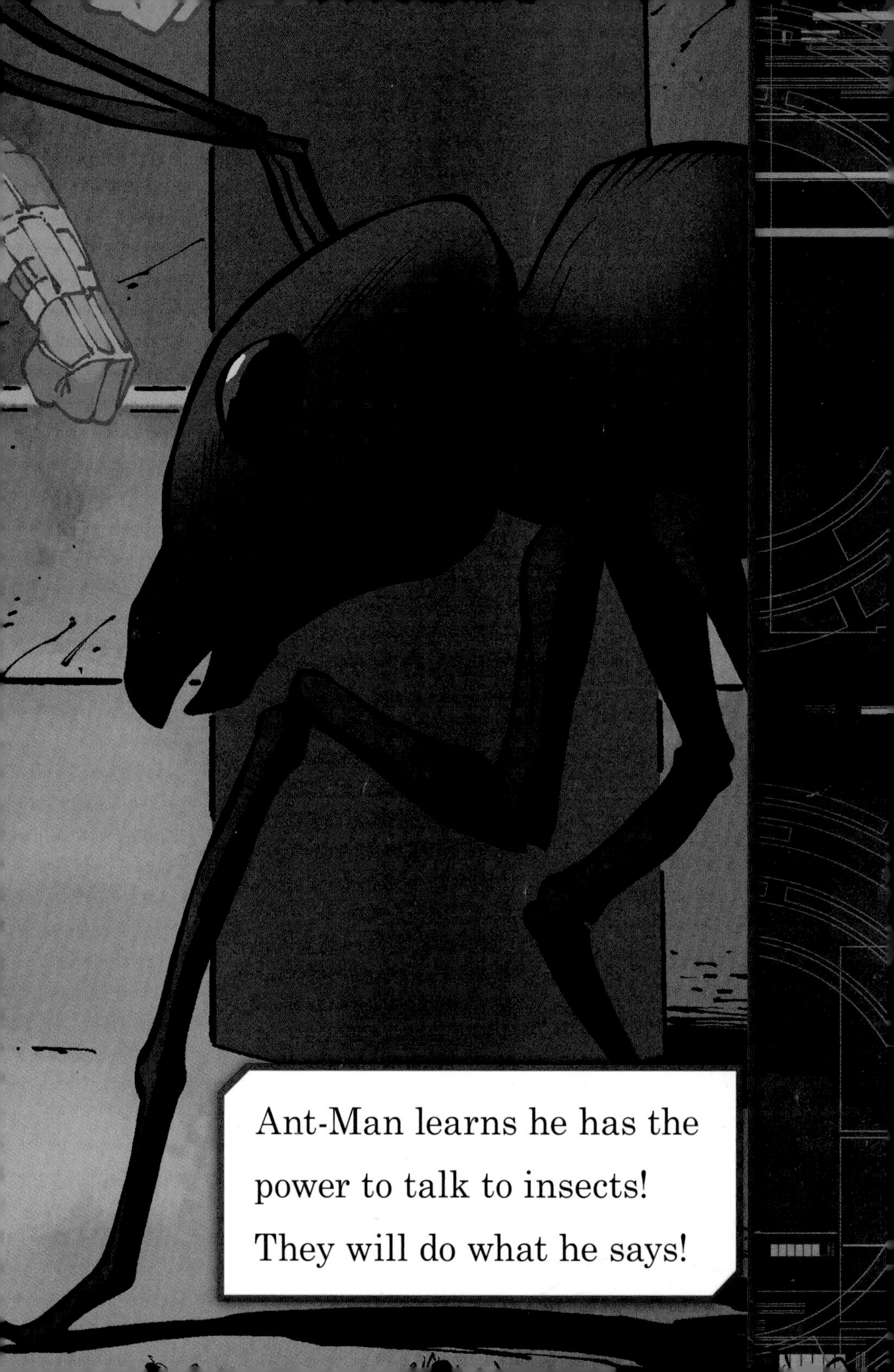
Ant-Man learns he has the power to talk to insects! They will do what he says!

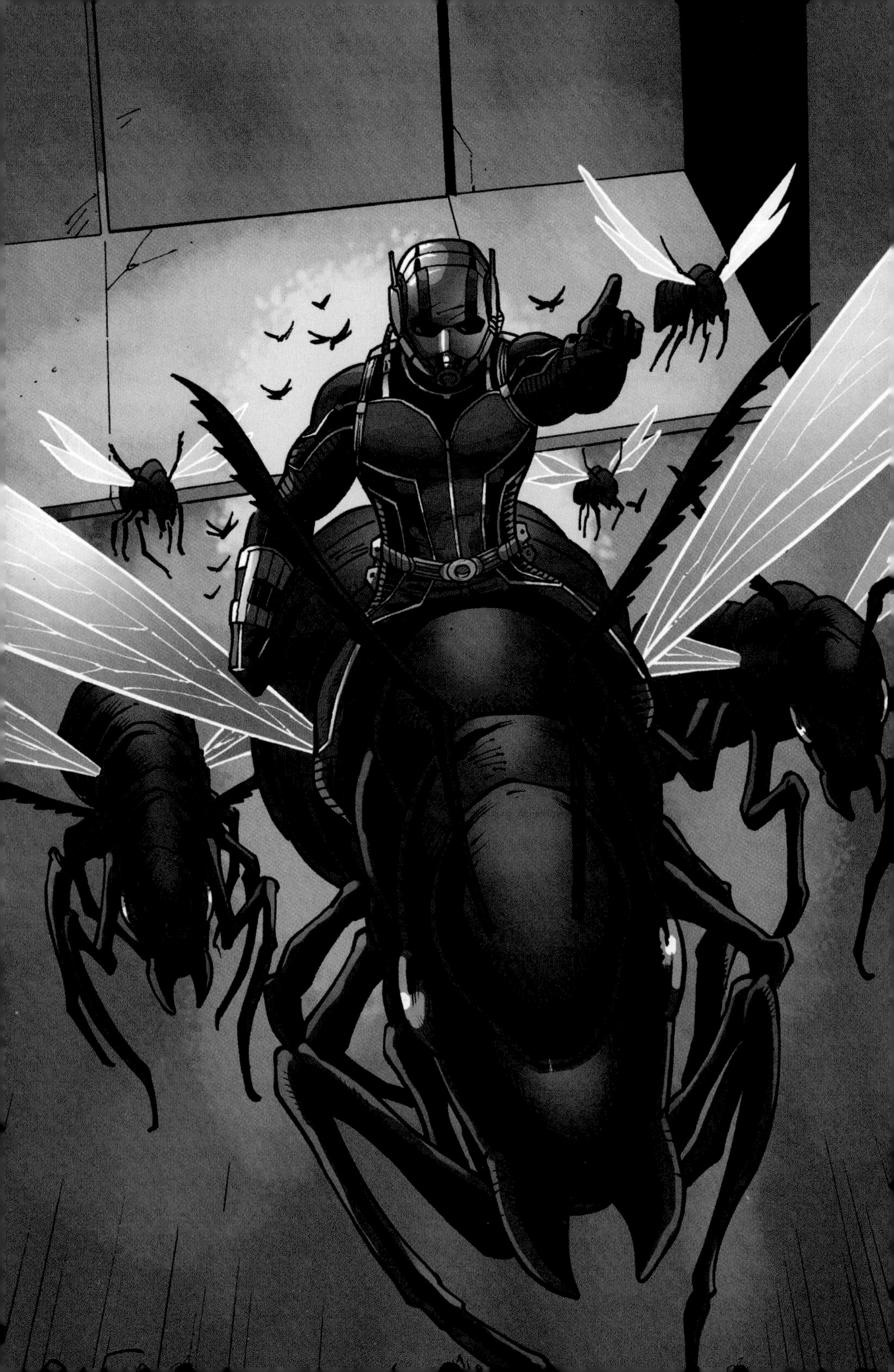

Now Ant-Man has an army of ants!
Ant-Man climbs onto one.
His name is Ant-Thony.
He leads the charge!
The ants fly away!

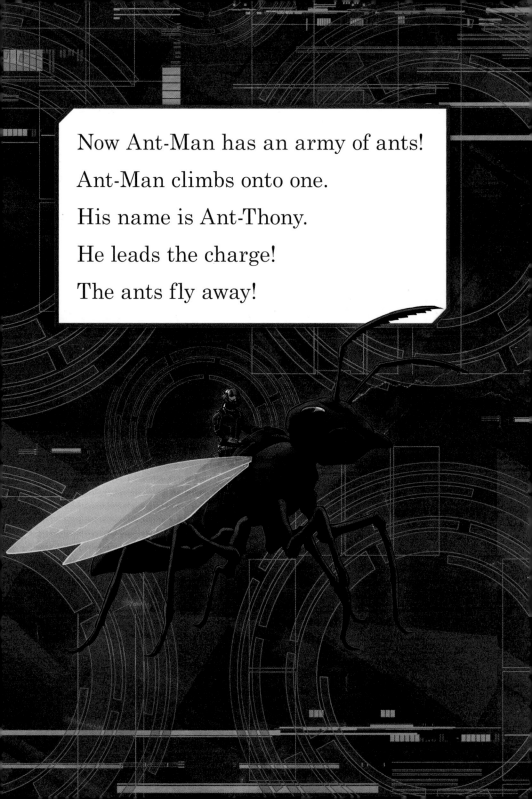

Ant-Man protects Cassie from a bully. Ant-Man does not like bullies.

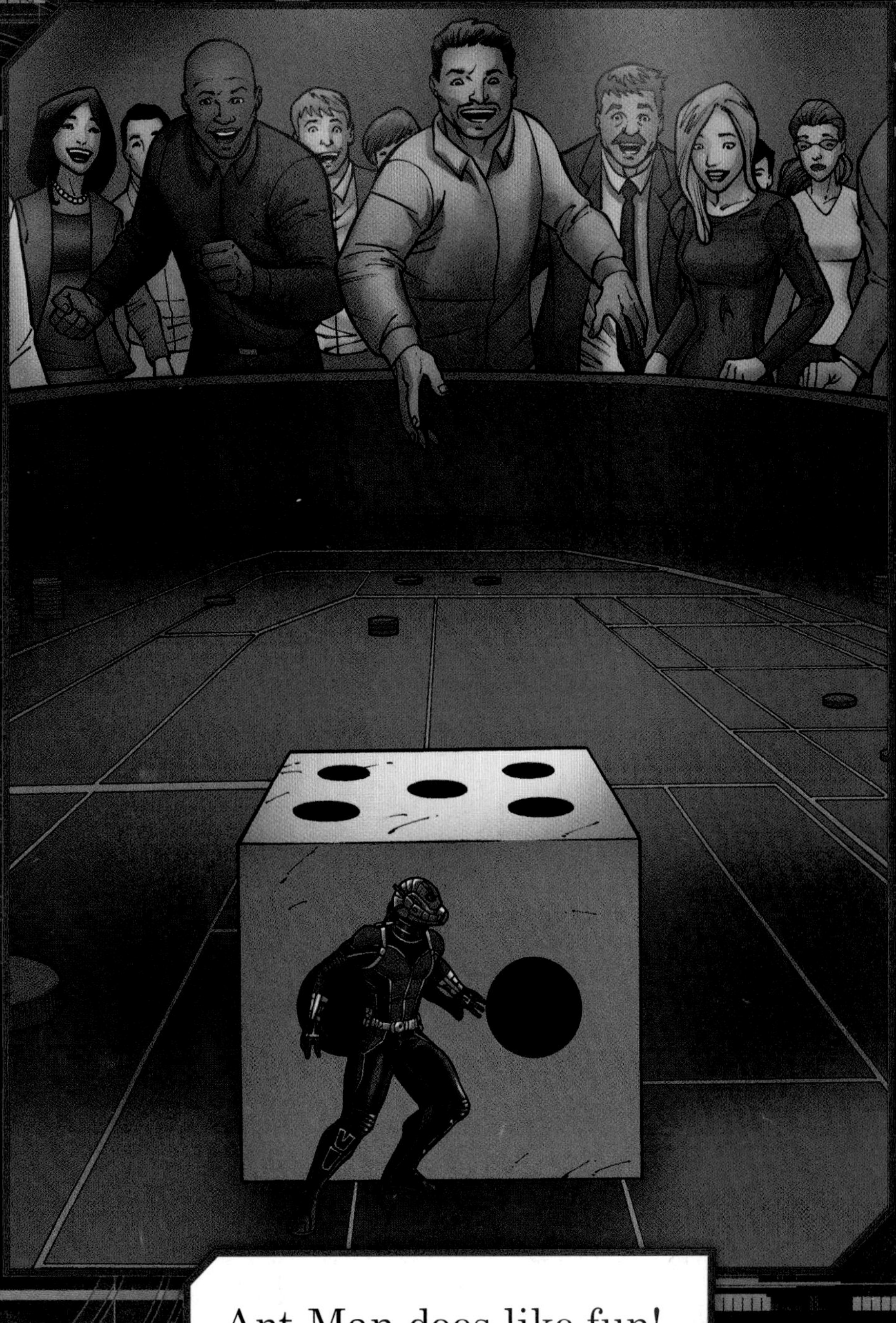

Ant-Man does like fun!

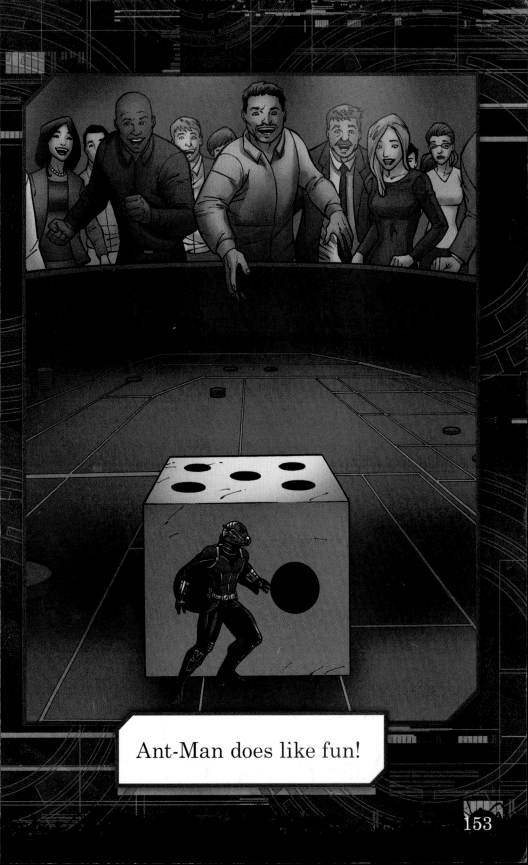

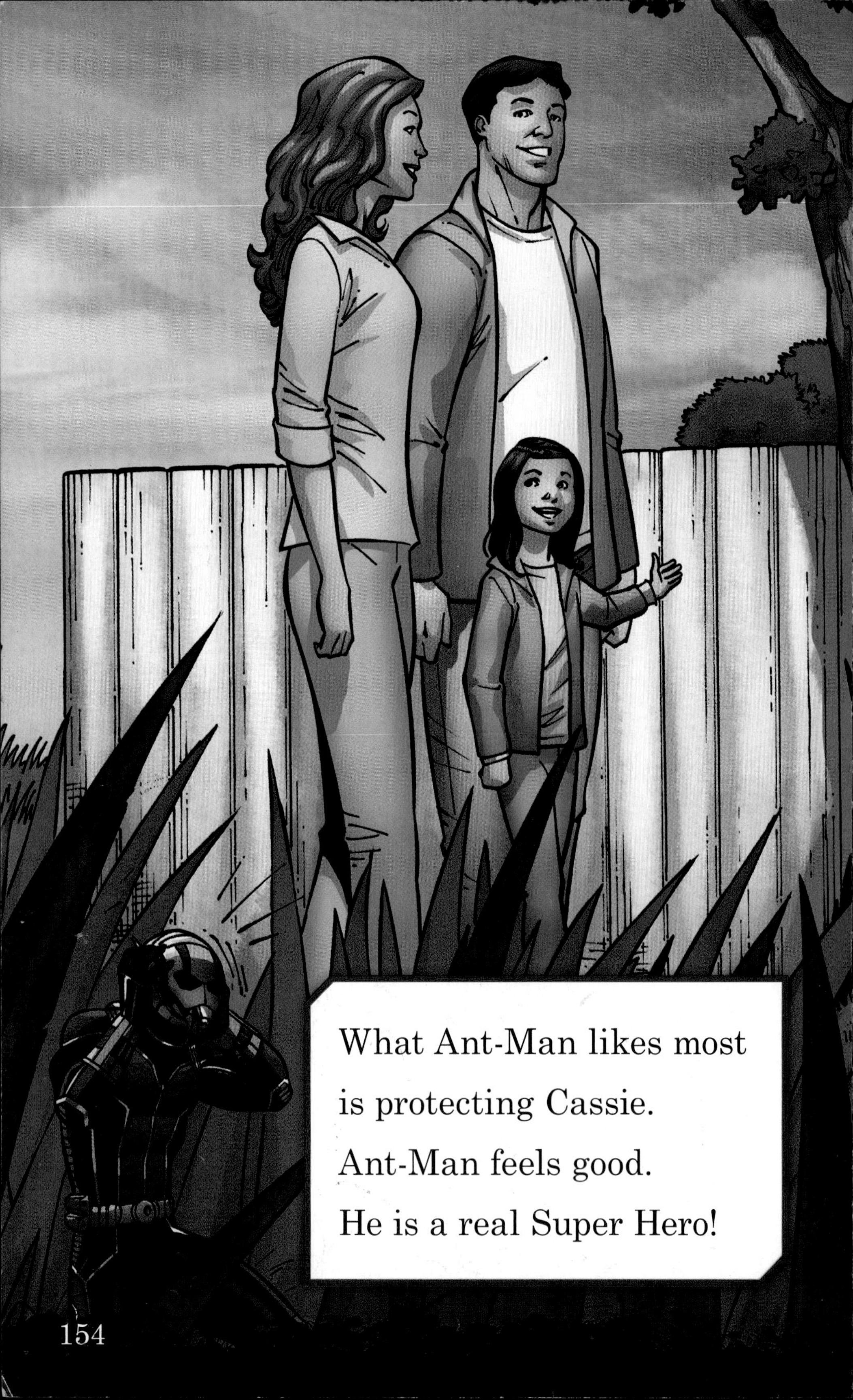

What Ant-Man likes most
is protecting Cassie.
Ant-Man feels good.
He is a real Super Hero!

MARVEL
GUARDIANS OF THE GALAXY
FRIENDS and FOES

By **Chris Strathearn**

Illustrated by Ron Lim, Drew Geraci, and Lee Duhig

Based on the Screenplay by James Gunn

Story by Nicole Perlman and James Gunn

Produced by Kevin Feige, p.g.a.

Directed by James Gunn

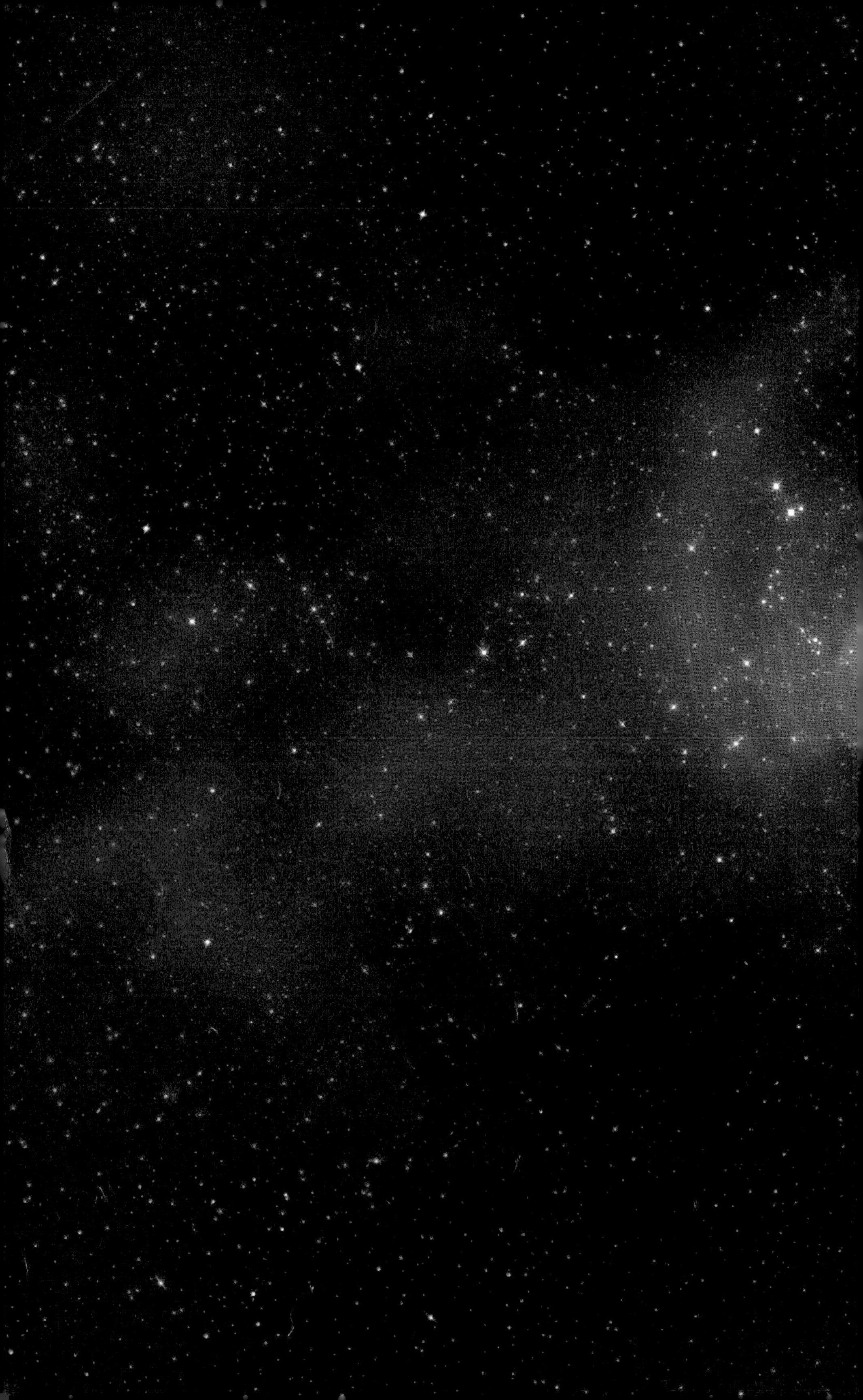

Attention, GUARDIANS OF THE GALAXY fans! Look for these words when you read this book. Can you spot them all?

Orb

spaceship

tape player

soldiers

A magic Orb is hidden
on the planet of Morag.
It is an object of power.
It can be used for good—or evil.

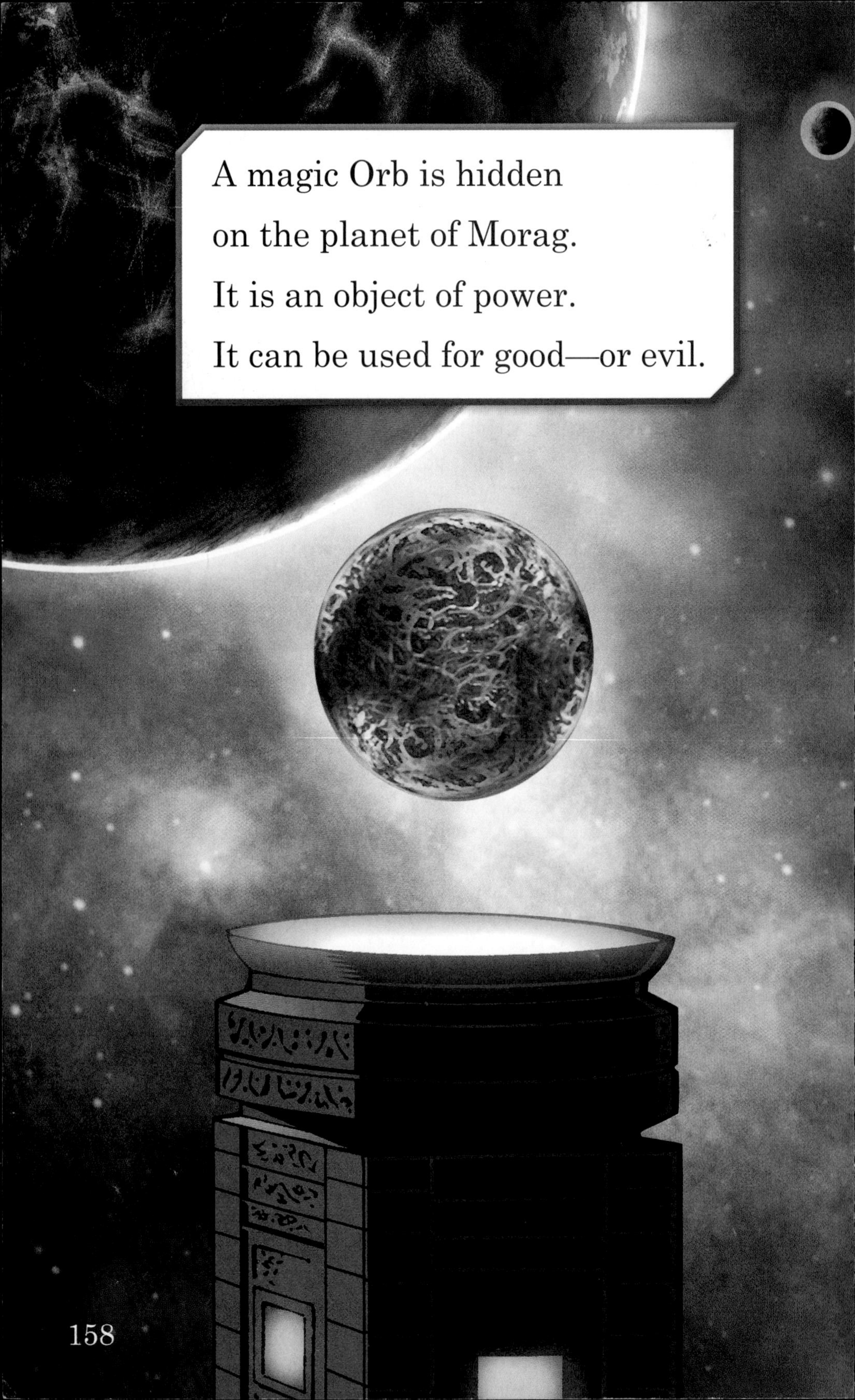

Someone must protect the Orb
and keep the galaxy safe.
If it were used for evil,
the Orb could destroy everything.

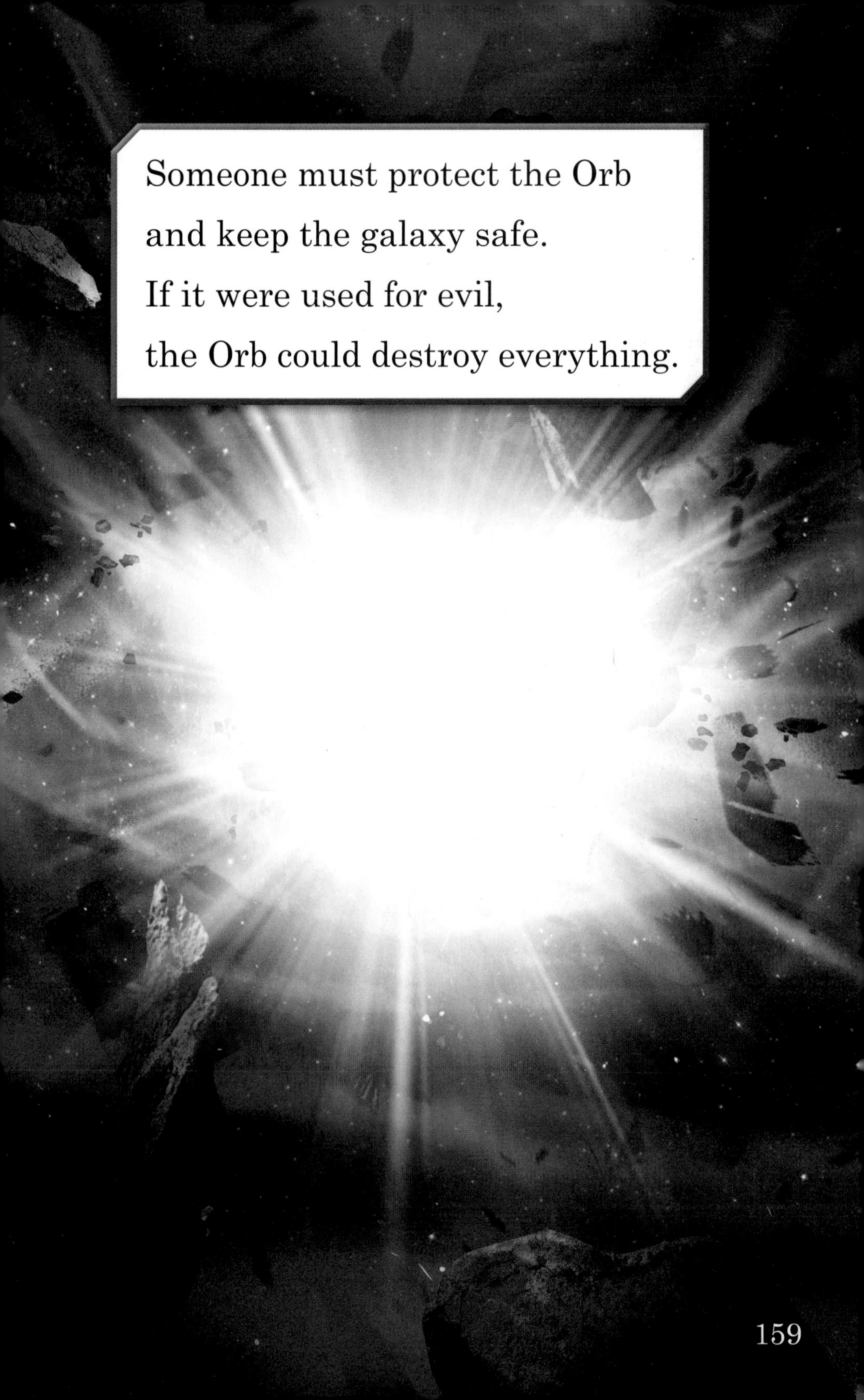

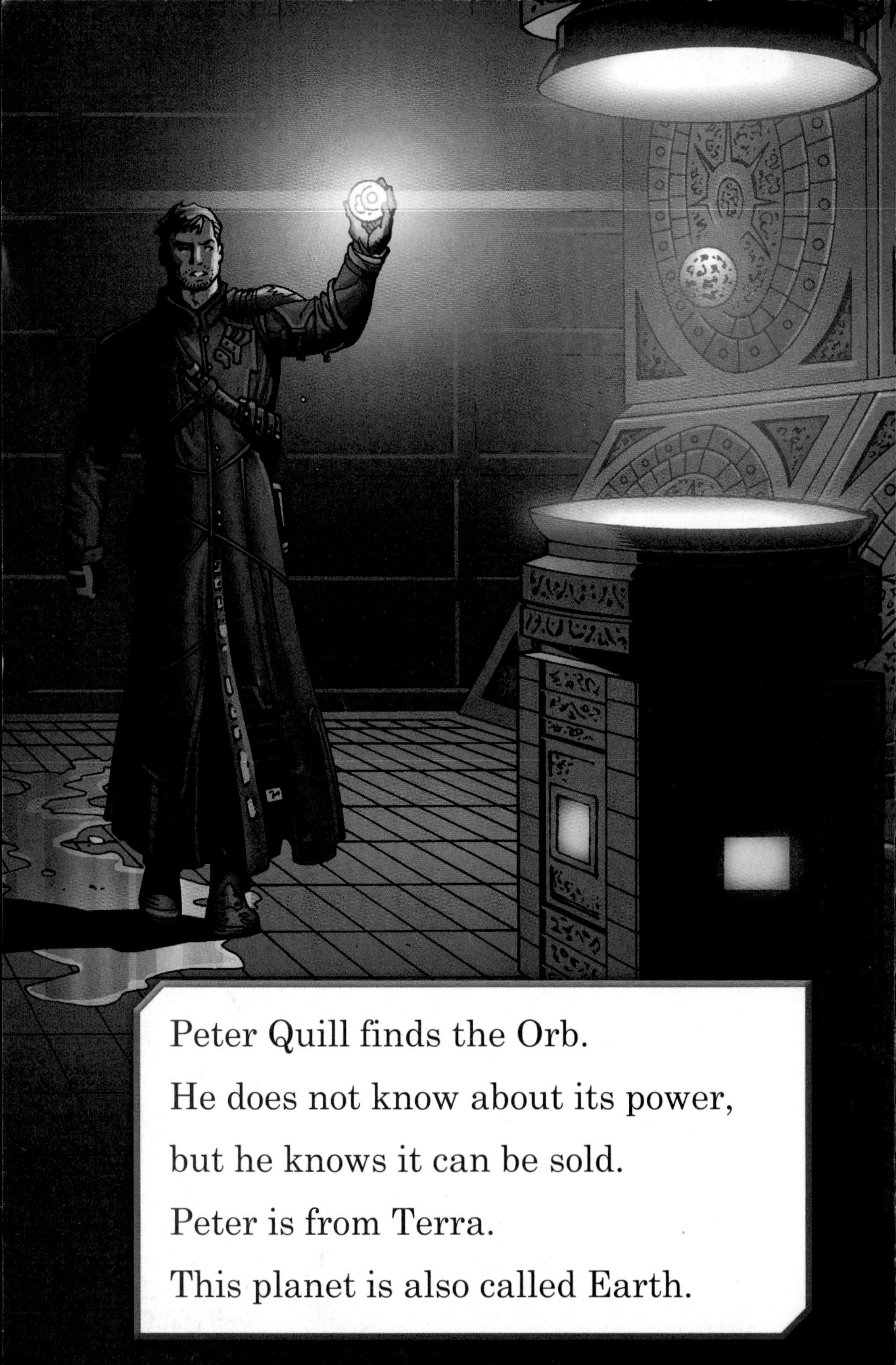

Peter Quill finds the Orb.
He does not know about its power,
but he knows it can be sold.
Peter is from Terra.
This planet is also called Earth.

Peter is a space adventurer.
He is also called Star-Lord.
His spaceship is called the *Milano*.
But thanks to his ankle thrusters,
he can fly without it!
His favorite thing is his tape player.

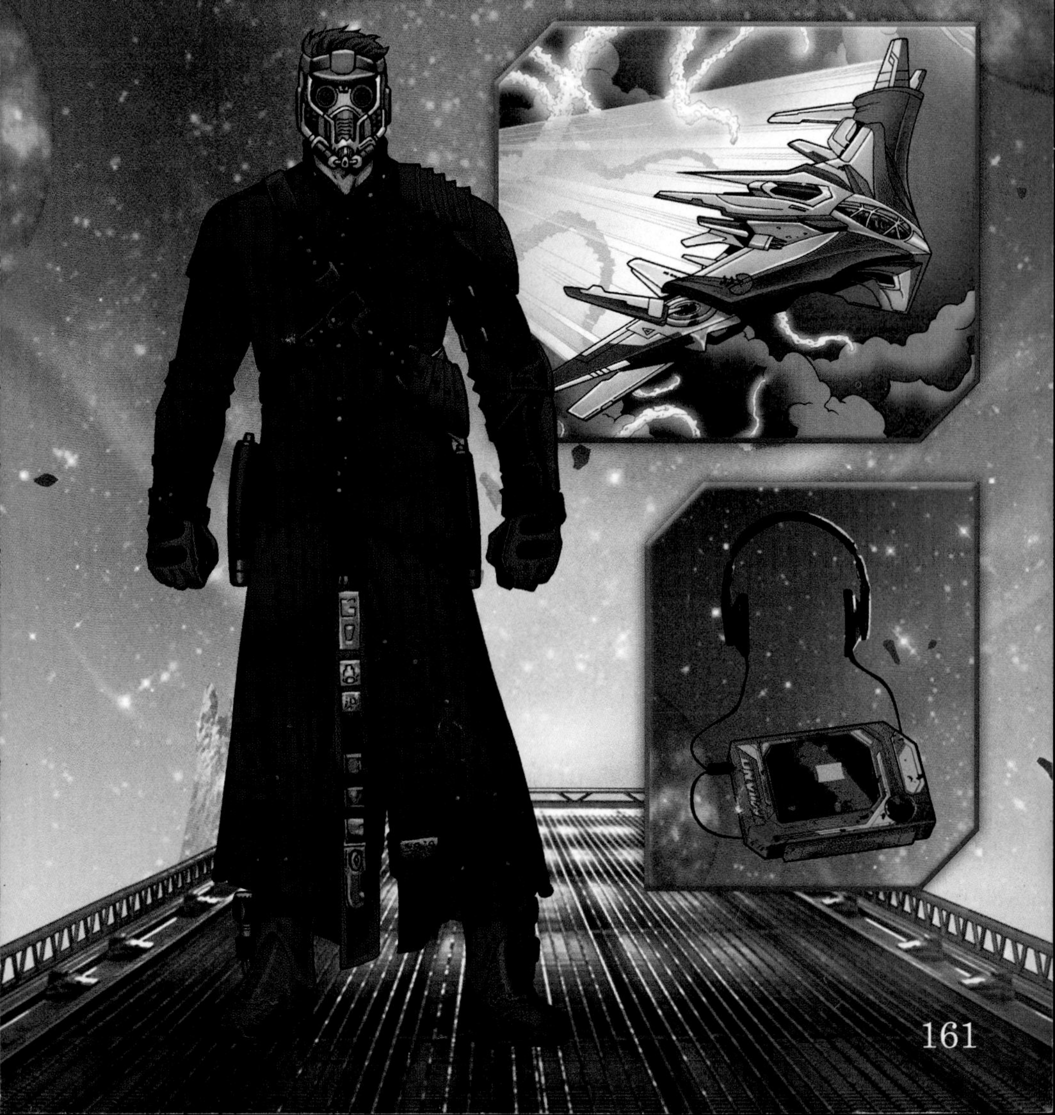

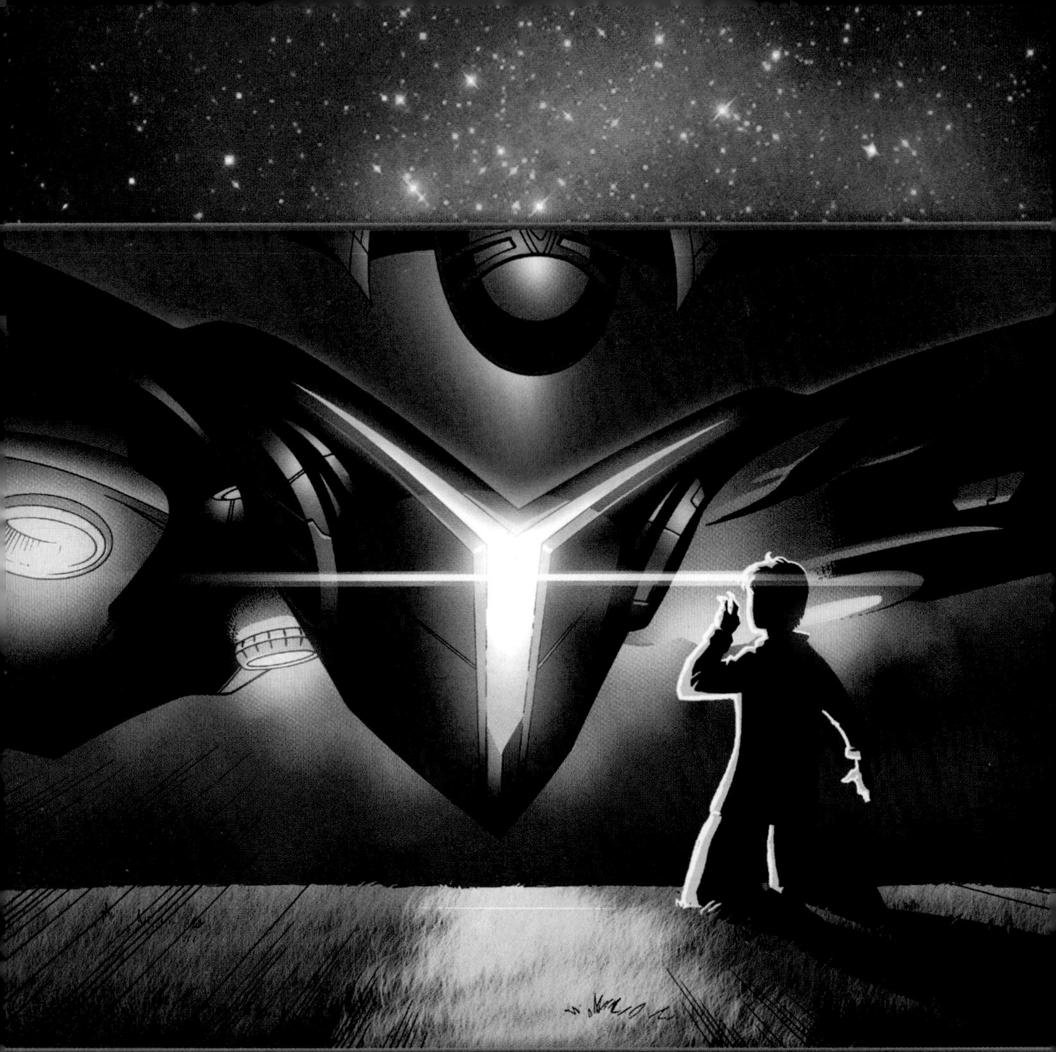

Peter grew up in space
with a group of aliens
called the Ravagers.
They find treasure and sell it.
Their motto is: “Steal from everybody!”

Yondu Udonta is the Ravager leader. He has blue skin and red eyes. Yondu finds out Peter has the Orb—and Yondu wants it!

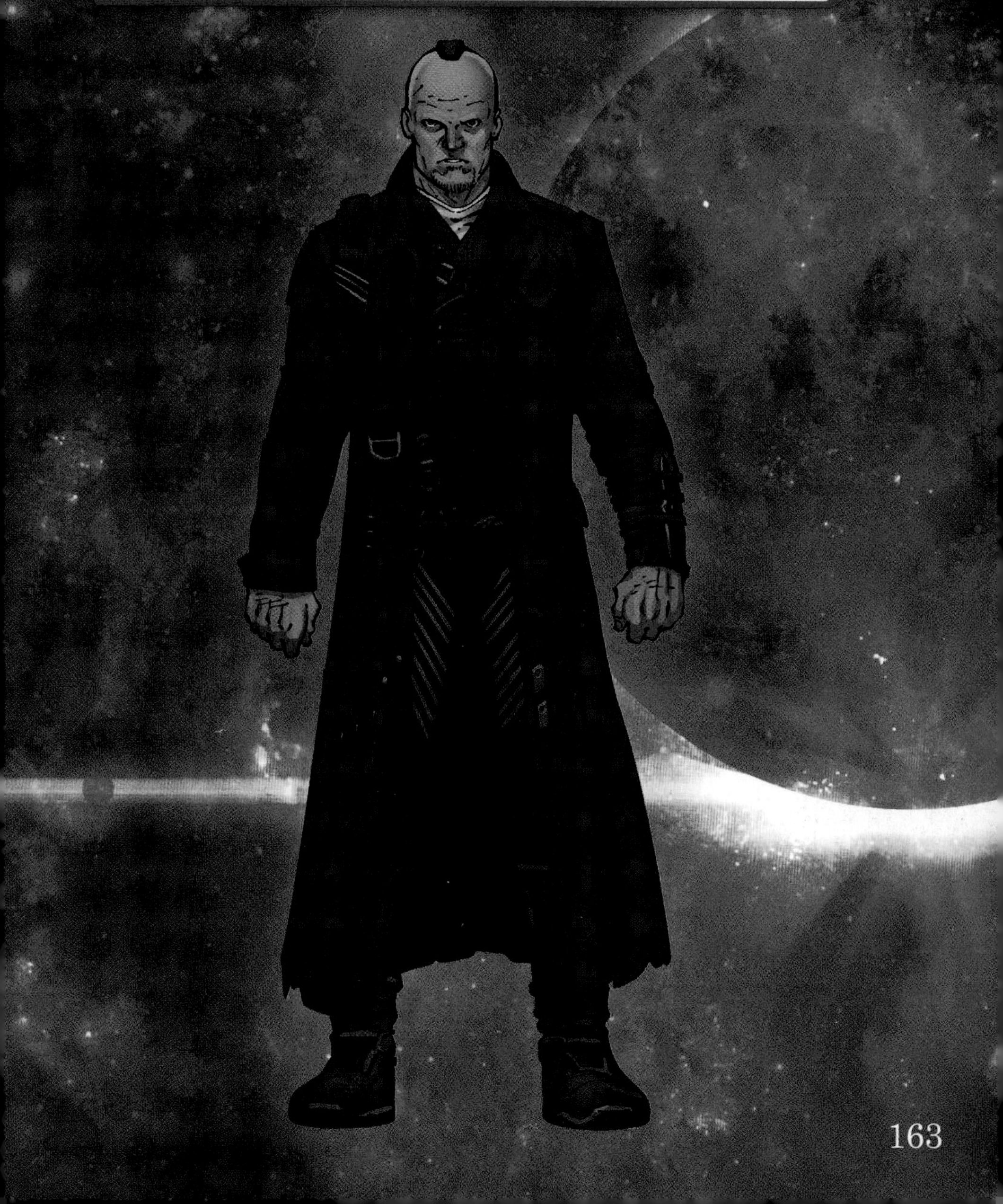

Peter needs friends to help him keep the Orb safe.

Rocket Raccoon is his friend.

Rocket is a short alien who looks like a raccoon.

He is small, but he is tough!

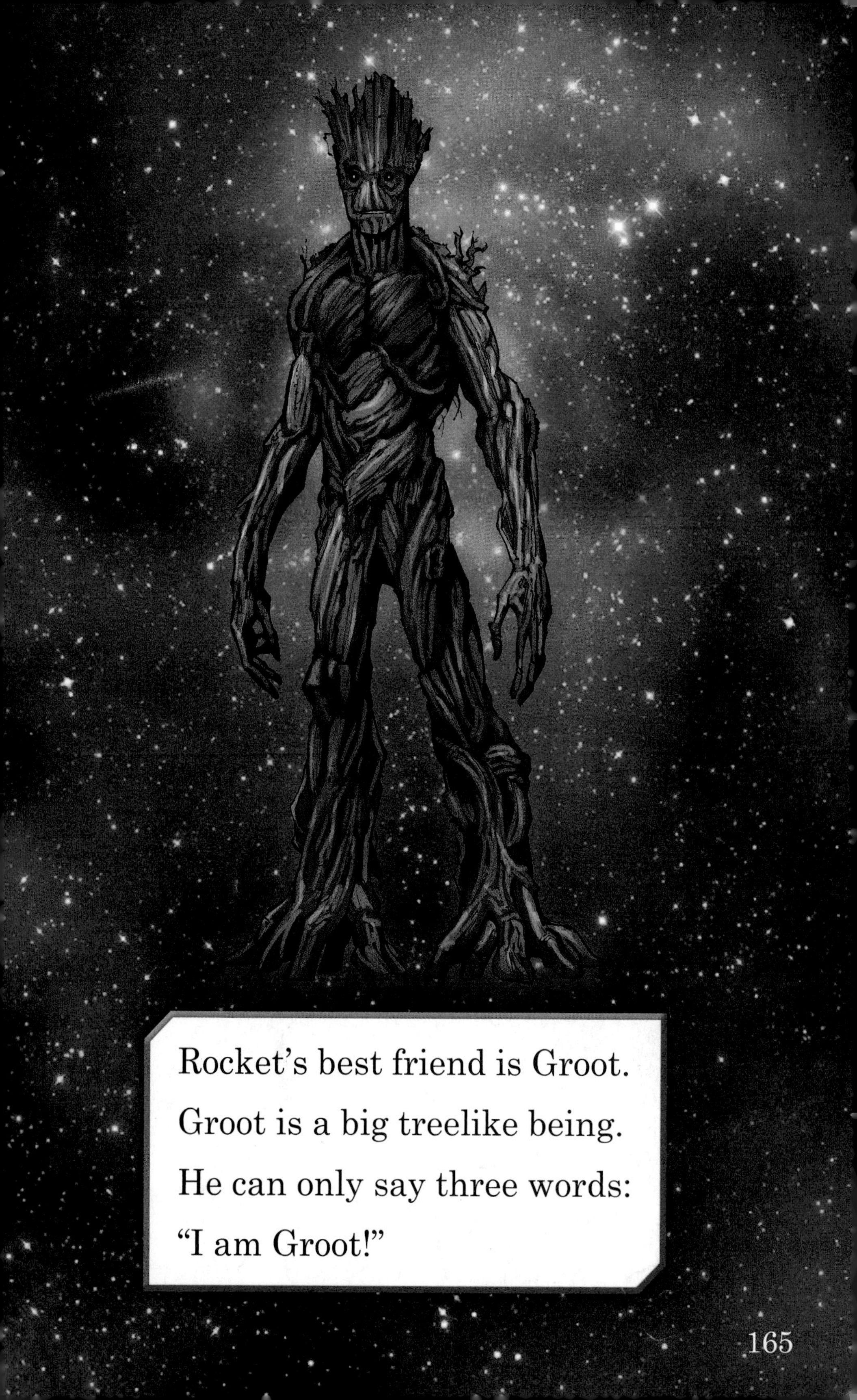

Rocket's best friend is Groot.
Groot is a big treelike being.
He can only say three words:
"I am Groot!"

Drax, another friend, is a skilled fighter.
His home world was destroyed,
and he does not like bad guys.
He is covered in tattoos.

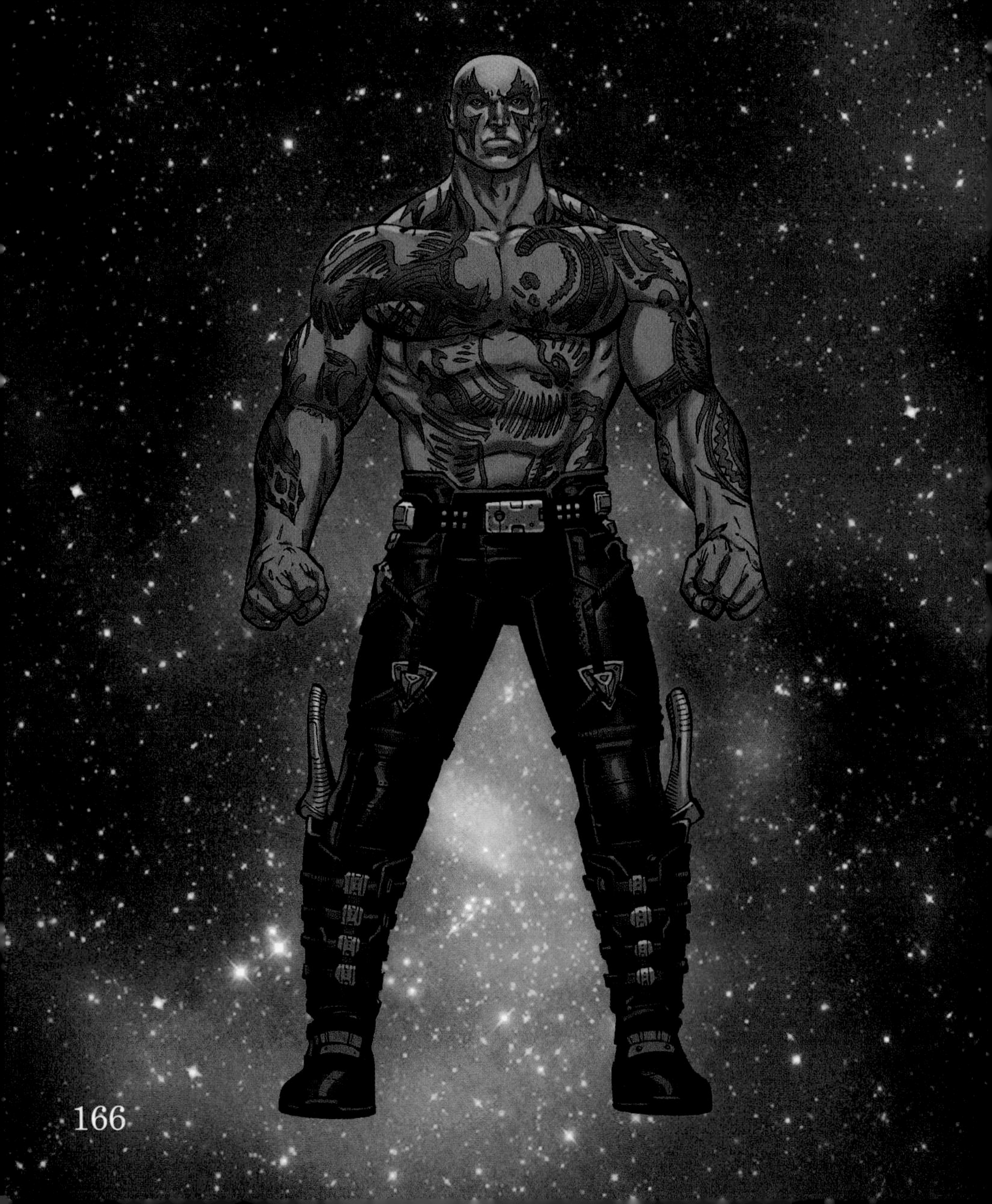

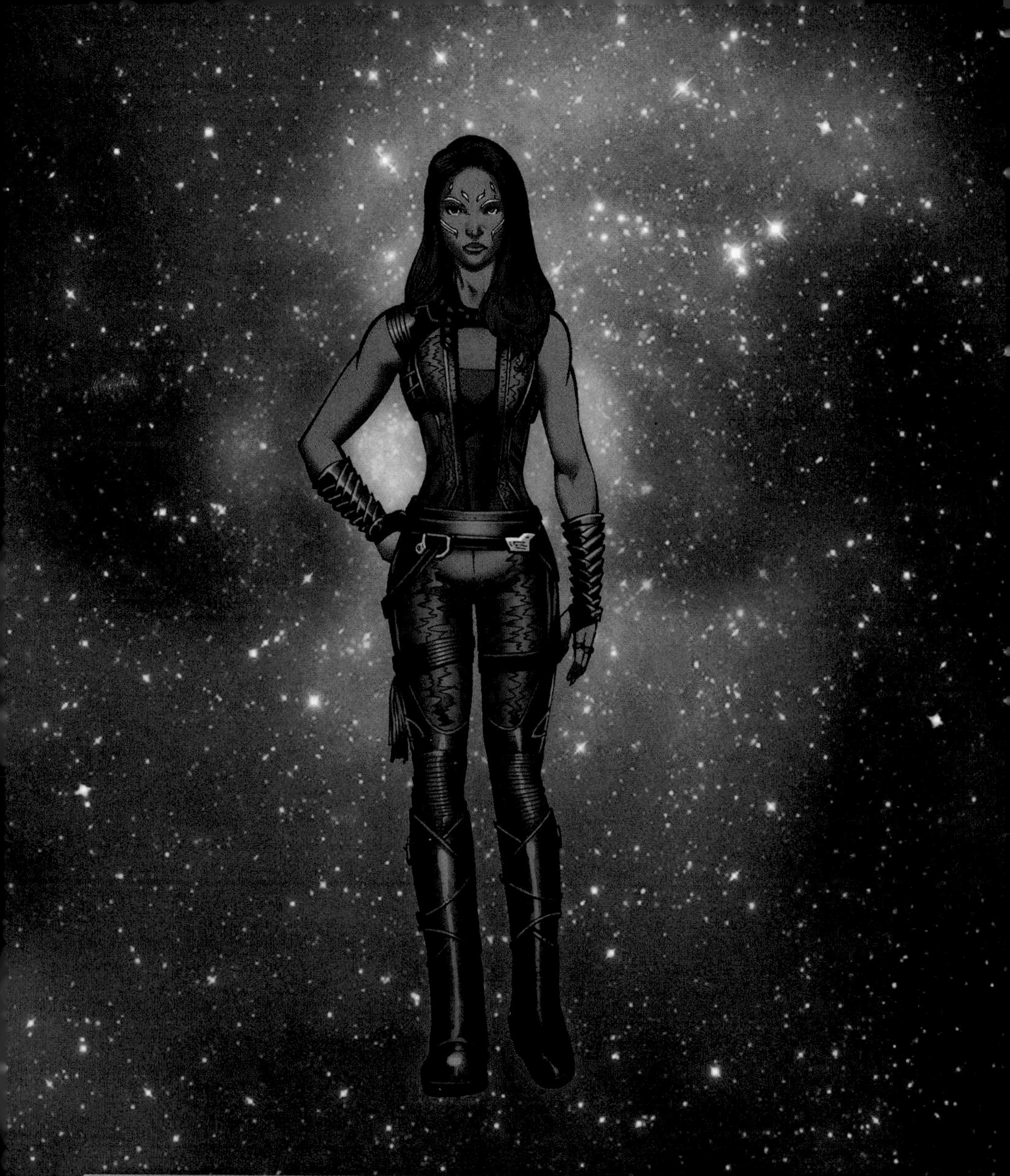

Peter also asks for help from Gamora,
who is the last of her alien race.
Her skin is bright green.
Drax and Gamora agree to help Peter, too.

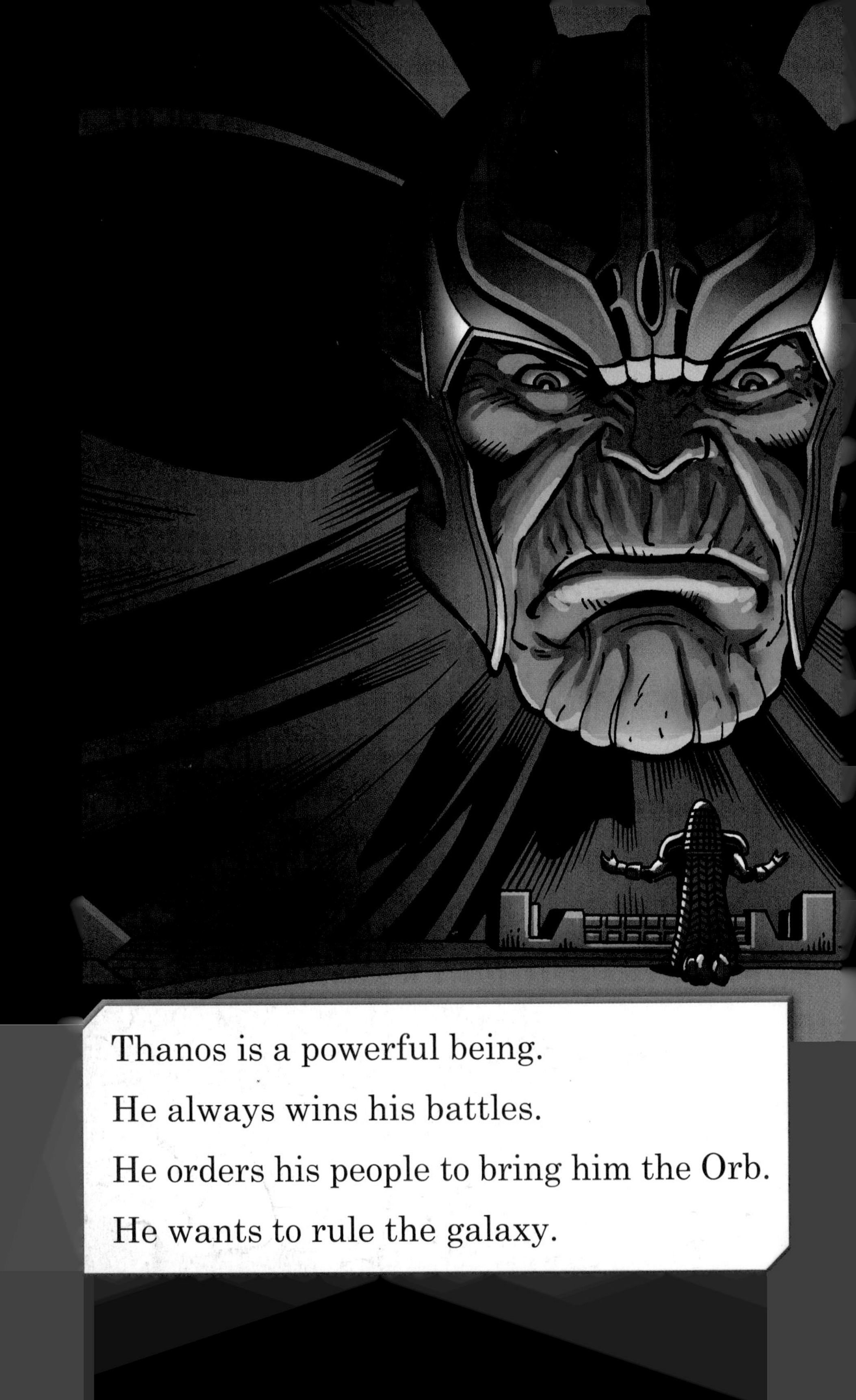

Thanos is a powerful being.

He always wins his battles.

He orders his people to bring him the Orb.

He wants to rule the galaxy.

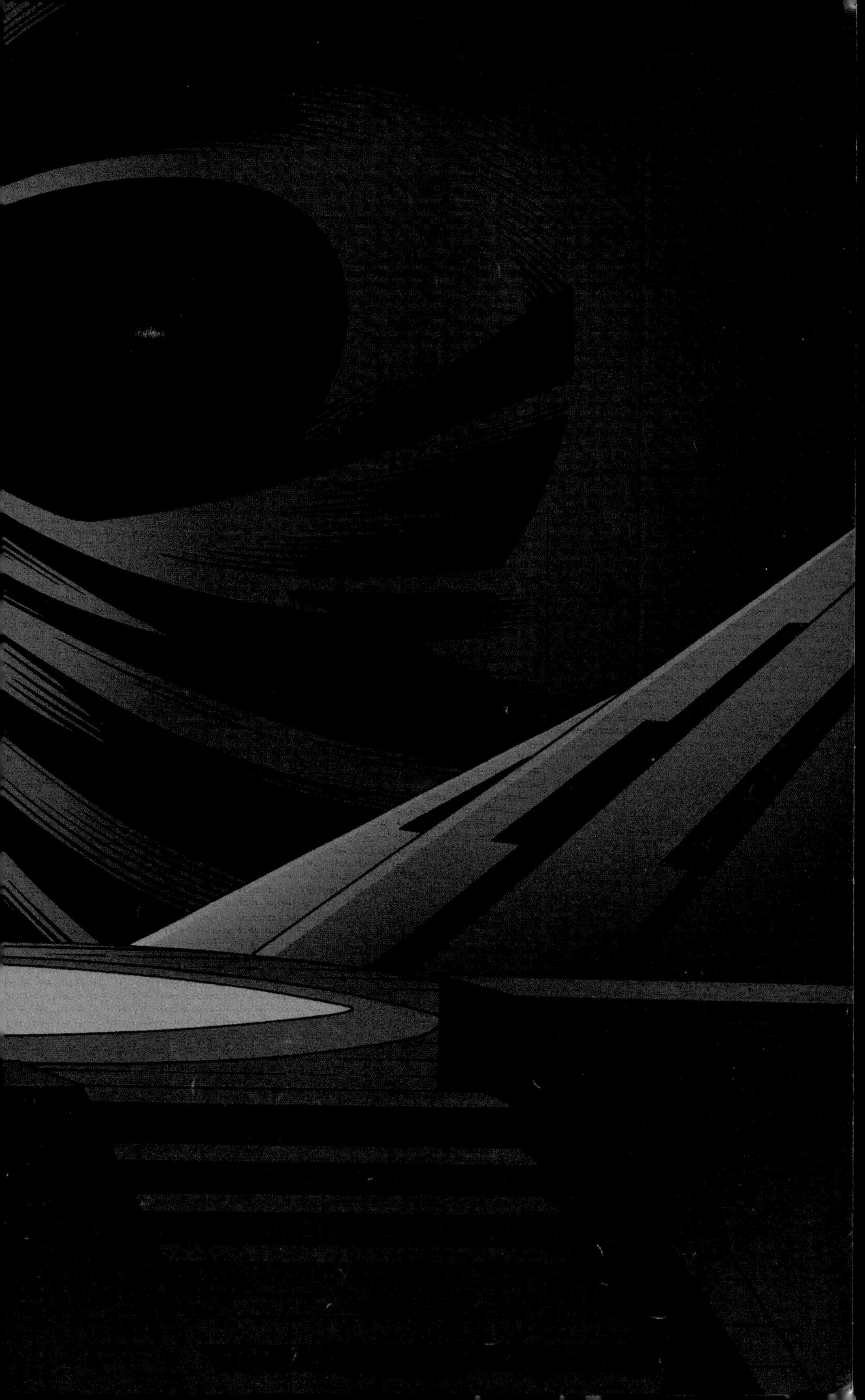

Ronan works for Thanos.
His Cosmi-Rod is a powerful weapon.
It makes everyone fear him.

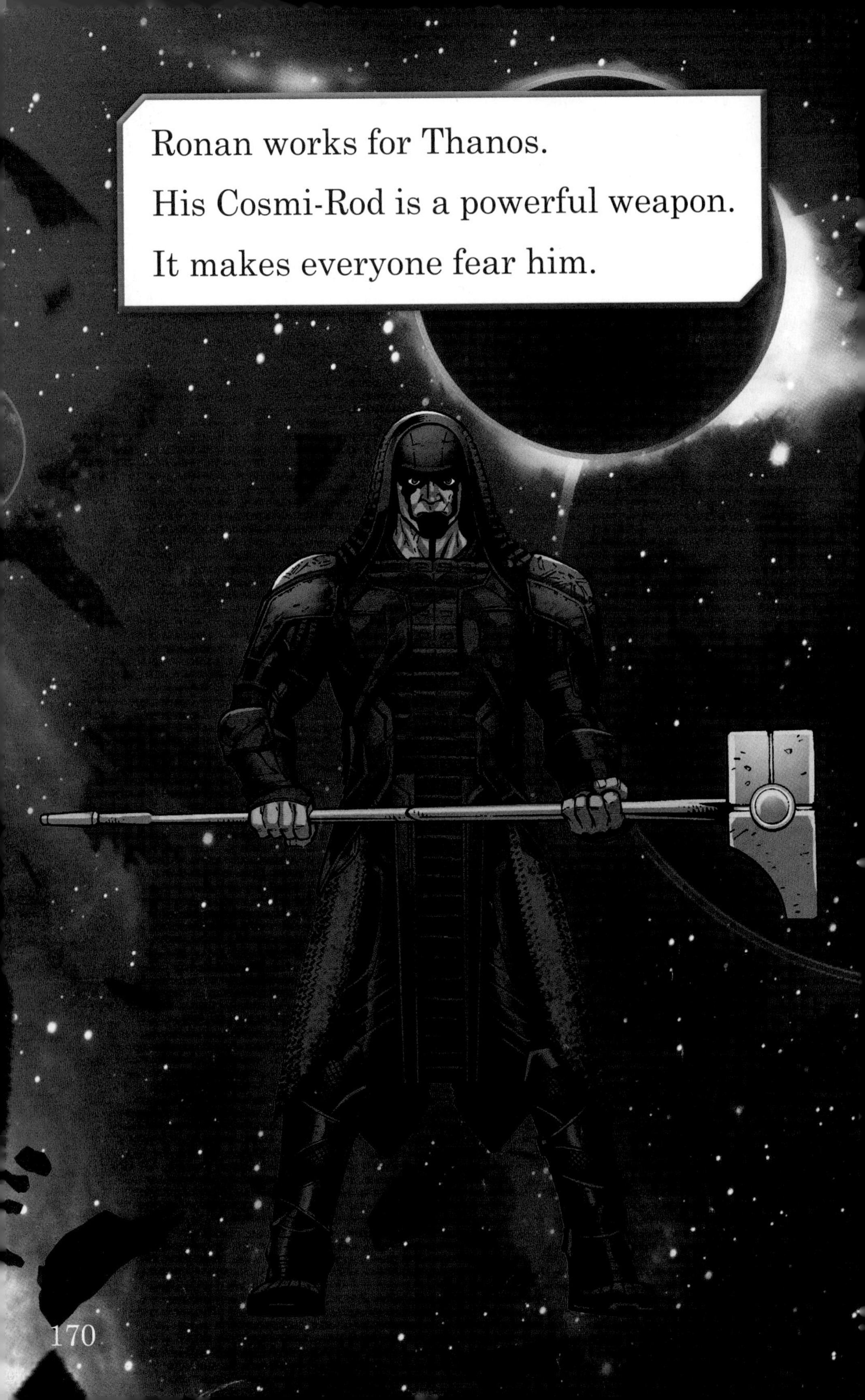

Korath works for Ronan.
He is part robot and very strong.
He leads a group of soldiers
called Sakaarans.

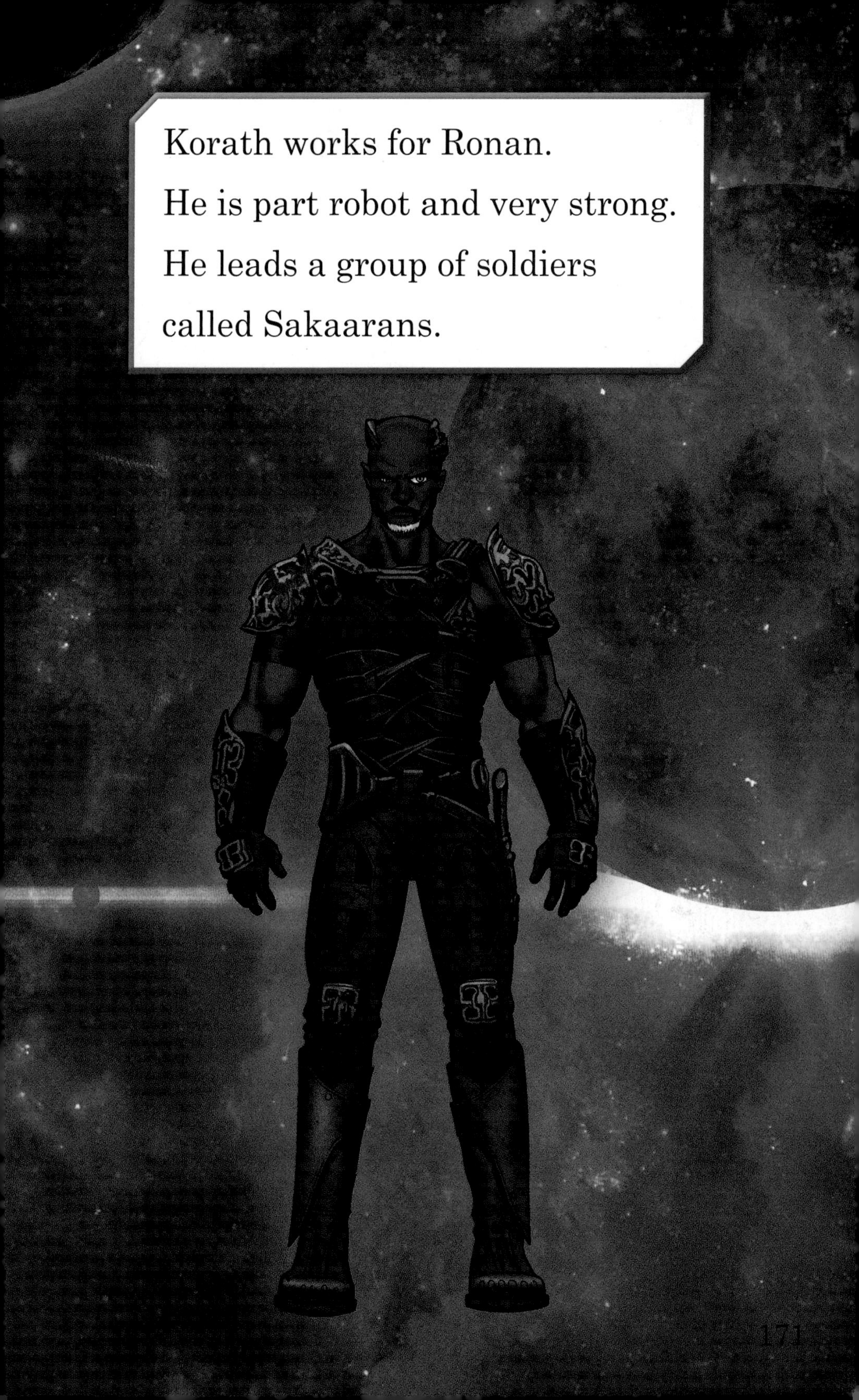

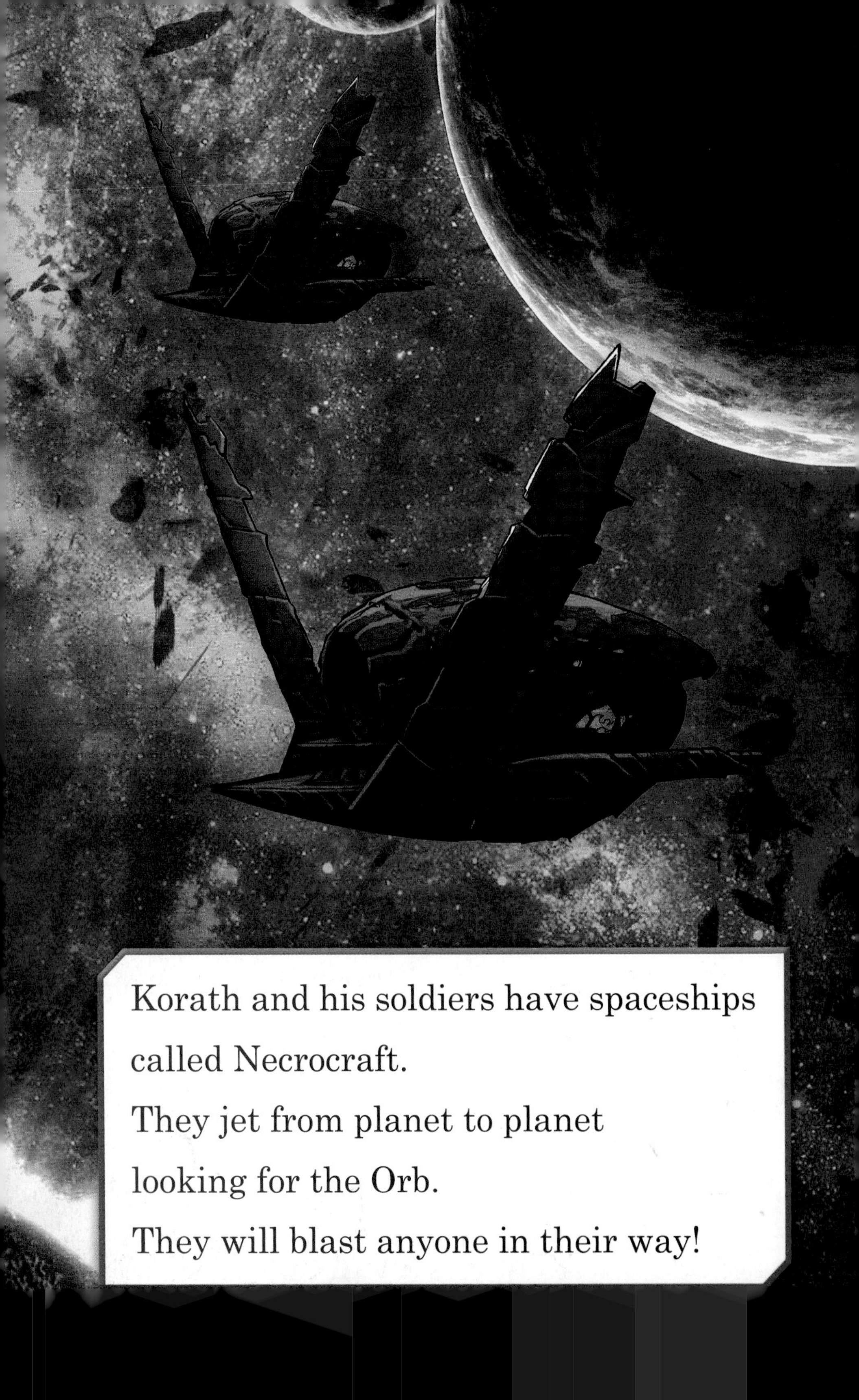

Korath and his soldiers have spaceships
called Necrocraft.
They jet from planet to planet
looking for the Orb.
They will blast anyone in their way!

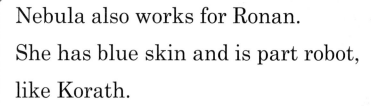

Nebula also works for Ronan.
She has blue skin and is part robot,
like Korath.
Nebula and Ronan set out
to find the Orb for Thanos.

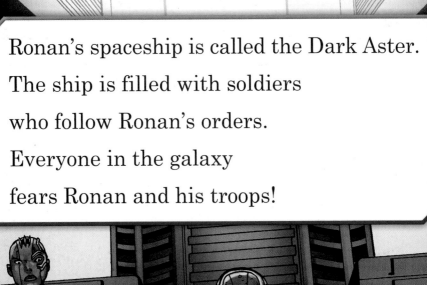

Ronan's spaceship is called the Dark Aster.
The ship is filled with soldiers
who follow Ronan's orders.
Everyone in the galaxy
fears Ronan and his troops!

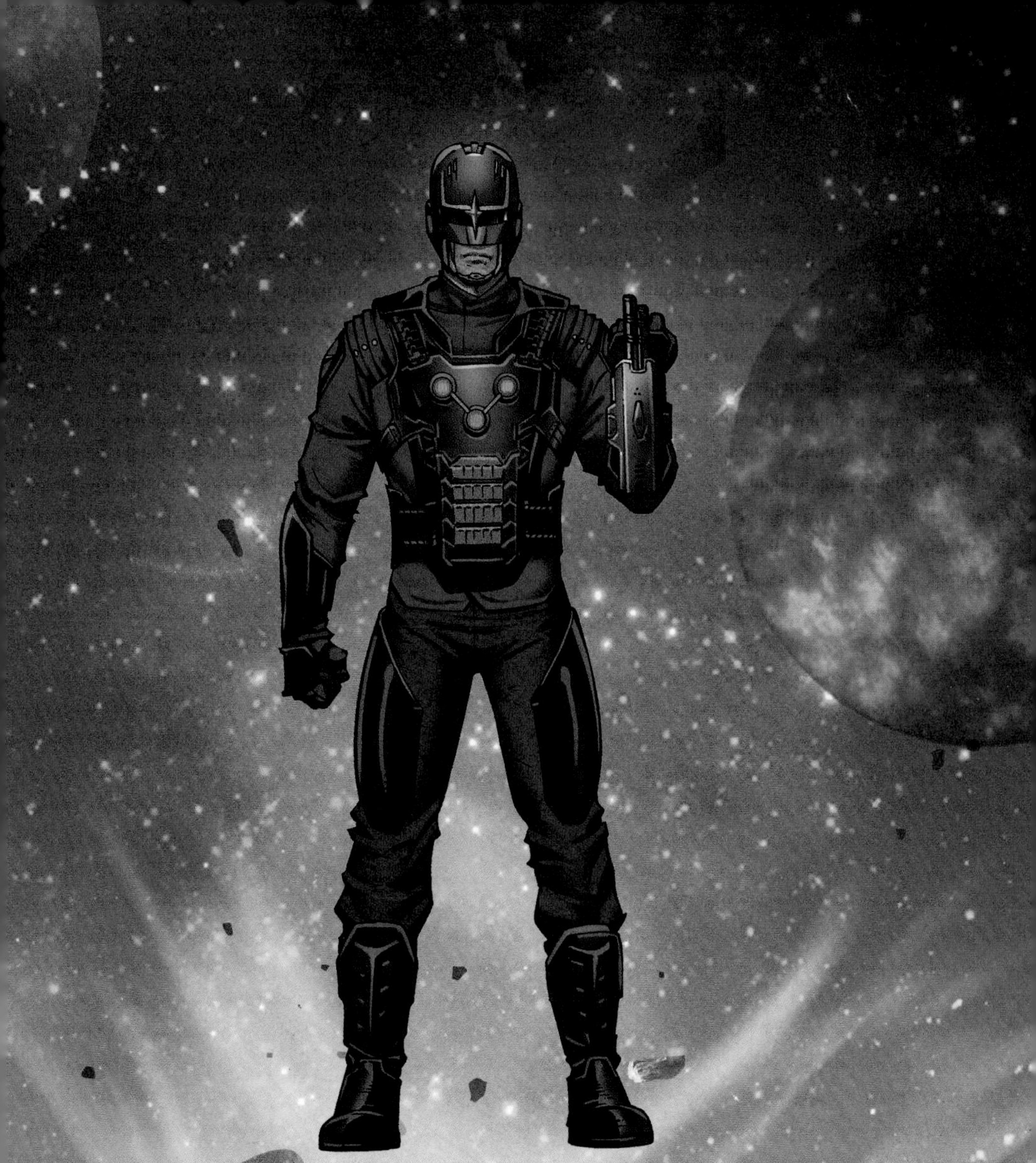

The Nova Corps is a group that polices the galaxy. They try to stop Ronan and other bad guys.

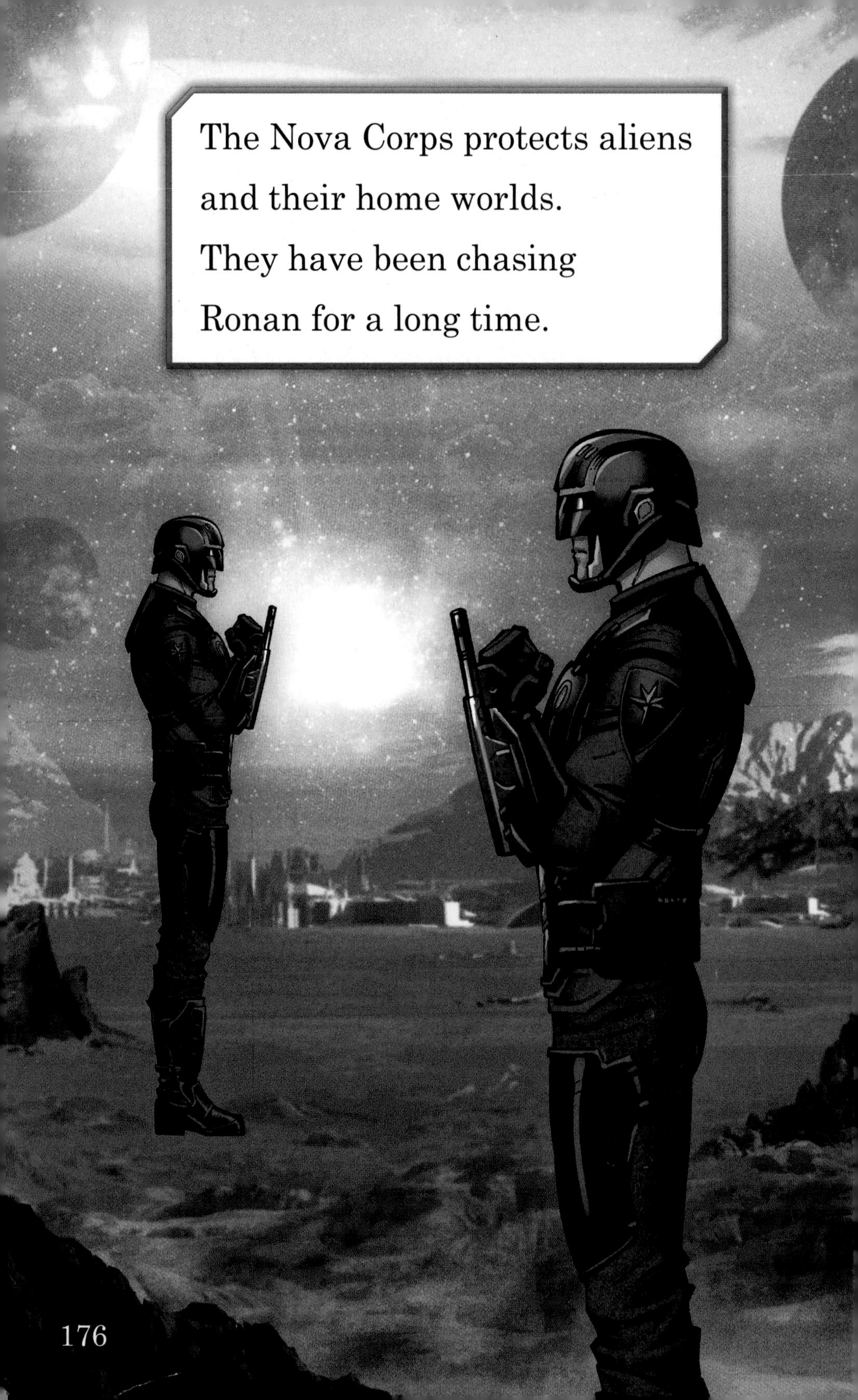
The Nova Corps protects aliens and their home worlds.
They have been chasing Ronan for a long time.

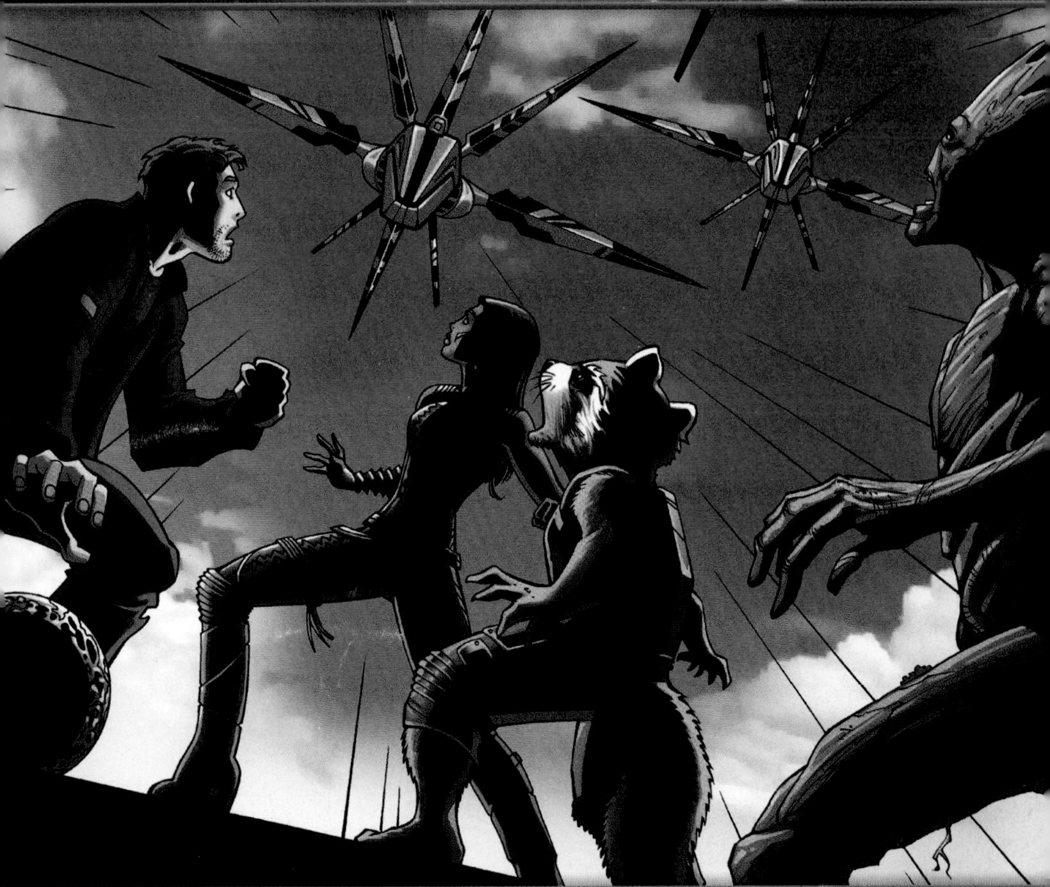

The Nova Corps fly in spaceships
called Starblasters.
The ships are fast.

Peter knows a lot of foes
are on their way to get the Orb.
Gamora says they should give the Orb
to the Collector.
The Collector will keep it safe.

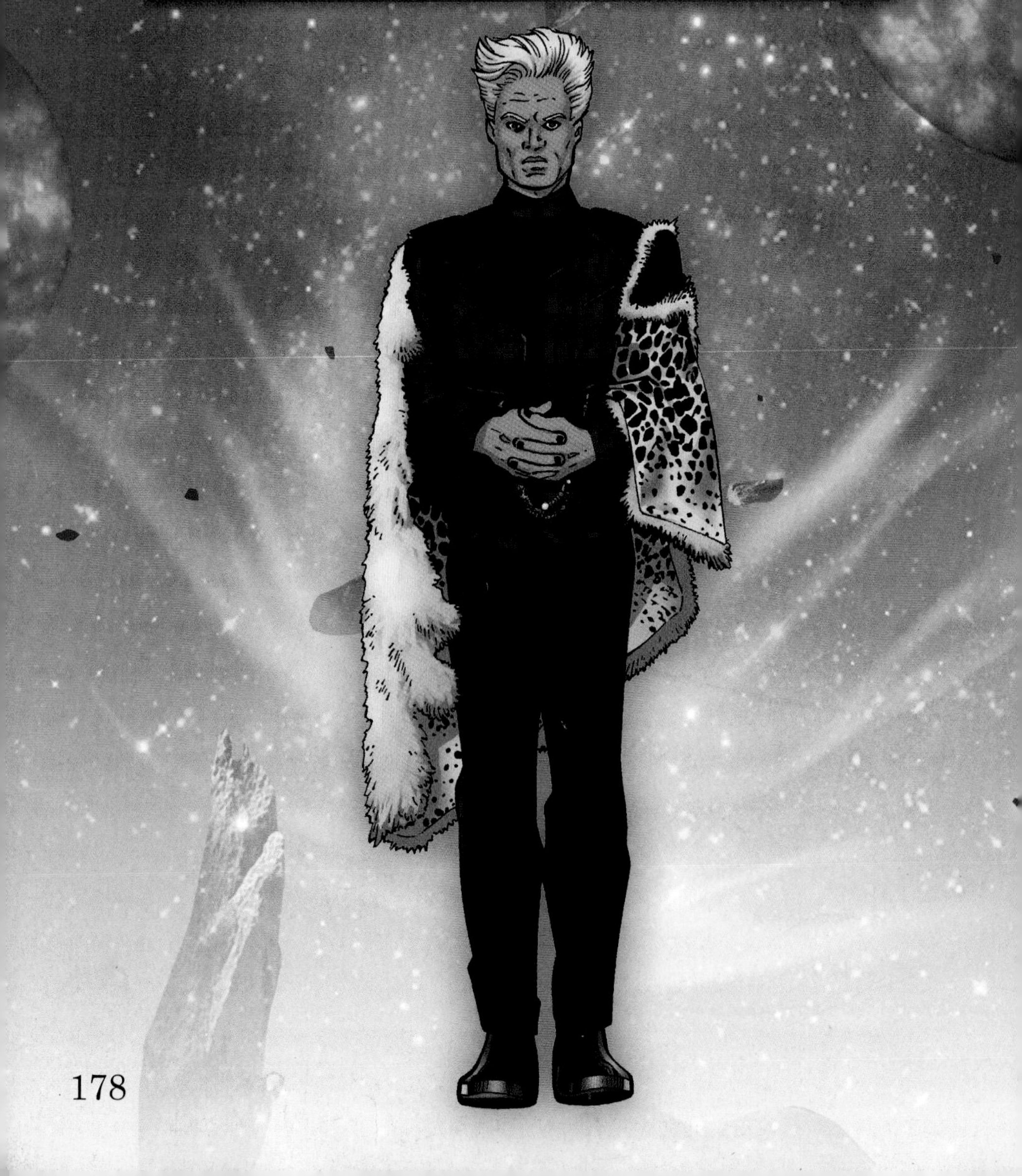

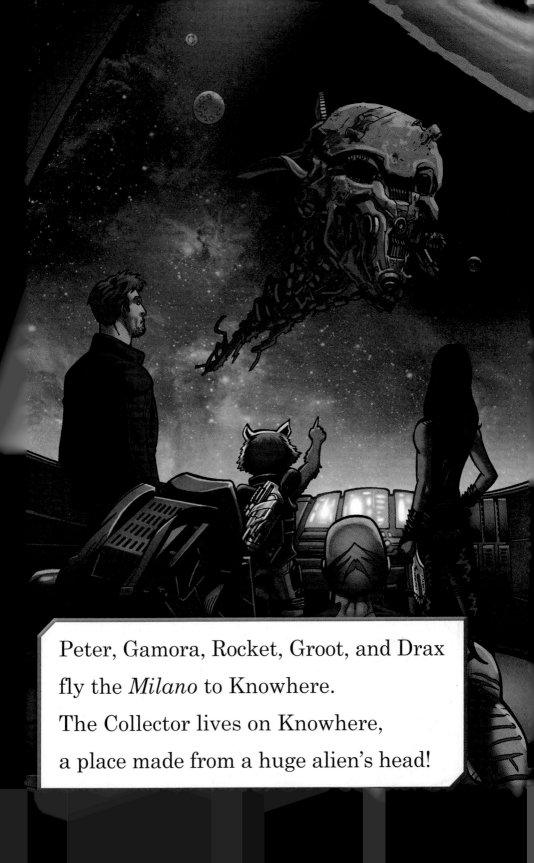

Peter, Gamora, Rocket, Groot, and Drax fly the *Milano* to Knowhere. The Collector lives on Knowhere, a place made from a huge alien's head!

The Collector has a lot of treasures.
He collects special items, plants, and animals.
Gamora gives him the Orb
to add to his collection.

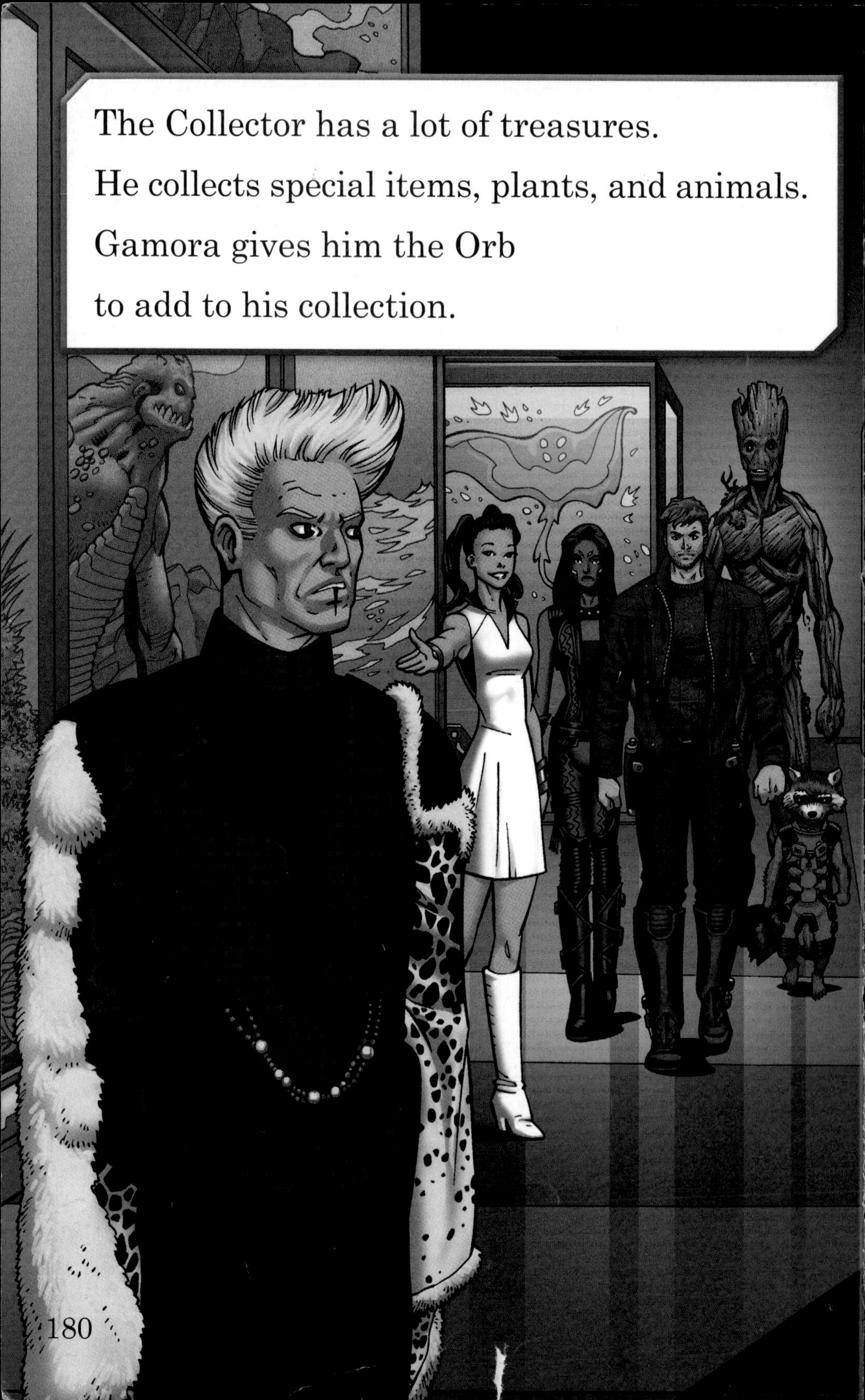

The Collector has a helper.
Her name is Carina.
When she takes the Orb from Gamora,
a powerful light flashes.
The Orb's power destroys
the Collector's home!

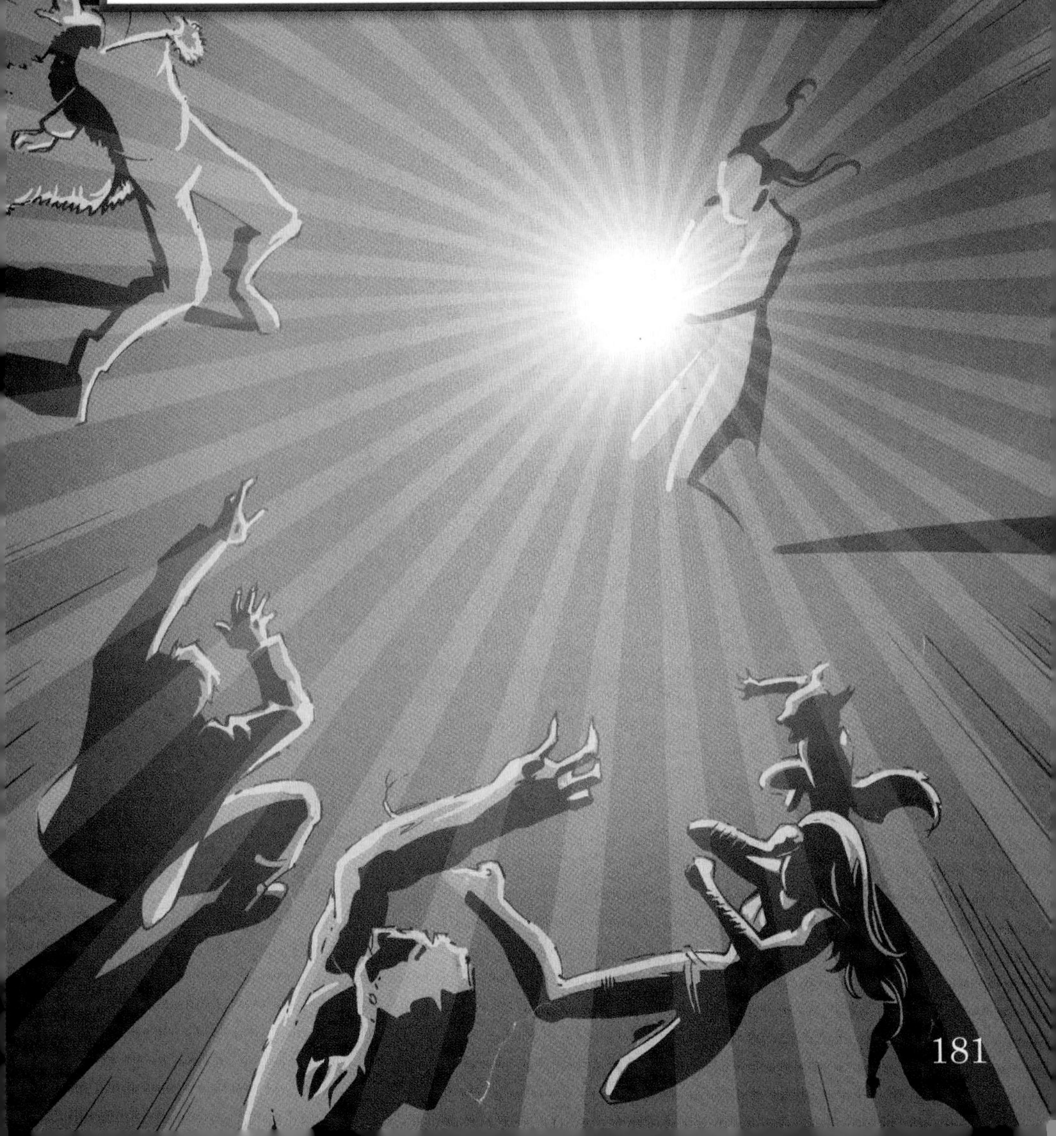

Just then, Ronan and his soldiers
appear on Knowhere!
If Ronan can get the Orb,
he will give it to Thanos!

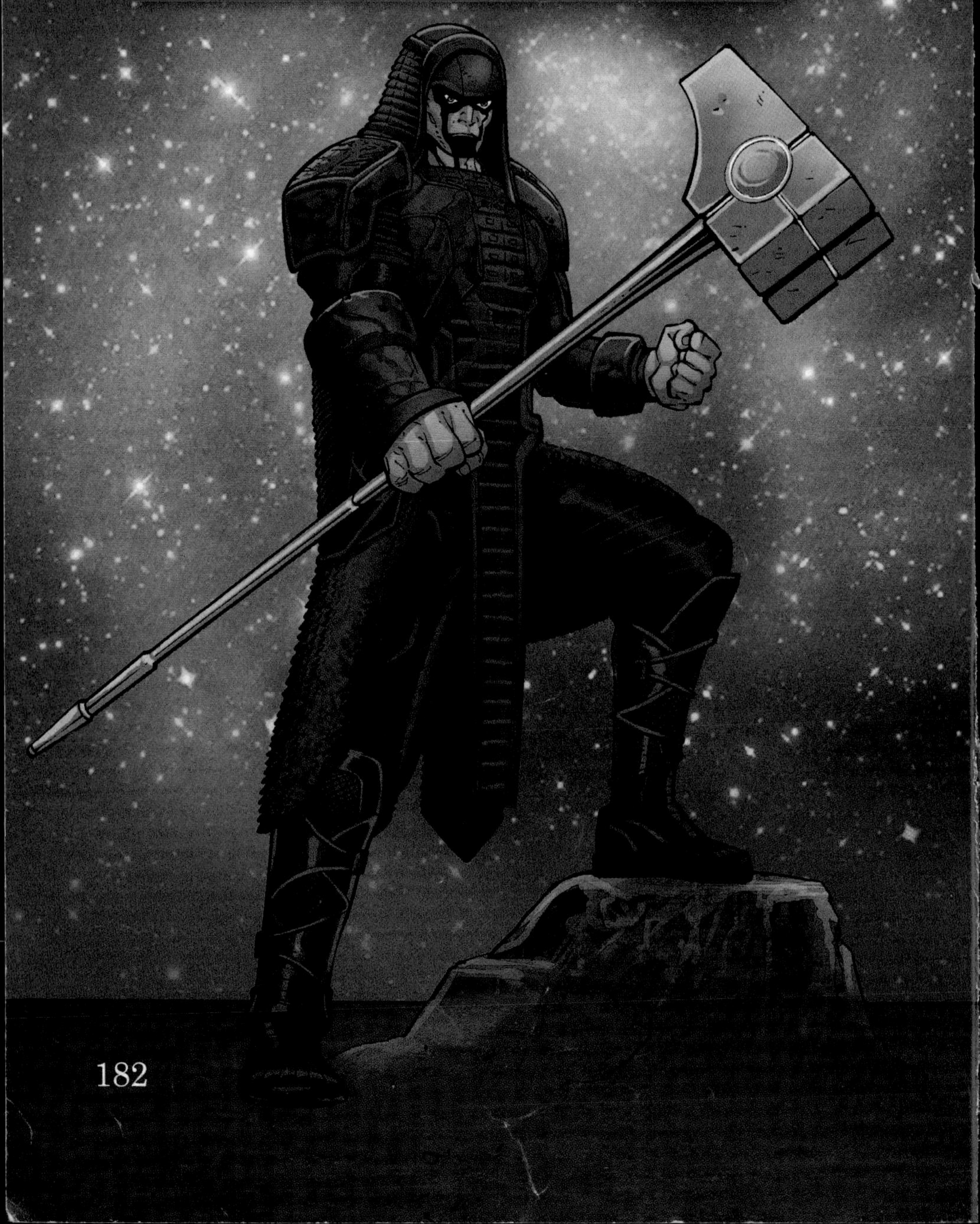

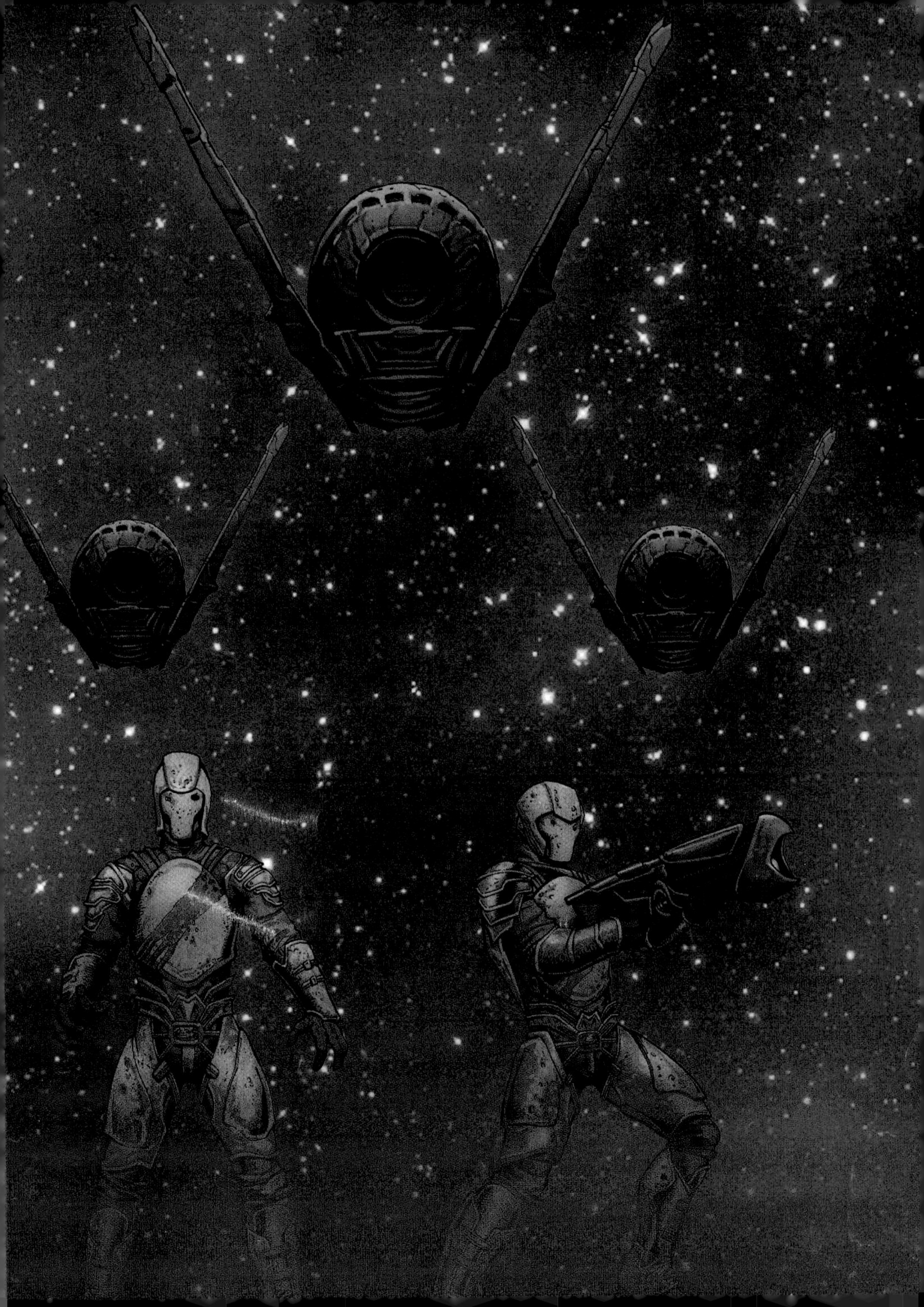

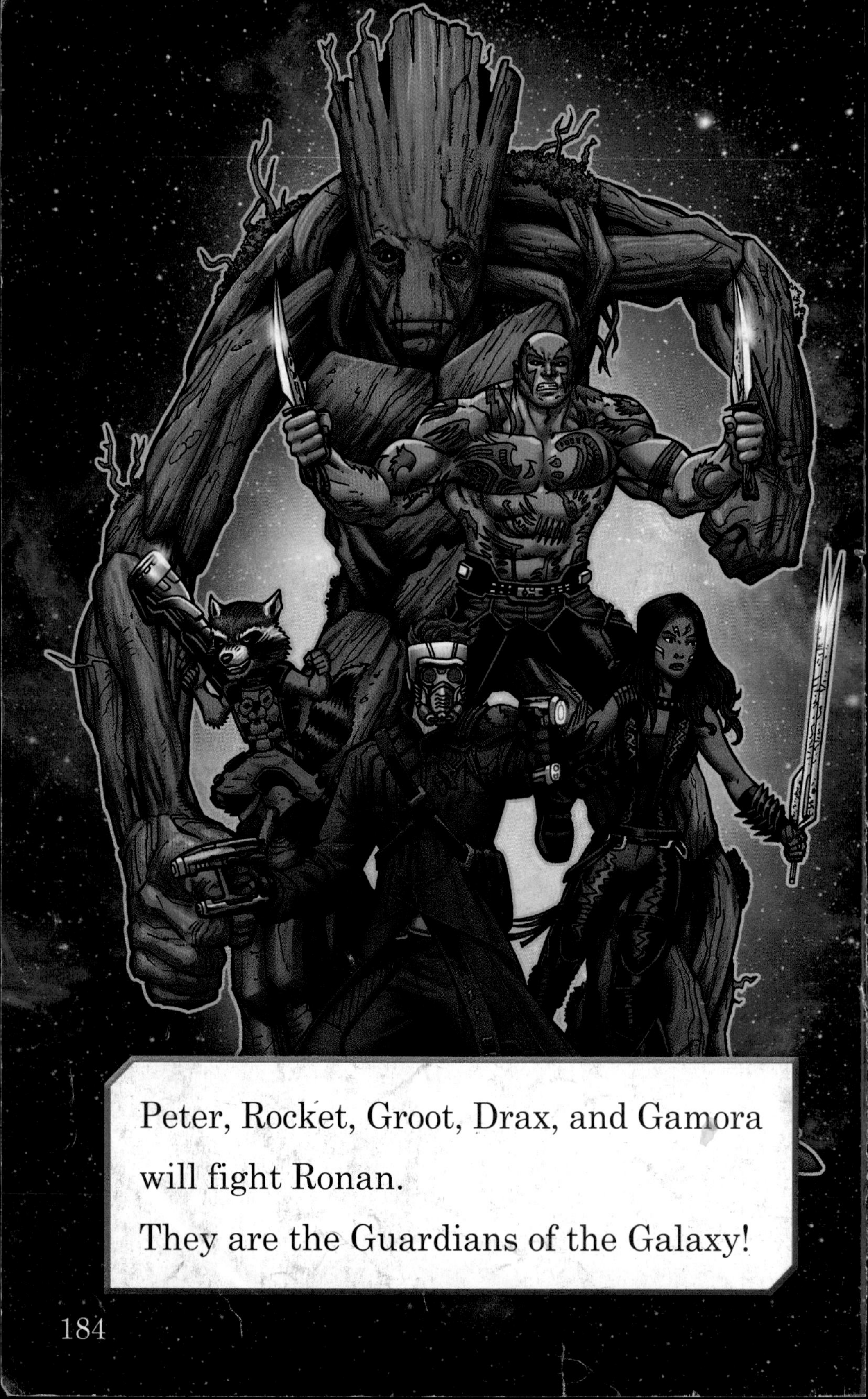

Peter, Rocket, Groot, Drax, and Gamora will fight Ronan.
They are the Guardians of the Galaxy!

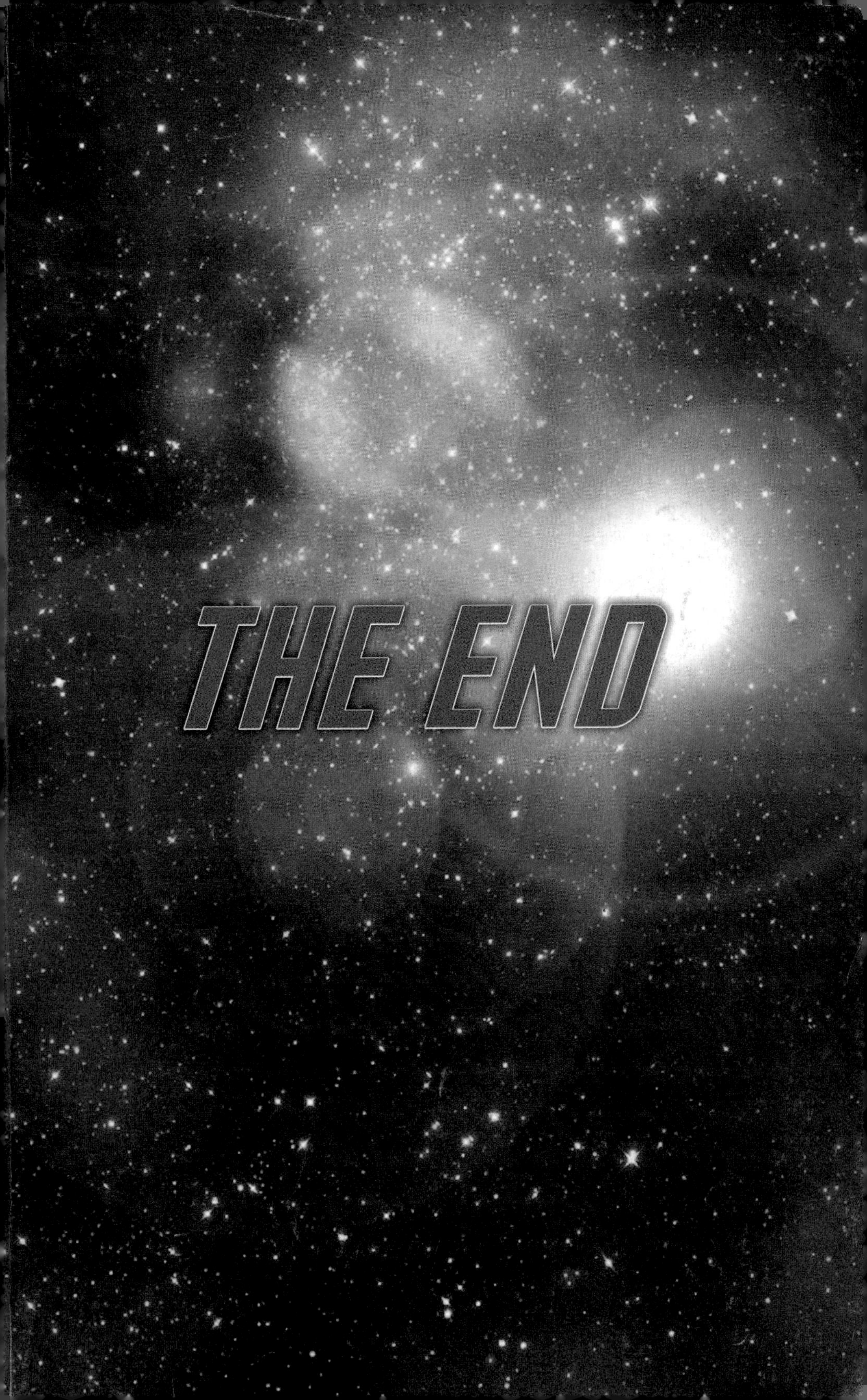
THE END

CHECKPOINTS IN THIS BOOK

Captain America: The Winter Solider: Falcon Takes Flight

WORD COUNT	GUIDED READING LEVEL	NUMBER OF DOLCH SIGHT WORDS
364	L	62

Avengers: Assemble!

WORD COUNT	GUIDED READING LEVEL	NUMBER OF DOLCH SIGHT WORDS
225	J	44

Avengers: Age of Ultron: Friends and Foes

WORD COUNT	GUIDED READING LEVEL	NUMBER OF DOLCH SIGHT WORDS
516	L	81

Avengers: Age of Ultron: Hulk to the Rescue

WORD COUNT	GUIDED READING LEVEL	NUMBER OF DOLCH SIGHT WORDS
317	K	64

Ant-Man: I Am Ant-Man

WORD COUNT	GUIDED READING LEVEL	NUMBER OF DOLCH SIGHT WORDS
486	K	68

Guardians of the Galaxy: Friends and Foes

WORD COUNT	GUIDED READING LEVEL	NUMBER OF DOLCH SIGHT WORDS
604	K	86

E MARVE   **FLT**
Marvel cinematic universe :reading
 rumble.

05/16